THE POLISH DETECTIVE

HANIA ALLEN

CONSTABLE

CONSTABLE

First published in Great Britain in 2018 by Constable

This paperback edition published in 2018 by Constable

1 3 5 7 9 10 8 6 4 2

A CIP catalogue record for this book
is available from the British Library.

ISBN: 978-1-47212-548-4

Typeset in Bembo by Photoprint, Torquay
Printed and bound in Great Britain by
CPI Group (UK) Ltd, Croydon CR0 4YY

Papers used by Constable are from well-managed forests and other
responsible sources.

Constable
An imprint of
Little, Brown Book Group
Carmelite House
50 Victoria Embankment
London EC4Y 0DZ

An Hachette UK Company
www.hachette.co.uk

www.littlebrown.co.uk

For Emma Cameron

Hania Allen was born in Liverpool, but has lived in Scotland longer than anywhere else, having come to love the people and the country (despite nine months of rain and three months of bad weather). Of Polish descent, her father was stationed in St Andrews during the war, and spoke so fondly of the town that she applied to study at the university.

She has worked as a researcher, a mathematics teacher, an IT officer and finally in senior management, a post she left to write full time. She is the author of the Von Valenti novels and now lives in a fishing village in Fife.

CHAPTER 1

It was when she glanced at it the second time that Jenn realised something was different. She squeezed the brakes hard, bringing the bicycle to a shuddering stop.

The scarecrow, bathed in May sunshine, stood where it always did in the middle of the wheat field. The clothes were the same: tatty straw hat with the floppy poppy, tartan scarf knotted under the neck, and the yellow shirt under the sky-blue workman's dungarees. The figure wasn't hanging right, though, making her suspect that someone had messed with it, probably those lads from the village dressing up in the clothes and scaring people. Instead of the pink head with its bulbous nose and creepy bowl-shaped smile, the face was white, the mouth open and smeared with red. Jenn swung her leg over the seat and propped the bicycle against the stone wall. She stared at the scarecrow for several seconds, and then climbed over the wall into the field.

With mounting anticipation, she made her way towards the figure, ignoring the green stalks catching at her ankles. She'd seen this scarecrow many times on her trips down the Liff Road and she knew everything about it, having helped Aleck, the estate manager, assemble and erect it a few years before. It hung with arms outstretched on crossed wooden poles. But, as she approached, she saw what it was that was different.

1

The woman's skin was the colour of ash, and her hair was plastered to her forehead, the brownish henna shade clashing with the red of the poppy. Her blue-veined hands were rigid, the fingers splayed. Jenn felt a growing tingling in her blood. From watching repeats of *Silent Witness*, but mainly from what Aleck had taught her about the process of decomposition, including the first stage of rigor mortis, she knew that the body stiffens after death, becoming flaccid after a time. She also knew that the degree of stiffness gives the police an estimate of the time of death. Whoever had dressed the woman and arranged her on the sticks would have known it too. Jenn reached out a hand and prodded the body. Underneath the soft dungarees it was rock hard. The woman had died with her eyes open, their expression one of horror, mingled with accusation. Peering into those dead eyes with their glassy stare, Jenn imagined how rigor would wear off. The softening eyes would cry real tears. The distorted mouth would become flaccid and slowly close.

Round the woman's neck was a chain to which was attached a card in a plastic sleeve. Jenn resisted the temptation to turn it over. Something she'd also learnt from *Silent Witness* was not to touch anything. Every contact leaves a trace.

She walked backwards, unable to tear her gaze from the woman's face, and then remembered that someone should call the police. With her heart thudding against her chest, she pulled the phone out of her jeans.

The phones in the room were ringing, but it was Detective Sergeant Dania Gorska who picked up first. 'It's the station controller, sir,' she said, the phone to her ear. 'Someone's reported a body on the Liff Road.'

DI Blair Chirnside was at the other end of the room, giving

instructions to the duty sergeant. He shouted across, 'Which part of the Liff Road?'

'Off the Coupar Angus, south of Muirhead. The lady didn't give a name. She said she'll wait for us there.'

'Let's go then, Sergeant.'

Protocol dictated that, as the junior officer, she should drive the staff Skoda, but Chirnside nodded to her to get in at the passenger's side and he slipped in behind the wheel. Was he being gallant or was he one of those men who felt uncomfortable with women driving? She'd been in Dundee for six weeks but Chirnside continued to maintain a respectful distance, which meant that she had little choice but to do the same. They were still at the dancing-around-each-other stage, something with which she was familiar from her time in London, where officers seemed to come and go with confusing regularity. But six weeks of formality was a record. She consoled herself by remembering that he behaved the same way towards the other female staff.

She risked a glance at his profile. He was a short stocky man in his mid- to late fifties, with hair that had more grey in it than dark. It was longish at the sides and back, but had almost disappeared on top, giving him the appearance of a monk. The pale spotty complexion suggested a bad diet. That, and the smell of stale tobacco that clung to his suit, made her wonder if he was heading for a coronary. His watery eyes and occasional wheezing and coughing suggested it might be his lungs that got him first.

Dania, who liked to know who her boss was, had asked around and learnt that he was single and lived with his elderly parents. A kindly man who didn't fly off into murderous rages like some senior coppers she'd known, he'd been good to her when she first arrived, making sure she knew her way around, and ensuring she was properly settled in.

They left West Bell Street station, a building that, with its many banks of windows, had a look of authority to it, and swung into the Marketgait. Dania had long since concluded that the reason God had invented sat-navs was because of the maze of hilly streets in Dundee's city centre. Chirnside turned left at Dudhope Roundabout and, with a few nifty lane changes, followed the twisting and turning Lochee Road until it became the Coupar Angus, taking them north towards the intersection with the A90. There were fewer buildings here, the houses and apartment blocks yielding to green spaces. She knew this route, as it took her to the retail park off Kingsway and also to the cinema complex near Camperdown Park.

'I'm sure you didn't think you'd be getting another case as quickly as this,' Chirnside said grimly.

She was used to cases piling up. Secretly, she was pleased she wouldn't be spending her Saturday-morning shift cross-referencing reports and entering them on to the database. Desk work wasn't something she relished, although she understood the necessity for it. What floated her boat was thinking laterally and solving problems, something she'd found she was good at, and which, along with her ability to ask the right questions at the right time, especially awkward ones, had accounted for her rapid promotion to detective sergeant.

'You did a cracking job on your first case, by the way, Dania.'

'It's kind of you to say so, sir.'

'I give praise where praise is due. I'm keen for you to make progress here. You've made an excellent start, and I've added a note to your record.'

This was more than she'd expected, and she felt a pure pleasure that her hard work and ability had been noticed. Her sole focus since her first day had been on a particularly challenging sexual-assault case, which had been running for months. She'd come in in the middle and it had been her input, acknowledged by the other detectives – grudgingly by some – that had brought it to a rapid and unequivocal conclusion.

Her fellow officers had begun by calling her 'Danuta', the name on her application form, until she explained that Polish allowed for certain diminutives, and it would be more than acceptable for them to use the usual form, 'Dania'. They nodded, smiling, and she realised that they might already know this, given the number of Poles in Dundee.

They'd been wary of her at first, thinking she'd want to act like a big shot from London, but an evening at their local, where she'd shown them how to drink vodka without setting their throats on fire, and told a string of Communist-era Polish jokes, had settled it. A perennial favourite was: where can you find the best view in Warsaw? The answer: from the top of the Palace of Culture and Science – a 'gift' from the Soviet Union. Why? Because it's the only place in Warsaw from which you can't see the Palace of Culture and Science. The laughter had told her she was one of them. It had been worth the huge bar bill. But she could see the unspoken question in their eyes – why had she left the Met? The truth, that her marriage had broken down, wasn't something she was prepared to share with them quite yet.

They passed the roundabout at Camperdown Park and the sign for Birkhill, and were immediately into countryside. She loved this stretch of road, overhung with huge trees. On the right was the sign for Templeton Woods and then, in quick succession, a notice for a pick-your-own-strawberries place, and the sign for Birkhill Cemetery. She wondered who would pick fruit so close to decaying corpses. It struck her that the minerals leaching into the soil might make the fruit taste better.

The trees gave way to fields and then they were cruising

through the villages of Birkhill and Muirhead. The sat-nav told them they would shortly need to turn left.

Chirnside slowed to a crawl as he approached the traffic lights. On the left-hand corner was Tiddlywinks Nursery School, the name painted on the white building in large, brightly coloured letters.

'Last time I was here, we found a man passed out just behind Tiddlywinks,' he said grimly. 'The needle was lying next to him.'

'He did it beside a *nursery* school?'

'Drugs are the scourge of this city, Dania. We have more drug deaths per head than the rest of Scotland.'

'How do the drugs come in, sir? Organised-crime groups?'

'Aye, they've infiltrated the city.' His expression hardened. 'It's my long-term goal to crack down on them.'

The lights went to green and they turned into the Liff Road.

To Dania's surprise, there was a police office on the right, complete with blue lamp. The notice on the door urged the public to contact 999 in an emergency, and 101 if they wanted to speak to someone. The building looked deserted.

They passed Muirhead Medical Centre and, a second later, they left the village. There was a sign, 'Red squirrels for $\frac{1}{2}$ a mile', and another on the right, welcoming them to Backmuir Wood. The thick woodland, its trees in full foliage, was separated from the road by a low dry-stone wall.

Chirnside hit the brakes. The sudden deceleration caused Dania to lurch forward and strain against the seatbelt.

A girl with blonde hair was standing in the middle of the tarmac. Seeing them, she lifted both arms above her head, staring fixedly.

Chirnside brought the car to a stop. He cut the engine, and he and Dania hurried out.

The girl was of medium height, with skin so pale that it was almost transparent, and a determined expression, accentuated by the frown lines between her eyes. Her hair was long and fine, the kind easily blown about in the wind. Dania felt a twinge of envy. Her own, also blonde, but shading into brown, was thick and heavy, and the only way she could manage it was by wearing it in a shaggy bob.

'Jenn McLaughlin,' Chirnside said, the words barely audible. 'It was you who called the station.'

Dania glanced at him, registering the shock on his face. Perhaps, like her, he'd expected someone older. But this girl looked in her teens. And she was someone he knew. He seemed incapable of speaking, so Dania said, 'We're from Tayside Police.'

'Aye, I know,' the girl said in a soft voice. 'I need to see your IDs.'

Frowning, Dania pulled out her card. Chirnside did the same.

Jenn gave Dania's only a brief glance. But she lingered over the DI's. Whatever the reason, she spent more time studying his image than the occasion warranted. When she handed back the card, she stared at him with an expression that could best be described as hostile. It left Dania wondering how they knew each other.

'You said you'd found a body, Jenn,' he said in a changed voice. He swallowed noisily, and then looked over his shoulder towards Backmuir Wood.

Dania knew what he was thinking: a druggie finding a lonely spot amongst the trees and unintentionally taking an overdose. She imagined the limp body, the empty eyes, the needle still in the arm. Something made her reach across and slip an arm round Jenn. The girl stiffened but then moved closer to the detective. Dania could smell the lilac-scented shampoo in her hair.

'Can you show us where he is?' she said quietly.

Jenn's response was to point into the field. 'There's a body inside the scarecrow. And it's a she, not a he.'

Dania felt her throat tighten. *A body inside the scarecrow?*

'Will you take a statement, Sergeant?' Chirnside said, his voice sounding strange.

'Yes, sir.'

The field's boundary wall was made of stones, but was overgrown front and back with weeds and grass. Immediately behind it, the farmer had erected a low wire fence. Chirnside stepped over it and almost ran across the corn.

The wind gusted suddenly, tugging at Dania's hair and whipping Jenn's across her face.

'Shall we do this in the car, Jenn?'

'If you like.'

They sat in the back of the Skoda. Dania pulled out her notebook. She was good at putting people at their ease, and yet there was no need with this girl: she seemed completely in control of herself, gazing unblinkingly with pale blue eyes.

'I'm Detective Sergeant Gorska,' Dania said with a smile.

Interest flickered on Jenn's face. 'You're Polish, aren't you?'

'Can you tell from my name?'

'From the way you speak. We've got some Polish girls in my class. They don't sound like you, though. But their parents do.'

'Which school do you go to?'

'St John's High. It's a Catholic school.'

Dania hesitated. 'How old are you?'

'Seventeen. I like your jacket, by the way. It's Black Watch tartan.'

'Jenn, can you tell me how you found the scarecrow?'

'I was cycling along the road and I happened to glance into the field.' She ran her hands down her jeans. 'I've seen that scarecrow lots of times, but it looked different today. So I went up for a closer look. I saw straightaway that someone had dressed a woman in the scarecrow's clothes. And that she was dead.'

'How do you know she was dead?'

The girl seemed to consider this. 'The obvious indicator is that her hands are rigid. That's rigor mortis.'

'What were you doing cycling along this road?'

'I was going to see Aleck. Aleck Docherty. He manages this estate,' she added, indicating the surrounding fields with a nod of her head.

'And he's a friend of yours?'

'Aye.' Her expression softened. 'I've known him all my life.' She looked behind Dania's head towards where Chirnside was standing staring at the scarecrow. 'I helped him make that. That's my old hat, the one with the poppy.'

She could have been describing herself in a photograph. 'Whose estate is this?' Dania said.

'It belongs to the local laird, Graham Farquhar. He owns the land as far as the eye can see. And then a bit more.'

'And where does he live?'

'Go all the way down that road, and it's behind the wood. Backmuir Hall. You can't miss it. Think Downton Abbey and you've got some idea.' She said it without a trace of irony. Or envy.

'I'll need your address, Jenn, as well as Aleck Docherty's.'

'I live on Oaktree Farm, north of Muirhead. Aleck lives further down this road. It's not far from Liff village. Keeper's Cottage. The name's on the gate.'

'Keeper's Cottage? What does he keep, then?' Dania said, trying a lame joke.

The girl looked at her steadily. 'He's a gamekeeper.'

'Ah.' After a pause, Dania said, 'Do you cycle down this road often?'

'Only when I go to see Aleck.'

'And were you here yesterday?'

'Aye, I dropped in to Keeper's after school.'

9

'Did you see anything unusual? People you don't normally see round here? A car parked on the road?'

'People don't really park here,' she said in a matter-of-fact way. 'I can't remember seeing anything out of the ordinary. I cycle along this road quite quickly.' She looked past Dania towards the scarecrow. 'I wouldn't have noticed anything today if I hadn't glanced across that field.'

'Did you stay long with Aleck yesterday?'

The girl narrowed her eyes, making Dania feel that she'd crossed a line. 'Maybe half an hour. I had to get home for tea.'

'And how are you feeling?' When the girl didn't reply, Dania added gently, 'It must have been a shock for you. It's not every day you find a dead body.'

'I'm used to finding dead bodies. The fields and roads are littered with them.'

'Yes, but they're animals.'

'But they're still dead.' She shrugged, as if to take the sting out of the remark. Dania had the strangest sensation that she was speaking to an adult.

'What do you do when you go to see Aleck?'

'I help him on the estate.'

'It's Saturday. Wouldn't you rather be with your school-friends?'

An expression Dania couldn't read crossed the girl's face. She shifted her gaze to a point behind Dania's shoulder. 'Your DI's coming back,' she said stiffly.

Chirnside was making his way across the field in long, loping strides.

Dania stepped out of the car, feeling the wind lift her hair. As Chirnside approached, she saw his face clearly. It was grey with shock.

He wiped the sweat from his upper lip. 'Call it in, Dania.' There

10

was an edge of panic to his voice. 'We need Forensics out here. And the procurator fiscal.'

'Got it.'

'What about the girl?'

'She seems okay.' Dania very nearly added, '*But are you?*'

'And the statement?'

'I've got everything we need for now.'

'We'll have to get her home.'

'She lives not far from here, in Muirhead. I think she could probably cycle home.'

Jenn was getting out of the car. They turned and looked at her. She returned their gaze without blinking.

And the thought crossed Dania's mind then that the girl *had* seen something, either here or elsewhere. Something that she didn't yet recognise as significant.

CHAPTER 2

It was now mid-morning and the Liff Road had been transformed. An entire section had been cordoned off and, because walkers in Backmuir Wood might use the exits in the boundary wall, police officers had been stationed along it at intervals. The area around the scarecrow was taped off, and rows of uniforms in reflective jackets were systematically searching through the wheat.

Dania, in protective suit and slippers, was getting her first good look at the victim. Seeing the pouched eyes and the hennaed hair, she realised she'd seen the woman before. It was when Chirnside lifted the ID card and Dania squinted at the photograph of the smiling face that it came to her: the woman had been interviewed, although Dania couldn't now remember in what connection, and her photograph had appeared in the *Dundee Courier*.

'Her name's Judith Johnstone,' Chirnside said wearily. He gestured to the ID. 'That's the crest of Dundee University.'

'She's wearing bright red lipstick.'

The remark caused the attending pathologist, who'd been standing watching the photographer, to turn. 'We haven't been introduced,' he said in a bass voice. He had a Mick Jagger mouth that smiled easily. 'I'm Professor Milo Slaughter.' He rolled his eyes. 'I know. Great name for a pathologist.'

'DS Dania Gorska.'

'So what were you saying about lipstick?'

'It's been applied heavily, which means it has to be done carefully. But it's been smeared.'

'Go on.'

'It suggests she's been overpowered. Someone placing a hand over her mouth? Or maybe she's been gagged.'

He threw Dania an appreciative look. 'We'll get an idea when we do the tests.'

'I'm wondering if it's a random killing, or whether she knew him.'

'Too soon to tell,' Chirnside said. He glanced at the pathologist. 'Time of death, Prof?'

'The body's in full rigor. We've measured the ambient temperature and I'll take the rectal when we get her down off the posts, but the more accurate potassium test can only be done in the lab.'

'Your best guess?'

'Yesterday afternoon.' He stared at the scarecrow. 'Strange way to crucify someone.'

Dania was about to press him, when a uniform called from the road. 'We've found her car,' he shouted to no one in particular.

'Definitely hers?' Chirnside shouted back.

'We checked with the DVLA.'

'So where is it?'

The man pointed south. 'Round that corner, there's a sharpish left turn with a sort of layby. It's parked there. A Honda Civic. The keys are still in the ignition.'

'Do you think she came to meet her killer, sir?' Dania said.

'It's possible.' Chirnside watched the photographer packing away his gear. 'Any idea how she died, Prof?'

'Too soon to say. There are no visible marks. You'll have to wait till we get her down.'

'There's been no attempt to hide the corpse, or who she is,'

Dania said. 'Clothes are sometimes removed to hide a person's identity but that's not the case here.'

Chirnside addressed himself to Milo. 'How quickly can you get the PM authorised?' he asked impatiently.

'Monday at the earliest. But I'll do a preliminary examination as soon as we get her back.'

'Right.' Chirnside marched off to speak to the SOCOs.

'He's in a bit of a hurry,' Milo said, an amused expression in his eyes.

'He's a detective inspector. They're always in a hurry.' She gazed at the scarecrow. 'Unusual thing to do,' she murmured.

'What is?'

'Pose a body like this.'

'You'd have to do it before rigor set in.'

'It's not impossible to dress a rigid corpse. We had a case like that in the Met.'

'True. But look at the arms. They're spread out. The legs too, although not as much. Once rigor's advanced, you need considerable force to move limbs apart. My guess is he posed her here within a few hours of killing her.'

'And once we have the time of death . . .'

'. . . you'll have some idea of when he brought the corpse here.'

'Assuming he killed her elsewhere.'

'And drove her car here with the body inside.'

Dania frowned. 'He might have killed her here. In this field. Or she was still alive when he put her on the posts.'

'Endless possibilities.'

'He took a great risk. This seems to be the main road to Liff village. And, along there, you can see the traffic on the Coupar Angus Road.'

'Suggests he erected this thing under cover of darkness.'

'That'd be my guess.'

Milo signalled to one of his staff that it was time to move the corpse. 'Will I see you later, DS Gorska?' he said over his shoulder.

'You will,' she shouted to his retreating back.

Milo's staff were working on loosening the soil underneath the scarecrow and, ordinarily, Dania would have observed the procedure. But she had the strangest feeling that she was being watched. She turned and stared into Backmuir Wood. Someone, or something, was in there. She took a few steps towards the road, peering into the mass of trees with their intermeshed branches. A sudden gust of wind made them come alive, the wood creaking and groaning. The gust died just as suddenly, leaving behind an uneasy calm.

Chirnside returned. 'They're taking her to the lab the way she is. They'll have to cut those sticks off her.'

'Is the van wide enough, sir?'

'It is if they turn her on her side. Amazing thing is, they've got extra-wide body bags.' He glanced at Dania. 'Let's go,' he added grimly.

As they walked up the road to where they'd left the car, her feeling of being watched returned. She stared again into the rustling woodland, wondering what was in there, yet seeing nothing.

Jenn pushed her bicycle into the yard of Oaktree Farm. She knew from the absence of the van that her mum was in Dundee's High Street, selling eggs and cheese at the farmers' market, something she did on the last Saturday of every month. She wouldn't be back now till late afternoon.

Jenn wandered into the kitchen and sat at the scarred pine table, resting her chin in her hands. The Polish detective had been insistent that she should go straight home, so she'd called Aleck to say that she wouldn't be coming over. A pity that, as he'd promised to let her drive his new tractor. She wondered if she should go over in the afternoon, but it was likely that the police would still be on the estate. They were probably on their way to interview him right now.

Her thoughts drifted to the scarecrow. Or tattie bogle, as it was known here. And her shock at finding the body dressed in the dungarees. So where would the woman's own clothes be? Would the police find them somewhere on the estate? If so, what would that mean for Aleck? He'd surely be implicated. The notion made her sit up sharply. She should ring him. But would he want her bothering him at a time like this? If the police were with him? Probably not.

She gazed through the dusty windows at the barn. If she held her breath and listened, she could hear the clucking of the hens as they foraged in the dust, and pecked at each other, and did the things hens do. Other than the herd of dairy cows, whose milk her mum used to make her award-winning cheeses, the hens were an important source of income, as were the acres of land they rented out to the neighbouring farmer because her widowed mother could no longer manage the crops.

The thought of her mum working so hard always galvanised Jenn into action. But she'd helped clean the kitchen the day before, rubbing down the whitewashed walls and mopping the flagged floor, even scrubbing the inside of the Aga. And the cows had been milked and the eggs collected, so there was nothing more to do on the farm. Her time was her own. There was home-work, of course, but that could wait.

She left the kitchen and took the stairs to the first floor. The second door on the left was ajar. She pushed it wide.

Despite facing south, the room was always chilly, and a faint musty smell lingered in the air. She flopped on to the wickerwork chair beside the blackened fireplace, and ran the toe of her trainer

16

across the rag rug. The shelf behind her sagged ominously. She'd have to do something about that before it collapsed under the weight of books. And the Swiss-cheese plant needed watering.

She got to her feet and studied her reflection in the wardrobe mirror. Her close-fitting jeans and t-shirt showed her muscular body to good advantage. It was the swimming, no question. Every weekday before school, she cycled to the Olympia Centre on East Whale Lane, and swam one hundred lengths in the training pool, trying to avoid careering into the grey-haired ladies. These women would chat to each other while doing their sedate breast-strokes, careless of the human torpedo in the left-hand lane. The pool opened at 10.00 a.m. on a Saturday. Perhaps she should go there now.

She sat down at the small dressing table and searched through the array of make-up items for the wand of pink lipgloss. After applying it to her lips, she smoothed away the excess at the corners. The effect was hardly transformative, as the gloss was the exact same colour as her lips. She wiped it away with the back of her hand.

She lay down on the bed, and reached behind her to finger the curtains falling over the sill. Her thoughts slipped back to the woman in the scarecrow. Jenn's knowledge of rigor came not just from listening to the forensic pathologist, Nikki Alexander, on *Silent Witness*, but because she herself kept the bodies of dead animals and birds in the woodland bordering Oaktree. They'd usually been run over by speeding drivers and were mostly rabbits and crows, although she'd been lucky enough to find a red fox. As often as she could, and at least once a week, she would visit the site to study the process of decomposition and the effects of insect activity.

She closed her eyes. She badly wanted to see Aleck. He'd likely be on his own, as his partner worked as a volunteer in the library on a Saturday. She could walk through Backmuir Wood and spy on Keeper's Cottage from the safety of the trees. Once the police left, it would be safe to go inside.

As always, once she'd made a plan, she was filled with a sense of determination to see it through. She sprang to her feet, and left her sister's bedroom.

CHAPTER 3

The procurator fiscal, a lean middle-aged woman with a cap of dark hair, peered over the corpse, watching Professor Slaughter cut away the clothes. He was bent over the body, giving everyone a good view of his comb-over hairstyle.

They were in Ninewells Hospital, in the cutting rooms of the Centre for Forensic and Legal Medicine. The University of Dundee, as Dania had learnt, was funded by the Scottish Crown Office to provide forensic autopsy and toxicology services, including medico-legal dissections, to the Tayside region as well as to Fife and Central. The room they were in had the same musky smell, overlaid with antiseptic, that Dania recognised from similar rooms in her time at the Met.

The woman's body, still posed on sticks, had been placed face down on two steel tables, her head protruding over the edge. The bags from her head, hands and feet had been removed, and Milo was working up the body, cutting through the legs of the dungarees with slow, deliberate movements. As he snipped the second of the two straps, he pulled the dungarees apart, and the sticks fell away, revealing the back of Judith Johnstone's legs. She was wearing tights and black knickers. The assistant gathered up the sticks and set them on another table, next to the scarecrow's scarf, which Milo had helpfully told the assembly was in the tartan known as Ancient Buchanan.

Dania, standing a few feet away, automatically made mental notes of what needed to be done: the sticks would have to be checked for prints, and the clothes sent off to be taped for fibres.

'She's not wearing shoes,' Chirnside said.

'They'd have removed the shoes to dress her,' Dania said, glancing at him. 'They wouldn't have bothered putting them back on.'

'Why not, do you think?' said the fiscal.

Dania shrugged. 'They may not have had time. Anyway, they had to dispose of her clothes. My guess is they disposed of the shoes in the same way.'

'Why do you say "they"? Don't you think this is the work of one person?'

'I thought at first that it might be, but now I'm not so sure.' She nodded towards the adjacent table. 'Look at the soil marks on those sticks. They were buried to a depth of a least half a metre. Someone would have held the body upright while another hammered the sticks in.'

'You don't think one person could do that?' the fiscal pressed.

'If it *is* one person, it would have to be someone strong.' Dania gnawed at her bottom lip. 'I suppose he could hammer in one stick, haul the body on to his shoulder, lift one leg up and slot the leg of the dungarees over the stick. He could then insert the second stick while the body was hanging off the first. So, yes, difficult, but not impossible. He'd have to be built like a wrestler, though. And tall, to get that first leg in.'

They were watching her with interest. A smile was playing about Milo's lips. He had warm, deep-set eyes, she noticed then.

'He could have stood on a box,' Chirnside said. 'The area around the scarecrow was pretty chewed up.'

'That would have made it easier.'

'Proceed, Professor Slaughter,' the fiscal said.

Milo cut away the yellow shirt, nodding to the assistant to catch the horizontal stick before it fell. Although the men could have used the hydraulic hoist, they lifted the stiff body and pulled away the scarecrow's clothes. Judith Johnstone lay face down in her black underwear and tights, her arms outstretched, her legs apart.

'There are no breakages in the skin,' Milo said. 'But there are striations on both wrists, consistent with ligatures. It looks as if she put up something of a struggle.'

'Anything under the hair?' the fiscal asked.

Watching Milo's long fingers feel around the woman's scalp, Dania thought that he would have made an excellent pianist. 'There's a laceration consistent with blunt-force trauma,' he said.

'Hard enough to have killed her?' Dania said.

'I very much doubt it. I think the intention was to stun her.'

'Knocked on the head and then tied up,' Chirnside said, drawing his shaggy brows together.

Milo signalled to the assistant to help him turn the body over. Under the harsh light of the overhead lamps, the woman's skin was like alabaster, and the contrast with the lipstick, some of which was smeared on to her teeth, couldn't have been greater. The blood-red open mouth and the look in her eyes gave her the appearance of something out of a vampire horror film. Only the freckles on her face, neck and breasts suggested she was human.

'No ligatures round the neck,' Milo said, his face close to the body. 'And no other visible marks.'

'Could she have been tied on to the posts, and then have died?' Dania said. 'Maybe something sudden? A heart attack?'

He straightened. 'It's possible, but we'll need the autopsy before I can pronounce on cause of death.'

'Was she raped?' Chirnside said gruffly, nodding at the ligature marks.

'We'll do the usual checks for semen and saliva. As far as I can tell, there's nothing under her fingernails.'

'If he raped her,' Dania said, 'why would he bother putting her knickers and tights back on? Unless it's part of the tableau.'

'If it is, then we're dealing with a sick individual,' Chirnside blurted.

The emotion in his voice made everyone look at him in surprise. He turned away and made a point of checking his phone. 'I need to get back to the station,' he muttered. 'Can you carry on, DS Gorska?' Without waiting for a reply, he hurried out of the room.

'There are tests I need to conduct before the autopsy,' Milo said, his voice level. 'I'll keep you informed.'

This seemed to be the signal that he wanted to be left to get on with it. The fiscal nodded at Dania and left.

She stood, uncertain as to what to do next. Milo and the assistant were pulling off the woman's tights. There was nothing she could do but try to catch Chirnside before he left the building. Otherwise, she'd have to make her own way back to the city centre.

It was not what she'd expected, she thought as she left the room – a boss who went weak at the knees at the sight of a corpse.

It was midday before Dania arrived at West Bell Street, having paid off the taxi. The open-plan room with the ranks squashed together, unlike the Met where the sergeants had their own area, had filled in her absence with officers come for the afternoon shift, and the air was thick with the smell of aftershave.

'The DI's with the chief inspector,' Fergus said, apparently anticipating her question. He nodded towards where an incident board had been set up. 'Said he'll brief us when he gets back.

Leave's been cancelled, by the way. Can't say I'm bothered. I could do with the overtime.' He smirked knowingly. 'I've got an expensive girlfriend.'

'Aye, right. She gets the best TV dinners money can buy,' someone snorted.

Fergus Finnie was the best-looking officer at the station. With his sandy-brown hair, laughing eyes and lopsided smile, Dania suspected he knew he was hard to resist. She'd worked closely with him on her recent case – it had taken her a while to get used to his rich Glasgow accent – but hadn't yet decided if he was someone she could trust. And trust was essential in this game. She'd met officers in London who said 'Yes' to their superiors and 'No' to their inferiors although, so far, Fergus hadn't exhibited that kind of behaviour. He tipped his chair back, balancing it on its back legs, and she had to suppress the childish urge to push it over. Although his desk was on the other side of the room, she occasionally found him looking over her shoulder at her computer screen. She wondered how he'd feel if she behaved the same way, but creeping across the room in a cat-like tread was a skill for which she was lacking the gene. At first she'd been flattered, but she soon began to find it annoying.

'So he abandoned you at the Slaughterhouse,' Fergus said with a smile like a sneer.

She dropped her bag on her desk, beside the framed photo of her family. Chirnside was her superior, and deserved her loyalty. 'Something came up and he had to leave,' she said.

Fergus's smile widened, but the look in his eyes suggested he didn't believe her. He was the only other detective sergeant in the team and was ambitious to the point of obsessiveness. Although he'd not said it in so many words, he'd made it clear to her, in a nice sort of way, that he intended to make DI before she did. Dania was determined not to let this happen.

'I take it the uniforms aren't back yet,' she said.

'They'll be out for ages.'

She checked the incident board. A blow-up photo of Dr Judith Johnstone, taken from her university ID card, was pinned up under her name and title: Reader at the Institute of Religions and Belief Systems. The word 'religion' caused Dania's mind to stray to something Milo had said. *Strange way to crucify someone.* At the memory of the woman's rigid corpse, and the position in which it had been posed, Dania felt the first stirrings of unease.

Fergus strolled across. He stood close enough to Dania that she could smell the heavy, camphor-like odour of his hair gel. 'We looked her up on the uni's website,' he said. 'Religions and Belief Systems. Sounds like a load of tosh to me.'

'What did they find in her car?'

'Just her handbag.'

'Phone?'

'Tech are running the numbers.' He blew out his cheeks. 'Strange one, isn't it? Stringing her up like that.' He glanced at Dania. 'What did the Slaughterman tell you?'

'The professor?' She gestured to the board, where Chirnside had listed the main points from the preliminary examination. 'It's all there,' she said.

Fergus's expression hardened. She could tell he wasn't impressed with the answer. He was looking for more, hoping to get a leg-up in the investigation, and shinny over their heads. But there was no more to tell.

'What about the person who found the body?' he persisted.

'Jenn McLaughlin? I need to enter her statement on to the system.'

The mention of the girl's name caused a few of the officers to exchange glances, something that wasn't lost on Dania.

'Jenn McLaughlin's come up again?' Fergus said. 'Talk about a bad penny.'

'What do you mean?'

'Her sister, Ailsa, went missing. It was not long after you arrived.'

'Did they find her?'

'In a manner of speaking.'

Before he could continue, the door banged open and Chirnside marched in. He strode to the incident board and beckoned everyone over. They crowded round expectantly as he pinned up a large sheet.

'Right,' he said, 'I've listed the tasks on this roster.' He addressed himself to Dania and Fergus, as it would be down to the two detective sergeants to organise the team. 'You both know what to do. Fergus, we need to show the victim's photograph around the villages off the Coupar Angus Road. Not just Muirhead and Liff but the ones further afield. I particularly want to know if anyone saw the victim's light blue Honda Civic, and who was driving it.' He ignored the groans from the rest of the room. Like everyone there, Dania knew how bad the public was at identifying and remembering makes of cars, let alone noticing who was in them. 'We also need to find out everything we can about the victim,' Chirnside went on. 'Who she was, who her friends were, what type of cornflakes she ate. The works.' He paused to draw breath. 'That's your job, Dania.'

'Pity there's no CCTV anywhere near where she was found,' someone said.

'We've not been able to track down the gamekeeper, Aleck Docherty. And the laird's away. But they'll surface soon enough.' Chirnside eyed his officers purposefully. 'Now get to it.'

★ ★ ★

25

The officers hurried to their desks, but Dania lingered, studying the roster. She glanced sideways to see Chirnside watching her.

'The fiscal's granted us the warrant to search Judith's house, Dania. You can get the keys from Sydney. Everything's already been through Forensics.'

'What about broadcasting an appeal for information on the television, sir? We did that a lot in the Met, and it often gave us results.'

Chirnside drew his brows together. 'This is Police Scotland. We haven't the resources the Met has.' He seemed to think better of his comment. 'We'll see how it goes,' he added, his voice softening. 'I'm not ruling it out. Look, I have to go. The chief inspector and I are giving a press conference.'

At her computer, Dania pulled up the victim's details. Fifty-three-year-old Judith Johnstone was unmarried and lived in Monikie, a village outside Dundee. Dania slung her bag over her shoulder. The first twenty-four hours after the discovery of a body were crucial, so lunch would have to wait. She spoke briefly to the remaining detective constables, then left the room.

Sydney, the elderly Evidence Room manager, was a cheery, wispy-haired Cockney. At their first meeting, he'd informed Dania that he had been born within the sound of Bow Bells and, on hearing that she'd come up from the Met, had hugged her fiercely. The fact that her accent betrayed her as being from Eastern Europe made no difference to Sydney, who on more than one occasion had referred to her as a 'Londoner'. At least he didn't use rhyming slang, which she'd never been able to get the hang of.

'So what can I do you for, Detective Sergeant?' He smiled, deepening the wrinkles crosshatching the corners of his eyes.

'I need to get the keys from the handbag that was brought in today. Judith Johnstone's.' Dania hesitated. 'And I'd like to examine the contents.'

'Right you are.' He peered over his half-moon glasses and

consulted a folder, which contained a printout of the information held on his computer. Deeply mistrustful of technology, he refused to use it, reminding everyone of the computer failure that would happen any day now, and which would leave every department paralysed except his own. The chief super had long since given up trying to persuade him to change, and grudgingly admitted that Sydney's methods in no way affected his performance. Provided the information was duplicated on the system, a task the chief super's secretary happily undertook, Sydney was left to run his department his way.

He took a plastic sheet and two pairs of latex gloves from a drawer. 'It's over here,' he said, nodding towards the right-hand aisle.

Dania followed him past shelves of bags, each meticulously labelled. There was a strong smell of stale dust and lavender floor polish.

He stopped and consulted his folder. 'Everything's been checked already, so we don't need the gloves.'

'Fantastic, Sydney. They ought to put you in mass production.'

'Don't get excited. It's bad for the heart.'

He pulled a plastic box down from the shelf. On a table near the back, he spread out the sheet, placed the box on it, and removed a woven shoulder bag. It was the kind with a flap, woven in a strong geometric pattern of browns and deep reds, such as she'd once seen on a Navajo rug. It closed with a magnetic clasp. He opened it and tipped out the contents, laying out the objects reverentially on the sheet.

The key ring held two Yales and a variety of key fobs. The other objects were a hairbrush, a blue Specsavers case, a squashed chocolate bar, a brightly coloured make-up bag, a black leather purse and a card wallet, thick with credit and store cards.

And a notebook.

She picked up the notebook and flicked through it. 'It's a diary,' she said, her heart racing.

'Seems like Dr Johnstone is another one of those people who do things the old-fashioned way,' he said, his tongue firmly in his cheek.

Dania unzipped the make-up bag. The cosmetics were an expensive brand. Powder compact, lipstick, and a duo eye-shadow palette in complementary shades of beige. No mascara or liner. The face powder was the pale mineralised type. She pulled the top off the lipstick and swivelled it up. The same vampire red she'd seen on the corpse. She replaced everything in the bag.

The credit cards were worth only the merest glance – the entries on Judith Johnstone's growing computer file confirmed that a bank check had already been initiated. The store cards included the usual Tesco, Boots and Debenhams, as well as Waterstones, Costa Coffee and the Odeon cinema. Inside the purse was roughly eighty pounds, most of it in notes.

'Forensics scraped the brush for hairs,' Sydney said helpfully. 'I reckon they're looking for ones that aren't hers.'

Dania threw him a quick smile. If the Met was anything to go by, most Evidence Room managers saw themselves as amateur sleuths.

'So how do you think the vote will go, Detective Sergeant?'

'I've no idea,' she said cagily. A definitive answer about the forthcoming EU referendum could lead to a prolonged and heated discussion, and the last thing she wanted was to hurt Sydney's feelings by cutting him off.

'It was just the house keys you wanted, was it?' he said.

She held up the diary. 'And I'll take this.'

A smile spread across his face. She could see that he believed the case would be as good as solved once the diary yielded its secrets. A detective, however, knew that things were never that simple.

CHAPTER 4

Dania's sat-nav informed her that Monikie lay approximately nine miles north-east of Dundee. She followed the Arbroath Road, negotiating the lunchtime traffic, and turned on to a filter which took her to a narrow but well-maintained B-road. Crop fields stretched out on either side, broken only by a line of trees on the eastern horizon. She wondered what the London lot would think if they knew that it was possible to drive in and around Dundee without spending the best part of an hour in a traffic jam. Some officers she'd known at the Met got to places faster by using the underground.

Whoever had been in the staff car last had left pizza detritus on the passenger seat, and the stale smell of cheese and pepperoni forced her to wind down both car windows and let the breeze blow through. After passing a couple of farms, the words 'Pitairlie Road' appeared on her sat-nav. She slowed on the approach to Newbigging, and passed through it at twenty miles per hour. It would never do for a police officer to be caught speeding, something that had recently happened to Fergus and which he was unlikely ever to live down.

Although she needed to concentrate on the road, she found herself thinking about Judith's diary. She'd given the contents only a glance before authorising their digitisation. Judith Johnstone seemed to lead a full life, but on Friday 27 May – Milo's best estimate for the date she'd died – the diary page was blank.

At the old red phone box, she turned off the road and drove straight on, glimpsing now and again the glint of water from the Monikie reservoir. Minutes later, the 30 m.p.h. sign told her she'd arrived in the village. As she passed the placard advertising the Café Byzantium, with the gates to Monikie Country Park beyond, she was sorely tempted to stop for a coffee. Perhaps on the way back.

'You have reached your destination,' came the sat-nav's sexy female voice. Dania pulled up outside a cottage made of weatherbeaten stone, with a slate-tiled roof. The scrap of garden was surrounded by a picket fence of bleached wood.

The street was deserted. She left the car, taking care to lock it.

She pushed against the tiny gate. Gardening didn't seem to be Judith Johnstone's thing. A straggle of unpruned rose bushes bent away from the walls, and grass grew between the flagstones leading to the entrance.

At the front door, Dania pressed her ear to the wood. Nothing. Although she had the keys and a warrant to enter, she felt uneasy about simply going in. There was no bell, so she rapped at the door.

'Hello?' she shouted, when there was no response. 'Is anyone in?'

She rapped again, louder now, and then tried the Yales. The key that unlocked the door had a red tag. She drew on a pair of latex gloves and pushed gently but firmly.

The room behind the door held a few pieces of prim and solid furniture, as well as a couple of sagging cane armchairs that looked as if they'd been bought second-hand. The sooty fireplace sheltered an arrangement of dried flowers in a pitted brass bucket. A worn blue rug covered the stone floor, made new again by the sunlight streaming through the window.

On the walls were framed black-and-white photographs of

places she recognised: Yellowstone Park, the Manhattan skyline before 9/11, the red San Francisco bridge. One showed a bronze statue of a Native American seated on a horse, looking towards the sky, his arms outstretched. The caption underneath read: Appeal to the Great Spirit.

Two books lay on the coffee table: *Oral Histories of Native Americans*, and *Ghost Dance Ceremonies in Native American Religion*. She leafed through the brightly coloured photographs. It seemed that Native American culture was one of Judith Johnstone's specialist subjects.

The other books in the room sat on a long shelf opposite the fireplace: the complete twenty-eight-book set of Scott's *Waverley* novels, bound in red leather. Dania wondered if they were worth anything, but a glance showed them to be modern reprints.

A CD deck and speakers stood in the corner beside a snazzy CD holder in what might have been a double helix. What was your taste in music, Judith? Classical? Or maybe something with a Native American theme?

Dania picked out CDs at random: Duke Ellington, Charlie Parker, John Coltrane, Dizzy Gillespie. Was this how you spent your evenings? Listening to jazz?

The bedroom was off the corridor behind the living room. There was a single bed, made up in the same M&S floral linen that Dania used and, next to it, an IKEA-style cabinet in blond wood. She pulled opened the drawers. Underwear and tights. A kidney-shaped dressing table stood under the window, with more of the same type of make-up that Judith had in her handbag. And a bottle of perfume: Le Baiser du Dragon by Cartier.

The only other piece of furniture was a double-doored mirrored wardrobe, which was so big that Dania wondered how it had been manoeuvred into the cottage. Inside were dark suits and an assortment of jumpers, shirts, and skirts, the labels mostly

Debenhams. A pair of knee-high black leather boots stood among the jumble of shoes.

She was closing the door when she spotted a long gown in raw black silk. It was a tailored dress in an old-fashioned style, with wide lapels, a hood and two large pockets. Was this what Judith wore to formal occasions? Dania, who was trying to get a sense of the woman from her clothes, imagined events at the university, with Judith wearing this dress, sipping a cocktail while chatting to men old enough to be young when this type of dress was in style.

Next to the bedroom was a spotless white bathroom, which looked recently renovated. The tiny cabinet over the sink contained a bottle of ibuprofen, a tube of extra-strong insect repellent, and an unopened packet of Elastoplast. In the larger wall cupboard were loo rolls, packets of toothpaste and dental floss, and dispensers of hand-wash gel. No contraceptives.

The contents of the small kitchen suggested that, unless Judith was about to do a big shop, she took most of her meals elsewhere. There were three eggs in the fridge, half a carton of skimmed milk, and an unopened packet of Jarlsberg. The wall cabinets contained the usual crockery, glassware and packets of dried goods. And Dania could now tell DI Chirnside what Judith Johnstone ate for breakfast: Tesco honey nut cornflakes.

Dania peered through the window, seeing little through the tangle of bushes behind the cottage. The locked kitchen door opened with the other Yale, and the neglect she'd seen in the front garden was mirrored at the back: the coarse lawn was choked with dandelions and, other than the shrubbery straggling the walls, the garden was bare.

She felt her jaw grow slack. In what could have been the geometric centre of the lawn, there was a gigantic totem pole. Although she stood at just under six foot, she had to draw her head back to see it in its entirety. Huge rough-hewn faces of animals and birds, painted in dull shades of red, brown and green, stared back at her. A fish, its lidless eyes gawking, held a small male figure in its mouth. Near the top was a set of outstretched wings and, as she gazed in astonishment, a dusty black raven landed on them and sent up a screech that nearly curdled her blood. It shifted its weight, dropping its head to look at her. She had the sudden sensation that the ponderous structure was about to topple.

'Can I help you?' The voice came from her right.

An oldish man, holding a dripping hose, was watching her from over the low wall that separated Judith's garden from his. His grey hair was held back in a tight ponytail, and he had a rugged complexion that suggested he spent much of his time outdoors. He gazed at her, suspicion growing in his huge liquid eyes.

She pulled out her warrant card. 'Detective Sergeant Dania Gorska. I'm with the Specialist Crime Division.' By now, Judith Johnstone's demise would be all over the media, so she added, 'I'm investigating a murder.'

'Aye,' the man said, shaking his head, and staring at her latex gloves. 'I heard it on the news. A bad business.'

'Can you tell me when you last saw Dr Johnstone?' Dania said, taking out her notebook.

He dropped the hose and kicked it away. 'Yesterday morning, the Friday. She left for work as per usual.'

'And what time would that have been?'

'Seven-thirty. On the dot.'

'On the dot?' Dania said, making a point of not hiding her surprise.

He rubbed his nose with the back of his hand. 'I take Bruce out for his walk then. He's my spaniel. Always do it at that time. Regular as clockwork.'

'I see.'

'And Judith always leaves the house at that time.'

Dania noted his use of the woman's first name. 'You knew her well?'

'Not well. She was hardly ever home. Worked long hours at the uni.'

'What about the evenings?'

'Ah now, she was often away out in the evenings.'

Dania glanced up. 'Out where?'

'Not a question I asked her. And she never offered to enlighten me.' His mouth formed into a smile. 'But she must have had an active social life. She always wore that black ball gown.' He paused, and Dania could see regret in his eyes. 'A fine-looking woman, she was.'

'Do you think she went to functions at the university?'

'Couldn't say. The few times we spoke, she often complained about how much work she had, so maybe she was expected to attend their fancy dinners and that.'

'Did she go with anyone? Did you see anyone call for her?'

'No one. She always went alone. In her blue car.'

Interesting. If Judith had indeed attended functions at the university, there'd be drink flowing. Dania made a mental note to check the contents of the woman's stomach with Professor Slaughter. And then she realised that nowhere in the cottage had she seen any alcohol. No beer. No spirits.

The man had anticipated her question. 'She drove herself back,' he said, smiling slyly. 'I'd hear the Honda through my open window. Had a bit of a rattle, that car. And she always jerked the handbrake like all women drivers.'

'Did she ever bring anyone home afterwards?' Dania said, watching his reaction.

He shook his head. 'I'd see him in the morning, wouldn't I? And Bruce barks at strangers.'

'He didn't bark at me.'

'He's at the vet's today.' A look of anxiety crossed the man's face. 'I may have to have him put to sleep. He's getting on a bit and can't see too well.'

'I'm sorry to hear that.' She paused. 'What time did Judith usually get in at night?'

'That depends. She stayed out longer in the summer.' He grinned, showing long yellow teeth. 'I mean, don't we all?'

Dania gestured to the totem pole. 'When was that erected?'

The man rubbed his nose again. 'Now you're asking. Last spring, I seem to remember. Judith had come back from America. Study tour, she called it.' He lifted his head back and squinted at the pole. 'She'd arranged for that to be shipped over. Must have cost her a few weeks' wages.' He nodded. 'Aye. Nice to have that kind of money. Although she probably bought it with one of them grants that university folk are always getting. It's likcly it was the taxpayers funded it. That'll stop once we leave the EU, mind.'

Dania recalled Judith's furniture and clothes. The woman wasn't exactly living the high life. 'Can you think of anyone who'd want to harm her?'

'Sorry. Can't help you there. I never met her lecturer friends.'

'What about in the village?'

He looked at Dania from under heavy brows. 'She didn't know anyone here. Never used the shop, or joined the bridge club at the Memorial Hall. Never went to church.'

'There's a church here?'

'It's in Kirkton.'

'I see. Well, I think that's it for now.' Dania took the man's name and address. 'Thank you for your time. If you can think of anything that might help, anything at all, please don't hesitate to get in touch.'

She left him staring at her business card.

After locking up the house, she slipped into the car and pulled away. In the rear-view mirror, she caught a glimpse of him stand-ing watching her, the card still in his hand. As she rounded the corner and sped away, although she couldn't remember, she had a niggling feeling that she might have jerked the handbrake when she pulled up outside the cottage.

It was nearly four by the time Dania reached West Bell Street, having stopped at the Kentucky Fried Chicken on the corner of the A92 and the Baldovie Road. She'd bought a Double Down, which she ate on the way to the car. Eating while walking was a bad habit she'd picked up in London.

The incident room was empty except for DC Laurence Whyte, who was sitting staring glumly into his computer screen. He was a young officer with a serious, boyish face, and she'd warmed to him from her first day on the job. With his shabby suit, and tie at half-mast, he was the polar opposite of Fergus, whose pressed clothes always looked straight off the rail. Laurence had striking brown eyes, but she rarely looked straight into them because he was too shy to look directly at the person he was talking with. He was the type who was willing, but was always in need of instructions. That he seemed to want to take those instructions from her and not from Fergus was not lost on Dania.

A leaflet was lying on her desk.

'I thought you might be interested in that, Sergeant,' Laurence said, looking at her sideways.

The circular advertised a forthcoming event, the opening of a museum dedicated to the Polish soldiers stationed in Angus dur-ing the war. It transpired that the Poles living in Dundee had been petitioning the council for a memorial for years. The council, permanently broke, had been unable to help, and a fund-raising committee had been set up.

'Where did you get this?' she asked, suddenly interested.

'Someone left a whole pile of them with the desk sergeant. Did you know there were Poles here during the war?'

'I knew there were soldiers in St Andrews. There's a bust of General Sikorski in Kinburn Park, and there's that Polish mosaic on the town hall building.'

'A mosaic?' Laurence said doubtfully.

'I think the Pole who designed it was killed in 1944, in the Warsaw Uprising. But, no, I didn't know there were Poles in Angus.'

'Didn't you spend your childhood in Fife?'

'My childhood was spent in Poland. We came to St Andrews in 2002, when I was fourteen. I've lived exactly half my life in Poland and half in the UK.'

He was looking at her with curiosity. 'You must know Dundee well, then.'

'Hardly at all. We came into Dundee to shop, so I know my way around the city centre. But that's pretty much it.' She smiled. 'My school-friends and I took the train to Edinburgh when we wanted a night out.'

'Why did your parents choose St Andrews?'

'They'd heard of the town in connection with the war. Many Poles came after the fall of communism.'

'Was that the start of the influx?'

'This was before Poland joined the EU.'

Her colleagues were constantly bombarding her with reasons why the UK should leave the European Union, the chief one being that there were too many immigrants in the country. She had long since wearied of the debates on television. But Laurence had shied away from that particular argument. He was more interested in how things had been in Poland before 1989, having

37

confessed to her that his favourite subject at school had been modern history.

'Some time, you'll have to tell me more about life under the communists, Sergeant.'

'I was too young to remember. The system fell apart the year after I was born.' She laid the leaflet aside. 'But I heard things from my parents. When the older Poles weren't talking about the war, they talked about the communists. Empty shops. Meat queues. Solidarity. How the new president, Lech Wałęsa, saw off the Russian tanks on the seventeenth of September, the anniversary of the day they first arrived. A nice story, but they didn't all leave on the one day. There were too many of them.'

'You're saying the Russian tanks that came at the start of the war never left?'

'That's right. If you knew where to look, you'd see them in the forests.'

'Must have been hard for your folks, relocating to a strange country, not knowing anyone.'

She shrugged. 'They soon got to know the other Poles here.'

'Your parents still in St Andrews?'

'They didn't take to life in the UK, and decided to move back to Warsaw.'

The silence lengthened. 'So did you find anything this afternoon?' he said.

Briefly, she told him what she'd discovered in Judith's cottage, and the gist of her conversation with the neighbour. 'I'm guessing the university is where her life was,' she said. 'And what about you?'

'We managed to track down some of the university staff, including a lecturer from her institute.' Laurence raised a knowing eyebrow. 'She never showed at her office yesterday.'

'Did they think that strange?'

'For Judith, yes. She had a meeting scheduled first thing.'

'Right, then, what we know so far is that seven-thirty a.m. yesterday was the last time anyone saw her.'

'You think she was snatched on the road into Dundee?'

Dania thought back to her drive from Monikie. There were plenty of places to ambush someone. 'Whoever did it must have known what route she'd take.' She pulled up an online map. 'There's one obvious route. Go down this B-road and then take the A92 into Dundee. I can't see her taking the parallel B-road to the north. The A92 is much faster.'

'My money's on a snatch somewhere outside Monikie, then.'

'What about her car, though? It was found not far from the body.'

'Okay, so maybe she wasn't snatched.'

'Or maybe she was, and someone else drove the car there. Forensics might be able to tell us.'

Laurence picked up a paper clip. 'The DI seems to be taking this murder quite hard. I think he was spooked by that tattie bogle.'

'Could it be because the victim is a woman? I remember officers at the Met who found the murders of women difficult.' She glanced at her colleague. A pulse was beating in his temple. But it was the expression in his eyes that said it all. If anyone was spooked, it was Laurence.

'I keep coming back to it,' she added, half to herself. 'It seems a strange way of disposing of the body. Almost as if you want to advertise to the world what you've done.'

'You think it might be something to do with this Institute of Religions and Belief Systems? A ceremony that went badly wrong?'

'And they left her there on those sticks? If something went wrong and someone died, surely they'd want to get rid of the evidence. Anyway, is there a religion or belief system where people dress up as scarecrows? I thought scarecrows were just meant to scare crows.'

But the exchange had set off a train of thought. She did a Facebook search for Judith Johnstone. Several people with that name came up, but she quickly found the one who worked at Dundee's Institute of Religions and Belief Systems.

She flicked through the folders. 'Judith's been all over the world, according to this.'

'Let's see, Sergeant.' Laurence moved his chair over. She smelt curry on his clothes, suggesting he'd managed lunch. Well, lucky Laurence.

'Wow, look at those photos,' he said.

Judith Johnstone had created a rich resource for her students. In addition to hundreds of photographs, there were pages on the major world religions, organisations such as Interfaith Scotland, and a link to The Pagan Federation's Facebook page.

Dania twisted a strand of hair round her finger. 'I can't see anything about scarecrows.'

Her desk phone rang. It was Tech, saying that Judith Johnstone's notebook had been digitised and returned to the Evidence Room. The contents were now available to view.

She pulled up the pages. 'Okay, Laurence, this is Judith's diary for 2016.'

'So, anything for yesterday?' he said eagerly.

'I checked that earlier. The page is blank.'

'No mention of that work meeting?'

'This must be her private diary. I'm guessing her work commitments are on a system at the uni.' She skimmed through the entries. 'There are some work events, actually, university receptions of one kind or another.' She thought of the black silk gown in Judith's wardrobe. 'There's a large number scheduled for the third week of June, when graduations take place.' She scrolled backwards.

'What's that?' Laurence said suddenly. 'There. April the twenty-ninth.'

'Yes, I see it. She's crossed out DM Banks and written LCM.'

'So who's DM Banks?'

Dania checked the Dundee directory, and then searched nationally. 'Lots of DM Banks but none that live locally.'

'Maybe she had two boyfriends, DM Banks and LCM.'

'But then why not write DMB instead of DM Banks?' Dania crossed her arms. 'Maybe they're not people. What does LCM stand for?'

When she saw Laurence's blank look, she tried an Internet search. The returns included Lowest Common Multiple, Life Cycle Management, Latent Class Model, Leeds College of Music, and London Canal Museum.

She scrolled back to the start of the year, and then went forward systematically, finding both DM Banks and LCM several times. 'Look, Laurence. Tonight. Saturday the twenty-eighth. DM Banks. Eight p.m.'

'Well, if it's a bloke, whoever he is, he's going to be disappointed.'

'And there are no DM Banks or LCM entries after today.'

'Maybe they don't set up lots of dates in advance.' He threw her a sideways glance. 'I mean, when you meet with your boyfriend, Sergeant, do you do that?'

He was trying to find out whether she was seeing someone. She smiled to herself. Let him keep trying.

'I think most people phone or text the day before,' she said. She glanced at her watch. 'I have to go, I'm afraid.'

Laurence moved his chair back to his desk. He nodded at the leaflet about the Polish museum. 'Let me know if you decide to go to that.' He studied his computer screen as though the answers to the mysteries of the universe were there. 'It's not for a while yet, but I could go with you, if you like,' he added, his voice tailing off.

DI Blair Chirnside let himself into the ground-floor flat on the Lochee Road. Although he had a place of his own in the West End, he was renting it out to a university lecturer and his family, and stopping with his folks. They'd reached the age where they needed help, but not the age where they were prepared to admit to it. So, rather than uproot them and have them live with him, he'd invited himself over on a semi-permanent basis and, without making a song and dance about it, quietly looked after them. This part of the Lochee Road, with block after monotonous block of terraced residential buildings crammed full of noisy students, wouldn't have been his first choice of living quarters, but it had the advantage that it wasn't far from the station. And his roots were here, his ancestors having been employed at the famous Camperdown Works, once the largest jute production site in the world, and Lochee's primary employer.

The stale smell of tobacco and burnt food greeted him as he opened the door, making him wonder if his parents had tried their hand at making supper. And yet he'd told them he'd be back in time to cook, as he'd filled the fridge the day before. He fought down his irritation. Ach, they were trying to be helpful. And they never knew what time he'd be home.

'It's me,' he shouted from the narrow hallway. He didn't expect a reply and he received none.

His parents were in the living-cum-dining room, sitting one on either side of the fake-coal electric fire. His mother was buried in the book of cryptic crosswords he'd bought her, and his father was reading the *Dundee Evening Telegraph*, known as the '*Tele*' although Dundonians pronounced it 'Tully'.

He felt the back of his throat as he walked in, less from the cigarette smoke that hung in the air and more from the fine film of dust that took the shine off the clumsy wooden furniture. He'd have to find time to clean the place, not easy given the high ceilings with their ornate cornice plasterwork, which was ideal for the spiders that so terrified his mother. And there was the washing. And the flowers that had been dead for days in the slim crystal vase. And he couldn't put off doing something about the loose carpet tiles for much longer or his parents would slip and break their necks.

The burnt smell, he realised on glancing at the dining table, was toast. The remains of afternoon tea − or what passed for it − lay scattered on the plastic tablecloth.

'Right then, I'll make a start on supper,' he said cheerfully.

His mother lifted her head. She was a fleshy woman with a florid complexion, and Chirnside had long since accepted that he'd inherited more of her genes than his father's. 'That'd be nice, son,' she said in her timid voice. She seemed anxious about everything, always fingering the neck of her heavy-knit roll-neck. 'Before you do, can you help me with this one? It's driving me mad.' She read out the clue. 'There's no anger in a French flower.'

He squinted over her shoulder at the words. 'Garonne,' he said, a few seconds later. 'It's not flower,' he said, making the word rhyme with 'flour', 'but flower, as in a river flowing. Garonne is an anagram of "no anger".'

'What's the Garonne, when it's out?' his father said, reaching for the pack of Dunhills beside the overflowing ashtray.

'A river in France.'

The man thrust a cigarette into his mouth and lit it with a plastic lighter. His face was dry and creased from chain-smoking.

'Why the devil they don't make the clues straightforward, I'll never understand,' he grumbled, shaking out the *Tele*.

'That's the whole point, Walter,' his wife said with a nervous quaver. She rolled her eyes at her son, and her face twitched into a smile, as though this were a private joke between them.

Chirnside smiled back. He'd always been good at crosswords, and had infected his mother with his enthusiasm. Helping her was one of the highlights of their time together, and the two of them would often leave his father to watch football on the large flat-screen TV.

'You're on the front page,' his father said suddenly. He held out the *Tele*. 'Did you know?'

Chirnside took the paper and stared at the image, feeling his teeth clench. Whoever had taken the photograph must have been in Backmuir Wood. It showed him and Dania in deep discussion with the Prof. Behind them, the scarecrow hung in the sunshine. At the memory of Judith inside that devilish contraption, Chirnside felt the pit of his stomach drop out. He scanned the text, wondering how the journalist had got her name so quickly. Maybe he'd overheard them talking. Or slipped a few notes to one of the uniforms, more likely. It hardly mattered now.

'Did you know the lass?' his father said, letting the smoke out of his mouth as he talked.

'Why do you ask?'

'You've got that look on your face. Were you and she stepping out, then?'

'Of course not,' Chirnside said hotly. He thrust the paper back.

His father wouldn't let it go. 'But you *did* know her. You told us you were off to some meeting with her.' It was a statement and not a question.

'Aye, I knew her. Not well, but I knew her. Now, can we leave it?'

44

The man tapped the page. 'And who's that girl you're talking to?'

'She's a detective sergeant, come up from the Met.'

'The Met, eh?' His father squinted at the photo. 'Nice lass. You should bring her round to meet us.' He looked up and grinned, showing his newly whitened dentures. 'Might make you forget the one who's propped up on that tattie bogle.'

His parents, his father in particular, couldn't understand that it was possible to work with a woman without having a relationship with her. The man was constantly prying into his son's private life, not realising that he simply didn't have one. Chirnside had always been awkward with women, and the few relationships he'd attempted had stopped before they'd really started. Aye, and that had been when he was young. Fortunately, he had filled his life in other ways, not just in the Force, but through his work with schools and colleges. It gave him enormous satisfaction to think that he might have made a difference in the lives of those youngsters. Wasn't that worth the sacrifice of not having children of his own? No, he couldn't complain. His life was full. And, if he could make it through the next few years, he'd retire on a full pension. The thought left him depressed beyond words.

'I'll get supper started,' he muttered, turning away.

Although the flat looked like something from the 1930s and, in an estate agent's brochure, would have been described as 'having character, and still maintaining some original features', the kitchen had been modernised by a wannabe chef who had installed the American-style island and granite worktops. Through the window, Chirnside could see the piece of weed-choked lawn that was shared by the other tenants and used as a drying green. His parents hadn't needed it since he'd bought them the monster washer-dryer. Now that his father was losing control of his bladder, the sheets required constant laundering.

Chirnside filled the kettle, set about defrosting the moussaka, and put the broccoli on to boil. He'd read somewhere that broccoli was one of the magic foods, whatever they were, but his parents never touched it. Yet they'd need to have something with the moussaka. He rootled around at the back of the freezer for the oven chips.

Half an hour later, he brought in the tray. He returned to the kitchen to fetch the teapot and the plate of bread, as his parents couldn't eat a hot meal without drinking gallons of tea and eating slices of bread, spread thickly with butter.

His father's knees cracked as he got up to shuffle to the table. He made no attempt to help his wife, and it was left to Chirnside to hoist his mother out of her deep armchair and assist her to her chair.

'So how did you know the lass who was killed, son?' his mother asked, without looking up from her plate.

He could see he'd have to tell them or they'd keep on badgering him. 'I met her once or twice at the uni. It was in connection with the outreach work I've been doing, trying to keep the youngsters away from the drugs.'

His father snorted. 'Ach, a waste of time, if you ask me. If they're going to do it, they're going to do it. You're not going to stop them. You're better spending your time catching criminals.'

Chirnside said nothing. He and his father had had this discussion many times. And he wanted to get his parents off the subject. Technically, he should have declared and taken himself off the case, as he knew the victim, although not well. But he wanted to stay on it. In fact, he needed to stay on it. He had a growing sense of foreboding that Judith hadn't been chosen at random. And that she would not be the only victim. The shock of seeing her strung up hadn't subsided, and it would be a long time before he would rid himself of the look of terror in those staring eyes.

CHAPTER 5

'I'm going out this evening, Mum.' Jenn reached into the sink and pulled the plug. The water drained slowly. Too slowly. It meant the sink was bunged up again. She'd have to do something as her mum no longer had the time to deal with trivia like blocked drains. Consequently, Jenn had become something of an expert when it came to sorting household problems. She'd even plumbed in the new washing machine.

The woman was putting away the dishes. 'Where are you off to? Aleck's?'

'I haven't seen him all day.'

Her mum turned and studied her, the way she did when she wanted to stop her daughter doing something but knew the battle was lost before it had started. 'He may be with the police,' she said, pushing her fair hair off her brow. 'That tattie bogle was found on the laird's estate.'

'Aye, I know. But the police will be long gone by now. And he might like a bit of company.' She paused, choosing her words. 'Unless you want help with the cows?' This was intended to produce the negative response that she desired. Her mum loved to be alone with her cows. Jenn would watch her rubbing their necks, coaxing them, speaking softly into their ears. The woman no longer had to call them in: the animals would see her approaching from a distance, and immediately clump across the field towards the gate. It was the best part of the day for her, especially in summer, when the sun seemed not to want to fall over the horizon. This empathy with cattle had made Jenn wonder whether her mum hadn't been a cow in a previous life.

'I'll bring them in myself, Jenn. You get off.'

She turned away so her mum wouldn't see her smile.

Fifteen minutes later, she was cycling down the Liff Road. Before it swung away towards the village, she slowed and came to a halt in front of a rabbit-hutch of a house. Each time she saw it, she was reminded of the dwarves' cottage in *Snow White*, and it would have been postcard perfect had it not been for the grimy windows and red-brown stain under the broken gutter. The sign on the gate said 'Keeper's Cottage'.

She propped the bicycle against the wall and, without bothering to knock, opened the door and let herself in.

As always, she paused, letting her eyes become accustomed to the gloom, although she knew the room well enough that she could have found her way in the dark. Even with eyes closed, she could have stepped over the holes in the sisal matting that covered the cracked brown linoleum. Wooden beams crossed the ceiling, giving anyone who wasn't a dwarf the sense that the timbers were about to fall. The soot-smelling walls were of blackened brick and, had anyone bothered to give them a couple of coats of magnolia, the room would have looked twice as large. As it was, the furniture, which consisted of a couple of wing chairs, a bookcase and chipped chest of drawers, and an old Formica-topped table, cluttered out the space. Which is probably how it is in cottages that could have belonged to the Seven Dwarves, thought Jenn.

On the chest of drawers was the silver-framed photo of Aleck's daughter, Seona, who'd died as a child. She would have been Jenn's age had she lived. Jenn had often wondered how he'd survived the loss of his only child. She, herself, had never known her father, who'd perished in a farm accident when she was a baby, but sorrow at the loss of Ailsa, missing for a month now, surely came close. Yet Aleck had also lost his wife, who'd died giving birth. Rabbie had once told Jenn that her clothes were still in Aleck's wardrobe, and the knick-knacks on the mantelpiece were hers.

Aleck was hunched over the table, working on his figures. He looked up as she entered, and his seamed brown face broke into a smile, which was a change as his mouth was usually turned down at the corners. He stuck his pencil behind his ear. 'Hello lass, I was wondering when you'd call by.' He had a gravelly voice, yet somehow managed to make it sound gentle.

She motioned to the sheet. 'Do you want me to check your maths?'

'Aye, if you would.'

She took the chair next to his. Maths — arithmetic especially — held no terrors for her and, in a matter of seconds, she'd run through the column of figures and established that he'd added them correctly. 'You should use the computer the laird bought for you,' she said softly. 'It would be quicker.'

'Ach, well, I'll enter the figures later, but I wanted to get the answer right on paper, in case the computer gets it wrong.'

She said nothing, nodding her agreement. She adored Aleck. He was the father she'd never known and, although she would never admit it, she felt closer to him than to her mother. Whenever she could, she spent time with him, learning the business of the estate. That he was prepared to spend time with her, she put down to his having lost Seona. They not only helped each other, but they seemed to Jenn to be two halves of a whole.

These last few weeks, however, she'd noticed a change in him, which had left her with a strange feeling of apprehension. He'd become moody, depressed even. And it wasn't just his manner that was giving her cause for concern. He no longer seemed to bother with his appearance. There was a great smear of dirt on his cheek, and his hands were grimy, with a black crust round the nails. Few farm managers were able to keep their hands clean, but he used to be meticulous about washing. He hadn't changed his checked shirt for weeks, and it was minging and so were his trousers. She wondered if it was his workload. There was always more to do in the summer months. But, although she helped him with the estate-management software, which was becoming increasingly complex, she could see that he was struggling.

He ran a calloused hand over his stubble in a familiar gesture. He seemed to remember something then. 'I've got a wee present for you, lass.' His old gamekeeper's coat, its pockets like bellows, was hanging over the back of the chair. He reached into it and removed something that could have been mistaken for a mouse. She recognised it immediately from the shape of its body and its short hairy tail.

'A vole,' she said, excitement in her voice. She'd been looking to add to her body farm.

'It's too fresh for you to see any rigor.'

'Where did you find it?'

'Backmuir Wood. I was there earlier today.'

She cradled the tiny lifeless body with its yeasty smell. 'Aleck, have the police been here?'

'An hour or so ago. Asked about the tattie bogle they found in yon field.'

'I see they've taken it away,' she said, not looking up.

'Aye, it'll be in the mortuary now.'

She wondered if the person who'd interviewed Aleck was the Polish detective with the intense, questioning eyes. Before she could ask, the door opened and Rabbie came in. Older than Aleck, his face ravaged with childhood acne, what was left of his hair sprouted in wings at the sides of his head. Seeing her, he smiled automatically, but she could tell he'd not really registered her presence, which was strange as he usually greeted her warmly. He went over to the bookcase and replaced something on the top shelf. Without looking, Jenn knew it would be one of his many books on plants and trees.

He gazed with deep affection at Aleck. 'Shall I put the kettle on, old thing?' he said hesitantly. He had a breathy voice, as though he couldn't quite get his lungs to work, and yet Jenn had seen him chop up logs with the strength and speed of a man half his age.

'Aye, go on then.' Aleck glanced up at Jenn. 'You staying for tea, lass?'

'Just one cup. Here, Rabbie, let me help you.' She slipped the vole into her jacket pocket, and busied herself with finding crockery. There was no doubt about it: the kitchen was in more of a mess than usual; neither Aleck nor Rabbie seemed to be bothering much. She ran the hot tap and washed the cracked mugs in the sink, taking care to scrub and rinse them thoroughly, in case Aleck hadn't.

The tea made, they sat at the table, sipping quietly.

'Library busy today?' Aleck asked, all of a sudden.

Rabbie shrugged. 'So so. I think people are reading less these days.'

'So is the laird back?' Jenn said to no one in particular.

Aleck regarded her over the rim of his mug. 'Tomorrow afternoon.'

'Do you think he's seen the news?' Rabbie said. 'That lady was found on his land.'

'If he hasn't yet, he soon will,' Aleck said grimly.

Jenn put her mug down. 'It's likely to have made the national papers.'

'A bad business,' Rabbie said, shaking his head.

Aleck was kneading his forehead, his eyes closed.

'You all right, Aleck?' she said gently, touching his wrist.

'Just a headache.' His turned his head with apparent difficulty and looked at her. 'The tea will help, lass.'

She stared into the bloodshot eyes with their heavy lids, unable to stem the rising tide of panic. Something was wrong. Aleck never looked like this.

He brightened suddenly and gripped her hand. 'Did I tell you I've bought a new tractor? A Massey Ferguson?'

She caught Rabbie's slight warning shake of the head. Aleck had told her about the tractor weeks before.

'Come round tomorrow, lass, and I'll show you how to drive it.'

'All right, then,' she said with a feeling of unreality.

They finished the tea in silence.

'Well, I'd better be on my way.'

'Don't forget to add that thing to the farm,' Aleck said, gesturing to her pocket.

'I'll do it now. So what time tomorrow?'

He rubbed his forehead. 'Afternoon would be best.'

'I'll come straight after lunch.'

'Aye.'

She said her goodbyes and left the cottage.

Twenty minutes later, she reached the woodland on the edge of Oaktree Farm. Under a cage of wire netting that she and Aleck had built together lay the remains of her dead animals. The netting prevented predators from tearing at them, and allowed her to observe the natural process of decomposition. She'd learnt everything she knew about what happens after death from Aleck, as he'd spent a lifetime observing it. He'd told her what to expect, how long each stage would last, and what the factors were that would determine it.

She was familiar with all but the 'fresh stage', where the muscles stiffen in rigor, because she usually found the bodies after rigor had worn off, and because rigor wasn't apparent in the smaller animals and birds. But she'd had ample opportunity to study the remaining stages of decay. The bloat stage, in which gases in the body expand and body fluids are pushed out of every orifice, was the most interesting, although the smell of putrefaction was unbelievably nauseating. The active decay stage was currently present in her rabbits, with the skin under the scraggy fur rippling as the larvae of the black blowfly feasted on the flesh. One animal was now at the advanced decay stage: the body had broken down to dry and no longer smelt.

The crows were starting to mummify, and no longer held her interest. She examined the fox, the only one of her animals to display rigor and, even then, it had been wearing off when she'd found it. It had been run over, and animal predation had resulted in lacerations that were visible through the matted fur. Cause of death: massive head trauma, consistent with the impact of a car. The skull had been forced in and splintered, giving her the opportunity to study the maggots crawling over the brains. The open wounds were particularly interesting as they sank after several days. Blood had been oozing out of the animal's ear, prompting her to ask the question: are there enough genetic variations in the species to allow identification by DNA? She would have to look up the answer.

She removed the vole from her pocket. It was perfect, showing no splits in the skin or other injuries, making her wonder how it had died. Aleck had done well to get it before its eyes had been pecked out. Her mind went back to the morning, and her discovery of the dead woman in the scarecrow. She, too, had displayed no obvious marks of injury. How long would it take the pathologists to establish cause of death? Nikki Alexander would have it done in a matter of hours.

Jenn laid the vole on the ground and made a mental note to come here frequently, as the weather was turning warm and it would speed up decomposition. She was already designing future experiments. She'd read that bodies decompose in water twice as slowly as in air, creating trapped gases which ultimately enable them to float. It would soon be time to put that to the test, for which she'd been lucky enough to find an old tank. But next on the list was the study of decomposition following exsanguination. For that, she would have to trap live animals, and would need help. She thought suddenly of Aleck, and a feeling of dread came over her. What was wrong with him? Was it the visit from the police? Or was it the laird returning, which usually meant more work? That would be it. Aleck was a conscientious estate manager, always wanting to do his best. The grip of anxiety loosened.

She glanced at the vole. Flies had already landed on its fur. She felt her pulse quicken. Excellent . . .

Dania let herself into the flat. On her way down Union Place, she'd glanced into the parking area where Marek kept his black Audi Avant. The space belonged to the owner of the block of flats opposite but, as the flats were occupied by students who didn't have cars, Marek was able to lease the parking place on a continuous basis. The Audi had been neatly backed in, suggesting that he might be home. It was when Dania ran up the two flights of stairs, opened the front door and was greeted by the rich smell of roasting meat, that the suggestion became a certainty.

Her brother, Marek, turned as she entered the kitchen. 'Ah, Danka, great timing,' he said.

She slipped into Polish, which they spoke when they were alone together. 'Something smells good,' she said eagerly.

He removed plates from the oven. 'Can you guess?'

'*Bigos*?'

His smile told her she'd guessed correctly. It was his favourite dish, and he cooked enough to feed an army and a circus. A traditional Polish recipe, which had many variants, he made it exclusively with pork, using different types of Polish sausage. The ingredients, which included sauerkraut and fresh cabbage, dried mushrooms, prunes and sour apples were much the same in most *bigos* recipes. The final touch was a glass of Madeira. It was a long-established custom to reheat the dish over the next day or two to let the flavours develop. All well and good in old Polish kitchens, Marek had said, but he no longer had the time. There was, however, the perfect modern-day equivalent – a slow cooker. He was by far the better cook, and loved it, which she exploited, as she had neither his skill nor his patience.

She watched him bustle about, draining the potatoes, and cutting the fronds of dill that he kept in pots on the windowsill. He was her twin, not identical, which was unfortunate as she would have loved hair like his. It was the colour of hay and he wore it short, but not so short that it obscured its natural wave. At six foot two, with his magnetic blue eyes, aristocratic appearance, careful dress and impeccable manners, he'd have no difficulty charming women into his bed. Whether he threw his favours around was something Dania had yet to discover, but it was hard to believe he didn't have a long line of moist-lipped women queuing up to come into his life. In the time she'd been living with him, he'd brought no one back, but he occasionally stayed out till the small hours, and she wasn't convinced this was solely on account of his job.

When he'd heard that she'd accepted the post in Dundee, he rang to say that she must move in with him. And of course she must stay as long as she wanted. The modern apartment, off the Perth Road, was in an excellent location and within walking distance of the town centre and the police station. It occupied the top two floors of the last building, giving the rooms on the corner breathtaking views of the river Tay and the rail bridge. There was plenty of space, he said, and the ceilings were high enough that they could have real candles on the Christmas tree without worrying about setting the house on fire.

She'd registered the anxiety in his voice, magnified over the phone, and knew that he still felt he should look out for her. She and Tony had split up a few months earlier, and what brother, especially a twin, wouldn't worry under those circumstances? When she arrived in Dundee, he said nothing, but she knew he'd noticed her wedding ring was no longer on her finger. He'd been brilliant about everything, even insisting she have his room. When she protested, he brushed away her objections by explaining that his work as an investigative journalist meant he was hardly ever home, so it was only right and proper that she have the master bedroom. That her work as a detective meant that *she* was hardly ever home didn't seem to enter into the equation. And he'd bought an upright piano. She played and he didn't, so there was no argument. She had to come. It was the piano that had clinched it.

'Shall we eat in the kitchen, Danka? I have to go out afterwards.'

Before he'd moved in, the flat had undergone a renovation, which included putting in a small dining room. When they ate there, it usually signalled making a night of it, with wine as well as vodka. Otherwise, it was used as an office, and he sometimes wrote his pieces at the dining table.

'The kitchen's fine,' she said, taking cutlery from the drawer.

He took the lid off the slow cooker, releasing an aroma that would have made even a vegetarian drool, and spooned the *bigos* on to the plates. He added potatoes, and then sprinkled them with dill.

As she carried everything to the table, he opened the fridge and took a bottle out of the freezer. The blue and silver label told her it was Wyborowa, the 40 per cent proof rye-based vodka that was so popular among Poles. He usually drank it with *bigos*, but tonight he offered it only to her, pouring water for himself.

'Not drinking, Marek?'

'I have to drive.'

She ran a finger through the rime of frost on the bottle, watching it build up under the nail. 'So, where are you going?'

'I'm meeting someone.'

It was a rule of theirs not to pry into each other's affairs, although volunteering information was fine, provided it was understood that anything highly confidential could go no further. They were still feeling their way, neither wanting to embarrass the other, but conscious that they were both investigators and might be in a position to help each other. Marek had a reputation for thoroughness and, having read his articles, Dania was impressed by his attention to detail.

His mobile rang. He muttered something under his breath. 'I'll have to take that. It could be him.'

He left the table, and picked up the phone on the windowsill. She made to get up and leave the room, but he signalled to her to stay. He listened to the message and then ended the call. 'The meeting's been cancelled.' The corners of his mouth lifted. 'Looks like I can have a drink after all.'

He brought over another glass, and she poured him a generous measure.

He raised the glass. '*Na zdrowie.*'

'*Na zdrowie.*'

'You know, Danka, I'm hearing that a lot in the pubs in Dundee.'

'Poles?'

'And Scots. They're starting to say it.'

'Do they drink vodka?'

'Not like we do,' he smiled.

'I'm on a new case,' she said, after a while. 'A murder.'

He didn't look up from his plate. 'I caught the news at midday. A woman dressed up as a scarecrow. Is that the one?'

'She was a reader at the Institute of Religions and Belief Systems.'

The remark made him jerk his head up. His gaze bored into hers. 'That's something of a coincidence.' He picked up his glass. 'I'm looking into reports of a Druid cult in Dundee. Some of the staff at the Institute of Religions and Belief Systems are rumoured to be members.'

'Druids?' she murmured. 'I thought they died out with the Romans.'

'There are such things as modern Druids. The ones at Dundee have been going for a while, I believe. My informant told me they were gathering tonight. He was going to take me there, but the meeting's been cancelled.'

'Where do Druids usually meet?'

He shrugged. 'In woodland, I think. And there's plenty of that around Dundee.' He took another sip. 'You know, I went to the Institute of Religions and Belief Systems, hoping to find out what I could about their connection with the Druid group, but the staff there politely side-stepped my more probing questions. They said their interest is academic only.' A smile crept on to his lips. 'But I think there's another way.'

'What?'

'I'm going in undercover. I've decided to enrol for their summer school.'

But Dania was only half listening. His mention of woodland had made her think suddenly of Backmuir. And Jenn McLaughlin. 'Marek, do you remember the case of a missing girl, Ailsa McLaughlin? It would have been about a month ago.'

'I do, as a matter of fact.' He took a forkful of *bigos*. 'I did a feature for *The Courier*. There have been several cases like hers this last year, teenagers who ran away to the big city.'

'You're saying she left home?'

'That's what the police are saying. Probably because a couple of these teenagers returned from London after running out of money.'

She could see he wanted to ask why she was so interested. But he didn't.

He refilled their glasses. 'Ailsa's sister — I forget her name — Janet, I think? — began a campaign for Ailsa to be found. She was on the radio a couple of times, pleading for anyone who knew what had happened to her sister to come forward.'

'So she didn't believe Ailsa was a runaway?'

'She thought something bad had happened to her.'

Dania chewed thoughtfully. She remembered the question she'd asked at the station: *Did they find her?* And the enigmatic reply: *In a manner of speaking.*

After they'd finished the *bigos*, Marek said with a shy smile, 'I'm afraid there's no dessert.'

'Never mind,' she smiled back. 'I'll make tea. Shall I bring it into the living room?'

'Please.'

She made the tea and poured it into two of the ornamental Polish glasses their parents had left with her before they returned to Poland. Instead of adding milk or sugar, she stirred in a generous dollop of the cherry jam she'd bought in the Polski Sklep on Dura Street. Shortly after she'd moved in with Marek, she shopped at Tesco, and bought a jar of Dundee's famous Keiller's marmalade, but it had proved too bitter for him. Like most Poles, he had a sweet tooth. Tomorrow, having promised to cook, she would prepare *kisiel*, the hot fruit jelly he loved so much. She could make it from scratch, blending the fruit in their new processor. Or she could use the packet she'd bought in the *sklep*.

In the living room, they sprawled on the sofa, facing the large picture window with the stunning view of Fife, and sipped the tea.

'Play something, Danka.'

'What would you like?'

'You know what I like,' he said, his voice drowsy from the vodka.

The piano stool held a large selection of the sheet music she'd brought with her from London. But what she was after was lying on top of the upright. It was Chopin's Étude, Op. 10, No. 3, which she'd been learning, often rising at 6.00 a.m. to get in two hours of practice before work.

As a child, she'd fallen in love with Chopin after hearing, one Sunday afternoon in summer, a student playing his music in Warsaw's Łazienki Park. The boy had been seated at a grand piano beneath the bronze statue of the composer, who was peering at him haughtily over his left shoulder, as if checking that his pianist was finger-perfect. Listening to the music drifting across the small lake towards the audience seated among the sweet-smelling bushes, she knew in that instant that she wanted to be that boy, wanted to play on that grand piano, under that statue. She started lessons and discovered a talent for the piano, helped by having fifth fingers that were nearly as long as her fourth. Her parents had hoped she would become a concert pianist, as her playing had reached the requisite standard, but by then she'd discovered another talent – a passion and a gift for solving problems. And so she trained to be a detective. And, although she sat at many grand pianos, she never did sit at the one under that statue.

She set the sheets on the rack, spreading them flat, and settled herself on the stool. There was no need to adjust the height, and the sheets were unnecessary, as she knew the piece by heart. She began slowly, *ma non troppo*, playing softly, the music gathering momentum and swelling towards a *fortissimo*. As the sound filled the room, her fingers moving mechanically over the keys, she let herself be transported by the music, until the initial melody returned, slowly dying away to the final muted chord.

The piece finished, she cast a glance over her shoulder.

Marek was snoring softly.

CHAPTER 6

Marek was wiping the remnants of shaving foam from his cheeks when the doorbell rang.

'I'll get it,' he shouted into the living room. He threw the towel into the sink, and left the bathroom.

He pulled back the locks on the front door. A young man in his late twenties stood peering down the stairwell, listening to the sounds of students squabbling. Hearing the door, he turned and gazed at Marek with an expression that was hard to read. Surprise was there, as was comprehension. But there was also envy.

'Yes?' Marek said with a smile. 'May I help you?'

'I was looking for Dania.' The man's gaze drifted down Marek's body. 'Detective Sergeant Gorska,' he added quickly.

'And you are?'

'A colleague. Laurence Whyte. I think she's expecting me.'

'Is she? She's said nothing to me.'

Fumbling, the man pulled a plastic wallet from his back pocket and held it out. It contained a warrant card, similar to Danka's. Marek studied the face with its stern expression, different from the shy smile of the man in front of him.

'Do come inside, officer.'

'Laurence, please,' the man said, stepping into the corridor.

'I'm Marek Gorski.'

'Gorski?' Laurence said in a tone of dismay. 'I didn't realise Dania was married.'

'I'm her brother.'

The fleeting look of relief on Laurence's face was not lost on Marek. 'Would you like some coffee, Sergeant Whyte? Or tea?'

'Um, it's Constable. And I can't stay. I'm working this morning.' Under Marek's gaze, he seemed to feel the need to keep talking. 'I'm going into town.'

'I see.'

'Is that Chopin I can hear?'

'It is.'

Laurence's eyes lit up. 'It sounds like one of his Ballades. It starts off quiet and then goes all manic. Specially at the end. I love Chopin's music. It makes me happy and sad at the same time. I have all Rubinstein's recordings.' He gabbled on. 'I've always thought that Chopin and Rubinstein were made for each other. Did you know that Rubinstein was the greatest Chopinist of the last century?'

'I did.'

'I've often wondered who was the greatest Chopinist of the century before.'

'That would have been Chopin himself.'

'Yes, of course.' A pause. 'And is that Rubinstein playing?'

Marek suppressed a smile. 'It's my sister.' He shouted over his shoulder. 'Danka! Someone for you.'

The music stopped abruptly. A moment later, Danka came to the door. Seeing Laurence, a look of surprise crossed her face.

'I was on my way to the station and thought I'd call by,' Laurence said weakly.

'My shift doesn't start till later.' She shrugged. 'But, okay, I suppose I could come now.'

'Are you sure you wouldn't like some coffee, Constable?' Marek said.

'I don't want to put you to any trouble.'

'It's okay, Marek,' Danka said. 'I've finished. Let me get my coat.' She searched through the pegs for her denim jacket. 'I'll see you this evening.'

Laurence shot him a glance as they took the stairs.

Marek watched them go. The suspicion that this man was hoping to find Danka early on a Sunday morning, alone and perhaps undressed, amused him. He felt the corners of his mouth lift as he remembered the look of dismay when the door opened and Laurence took in his height and build. Danka had obviously not told her colleagues she was staying with her brother. Still, the lad looked harmless. Marek hoped he hadn't frightened him off.

He glanced at his watch. There was plenty of time.

'Your brother's quite scary,' Laurence was saying as they headed down the Nethergate.

'Not really. Not when you get to know him. He's a complete softie.'

They were nearing the Phoenix, the red-painted pub on the corner of Tay Street Lane.

'I didn't realise you were on a later shift,' Laurence said, 'or I wouldn't have disturbed your piano practice.'

Dania was about to remark that the shift roster was displayed prominently on the incident board when she heard a child screaming. It wasn't the sound children make when they're tired or angry. This was a full-throated scream of terror. It was coming from behind the Phoenix.

She glanced at Laurence, and then rushed into the narrow lane. To the left loomed a row of tall tenement buildings and to the right, behind the Phoenix, was a line of large bins. The screams came from the passageway beyond. And they were growing louder.

She pushed the bins aside, searching frantically. A small blonde girl in a flower-print dress was holding on to a pushchair, pointing at a woman sprawled on the ground. She had tangled dark hair and her jeans were pulled down, exposing her underwear. Hunched over her, a man in a camouflage jacket was riffling through a handbag. Seeing Dania, he dropped the bag and sprinted down the passage.

'Police! Stop!' she shouted. She ran after him but he pushed over one of the bins, blocking her path and littering the passage with empty bottles. She tried to dodge them but slipped and fell heavily on to her side. At the end of the passage, he jumped over a low wall into a private car park and disappeared through an archway. Beyond was the West Marketgait, where he could lose himself. She scrabbled to her feet, kicked away the coloured glass and rushed after him. By the time she reached the main road, he'd already crossed it and was slipping into Debenhams.

The lights had been in his favour. She'd arrived just as they turned green. Even if she made it to the department store, he'd be long gone through one of the exits into the Overgate. She called it in, requesting the uniforms to scour the area. With luck, they'd pick him up, or find him on the store's cameras. There couldn't be too many men with orange-red hair and wearing camo jackets.

She returned to Tay Street Lane. Laurence was crouching beside the pushchair, trying to calm the hysterical child. It was then that she saw what she'd missed earlier: a shaven-headed man, also with his jeans half down, slumped against the wall. Both man and woman were holding needles in their clenched hands. They'd injected into the groin.

Laurence had followed the direction of her gaze. 'They took a huge risk,' he shouted over the noise the child was making. 'They might have hit the femoral artery or the nerve. It could have killed them.'

She stared at him. She'd thought it was rape but saw it now for what it was: a couple shooting up and passing out, and a stranger, drawn by the child's crying, seizing an opportunity to steal the woman's money. She felt anger surge through her. She didn't know where to focus her rage – on the opportunistic thief who'd left the users to their fate, or the couple who'd injected in full view of a child.

Laurence had picked up the girl, and was cuddling her and making soothing noises. 'The paramedics are on their way,' he said, glancing at Dania. 'And I've phoned social services.'

'That was quick thinking.'

'I've done this before.' He smiled bleakly. 'We don't usually get it so close to the city centre. Tells you how bad things have become.'

A short walk from where Marek lived was the Dundee Contemporary Arts centre, or DCA. A favourite place of his, where he met many of his contacts, the DCA was an art venue which housed, on upper and lower levels, two galleries, a print studio, a visual research centre run jointly by the DCA and researchers from the nearby Duncan of Jordanstone College of Art and Design, a cinema and a café bar. He was glad now that he'd rented in the city centre. He'd considered a place in Broughty Ferry, a former whaling village, which had been transformed by the jute barons who'd built their stunning residences there, but the flat on Union Place, so close to where he worked, had proved irresistible.

At a few minutes before 10.30 a.m., he pushed through the DCA's glass doors and made his way down the stairs to the bar. A sweet buttery smell permeated the room. He knew the barista, a Pole from Kraków, and exchanged a few words before declining his offer of a bottle of the Polish beer, Tyskie. Marek told him he was here to meet a lady and, with a knowing smile, the barista directed him to the far corner, where a woman with wavy black hair was sitting at the window. Her head was bent, and she was absorbed in her mobile.

'Dr Peterkin?' he said, hurrying over. He'd arrived early, but she'd arrived even earlier. Keeping people – especially ladies – waiting was something he avoided at all costs, and it bothered him that she'd been sitting here alone.

The woman jumped. She had a pale oval face and large grey eyes, and was dressed in a navy suit with pleated skirt. She stared up at him.

'I'm so sorry. I didn't mean to startle you.' He offered his hand. She placed hers in his, and he lifted it to his mouth, brushing it with his lips. As he bent forward, he caught a trace of her powdery perfume. 'I'm Marek Gorski,' he said, releasing her hand. 'I do apologise for keeping you waiting.'

A faint flush appeared on her cheeks. She continued to stare at him, her lips slightly parted.

'I'm here for our meeting, Dr Peterkin. I'm applying for the summer school.' He smiled. 'Druidism?' he added when there was still no response.

'Yes, of course.' She seemed flustered, as though she'd forgotten something. 'Do please sit down. You're early.'

'I try never to be late. But please don't let me disturb you.' He gestured to the mobile in her hand. 'Shall I get us some coffees while you finish your message?'

'That would be lovely. Black, no sugar, for me.' She had a soft but clear voice and spoke with an educated Scots accent.

He left the table and, when he returned, the mobile had been put away.

'Thank you for agreeing to meet me, Dr Peterkin.' He hesitated. 'Specially in view of the dreadful news.'

She stiffened and he wondered if, by alluding to the scarecrow murder, he'd made a gaffe. The colour leached from her face and a look of fear came into her eyes. Her hands shook as she lifted the coffee to her lips.

'I'm so sorry,' he murmured. 'That was insensitive of me.'

'No, no. Please don't apologise. It's natural that everyone should want to talk about it.'

'Of course, you must have known Dr Johnstone.'

'She was my line manager. A lovely lady. The series of summer schools was her idea, actually.' The woman was still trembling, her hand playing with the bow at her throat as though, by this act, she could dispel the memory of what had happened. 'We'd thought of cancelling but decided against it.' She looked directly into his eyes. 'It's what Judith would have wanted. For them to go on. Particularly the one on Druidism, which she herself designed.'

'I understand.' He smiled. 'And I'm glad to hear that.'

'So what is your interest in Druidism, Mr Gorski?'

'Please call me Marek.' This was the question he knew would be asked. He decided to play the innocent. 'It was simple curiosity, Dr Peterkin. I know nothing about Druidism and thought that evening classes would be an excellent way to learn.'

She smiled brightly. 'Let me ask you, then, when you hear the word Druid, what do you think of?'

He sipped his coffee thoughtfully. 'Old Celts with long beards, wearing robes, and gathering round Stonehenge?' he said, raising an eyebrow.

'Which is what the majority of the population would say. Certainly the ancient Druids were members of the Celtic learned class, in other words, priests and teachers. But modern Druidism is different, although it has its roots in the ancient practices. What you will learn in the summer school is the history of Druidism, but also what neo-Druidism is.'

'Is there a textbook I need to buy? The equivalent of a Bible, perhaps?'

'Absolutely not. We have no sacred text. In fact, there is no universally agreed set of beliefs amongst Druids.'

'But surely there must be some sort of dogma.'

'Dogma is too strong a word. There are indeed a number of ideas that most Druids hold in common, and that help to define the nature of Druidism today.' Her colour had returned. She leant forward, and he was struck by the fire in her eyes. 'It is a spiritual journey, Marek – a religion to some, and a way of life for others – but each Druid must find the Path for him- or herself.'

Listening to the confident, eloquent way in which she spoke, he suspected that this little speech was one she had delivered before.

'Unlike other religions,' she went on, 'there is no central authority over the entire movement, no religious leader. You look surprised, but it works extremely well. And we view the natural world as sacred. Many of us involve ourselves in environmental issues, thereby acting to protect areas of the natural landscape that are under threat from development or pollution.' She was sounding more and more like a manual.

'A worthy cause. Who can argue with that? But you said "series of summer schools". So are there others?'

'Druidism connects with the other Earth-ancestor traditions.' She must have seen his blank look because she added, 'For example, Native American, the Maori and Huna, Aboriginal,

69

Romany, and the indigenous spiritualities of Africa and Asia. Judith envisaged summer schools in all these traditions. But Native Americanism is the only other one that we have prepared this year. It was a great interest of Judith's, you see. She travelled widely around the United States, visiting and learning from Native Americans. But that course may not now go ahead, as it was Judith herself who was to teach it.'

He nodded sympathetically.

Dr Peterkin smoothed her skirt. 'After the summer school, many of our students go on to enrol for a full course at the institute.' She must have mistaken Marek's look because she said, hurriedly, 'I realise that not everyone is able to study full time, so we offer an equivalent course by correspondence.'

'Ah, I see.'

'The curriculum follows the three grades, or levels, of Druidism: the first is that of the Bard, the second is the Ovate, and the third and final is the Druid. The course is designed so that the student can study at his or her own speed.' She played with her teaspoon before placing it neatly back in the saucer. 'Some summer-school students become so enthused that they don't wait until autumn to put into practice what they've learnt. They discover a way of living that avoids many of the problems of intolerance and sectarianism that other world religions have established.' She lifted her gaze to his. 'But I should reassure you, Marek, that we would in no way try to convert you.' She had the sort of light in her eyes that made him suspect that this was precisely what the summer school's purpose was. 'I take it from your name that you're Polish,' she added. 'And therefore a Roman Catholic?'

He threw her a smile. 'You're correct on both counts, Dr Peterkin.' He wondered if the interview would now come to an end and he would be denied a place.

She looked at him dreamily. 'The summer school starts next week. We look forward to seeing you there.'

'Thank you. I'm delighted to hear it. Now, another coffee?'

'I'm afraid I can't stay. Work calls.' Her hand drifted to her throat and she fingered the bow, more confidently this time.

'You must be run off your feet, teaching through the summer as well as during term time.'

'We academics are used to that. Most evenings, I don't leave my office till seven.'

As she pushed her chair back, he sprang to his feet. He bowed, and then reached for her hand and kissed it lightly. 'Thank you for your time, Dr Peterkin. I'm most grateful.'

She seemed in no rush to take her hand away. 'Thank *you* for the coffee,' she smiled, inclining her head. She picked up her handbag and left, her court shoes squeaking on the floor.

He lingered, sipping the remains of his coffee, wondering if he would learn anything about the Druid cult from the summer school. He went over the conversation. There were enough clues in what Dr Peterkin had said – *We view the natural world as sacred. Many of us involve ourselves in environmental issues* – to convince him that not only was she a lecturer, she was a practising Druid. He glanced at his watch. He should be able to make St Joseph's easily: the church on Wilkie's Lane had a Polish priest who was saying Sunday Mass in Polish at midday.

The place was now buzzing with people. A toddler with heavy cheeks and enormous eyes was seated at the adjacent table with two women, one elderly. As Marek was about to go, the younger woman, a brunette of slight build, caught his eye and said, 'They seem to have forgotten about our order. Could you watch he doesn't fall off the chair while I go to the bar?' She glanced at the older woman, and then smiled at Marek, as if to suggest that

71

she couldn't trust her elderly companion to watch the toddler. With a few words to the woman, she hurried away.

The little boy's face crumpled and he took a huge breath, ready to start wailing. Marek whipped the handkerchief out of his breast pocket and quickly folded and knotted it so it resembled a mouse, complete with tail and tiny ears. The boy forgot he wanted to cry. His eyes blazed with interest. Marek balanced the mouse on his cupped hand and stroked it. Then, with a sudden movement of his upturned fingers, he launched the mouse into the air with such speed that he only just caught it by its tail.

The boy squealed with delight. 'Again,' he commanded.

So Marek did it again, and again, and again, until the young woman returned.

'That's a neat trick,' she said, admiration in her voice. The elderly lady was rocking with laughter.

The boy held out his arms to Marek, his whole body trembling with anticipation.

Marek placed the mouse in the toddler's hands, and smiled at the young woman. 'My compliments,' he said with a small bow.

As he wandered through the café and out on to the Nethergate, he thought again about his conversation with the trembly-voiced Dr Peterkin. Something niggled. Something he only now remembered. When he'd made reference to the scarecrow murder, he'd seen grief in the woman's eyes. That was natural: she knew the victim. But there was another emotion which she had tried, but failed, to mask – fear, bordering on terror.

When Dania and Laurence finally arrived at West Bell Street, they walked into a crowded incident room. Desks had been rearranged, with people huddled over computer screens or gathered round the whiteboard.

DI Chirnside called Dania over. 'I see you've had your first taste of what ails this fair city.'

'Yes, sir.'

'There was a child, you said?'

'A little girl. She'll be going into child protection.'

'And the parents?'

'The paramedics didn't take long about it.' She kept her voice level. 'They pronounced life extinct at the scene.'

He studied her with an expression of concern. 'You've seen this in London, I've no doubt.'

'Never in such close proximity to a child,' she said through clenched teeth. She felt her cheeks flush with anger. 'If they hadn't been dead already, I'd have been tempted to kill them myself.'

He nodded, patting her arm gently. 'By the way, Judith's autopsy is set for tomorrow afternoon. I'd like you to be there.'

'Yes, sir.'

'I'm about to update the press, but I'll be back for this afternoon's briefing.'

'Right.'

'And can you check the cameras? The system hasn't been able to pick up the victim's vehicle registration.'

She knew what this meant. Judith's car registration may have been recorded, but the system hadn't recognised the characters. Such images were marked for attention, and it was then up to an officer to see if he or she could identify the alphanumeric characters.

It was too late to try to hide her feelings. Chirnside had registered her disappointment. 'Look, I know it's a thankless task,' he said with a kindly smile, 'but it has to be done. And, with your eye for detail, you're the one to do it.'

'Of course, sir.' She'd planned to spend her time doing something different. That would now have to wait.

She watched him leave the incident room, thinking that he seemed more like his old self, his shoulders back and his stride more purposeful.

She powered up her computer and signed in. An hour later, she'd finished viewing the images flagged with unreadable plates, none of which was from a light blue Honda Civic. But the system wasn't foolproof. She would have to do this the hard way. On a parallel screen, she pulled up a map of Dundee, which included the positions of the fixed cameras that formed part of the city's Automatic Number Plate Recognition system, or ANPR.

Suppose Judith had left Monikie at 7.30 a.m., and had taken the most direct route, how long would it have taken her to reach a road with ANPR cameras? And which road was it? Dania traced the route until she found the first set of cameras, on the A92. Leaving a wide margin for error, she systematically checked every light blue car that passed the camera at the time Judith would have reached it.

Two hours later, her eyes smarting from staring at the screen, Dania was forced to admit defeat. Although there were many light blue cars, some of which were Honda Civics, there was none with Judith's registration number.

Another possible explanation for the absence of the number plate from the record was that the car had not been taken on to roads with cameras. That would require a huge detour. Yet, why would Judith do that? Wouldn't she want to get to work as quickly as possible? She had a meeting that Friday morning. The A92 was the obvious route. It was fast, and would have taken her straight into Dundee.

Okay, suppose Judith *had* decided to avoid the cameras. She could have taken the B-roads west to the A90, and approached the city from the north. And yet, even with this detour, she couldn't avoid every camera in and around Dundee. The problem was in the timing. They had no idea when the Honda had been driven to the Liff Road. It would be a mammoth task to check every recording. Dania let her head drop back, and stared at the ceiling.

Chirnside's voice dragged her from her thoughts. 'Can everyone gather round, please?' he shouted to the room.

She glanced at her watch. It was after two, and she hadn't noticed that she'd worked through lunch.

'Right then,' said Chirnside, 'let's take stock and see where we are.' He pinned a sheet on to the incident board. 'We found the deceased's mobile in her handbag. The numbers have just come in from Tech. They're mostly from the university, and this is a record of calls she made and received, going back several weeks. As you can see, she rarely used her mobile. And, before you ask, it was switched off, so we couldn't plot her movements on the day she was killed. She didn't have a home landline. So that leaves her emails. They're on the university's main server, but the IT people are having a devil of a job with it as it keeps crashing.'

'Anything on her laptop, sir?' Laurence asked.

'Tech pulled only lecture notes and similar material.'

'What about family?'

'None that we could find. Her parents are dead. No brothers or sisters. No husband or children.'

'Did she have a boyfriend? Or a girlfriend?' someone at the back said. This produced sniggers, which died down when they saw Chirnside's glower.

'So what did you find in the villages, Fergus?' he said.

Fergus's sour voice came from behind Dania. 'We walked our feet to stumps, showing her picture everywhere. A complete waste of time.'

'Posters? Any of the public ring in?' Chirnside was starting to sound desperate.

'Nothing, boss. Although it's early days.' The speaker was DC Honor Randall, one of the few female officers, and the only one who referred to Chirnside as 'boss'. She had a short, severe hair-cut, which did her no favours and, with her furrowed forehead and crabbed expression, she looked permanently constipated. The fact that she was stick-thin amazed Dania, because she couldn't do a day's work without getting through several packets of toffees, which she never offered around.

'What about the victim's car? Was it seen in the area around the Liff Road?' Chirnside said. 'Okay, I can tell from your faces.'

'About that, boss.' Honor wasn't usually big in the words department but, when she had something to say, she couldn't get it out quickly enough. And the faster she spoke, the more pro-nounced her London accent became. 'The Liff Road is busier than you think. Lots of cars travel along it between the Coupar Angus Road and Liff village. They have to slow down at that layby where the deceased's car was found.' She glanced round the room, as though for corroboration. 'We must have interviewed the entire village. Not one single person remembers seeing the Honda on Friday. Not one.'

'I checked with her neighbour,' Dania said. 'Judith left home punctually at seven-thirty a.m. She had a meeting scheduled for that morning but didn't show. We're assuming she, or somebody else, drove the car to the layby straight after she was kidnapped. But maybe that assumption's incorrect.'

They were looking at her expectantly.

'It's possible the car was driven to the layby in the evening.'

'Then where was it all day?' Chirnside said.

'She may have been held somewhere in the city.'

'He took a hell of a risk if he did that.'

'Not if she was tied up and gagged,' Fergus said.

'I meant a risk with the car. Judith's non-appearance at her meeting could have been reported later the same morning. The car could have been spotted before the kidnapper had a chance to drive it to the layby.'

'It could have been kept in a garage,' Dania said.

'I wonder why he didn't kidnap her on the way home *after* work.'

'Grab her in the middle of the Perth Road?' Fergus said incredulously.

'Follow her home and do it on a secluded road near Monikie. It has the advantage that he wouldn't need to keep her and the car hidden for most of the day.'

'He'd need to know what time she normally finished work.'

'If he did it in the morning, he'd need to know what time she normally *started* work.' Chirnside rubbed his cheek so hard it left a mark. 'We have to establish where she was all of Friday. That means getting a handle on the car's movements.' He looked pointedly at Dania.

'I'm still looking at the ANPR, sir.'

'Okay, let's move on. There's nothing irregular about her bank account. Regular income in, and regular direct debits out. Her credit card shows less than usual activity. Probably accounts for why her savings account had quite a bit in it.'

'From what I saw in her cottage, she wasn't living like a millionaire,' Dania said. 'The neighbour seemed to suggest that her life was at work. She never brought anyone home. She was away in the evenings, wearing a ball gown. Could have been to attend university functions.'

'Nice work if you can get it,' someone sneered.

'I interviewed her colleagues,' Laurence said. 'No one had a bad word to say about her. Highly conscientious. Devoted to her students. Respected by her staff. Worked long hours. The phrase that came up most was a "good person".'

After a silence, Chirnside said, 'Okay, everyone. Keep at it.'

Dania returned to her desk. A sandwich lay next to the keyboard. Ham hock and chutney.

'I had an attack of generosity, and thought you might like that,' Laurence said, peering at his screen. 'I think you're starting to look thin.'

'The older Poles I know tell me I'm too thin for a Polish woman.' She smiled. 'Thanks. How much do I owe you?'

'You can buy me a drink after work.'

She kept her face straight. 'I don't drink on a Sunday.'

He looked stricken. 'Really?'

She loved the way none of them got her sense of humour. Winding them up was one of the highlights of her day. She pulled the wrapping off the sandwich. 'So who benefits from Judith's death?'

'We've drawn a blank on that one.'

'What sort of enemies would a woman like that have?' Dania said, biting into the sandwich.

Fergus had ambled over and was listening to the conversation. 'My money's on an ambitious career academic who wants promotion, but is surrounded by equally ambitious and competent academics who are also in the running for promotion.'

Dania felt her lips twitch. Fergus could have been describing himself. 'Stringing someone up as a scarecrow is surely going over the top, even for a rival academic,' she said. 'Don't you think?'

'So what's your theory, Sergeant?' Laurence asked her.

She put down the sandwich. 'Judith was researching Native Americans and their customs. And who knows what other groups and sects. Many ancient tribes sacrificed humans. You did say yesterday that it might have been a ceremony that went wrong,' she added, noting the expression of horror on Laurence's face.

78

'Yes, but yesterday I was joking.'

'Well, I don't think anyone's joking now. Judith's death wasn't accidental. And it may not have been simple murder.' Dania threw the cellophane into the waste-paper bin. 'It may have been ritual human sacrifice.'

CHAPTER 7

Dania was watching the young woman with the dark hair. She was distinctly nervous. And with good reason. She was one of two people come to identify Judith Johnstone – a necessary procedure before a post mortem can begin. It was usually carried out by a near relative, but none could be found, so university colleagues had been asked to come in. The first, a young man with troubled eyes and a tiny plait in his flowing beard, had made the identification in a ringing voice bordering on hysteria. He hadn't waited to be shown out of the viewing room, but had run into the corridor. The second was a woman in her thirties. She was staring at the figure on the trolley, whose face, but not body, was visible.

'Are you sure that is Judith Johnstone?' DI Chirnside said gently.

The woman brought a handkerchief to her mouth and then let her hand drop in a gesture of defeat. Her nose was bubbling. 'Yes, Inspector, that's Judith Johnstone,' she said in a clear but resigned voice.

'Thank you, Dr Peterkin.' He nodded to the female officer standing a little way behind. She touched the woman lightly on the elbow and guided her out of the room. A second later, the sound of sobbing reached them from the corridor.

Dania let her gaze rest on Judith Johnstone's face. Had she been asked, she'd have said it was that of another woman. The eyes were closed, and the red lipstick had been wiped away, revealing a rough, pinched mouth. Only the freckles and the hennaed hair, now neatly combed out, gave the requisite clues as to the woman's identity.

Milo Slaughter and the procurator fiscal had been waiting discreetly by the door. Milo now came forward and nodded to his assistant, a young man with a pallid indoors complexion and fair hair cut short at the sides. He wheeled the trolley away.

As everyone left the viewing room, Dania glanced along the corridor, but Dr Peterkin had disappeared. Dania had recognised the name the instant she'd heard it: this was the woman Marek had met the day before, the lecturer on his Druids course. There'd been no reaction from Dr Peterkin, however, when she had been introduced to Detective Sergeant Dania Gorska. Perhaps, like some, she didn't recognise the female equivalent of a name like Gorski.

In a chamber adjacent to the dissection room, everyone gowned up.

'Have you been able to get a handle on time of death yet, Prof?' Chirnside enquired.

Milo was pulling on white rubber boots. 'I'd say six p.m. on the Friday evening, give or take a couple of hours. I can't be more precise as I don't know how long she was outside. The ambient temperature is a contributing factor.' He finished tying on his heavy-duty green apron. 'Are we ready?' He paused and surveyed the room. 'Then let's make a start.'

The cutting room at Ninewells had a viewing window, which was usually crowded with students, but, in cases where crime was suspected, students were not allowed to watch. Dania could imagine their disappointment. The murder of an academic in such unusual circumstances had knocked even the EU referendum off the front page of *The Scotsman*.

The two pathologists lifted Judith Johnstone's body on to the stainless-steel dissection table. Milo, a man who commanded a room simply by his presence, adjusted the microphone above his head, while the assistant removed the sheet covering the body.

'The victim is a white female in her early fifties,' Milo said. 'She appears to be in good health.' He bent over the corpse, studying every inch of her. 'There are deep striations on both wrists, consistent with ligatures, but none round the ankles or neck. And no other breakages on the skin, although there is laceration under the hair consistent with blunt-force trauma. There are no distinguishing features, other than freckles on her face, neck and chest.' He motioned to the assistant to take photographs.

'Did you check for evidence of rape, Professor?' Dania asked.

'We did, and there was none. We swabbed the entire body. There was nothing suspicious.'

'And the fingernails?' queried the fiscal.

'Nothing. Same with the nasal cavity.'

'What about her mouth?' Dania said. 'The lipstick was smeared.'

'I haven't forgotten, Detective Sergeant.' He smiled faintly. 'You were right about the gag. We found traces of adhesive round her mouth.' He bent over the corpse again. 'No petechial haemorrhaging in the upper part of the face or eyelids. So she wasn't suffocated.' He felt gently around the neck. 'The hyoid bone is intact. We can therefore rule out strangulation.' He gestured to the assistant, and they turned the body over. Milo made the same careful examination. 'And no distinguishing marks on the back,' he said finally. 'I should add that we took X-rays earlier. There's no evidence of fractures.'

After the assistant had taken more photographs, they returned the corpse to the face-up position.

They'd been standing for nearly thirty minutes. Dania risked a glance at Chirnside. The room was deliberately kept cold, but it was warm under the lights so either he was sweating from standing under them, or he was anticipating what was about to happen.

The assistant brought over a tray of instruments. After choosing a scalpel, Milo made a rapid T-shaped incision from shoulder to shoulder, followed by one from neck to groin. He exchanged the scalpel for a pair of rib cutters and, with confident movements, opened the chest cavity. With the flesh parted, Judith Johnstone's breasts hung sideways over the edges of the table. A musky, meaty smell filled the room.

He lifted out the sternum and attached ribs, exposing the lungs and heart. 'The condition of the lungs appears normal,' he said, lifting each one out in turn. 'They're not hyperinflated, so she didn't drown. And she wasn't a smoker. ' He placed the lungs on the scales, and then moved them to a side table, where he cut through the tissue, working silently.

This wasn't Dania's first autopsy, and she knew that patience was required. She was also regretting having skipped lunch. Depending on the findings, an autopsy could last several hours, and Milo had a reputation for thoroughness.

He returned to the dissection table. 'I'm checking the pulmonary artery, but there's no evidence of a blood clot.' He cut around the heart and removed it, turning it over and peering at it. Dania wondered how he could bring his face so close.

'No sign of stenosis,' he said, cutting through the organ and examining the blood vessels.

'Remind me what stenosis is again?' the fiscal said.

'A narrowing of one of the major coronary arteries. It's the most common cause of sudden cardiac arrest. But there's no obvious damage to the wall of the left ventricle, which is what one would expect in such a case.'

'Spell it out for us, Prof.'

'I'm looking for what caused her heart to stop. We checked with her GP. Judith Johnstone had no history of problems such as coronary atherosclerosis, or inherited cardiac rhythm disturbances. On the surface of it, the heart appears normal. But something may have caused a ventricular arrhythmia, a quivering of the heart, if you like, leading to sudden death. A sudden rush of adrenaline reaching the heart can cause that. And it can happen in a normal healthy person.' He dropped the heart into the metal basket held by his assistant, leaving him to weigh and record it.

Dania glanced at the chrome clock on the wall. She wondered how many students, feeling their stomachs churn with hunger, had bitterly regretted not eating before an autopsy. And how many, feeling their stomachs churn with nausea, had regretted that they had.

It was the turn of the liver, which Milo pronounced to be in excellent condition. He removed the stomach and emptied its contents into a bowl. 'There's an abnormal quantity of liquid,' he said. He bent over the bowl, inhaling, and then straightened and stared directly ahead.

'Well?' the fiscal said. 'Had she been drinking? Is that it?'

'I can't smell alcohol. And her liver suggests that she rarely drank.'

'What then?'

'It's not a smell I recognise. Pathologists can usually identify stomach contents with a degree of accuracy, but this has me baffled.' He shook his head with an expression that suggested he was annoyed with himself for not knowing. 'We'll have to wait for the results of the toxicity tests.'

'And how long will that take?'

'Up to three or four weeks.'

'You realise this is a murder case, Professor Slaughter.'

He turned his gaze on her. 'Is it?' he said sharply. 'I've seen no evidence of it so far.' He seemed to regret his mild outburst. 'I can fast-track the tests. You're in luck that teaching is over for the year.'

'Thank you,' she muttered.

He felt the intestines gently. 'She hasn't eaten for several hours.'

'And yet there's liquid in her stomach,' Dania said.

'Indeed. Most unusual.' He and the assistant carried the intestines to the sink, where they washed out the contents into a large bowl. The smell of excrement reached them.

She caught Chirnside glancing at his watch. They'd been standing for nearly two hours.

After several minutes, Milo returned. 'I'm about to examine the brain.' He waited.

This was a clear invitation to leave. No one moved.

'Very well, then.' He made an incision from behind the corpse's left ear, over the crown of the head to behind the right ear. With a slow deliberate movement, he peeled back the corpse's face, bringing some of the red hair with it. He repeated the process at the back of the skull.

He picked up the Stryker and cut a cap in the skull. This was the part Dania hated, the saw's whining noise, its tone rising and falling as it bit through bone. He tried and failed to prise off the cap. With a gesture of frustration, he picked up a tiny hammer and gave the skull a sharp tap. The bone fell away, exposing the brain. He continued to speak into the overhead microphone in a medical language that none of them understood.

After several minutes, he said, 'Nothing out of the ordinary. A more extensive examination will have to wait until I've removed the brain.' He chose a scalpel from the tray. 'I'm about to sever the cranial nerves and spinal cords.'

He was reaching into the skull when there was a crash behind them.

Dania wheeled round. The procurator fiscal had fainted.

Deep in thought, Dania locked the front door behind her and dropped her bag in the corridor.

The voice came from the dining room. 'Danka! How was your day?'

'I've been to an autopsy.'

Marek was seated at the table, his laptop open, his pale blue jacket slung over the back of the chair. 'I've never understood how anyone can watch one of those,' he said, lifting his head.

'It goes with the job, I'm afraid. What about you?'

'I'm finishing a report.' He smiled. 'Can you guess what it's about?'

'The EU referendum?'

'Correct. You know, when I switch on the radio now, every programme is about the referendum. It either starts or ends with The Clash's "Should I Stay or Should I Go?" or "Making Your Mind Up" by Bucks Fizz.'

'They're better songs than that schmaltz coming out of your laptop. What is it, anyway?'

'Ah, you'll like this, Danka. This is Mieczysław Fogg.'

'I don't know the name.'

'Our parents used to listen to him. This is a tango, "Ostatnia Niedziela". Do you know how to tango?'

'Do you?'

'I've been going to classes.'

'Show me, then.'

He got to his feet. With his arm round her waist, he swung her around expertly, avoiding the dining-room chairs, and danced her into the corridor. His face close to hers, he manoeuvred and spun her expertly, finishing by bending her backwards over his arm.

'Impressive,' she said. 'How long have you been learning?'

He lifted her upright. 'Nearly a year.'

'Do you go with anyone?' she asked, following him back to the dining room.

He smiled over his shoulder. 'I don't need to. There are always more women than men.'

'And I bet they queue up to dance with you.'

'All I can say is that, if men knew how passionate women become when they do the tango, they'd be signing on in droves. The classes have finished for this year. But next year I'm moving up to the advanced class. You should come along.'

'I've got two left feet.' She pulled up a chair beside him. 'Can you help me with something, Marek?'

'Of course.'

'Can we do a search on scarecrows? I want to see if there are pagan connections. Or connections to human sacrifice.'

'I'm guessing this has to do with the recent murder,' he said, raising an eyebrow. 'You think Judith Johnstone was killed as part of a human sacrifice?'

'Our main problem is that we're getting nowhere with motive. I'm prepared to consider anything.'

He typed in the search terms and hit 'Enter'. A second later, the screen flooded with links.

'There seem to be a number of fantasy writers who write creepy stories about scarecrows, Danka.'

'I'm looking for something more solid. Try this link here.'

The text of a scholarly article appeared on the screen. The gist was that there is no evidence that scarecrows are anything other than a device for keeping birds out of cornfields.

She thought of the totem pole in Judith's garden. 'Okay, try Native Americans. It was one of Judith's areas of research.'

'And human sacrifice?'

'As well.'

What came back were pages of someone's dissertation. The summary told them that there were North American peoples who did practise human sacrifice, but it could best be described as ritualised torture, and the unhappy victims were mainly captured enemy soldiers. As for killing women, children, and others whom they didn't meet in battle, and were therefore not worthy opponents, it was considered shameful.

Dania sat back, picking at her lip.

'I have an idea,' Marek said. 'Let's look for *Druids* and human sacrifice.'

She shot him a look.

'It's a hunch, Danka. Judith Johnstone wrote the course on Druidism. That suggests more than a passing interest.' He changed the search terms. 'Ah, here's something,' he said, scrolling down. 'The Celts appear to have performed human sacrifice as part of their religious rituals. And Druids were the religious and scholar class.'

'What's the evidence for that?'

'None other than Julius Caesar. In *De Bello Gallico*, he writes that the people of Gaul are completely devoted to religion and, when things get bad, they sacrifice human victims. And it's the Druids who are the administrators of these sacrifices.'

'Look at this bit, Marek,' she said, pointing at the screen. 'Effigies of great size are interwoven with twigs, the limbs of which are filled with living people and set on fire from below, and the people are deprived of life, surrounded by flames.'

'A wicker man.' He paused. 'A scarecrow isn't a million miles away from an effigy interwoven with twigs.'

'Could Judith have been killed as part of a Druid ritual? It's a possibility we have to consider.'

'But she wasn't set alight.'

'There could be a number of reasons for that. Maybe they were disturbed before they could light the match.' Dania imagined the crowd gathered on the Liff Road, waiting for their companions to return from Backmuir Wood with the branches that would be piled around the foot of the scarecrow. She peered at the screen. 'It definitely says the victims have to be *living* when they're set on fire.'

'That's nice. But she was found dead, yet not burnt. I might learn more about this at the summer school. The course includes the history of the ancient Druids. Shall I make a point of asking Dr Peterkin about wicker men?'

But Dania was only half listening. She was piecing together the forensic evidence. Judith had been hit on the head, although not hard enough to kill her. There was adhesive round her mouth, so she'd been gagged. And her hands had been tied. *She hasn't eaten for several hours. There's an abnormal quantity of liquid.* Maybe the intention had been to purify her system by giving her a ritual drink before the sacrifice. But she'd cheated them by dying before the fire was lit. Milo had still to return a verdict on cause of death, but something had to account for the look of horror in Judith's eyes. The announcement that she was about to be burnt alive would have done it. Easily.

But what sort of people were prepared to burn someone alive in a ritual ceremony? Were they modern-day Druids? She felt a constriction in her chest. With a growing feeling of dread, she gripped her brother's arm. 'We don't know what we're dealing with here,' she said, her gaze fixed on his. 'For heaven's sake, Marek, be careful.'

CHAPTER 8

On Wednesday, Dania arrived at the office early, having abandoned her piano practice. When she played, her brain slipped up a gear and, in the middle of Chopin's Waltz in A minor, a piece she knew so well that her fingers did the thinking, she'd let her mind roam freely. And suddenly she had it. Why Judith's car registration hadn't appeared on the cameras.

Marek had been slicing *kiełbasa* in the kitchen, the sleeves of his black shirt rolled up to the elbows. Around the chopping block were plates of cheese, paprika, pickled herring, and slices of the black rye bread with caraway seeds that he loved so much. 'Coffee's brewing, Danka,' he said over his shoulder.

'I've got to go.' She picked up a piece of bread and two slices of cheese. 'I'll see you this evening.'

She left him staring at the mountain of food.

At her desk, she wrote down the registration of Judith's light blue Honda Civic in big letters on a sheet of paper. If she herself wanted to cheat the system, how would she do it? There was little she could do with the numbers, but there were two obvious possibilities with the letters. The 'C' could be filled in to make the letter 'O' and the bottom of the 'L' could be masked to make it look like an 'I'. It helped greatly that the letters in a Honda Civic's number plate were without serifs.

If her hunch was correct, there were three possibilities: the letter 'C' alone had been altered, or the letter 'L', or both. She launched the ANPR system, entered all three registrations, and did a search for Friday 27 May. As she had no idea how long it would take, she decided to go hunting for a proper breakfast.

She left the building and, dodging the early-morning traffic, crossed the Marketgait. Opposite the Sheriff Court was an archway that led to one of her favourite eating houses. As well as selling the sort of homemade cakes the gods would have eaten on Mount Olympus, it did the best fry-up in town. She'd been careful not to tell Marek that she preferred full Scottish breakfasts to paprika and pickles, as she knew he'd be scandalised. Her problem was that he'd heard her talk about this place and, as his offices weren't far away, it was simply a matter of time before they bumped into each other here.

The hot sweet smell of scones hit her as she opened the door. The owner, a great hulking Dundonian with a lined face and dark bushy eyebrows, grinned as she entered. She didn't even need to place the order for the all-day breakfast and pot of builder's tea.

'So, how do you think the EU vote will go, bonnie lass?' he said, piling her plate high with bacon and sausages. 'It would be a pity if you had to take yourself off back to Russia.'

'It's Poland, actually.'

'Same thing, isn't it? Are they not both in the Soviet Union?'

She nodded, saying nothing. Balancing the tray on one arm, she lifted the stainless-steel teapot and crisscrossed past tables to the one at the window.

Half an hour later, she was back at her desk. The room was starting to fill as officers arrived for their shifts.

She stared at the screen. At first she didn't believe it, the light blue Honda Civic with a registration plate identical to Judith's, but with an 'O' instead of the 'C' and an 'I' instead of the 'L'. She followed the route it had taken on Friday 27 May, westwards towards the Coupar Angus Road, appearing on several cameras on the A92 and Kingsway.

With her heart thumping wildly, she examined each image in turn. Not all were usable, as it depended critically on the position of the cameras, but several had clear shots of the driver. And he looked nothing like Judith Johnstone.

Whoever was at the wheel was wearing a grey beanie hat, large sunglasses, black leather gloves and a blue boiler suit. The clothes were suspicious in themselves – who would wear smart leather gloves with a boiler suit? But she knew what a practised barrister would say: even though the DVLA would almost certainly confirm that this registration number had never been assigned to a Honda Civic, the plate could simply have been stolen and screwed on to any old light blue Honda. She would have to find stronger evidence to convince a jury that the car in this image was Judith Johnstone's. And, as she flicked through the images, she realised that perhaps she already had. The hubcap on the front wheel on the driver's side was different from the others. Judith must have lost it and had it replaced with one that didn't match. If Dania's theory was correct, then the Honda they'd found on the Liff Road would also have a different hubcap on the driver's wheel. Even a lawyer would have to admit that that was too much of a coincidence.

She picked up the phone.

An hour later, she was signing in at the entrance to the vehicle pound's clean room. Kimmie, a cheerful Australian with blue-green eyes, a creamy complexion, and dark glossy hair which she usually wore in a messy pile on top of her head, ran the place with an efficiency that left everyone breathless. Her success rate was staggering, and Dania had often wondered what kept the girl in Dundee. She'd worked closely with Kimmie on the sexual-assault case, and found her to be a no-nonsense, straight-talking scientist. When she didn't know the answer to a question, she said so, instead of trying to make out that she did. Dania had immediately recognised the girl's ability, and had run her theories past her, something that Kimmie evidently appreciated. Consequently, a rapport and mutual respect had developed between the two women.

Dania held up a copy of one of the stills from the ANPR system. It was taken from the driver's side, and showed not only the driver, but both front and back hubcaps to best advantage.

Kimmie examined the image. 'I'm about finished taking the evidence,' she said with a strong Australian accent, 'but from what you told me on the phone, there's one more test I need to make.'

'Which is?'

She grinned. 'Check for traces of adhesive on the number plates.' She nodded towards the Honda Civic. It was in the middle of the room, covered in fingerprint dust, making it look as though it badly needed a trip to the car wash.

'May I take a peek at the hubcaps?'

'Sure, but you'll have to gown up.' Kimmie pointed to a line on the floor. 'This is as far as you go in your civvies.'

'No problem. I'm used to it.'

'The changing room's next to the office.'

Dania pulled on suit and slippers and followed Kimmie into the clean room. The walls and floor had been painted white, which, as Kimmie informed her, showed up the slightest trace of foreign matter and, Dania thought, made the Honda look even filthier than it was.

They examined the front wheel on the driver's side. And there it was – the hubcap was different from the others. And identical to the one in the photo. Dania closed her eyes briefly. This was the breakthrough she'd been looking for. Their first piece of solid evidence. Her heart was clubbing away in her chest.

'Congratulations, Sergeant,' Kimmie said lazily.

'When can you let me have the results of the adhesive test?'

'By tomorrow morning.'

'That quickly?'

'Ah, come on now. I'm a woman, same as you.'

'While I'm here, can you tell me anything else about the car?'

Kimmie folded her arms, and her voice became businesslike. 'Right, so inside, there are loads of dabs in the places you'd expect. Keys, handbrake, dashboard controls, driving mirror, steering wheel. Although you mostly get smeared prints on the wheel as people slide their mitts over it.' She looked thoughtfully at the car. 'On the outside, it's mainly the door handle and the petrol cap. But all the dabs are Judith Johnstone's.'

'Fibres on the driver's seat?'

'About that. The upholstery was the cleanest I've seen in a car. Not even chocolate wrappers, like in my old banger. I think someone ran a Hoover over it. I'm afraid Judith Johnstone didn't leave anything of herself behind.'

'I noticed a hairbrush in her handbag. Anything there?'

'You think the killer combed his hair before putting that beanie on?'

'I was thinking more that, if she knew her kidnapper well, he might have borrowed the brush on a previous occasion.'

'Right, I get you. But we only found her hairs.'

'We think she might have been kidnapped and driven to the Liff Road in this Honda. We can't tell from the camera images, but she could have been lying unconscious in the back seat.'

'If that's the guy who put her there,' Kimmie said, tapping the photo, 'then he's forensically aware. Didn't bother wiping the prints away because, with those gloves on, he knew he wouldn't be leaving any. But he wasn't completely sure that a stray hair wouldn't pop out of that cap so he vacuumed everything.' She scratched her chin. 'Mind you, most people know to take those sorts of precautions.'

'And the floor? Was there anything around the pedals?'

'A bit of mud and gravel. We tested the soil. Nothing out of the ordinary.'

'No shoe prints or boot prints?'

'Zippo.'

'What was in the glove compartment?'

'Owner's manual, roadside assistance paperwork. Usual stuff. There were prints other than hers but we eliminated them.'

'How?'

'They belonged to the previous driver. We got his name from the DVLA and tracked him down.' Kimmie said it as though it were a trivial exercise. Dania reckoned that, to someone of her abilities, it probably was.

'What about the scarecrow's clothes?'

The girl closed her eyes briefly. 'Christ, that scarecrow. But, no, there's no organic matter there, if you don't count the bird mess.' She grinned. 'Birds these days are wise to scarecrows. It's humans that scare them, not bits of straw dressed in weird clothes.' She must have read Dania's expression because she added, 'Live humans is what I meant.'

'And the sticks?'

'No usable dabs.'

'I don't suppose there were footprints round the scarecrow?'

'Everything was trampled.' She paused. 'I'll be sending over my final report tomorrow.'

'Great. And thanks.'

'No worries. Anything else, just ask, okay? We sheilas can't let the guys have all the fun, right?'

★ ★ ★

Chirnside was reading at his desk, and glanced up in alarm as Dania hurried in without knocking. Breathlessly, she explained her hunch that Judith's number plates had been altered, describing what she'd found on the ANPR, and finishing with the explanation about the mismatched hubcaps. She laid on his desk the photograph of the driver with the beanie.

He picked it up and scrutinised it. 'Good work, Dania,' he said, excitement in his voice. 'And we're getting the forensics tomorrow, you say?' He studied the image. 'You can't see much of the face. But someone might remember the beanie and sunglasses.'

'Hard to tell what sort of build this person has.'

'Are you wondering if he could lift a body on to those sticks?'

'It's the first question you ask, isn't it?'

'Actually, my first question is: why did he do it?' Chirnside pushed his reading glasses up and wiped his eyes. 'What's your theory?'

'Judith had an interesting line of research. Native Americans, and other religions. Pagan groups exist today. It could be a ritual.'

'Are you saying there's a modern-day pagan sect operating in the city of Dundee?'

Dania could see he thought this far-fetched. 'It's possible, sir.'

He got to his feet and paced the room. 'Let's go with that for the moment,' he said, stopping and staring at her. 'So my question is this: why would a group of pagans want to sacrifice someone like Judith Johnstone?'

'I don't know, sir,' Dania said, feeling suddenly tired. 'We haven't enough information. We don't know who the pagans are. Maybe we should appeal to the public.'

His gaze drilled into hers. 'Sergeant, we have to walk a fine line between informing the public and keeping information back. How do you think people would react if they thought a group of pagans was going round stringing up women and leaving them for the corbies to feast on?'

'When you put it like that, they'd react strongly. But surely they'd react equally strongly if she'd been shot. Or had her throat cut.'

When he spoke, there was a slight shake in his voice. 'There's another possibility. We had an incident here a year or so back. It was at a summer festival, Willowfest, I think it was called. It was held on Dundee Law, in the evening.'

Dania had been up Dundee Law only once when, shortly after her move to Dundee, Marek had taken her to the observation point, more for the stunning view of the Sidlaw Hills than to see the war memorial. A stiff wind had come up suddenly, and she'd lost the silk scarf Tony had given her on her birthday.

'We sent the uniforms there to make sure there was no un-pleasantness,' Chirnside continued. He ran a hand across his face. 'It seemed harmless enough, lots of talks about woodland, and moon worship, that sort of thing. A few songs. But it soon turned nasty.' His expression hardened. 'A group of townspeople decided to take matters into their own hands. But these weren't the usual antisocial elements who are always spoiling for a fight. No, they were respectable citizens, churchgoers – pillars of society, you might say.'

'So what happened?'

'They descended on the group like poison gas. And they were armed. Some had baseball bats. I bet the Law's never seen any-thing like it since Bonnie Dundee raised the Royal Standard. Or even since the lava flowed. Uniform were totally outnumbered. Had to call for backup. By the time it arrived, the damage was done. Lots of bruises and broken bones.' He sat down wearily. 'We made so many arrests that the cells were full. When the cases came to court, it was always the same story. These God-fearing

Christians simply weren't prepared to tolerate what they referred to as black magic and devil worship in their city.'

'What about this Institute of Religions and Belief Systems? What does the public think about that?'

'There was a huge outcry when it was set up a couple of years ago.'

'It's as recent as that?'

'Most of the staff were employed in other departments, but it was Judith Johnstone who pressed for an institute of their own. Eventually, she got it. And then the fun began.'

'What sort of fun?'

'Bricks through windows, slogans on walls, human excrement through letter boxes.' He hesitated. 'And a few death threats. We took them seriously, of course, but nothing came of them. Judith insisted on going on Radio Tay and explaining that the institute was purely academic. Teaching and not preaching, she said. Students learn about the history of ancient pagan cultures, and what these cultures are like today. But nothing more. No attempt to convert them. She took regular slots on the radio after that. Always made sure the institute was seen in a good light. And everything settled down.'

The implication of what he was saying filtered into Dania's mind. She'd thought Judith's death was the result of a pagan ritual, and the reason she'd been chosen as the victim would become clear in due course. But perhaps it was nothing to do with pagans. The exact opposite, in fact. Milo's words sprang into her head. *Strange way to crucify someone.* Could that be it? A message from the Christian community to the institute? If so, then the person who'd set up the institute would be the obvious choice of victim.

Chirnside gestured to his papers. 'These are the transcripts of the interviews with the staff at the institute. They say the same as Judith, that they're academics. Nothing more, nothing less.'

'And you believe them?'

He frowned. 'I don't think they're members of a pagan cult. Some go to the same church I do.' He was silent for a moment. 'By the way, the uniforms picked up that thief, the one you chased out of Tay Street Lane. Your description was spot on. He was seen on Debenhams' CCTV and we managed to get a firm ID.'

'I'm guessing he stumbled across the users and saw an opportunity.'

'It was wasted; there was only small change in the woman's purse. He said he went there looking to buy from a pusher.'

'Looks like the couple got there first. Did he give a description of this pusher?'

'Aye, eventually, after the interrogating officer threatened to book him for all sorts of offences, real and imaginary. The pusher's from Glasgow, top of the list of their most-wanted. He goes by many aliases. The description we have of him is that he's missing two fingers from his left hand, chopped off with a cleaver in a turf war between dealers. And he walks with a pronounced limp.'

'Toes chopped off?'

'No idea. But now that we know he's in Dundee, we'll get the word out. If we can find him and break him, he'll lead us to the big guys.' Chirnside's eyes blazed with crusading zeal. 'For the first time, we might be able to make a real difference.' He seemed to remember himself then. 'On a completely different subject, Dania, I understand you're a brilliant pianist.'

She blinked in surprise. 'I've played for years, but I'm certainly not brilliant. You need to practise for longer than I have time for.'

'I have it on good authority that you are,' he said with a crooked smile. He shuffled his papers. 'The reason I'm bringing this up is that there's going to be some sort of monument to the Poles who were here during the war.'

'Yes, I've heard about that.'

'Good. Well, I was thinking. The Force needs to be represented at the opening ceremony and I thought it would be appropriate if our representative was you. Would you mind?'

She felt herself flushing. 'Not at all. I'd be honoured.'

'And I wondered if you would give a concert at the Caird Hall. Play some Polish music. Folk dances. That sort of thing.' He looked at her with a kindly smile.

She didn't answer immediately. He took this as a negative sign. 'I expect you'll want to think about it. But if you decide to take it on, and I hope you do, will you go and see Sir Graham Farquhar? He's the chairman of the fund-raising committee, and the driving force behind it.' When she still didn't answer, he added, 'So will you think about it?'

She nodded.

'Sir Graham lives at Backmuir Hall. Behind the wood.'

Think Downton Abbey and you've got some idea.

'There's no rush. But may I tell him to expect you?' Chirnside added hopefully.

She smiled. 'Of course.'

CHAPTER 9

Kimmie had been as good as her word. She'd sent in her final report on the Wednesday evening, earlier than promised, and it was waiting at the station when Dania arrived early on Thursday.

To her delight, Kimmie's tests clearly showed that the number plates of the Honda found on the Liff Road had been altered. Adhesive tape had been stuck on to both front and back plates to make the 'C' look like an 'O' and the 'L' like an 'I'. She'd sprayed the plates with a chemical that turned green on contact with the kind of glue found on adhesive tape. The results were unequivocal.

Dania spent the following hour plotting the route the Honda had taken through Dundee on the Friday Judith had gone missing. She'd have it computerised eventually but, right now, what she needed was to get it up on the incident board where everyone could see it. Chirnside was still with the chief inspector, but she decided this couldn't wait. After calling everyone over, she explained what she'd found on the cameras for Friday 27 May, and what Kimmie had found on the Honda's number plates.

A few officers were grinning and nudging each other. Others were looking reserved, as though trying to find another explanation. Dania was one of those rare detectives who welcomed scepticism, having discovered early on in her career that no one had a 100 per cent hit rate, and a heated discussion could cement a good working relationship.

'I checked with the garage Judith used,' she went on. 'Their records show that she lost that front hubcap earlier this year.'

'Probably going over a pothole,' someone sneered. The state of the roads in and around Dundee was a familiar gripe amongst the officers.

'The garage said they weren't able to get an exact replacement, so they fitted another model. This one,' she added, tapping the photograph.

There were murmurs of approval. She felt their excitement, just as she'd felt it when she had made the discovery.

'Okay, now take a look at the map.' She ran a finger over the thick red line. 'This shows the route taken by the Honda. I've added the times that it appears on the cameras. The first appearance is here, on the A92, and the last is just here, on the Coupar Angus Road. Unfortunately, there are no cameras anywhere near the part of the Liff Road near Backmuir Wood.'

'That would make it too easy,' Fergus said sourly.

'The Honda appears on that Coupar Angus Road camera at eight-twelve a.m. And then it disappears.'

'So where was it all of Friday? No one saw it in the layby.'

'If we knew that, we'd catch our killer.' She handed out the photos of the driver. 'And I think this is our prime suspect.'

She waited while the officers pored over the image.

'I guess we know what's next,' Fergus said, looking up. 'We need to do the footwork round those villages again, street by bloody street.'

'It's a long shot, but someone might recognise that boiler suit. If you look, you'll see a tear in the left shoulder.'

'What about the girl who found the body? Jenn McLaughlin?'

'I'll talk to her. She'll be at school now, but I'll try her house later this afternoon.'

'Rather you than me.'

'What do you mean?' Dania said, surprised by his tone of voice.

'There's something not quite right about that girl. I can't put my finger on it.' He shook his head. 'We interviewed her in connection with her missing sister. She was gutted that Ailsa had run off.'

'That's natural, isn't it?'

'Yes, but it was more than that. It was like everything she'd ever wanted had been taken away from her. And the way she stares. It gives me the willies. You're welcome to her.' He looked at Dania without enthusiasm. 'So if we're knocking on doors again, shall we draw up a roster, or what?'

Whenever they did this, there was always bickering about who went where.

Dania kept her expression blank. 'Thanks for volunteering to do that, Fergus.'

Dania remained at her desk after the officers had gone. Her conversation with Fergus about Jenn and her sister had triggered the memory of something she'd intended to do, but events had overtaken her. She should be getting on with finding Judith Johnstone's killer, but curiosity got the better of her. A few taps at the keyboard and she was reading about the case of Ailsa McLaughlin.

On Saturday 30 April, Ailsa had been reported missing by her mother. The woman claimed that Ailsa and her friend, Kerry Campbell, had been out the night before, and had failed to return home. The reason the case was marked closed was that Ailsa had subsequently sent text messages to her family to say that she and Kerry were living in London, had started a new life, and wouldn't be coming back.

But there was more. As part of the investigation, Jenn had also been interviewed. She claimed that her sister would never have run away. Why would she? She'd been admitted to Dundee University and was due to start her course at the Institute of Religions and Belief Systems in September. The statement had been taken by DI Chirnside.

Dania let out a breath. This was only a month earlier. And yet, when he and Dania had been called out to the Liff Road, Chirnside had made no mention of this case. Then again, why would he? The case was closed. The missing girls had simply chosen to live in London.

The file contained a list of the other missing teenagers, and a note that their names had been added to the MisPers database, with police in cities around the UK alerted. Someone had added a few lines to the effect that several of the teenagers had returned to Dundee, although neither Ailsa nor Kerry Campbell was amongst them. Attached to the file was a report by Chirnside of his outreach programme to Dundee's secondary schools. The gist was that he strongly warned the pupils that running away is an incredibly risky thing to do, and stressed the dangers from drugs, prostitution and human trafficking.

There was nothing new about teenagers running away. And yet it seemed strange that a girl who'd won a place at university would give everything up for the lights of the big city.

There was a link to the first of Jenn's radio interviews. Dania pulled on the headphones. The interviewer, a sensitive but clearly sceptical woman, was trying to get Jenn to explain why she thought Ailsa and Kerry hadn't simply left home. Listening to Jenn struggling to keep from breaking down, Dania felt a sudden anguish. This was not the composed girl she'd met nearly a week before. That girl was subdued, as though an inner spark, the very essence of her, had been extinguished.

There were articles in both the *Dundee Courier* and *The Scotsman* about Jenn's campaign to find the girls. The headlines were startling: 'Where are Ailsa and Kerry?' and 'What Happened To My Sister?' One photograph showed a distraught Jenn, staring open-mouthed into the camera. The substance of the articles was always the same. When asked about the text messages Ailsa had sent from London, Jenn said she had no explanation. She just knew that the girls hadn't run away. She had set up a Facebook page requesting that, if anyone knew what had happened, they should leave a post. The story was one of those nine-days wonders, and soon disappeared.

Dania checked the Facebook page. There was little there: expressions of sympathy, suggestions as to where to look in London, names and addresses of hostels, and some nasty comments saying that of course the girls had left a dump like Dundee, and Jenn needed to get a grip. But nothing concrete. She tugged off the headphones, deep in thought.

She was still staring at the screen when Chirnside arrived from the press briefing. One look at his face told Dania how it had gone.

'Bloody journalists,' he said, slamming the door behind him. 'What do they expect? It's only a few days since we found the body. They've no idea what it takes for a case like this to be resolved.'

He glared at the incident board. Dania hurried over and took him through the substance of her earlier briefing, leaving nothing out. He listened without interrupting.

'So why aren't you out with the others?' he said in a tone of voice she'd not heard before.

'I'm on my way, sir.'

She grabbed her jacket and hurried out of the room.

It was after four before Dania found Oaktree Farm. At Tiddly-winks Nursery School, she'd turned right into Muirhead and had naïvely thought that, once she was through the village and past the houses that spilled out at the other end, the farm would be easy to find. In the end, she stopped at a farmhouse, braving snarling dogs, and was put on the right road. Even then, she failed to find the front door, and came in at the back.

As she pulled into the yard, a door opened on the left and Jenn appeared. She was wearing black trousers, a blazer with a school badge and a white shirt. Dania switched off the engine and left the car, the fetid smell of the farmyard filling her nostrils.

'Hello, Jenn,' she said in a friendly tone. 'Do you remember me?'

'You're Detective Sergeant Gorska. The Polish detective.'

She'd forgotten the girl's unblinking stare. 'You've got a good memory.' She glanced around. A clucking noise came from the barn. 'Is your mother about?'

'She's away selling the eggs. But she'll be back soon.'

'May I come in?'

'Of course.'

She followed the girl into an old-fashioned farm kitchen with white walls and flagstone floor. A wooden table with books scattered across the surface took up much of the space.

'I hope I'm not disturbing you, Jenn.'

'I've not got a lot of homework today. Would you like some tea?'

Dania had been on her feet for hours, showing the photograph around. 'That would be great. Milk, but no sugar.'

As the girl bustled around the kitchen range, Dania cast a sur-reptitious glance at the books. Jenn was studying trigonometry.

Under the maths text was *Le Petit Prince* by Antoine de Saint-Exupéry.

She turned on the tap, startling Dania with the gurgle of noisy plumbing, and put the filled kettle on the Aga. 'I'm guessing you're here to question me, Detective Sergeant.'

The formality in the girl's tone took Dania by surprise. 'We're questioning everyone in Dundee and the outlying villages,' she said, feeling defensive all of a sudden.

'About the scarecrow murder?'

She took the photograph out of her bag. 'I want you to look closely at this, and tell me if you recognise the man who's driving.'

The girl studied the photo, frowning in concentration. 'It could be almost anyone. Lots of farm workers dress like that.'

'You can't see much of the face, I'm afraid.'

'Pity his hair's hidden under that hat.' She turned her clear-eyed gaze on Dania. 'Is this the man who killed Dr Johnstone?'

'We think he might be.'

A look of something that could have been excitement crossed Jenn's face. She went back to studying the photo. 'He's wearing driving gloves,' she said suddenly. 'Except they're a bit on the posh side.'

'He's driving Dr Johnstone's car. So he doesn't want to leave his prints behind.'

'Do you think she was in the car when this photo was taken? Maybe she was in the boot.'

'I can't tell you any more, Jenn.'

The girl handed back the photo reluctantly. 'There's something familiar about him. I don't know what it is. Maybe the way he's holding his head. I'm sorry, as I'd really like to help you.'

'Can I ask you something else, in that case?'

'Aye, go on.'

The kettle started to whistle. Jenn turned and reached for the mugs from the overhead cupboard.

'It's about your sister, Ailsa. And her friend, Kerry.'

The girl stiffened, and then turned slowly, the mugs in her hand. Her expression was hard to read. 'What about them?'

'I came across their names when I was researching Judith Johnstone. There's a mention of Judith's institute in those news-paper articles about Ailsa and Kerry. I've not been in Dundee long, so I missed the story. Can you tell me what happened?'

'There's not a lot to tell,' Jenn said, dropping tea bags into the mugs. She poured from the kettle. 'The articles more or less said it.'

'Ah, but journalists tend to leave out details they think are unimportant. But, often, those unimportant details turn out to be the only important ones.'

A look of respect crept into the girl's eyes. 'What do you want to know, exactly?'

'I want to hear why you think Ailsa would give up her uni-versity place and run off to London.'

'That's just it. I don't think she would.'

Jenn took a carton of milk from the massive fridge, giving Dania a view of dozens of animal magnets as she opened the door. She brought the milk to the table and pushed it across. Her eyes took on a wistful expression. 'She was so excited. Talked non-stop about her new course. She'd been speaking to Dr Johnstone, who was very encouraging. She was going to try to get her a place on the summer school without having to pay. Said she could arrange a sort of junior scholarship.'

'That was kind of her.'

'Aye, I think she was a kind lady, from what Ailsa said.'

Dania stirred the tea. 'And when was the last time you saw your sister?'

'At supper that evening.'

'Here?'

'We always eat here, at this table. She was still fair excited by that summer school.'

'And then?'

'She and Kerry went out.'

'Do you know where?'

'She didn't say.'

'Did Ailsa have a boyfriend? Or did Kerry?'

'Not that I know of,' Jenn said doubtfully. She wrapped her hands round her mug as though trying to warm them. 'The next day, Mum realised that her bed hadn't been slept in. It was the first time we'd seen that. If Ailsa was out late, she always came home.'

'No sleepovers?'

'Sleepovers are for kids.' She shrugged. 'Anyway, Mum called the police. They sent someone round. The DI who came with you to see the scarecrow.'

'DI Chirnside.'

'Aye, that's him. He came to our school once, and gave a talk about not running away. And saying no to drugs. We get that all the time from the teachers,' she added dismissively.

'So what did you tell DI Chirnside?'

'I told him what I've just told you. He said he would investigate. But the next day, the Sunday, we got a text from Ailsa, saying she was in London with Kerry. We've had a few more since then.'

'What do the messages say?'

'That they've both moved to London and decided to stay there. They're looking for jobs.'

'How do you feel about that?'

'I don't believe it.'

'Or you don't want to believe it?'

'Would *you* have believed it?' the girl said hotly. 'It's so completely unexpected.'

'If Ailsa had been planning it for a while, do you think she would have told you?'

'Aye, she would. She told me everything. Mum said it must have been a spur-of-the-moment thing.'

'Jenn,' Dania said, putting her mug down, 'if you're getting these texts, why do you think something bad has happened to the girls? Ailsa is sending messages from London saying they're doing fine.'

'At first I thought they were being held somewhere against their will,' she said in a flat voice. 'And I still think that.'

'And made to send those texts?'

'It would explain why they never ring. If they'd been forced into prostitution, I'm sure we'd hear something odd in their voices.'

'Did you say all this to the DI?'

There was genuine pain in the girl's eyes. 'He didn't believe me. He refused to have them listed as missing.' Her expression softened. 'But thank you for taking an interest. No one else seems to be bothered.'

Dania took a mouthful of tea. 'Tell me about Ailsa. What's she like?'

Jenn thought for a moment. 'She works very hard. And she has loads of friends. They're always hanging out.'

'Is there anything in particular she likes doing outside school? Does she have any hobbies?'

'She loves nature. I think she feels perfectly at peace in the woodland, or by the river. Whenever she gets the chance, she goes to Backmuir Wood. You know the place I mean, down the Liff Road?'

Dania nodded. It was where they had found Judith Johnstone's body.

'I go there a lot myself, now,' Jenn went on.

'To be near Ailsa?'

'To be near her spirit,' she said defensively. She looked away.

Dania hoped she hadn't embarrassed the girl. Or upset her. But the use of the word 'spirit' made her wonder whether Jenn was starting to believe, not that her sister was being held somewhere, but that she might be dead.

'What do you think of this EU referendum debate, then?' Dania said, trying to sound cheerful.

'We've been following it at school.' Jenn played with her mug. 'If we Brexit, does that mean you'll have to go back to Poland?'

'It won't come to that. People are too smart to vote to leave, like they're too smart to vote for Donald Trump.' She drank down the rest of her tea. 'Anyway, the Scots seem to like the Poles. Down south, I met many who thought that Europeans are swarming to the UK to steal directly from British pockets.'

'So were you born in Poland?'

'In Warsaw.'

'What's it like there?'

She wondered what the girl knew about Poland's history. 'The Warsaw you see now is only seventy years old. They rebuilt the old part of the city using eighteenth-century paintings as a guide.'

'That's amazing.'

'The paintings were by Canaletto.'

'So when did you leave?'

'When I was not much younger than you. My parents came here in search of the promised land.'

'Did they find it?'

'I don't think so. They went back to Poland a few years later.'

'What was it like growing up in a strange place?'

'We kept up our Polish customs and language.' She grew thoughtful. 'We were British at school. At home, though, we were expected to be Polish.'

'Do you feel like an outlander, then?'

'That's a hard one. I do sometimes. I got some choice verbal abuse in London.' She grinned. 'Usually when I was making an arrest.'

'Maybe it was the arrest they objected to, and not the fact that you're a foreigner.'

'Maybe it was both. I don't miss it, though. London and the Met. The police station I worked in was huge, and you never really got to know anyone. I much prefer it here.'

'I sometimes feel I don't fit in. My schoolmates are posh. They think folk from round here have shaggy hair and live in the woods.' Jenn stared into her mug. 'I've never been able to make friends like Ailsa did.'

Dania could see it had been an effort for the girl to make this confession. 'Well, they're the ones who are missing out, Jenn. You shouldn't let it bother you.'

The girl's expression brightened. 'I've got all sorts of plans for the future. For when I leave school.'

Dania was put in mind of the Jewish saying that her mother had been fond of quoting: If you want to make God laugh, tell him your plans for the future.

'I'm hoping to go to uni,' Jenn went on, 'but not the one here. I want to study abroad under the EU's Erasmus Programme.'

'Have you chosen your course?'

'When I was little, I wanted to be a detective.'

'Well, it's a lot less interesting than you see on the telly,' Dania said, smiling.

'But now, I'd like to do something with forensic pathology. There was an Open Day at Ninewells a few weeks ago. It was amazing.'

'Did you meet Professor Milo Slaughter?'

Before the girl could reply, Dania heard the sound of a motor, and a vehicle pulling up outside.

'That's Mum's van,' Jenn said, getting up. She busied herself tidying away and washing the mugs.

'I need to speak to her alone, Jenn.'

'No problem. I've got chores to do around the farm.' She glanced at the photo on the table. 'Can I keep that? There are a lot of farm workers round here. I might see someone who looks like him.'

'Yes, of course. I've got plenty of copies. My phone number's on the back.'

The door opened and a tired-looking woman came in. She had a nest of fair hair, and the same pale blue eyes as Jenn. There were two deep lines on either side of her mouth.

She stopped as she caught sight of Dania.

'Mrs McLaughlin?' Dania said, getting to her feet. She pulled out her ID. 'I'm DS Gorska from the Specialist Crime Division. May I speak with you for a minute?'

'Surely,' the woman said. She took off her coat, revealing muscular arms and dark sweat stains under the armpits.

'I'll be in the barn, Mum.'

The woman made no comment as her daughter eased past her into the yard.

'Mrs McLaughlin, I'm investigating the murder of Judith Johnstone.'

'The tattie bogle murder?'

Dania handed her the photo of the driver. 'Have you seen this man before? Please take your time.'

The woman peered myopically. 'I can't say that I have.'

'There's a tear in the boiler suit. In the shoulder.'

She handed the photo back, shaking her head.

'This man's our prime suspect,' Dania said. 'Jenn's asked if I can leave this with her. She said she might be able to recognise one of the farm workers.'

113

'Aye, well, she's always outdoors, that one. Just like her sister.'

It was the segue Dania was looking for. 'Can I ask you about Ailsa, Mrs McLaughlin? Jenn said she's gone to London. How is she getting on?'

If the woman found it odd that a detective was enquiring after her daughter, she gave no indication. 'She seems to be doing fine. Said she's got a job. It's in a fast-food place, ken, but it's only a stop-gap till something better comes along. You don't mind if I start getting supper ready while we talk?'

'No, of course not.'

Mrs McLaughlin hauled a deep pan from a cupboard under the sink, let the hot tap run for a while, and then filled the pan with water. 'Ailsa always likes to do things her own way. As a child, she went up the snakes and down the ladders. But she has a good brain,' she added, lifting the pan on to the largest plate on the Aga. 'She studied sciences at school. She was about to enrol at the uni and do engineering.'

Engineering? Really? Ailsa clearly hadn't let her mother in on her real intentions . . .

'When did you last hear from her?' Dania asked.

'Last Saturday.'

'And is she still in touch with Kerry Campbell?'

'Oh aye, the two used to be inseparable, and still are, from what I can gather. I suspect they've joined one of yon groups. They must exist in London, too.'

'What kind of group?'

'Druids. Both Ailsa and Kerry were members of a – what did they call it? – a Grove.'

Dania felt the blood pounding in her ears. 'Here in Dundee?'

'She never told me where they met. That's because she knew I didn't approve. My girls were baptised as Catholics, you see. Ailsa seemed to think she could become a Druid and be a Catholic at the same time. Somehow I think they're mutually exclusive, but what would I know?'

'Did you ever meet any of the Druids?'

'They keep themselves to themselves, from what I can gather. They don't seem to socialise. Unless their gatherings are social events. Excuse me a second.' The woman disappeared into the yard and returned a few minutes later with a limp hen. Dania was relieved to see she'd had the foresight to wring the bird's neck in the barn.

'Mrs McLaughlin, don't you think it was out of character for Ailsa to leave like that? Without saying goodbye?'

'I did to begin with. All her clothes are still in her room. The girls left in whatever they were wearing.'

'That Friday?'

'Aye. It was the same with Kerry.' The woman gazed through the window. 'I wondered about it often after that first text. But then I remembered what it was like to be that age. Eighteen.' She smiled wistfully. 'Your whole life in front of you. There are so many opportunities for girls these days. Not like when I was young. Maybe they wanted to take those opportunities in London.' She said it without resentment.

'It seems to have hit Jenn hard that her sister left so suddenly.'

'They've always been close. Even when they were wee bairns. Always played together and never bickered about anything.' She hesitated. 'I worry about Jenn, to be honest. She's not like other girls.'

'Oh? In what way?'

'She's not interested in the things girls her age should be. You know, dressing up and wearing make-up, going to the cinema. Having boyfriends.' The woman held the hen by its legs and lowered it into the bubbling water. 'She's always away in the woods. I've no idea what she gets up to there.' She lifted and

115

lowered the hen repeatedly. 'And now that Ailsa's in London, she's spending more time with Aleck.'

'Aleck Docherty?'

'Aye. He's a kindly man. He's been good to Jenn. And to me. I know I can rely on him if I need help.'

After a pause, Dania said, 'Well, I'd better leave you to get on. Thank you, Mrs McLaughlin. I expect your husband will be coming home soon.'

'I have no husband.' She lifted the hen out of the pot and took it to a small working table under the window. 'He died many years ago. It'll just be Ailsa, Jenn and myself for dinner now.' She paused and corrected herself. 'I mean just Jenn and myself.' She bent her head and pulled out the scalded feathers with rough, precise movements.

Dania slipped the latch and left.

CHAPTER 10

It was five, and Marek was unlikely to be home. Dania wondered about getting back to West Bell Street but then remembered Chirnside's request to drop by and see Sir Graham Farquhar. As she was in the area, she might as well do it now. And if Backmuir Hall really did look like Downton Abbey, she was keen to see it.

She drove back through Muirhead, crossed the Coupar Angus, and headed straight down the Liff Road. It was strange seeing the place again, the thick woodland on the right and the acres of field on the left. The spot where the scarecrow had stood was marked with a police sign but, other than that, there was no evidence that a crime had taken place almost a week earlier.

All she knew about the location of Backmuir Hall was that it was 'behind the wood'. It should have been easy to find by following the Liff Road, but 'behind the wood' could mean almost anywhere.

She drove around for a while, and then, seeing the sign, turned on to a rutted road, immediately changing down a gear. As she swerved to avoid the potholes, she noticed to left and right what might have been huge jumbles of wrecked cars amongst the trees but were, on second glance, works of art. She cut the engine and left the car.

The sculptures were of varying sizes, the smallest a mere couple of metres in height, but the largest towered over her and would have needed a forklift truck to lift it. They were made of scrap metal, welded together and painted in cartoon colours, and she wondered if the artist had bought the parts from a car-crushing plant. She also wondered what they were doing on a laird's estate.

As she was turning away, she thought she saw movement in the trees. A deer perhaps? She stood still, hoping to see it again, but there was nothing. Or almost nothing. A shadow moved, smaller than a deer, and then disappeared. She walked back to the car with the very definite feeling that someone was spying on her.

The pitted road grew more treacherous and she reduced her speed to a crawl, praying she wouldn't get a flat tyre. And then, as she rounded a bend, she caught a glimpse of the hall through the trees. It looked like a photo from *Country Life*. Not exactly Downton Abbey, more a smaller version of Wuthering Heights. Whoever lived here valued his privacy, as the building was well set back from the road and hidden by woodland.

The trees thinned suddenly, and she saw it beyond the big stone gateposts, a looming red-stone structure with gables and turrets, ivied walls and windows meshed with metal. Its most striking feature was the huge flagpole, from which a saltire hung limply. In front was an electric-blue Porsche Boxster with its hood down. She pulled up behind it.

The front door was wide open. She looked for a bell or knocker and, finding none, stepped into what looked like an ante-room. A jumble of coats and jackets fought for space on two large coat-stands, above a row of walking boots and wellingtons.

Opposite the entrance was a door. Uneasy about simply walking in, she called out, 'Hello?' and then, when there was no reply, 'DS Dania Gorska. I'm here to see Sir Graham Farquhar.'

Maybe she should have rung ahead. Sir Graham could be anywhere on the estate. But, what the hell, she was here now. After waiting and listening for nearly a minute, she pushed the door, which opened smoothly on to a wide corridor. Pressed against the right-hand wall, as though frightened, was a long line of identical throne-like chairs.

Off the corridor, on the left, was an enormous living room with dark gleaming furniture and the kind of sofas you can get lost in. A spherical vase of white lilies stood on a sideboard, the sweet scent filling the room. Instead of a stag's head above the enormous fireplace, there was a gilt-framed portrait of a kilted man wearing a feather bonnet. He looked around sixty, and had bushy hair and an even bushier moustache, and was scowling at everything that took place in the room. She peered at the title: Sir Graham Farquhar of Backmuir. At least now she knew what the laird looked like. Next to the portrait was a romantic oil of a group of women pointing towards the sea.

What caught her eye, however, was the grand piano in front of the casement windows. It was a Mason & Hamlin, the name imprinted on the black lacquer. She strolled over and lifted the lid. The keys were in perfect condition, suggesting that the instrument was rarely played and was likely to be out of tune. Running her fingers over the scale of C, she was pleasantly surprised to discover that, not only was the piano in tune, it had a strong but blissfully mellow tone.

There was still no sign of Sir Graham, so she pulled out the stool, sat down, and adjusted the height. She was tempted to play Scott Joplin's 'Pine Apple Rag', but the piano's timbre was wrong for that, and so was the laird's grand living room, come to think of it. She stared through the leaded-glass windows for a few seconds, seeing more of the twisted-metal artwork in the distance, and then brought her fingers down on to the keys. The piece she played was Chopin's lively Étude in E minor, Op. 25, No. 5, known as the 'Wrong Note' étude because of the dissonance at the start and the end, although the melodic middle part was more recognisably Chopin. Somehow, though, everything came together, and anyone thinking they could get away with playing the odd wrong note would be sadly disappointed.

As she finished, she heard a snuffling behind her and turned to see a West Highland terrier with paper-white hair, its paws up as though begging. Leaning against the far wall, his arms folded, was a man in his thirties. He had a gangling frame and a slight pot-belly, and he was looking at her with an expression of delight on his face.

Embarrassed to be caught out, she got quickly to her feet.

He clapped his hands enthusiastically. 'Bra-*vo*, madam,' he said, coming forward. 'Please don't stop.' He had a deep olive-oil voice that was somehow at odds with his appearance.

'That's the end of the piece.'

'Well, indeed. But do play more.'

'I'd love to, but I'm not sure Sir Graham would approve.'

'Oh, he definitely would.'

'How do you know?'

'Because he's telling you so.' He bowed then, the action caus-ing his auburn hair, which was cut in a floppy style, to fall over his eyes. He brushed the fringe away.

She stared in surprise at this man in sweatshirt, skinny jeans and pointed shoes. Confused, she glanced at the portrait.

He must have guessed her thoughts. 'That's my grandfather,' he said. 'I come from a long line of Graham Farquhars. Just don't ask about my father,' he added with a well-groomed smile. 'He's the black sheep of the family and we don't talk about him.'

'Detective Sergeant Dania Gorska. West Bell Street Police Station. DI Chirnside suggested I come to see you about the memorial to the Poles. He's asked me to be the Force's represen-tative at the event.'

Sir Graham cracked his knuckles. He had long bony fingers. A pianist's hands. 'Oh, yes,' he said, smiling broadly. 'And you're Polish?' He held out his hand, palm upwards.

She placed hers in his, and he lifted it to his mouth. But, instead of touching his lips lightly to her hand as Poles do, he slobbered over it. 'I simply love all that folderol when Polish men greet women,' he said, straightening. 'Now, may I offer you a glass of vodka?'

'I'm afraid I'm on duty.'

'Ah, a pity. Perhaps another time.' His gaze held hers. 'I suppose we'd better get down to business, in that case.' He gestured to the nearest sofa. 'Do please make yourself comfortable. Oh, I should have asked. Would you like some coffee?'

'Thank you, but I'm fine.' She took a seat, amused to see the terrier jump on to the sofa and curl up on her lap.

'Tippex! Get down!' Sir Graham picked up the dog and took it to the window, where he flung it outside. 'He much prefers chasing rabbits,' he said apologetically. 'Although they easily out-run him, thank goodness.'

He fetched a folder from the sideboard and sat so close to her that she wondered if, like Tippex, he was going to curl up in her lap.

'Now, the date for the unveiling is July the thirty-first,' he said, 'which is a Sunday. I thought we could begin the proceedings with my giving a brief talk about our strong Scottish–Polish connection. Not just about the tens of thousands of Poles stationed here during the war, including the impact they had, and how well they were received.' His gaze held hers. 'And the effect they had on the female population. But I could also mention the tens of thousands of Scots who migrated to Poland during the seventeenth century, the trade with the Baltic towns, and so on.'

She could see he'd done his homework.

'And, of course, emphasise the strong cultural and economic benefits to Scotland of the more recent Polish migration. I would finish by saying a few words about the work of my fund-raising committee. Originally there was talk of a monument, but we've been able to do one better. We've managed to raise enough to create a small museum. It will be housed in rooms in one of the university buildings, as this is a joint venture with our academic colleagues.'

'Promoting town and gown relations?'

'Quite so. Their historians are busy collating the materials for the exhibition. We've had many contributions of memorabilia from descendants of the soldiers.' Sir Graham shifted his weight, inching closer. 'The idea of a concert came from one of the Poles on the committee.' He smiled disarmingly. 'Inspector Chirnside volunteered the information that you play magnificently. And, having heard you myself, I would have to say that that's something of an understatement.'

'Well, I—'

'Oh, do say that you'll play.'

'Of course I will.'

He looked as though he'd won the lottery. 'Smashing. And, to seal the deal, I really will have to insist that you partake of an alcoholic beverage with me.' He must have seen her hesitation. 'Surely you're no longer on duty. And the sun's over the yardarm.' He glanced through the window. 'Well, maybe not here. But it definitely is somewhere in the world.'

She laughed. 'I can't really refuse, can I?'

'Excellent.' He jumped to his feet and left the room.

She sauntered over to the window. Beyond the patch of crazy paving, steps led down to a vast lawn with grass like velvet. It was hedged on one side with holly bushes, and screened on the other by spreading trees. Laid out across the lawn were flowerbeds where roses grew in yellow and white bursts. Tippex was indeed trying, and failing, to catch rabbits, which were running round the rose beds and into the bushes. He gave up and, panting, lay down briefly, and then, a sudden flash of fur, and he sprang up again.

The lawn disappeared into a field which unfurled itself almost to the horizon. It was in this field that she counted over half a dozen of the crumpled-metal art pieces, some monochrome, others multicoloured.

Sir Graham arrived with a tray. 'Do you like the sculptures, Sergeant?'

'I'm a Michelangelo person, myself.'

'I'm creating a sculpture garden. What you see is a work in progress.'

She wondered what it would look like when it was finished. Probably more of the same, as far as the eye could see.

'I've been greatly influenced by John Chamberlain,' Sir Graham went on. 'Constructing the pieces is time-consuming, but I enjoy the work.'

'You make these yourself?' she said, amazed.

'Indeed. It satisfies one's inner creative urge.' He set the tray down on the coffee table. 'I have a friend who gets me the car parts. I weld them together, and some of them I paint. Now, this is Żubrówka,' he said, watching her reaction closely.

The vodka, flavoured with a grass that grows in the Białowieża Forest in northeast Poland, was her favourite. 'You have excellent taste, Sir Graham.'

'I first came across it in Somerset Maugham's book, *The Razor's Edge*. Do you know the one?'

'I'm afraid I haven't read it.'

'One of the characters – I forget who – refers to drinking it being like listening to music by moonlight. He had a great way with words, did Somerset Maugham.' He poured the pale green liquid into two glasses.

'Did you study literature?'

He glanced up. 'Yes, at Oxford. I went to school there, as well as up to university.'

Which would explain his upper-class English accent, thought Dania.

He handed her a glass. Raising his, and clicking his heels together, he said, '*Za zdarowie.*'

'That's Russian.'

'Oh dear. What should I have said?'

'*Na zdrowie.*'

'I'm always muddling them up.' He seemed keen to get it right. 'So, do we throw it down, or do we sip?'

'This is flavoured, so I'd sip.'

'Excellent. Now, as to the concert, do you have any pieces that you'd particularly like to play?'

'I'm assuming you'd want a Polish composer.'

'Well, of course, it would have to be Chopin. Unless you'd prefer another?'

'No, I think Chopin.' She took a mouthful, holding the liquid in her mouth before swallowing. 'So how long will the concert be?'

'There'll be a reception afterwards, so I'd say not too long. Could you play perhaps two or three shortish pieces? Or one longer one? Have a think about it. The choice, of course, will be entirely up to you.' He widened his eyes. 'It's sure to be a scintillating success. The Caird Hall will be full of Poles.'

She smiled. 'So, no pressure.'

'You have a lovely Polish accent, you know.' A look of mild alarm crossed his face. 'I hope you're not trying to get rid of it.'

'I don't think I could, even if I wanted to.'

'What made you come up to our City of Discovery?' he said, taking a sip of Żubrówka.

'It was work. An opportunity came up. I'm the type of person who takes opportunities.'

'Have you been here long?'

'Only a few weeks.'

'You may pick up a bit of a Scottish accent, despite yourself.'

'You haven't though.'

'Well, I have to admit, I'm not often here. I have interests to take care of in London.' He cradled the glass in his hands, and then lifted it to the light. 'I expect you're working on this dreadful scarecrow murder.'

She watched the pale green liquid catch fire. 'The whole station's involved,' she said, not prepared to say more.

He looked at her, but his eyes had lost their focus, as if he were seeing something else entirely. 'Poor Judith. She was such a nice lady. Very caring. You could tell that from the way she spoke about her students.'

'You knew her?

'No, no,' he said hastily. 'I mean, that's what they're saying about her in the papers.'

The papers had made no mention of Judith's relationship with her students. The laird was lying. In Dania's experience, it wasn't uncommon for members of the public to want to distance themselves from murder victims. It didn't mean they were guilty of the crime. But the laird's clumsy lie had piqued her professional interest. She kept her attention on him, watching the various emotions come and go on his face. It struck her that, if this was how he looked at board meetings, the opposition would wipe the floor with him.

'I feel bad that that poor lady was found on my land,' he said, a hunted look in his eyes.

'About that, Sir Graham, we've been wondering why the body was left in such an exposed location. There must surely be places on the estate which are more secluded.'

He seemed surprised. 'Indeed. There are many. The estate straddles the Coupar Angus Road. But do you think the killer comes from the estate?'

'I'm not suggesting that, no. I'm merely wondering about the location.'

'Where would you hide a body, Sergeant?'

'That's just it. It wasn't hidden.' She took a thoughtful sip. 'If it were me, I'd bury it somewhere in Backmuir Wood.' His sudden look of anxiety wasn't lost on her. But, then, the thought of a body interred so close to one's home would fill anyone with apprehension.

In the thickening silence, she realised that he was studying her. The look of anxiety had vanished. In its place, she saw curiosity. And suspicion.

She finished the vodka. 'I really should be getting back. Thank you for the Żubrówka, Sir Graham. And for letting me play your piano. The tone really is beautiful.'

'Well, thank *you* for dropping by, Sergeant. You've made a dull day brighter. But indulge me by letting me show you the back garden before you go. I'm particularly pleased with my latest creation.'

She smiled her acceptance.

He led the way down a corridor lined with Impressionist paintings, and through a strongly reinforced back door. A sudden breeze bore the scent of roses, making her wish she had a place with a garden. The house she'd lived in in London was a mock-Tudor semi. It had a tiny garden, but the soil was like clay and she and Tony could never get anything to grow.

Talking all the while about having to guard against the

126

encroachment of nature, Sir Graham steered her across the crazy paving, down the steps and towards the lawn which, she now saw, opened out in the shape of a fan. Tippex, who was lying on the grass, leapt up into the begging position. Sir Graham paused to pet the dog, tickling it behind the ears, and then took Dania into the sculpture field with Tippex panting along behind them.

'So what do you think of it, Sergeant?' he said, stopping in front of a large piece of art.

To Dania, it looked as though a giant had picked up pieces of painted metal and crushed them in his fist. The colours, however, mainly creams and browns with dark red thrown in, looked fresh. She was finding that, the more of the artwork she saw, the more it grew on her. Tippex seemed to have other ideas. He padded over to the piece and let everyone know precisely what he thought by lifting his leg and peeing against it. She could almost hear Sir Graham grinding his teeth. It was clear that this was where his heart lay, and not in managing his estate. An accident of birth had catapulted him into his current position, and she guessed that, given the choice, he'd prefer to play the bohemian rather than the laird.

'How long does it take to make one of these?' she said.

'Oh, several weeks, months even.' He pulled a face. 'It can get a bit messy, so you have to wear protective clothing. I go through a large number of boiler suits.'

Without taking her eyes off the structure, she said, 'And do you have to protect your hair too?'

'Of course.' He cracked his knuckles. 'When you're spray-painting, it goes absolutely everywhere.' After a silence, he said, 'Well, it's been a great pleasure, Sergeant. I hope we'll meet again before too long.' He held out his hand.

She placed hers in his and let him slide his lips over it.

It was when she was back on the rutted road, bouncing over

the potholes, that she realised she hadn't asked him where he did his welding and spraying. She'd very much like to see the place.

I go through a large number of boiler suits. The unbidden thought slipped into her mind that perhaps she'd find a grey beanie there too.

Sir Graham Farquhar watched the car bump down the drive. He really should get that stretch of road properly paved as it didn't do to have his visitors getting seasick. And definitely not the stunning Polish detective with the sexy accent, whom he'd clearly impressed with his in-depth knowledge of Polish customs. Lucky Blair Chirnside to have her on his team, especially if her brains matched her beauty. He wondered how far on they were in catching Judith's killer.

At the thought of Judith, his mind strayed to the time she'd called round unannounced, asking if her Druid group could use his land for one of their meetings. She'd been quite subdued and had been unable to look him directly in the eye. Strange woman. Of course he'd objected. The last thing he wanted was those heathens on his land. Not only would they light fires and burn down the trees, they'd poison the air with their pagan singing and chanting. His father had been a kirk elder, as had his father before that, and they would be rolling in their graves at the thought. So where would the Druids meet now? he wondered.

He strolled round the side of the house and into the rose garden. It would soon be time for Rabbie. Their joint plans for re-landscaping were coming along nicely. The man had made some interesting suggestions, which involved uprooting the screen of yew trees and creating a water garden with exotic plants. It would be a mammoth task, as those yews were ancient, planted by one of his ancestors centuries earlier, and God knows how deep the roots went. But as well as obviating the need for constantly raking up the leaves, uprooting the yews had the advantage that it would open up the space behind the house and make room for more of his artwork. He would leave the area around the holly bushes untouched, though, as the ground there was a yellow flood of daffodils in the spring.

Tippex, who spotted Rabbie first, made a mad dash towards the field. Seeing Sir Graham, the man raised his hand in greeting, and then dropped into a crouch to play with the dog.

CHAPTER 11

Marek was sitting upright on the sofa, the laptop on his knees, staring in dismay at the email. It was from Dr Peterkin, telling him that she'd discovered he was an investigative journalist and, although his motive for enrolling on the Druidism summer school may well be genuine, she couldn't take the chance that he wouldn't write an article that would put the institute in a bad light. It should therefore come as no surprise to him that, having given the matter due consideration, she'd had no option but to deny him a place on the course.

He swore softly in Polish, and slammed down the lid. He should have used a false name, although he couldn't then see how he'd have got round showing his passport at the institute's office, something he would have had to do at enrolment. But how had Dr Peterkin discovered who he was? Unless she'd chanced upon his recent series of articles about the effect of a possible Brexit on the Polish population of Dundee. That might be it. The name 'Gorski' would have stuck in her mind.

In the kitchen, he quartered a lemon and, after pouring a half-measure of Wyborowa into a glass, squeezed one of the pieces into it. He sat at the table, sipping and thinking through his options.

All was not lost. That morning, his informant, Gerry, a member of staff at the institute, had rung to say that the Druid group was meeting at eight that evening somewhere around Monifieth, and he'd be in touch again about picking him up. Marek glanced at his watch. It was now after five, and he'd heard nothing. Gerry was usually more punctual than this. Best to give him a call.

Gerry picked up after two rings. 'Yes?' came the voice. He always sounded as if he was going to start sobbing.

'It's Marek. Are we still on for tonight?'

A pause. 'Um, no can do,' came the reply. 'You see, we've been warned against talking to the press.'

Marek swore silently, using an even stronger Polish word. This would be Dr Peterkin's doing. 'I give you my word, Gerry, that I'll never use your name. Or even tell anyone that my source comes from the institute.'

Another pause, in which he could hear Gerry breathing. 'It's more than my job's worth, Marek. If anyone finds out, my contract here won't be renewed. You've been a good mate, but please don't ring me again.' He ended the call.

Marek reached for the Wyborowa, sorely tempted to finish the bottle. Gerry had been his only way in to that Druid group. But, as he unscrewed the cap, he realised there was another avenue open to him. He could go to Monifieth and try to find the group himself. Problem was, he had no idea where they were meeting. He screwed the cap back on and opened the laptop. So where would Druids meet? Gerry's 'somewhere around Monifieth' was on the vague side. Could it be Broughty Ferry? The fifteenth-century Broughty Castle? Not ancient enough. There was a Holy Well at Balmossie Den, near the remains of an old chapel. Too Christian, perhaps. Ardestie Earth House might qualify. He leant back and ruffled his hair. Maybe he should follow Gerry. But he had no idea whether the man actually attended these meetings or just knew where they were held. Anyway, he didn't have Gerry's address, so he might as well forget it.

But there was one person who definitely *would* be at the meeting. And she was probably still at work. *Most evenings, I don't leave my office till seven.* It was a long shot, but it was the only shot he had. He grabbed a piece of cheese from the fridge. A quick text to Danka that he would be home late, and he ran down the stairs and out of the flat.

Marek was sitting in his Audi, watching the front entrance of the building that housed the Institute of Religions and Belief Systems. The only car park was outside the main entrance, something he'd established when he'd visited the institute some weeks earlier. Fortunately, there were no double yellow lines on this part of the Perth Road. Not that that was ever a problem. He knew the traffic wardens in this area of town, and most were only too glad to look the other way when he slipped a couple of notes into their hands.

If his hunch was correct, and Dr Peterkin was working late, she'd most likely go to the meeting straight from her office. He unwrapped the cheese and chewed it thoughtfully, his gaze never leaving the building.

It was nearing 7.15 p.m. when the front door opened. A dark-haired figure emerged. He felt a tingling in his blood as he recognised Dr Peterkin. Although he was wearing wire-rimmed spectacles and had covered his hair with his orange Dundee United hat, he sank lower into the seat.

With hurried steps, Dr Peterkin tripped down the path towards the car park, and climbed into a red Volkswagen Polo. As she started the engine, he turned the key in the Audi's ignition. A few seconds later, the Polo eased into the Perth Road. He took up position behind it, matching his speed to hers.

He was an old hand at tailing, especially slow, careful drivers who signalled their intentions. He kept a respectful distance, even letting cars overtake and pull in between them. At the junction with West Marketgait, she turned right, and followed the road past the Discovery Point and the site of the new V&A Museum of Design. Ignoring the intersection with the Tay Road Bridge, she cruised comfortably past the century-old Maritime Building, which had belonged to the famous shipping company, Dundee, Perth & London, but had recently been bought by a developer. She changed lanes and pulled into Gallagher Retail Park. Marek followed her, steering the Audi into a parking spot a short distance away, from where he had an uninterrupted view of the Polo.

She left the car and hurried into the Marks & Spencer Simply Food shop. Fifteen minutes later, she emerged carrying a huge bouquet of flowers and a large bag, which she hauled to the car and dumped in the boot.

They left the car park, Marek maintaining his distance, and continued along East Dock Street. One of the least appealing areas of Dundee, the street consisted of old gasworks and metal foundries, billboards to left and right, and garages and showrooms. The industrial landscape gave way to two-storey houses, and improved greatly the further east they travelled. The route eventually hugged the shoreline, giving him a view of the Tay.

They turned northwards, taking what was known as the Dundee Road through Broughty Ferry, with its gardens and villas and teasing glimpses of the river. After passing the sign to the castle, they veered on to the Monifieth Road, past rows of terraces and double-fronted houses. Marek felt like laughing. It had been so easy. He wondered, though, how well he'd have coped had Dr Peterkin not been a stickler for keeping within the speed limit.

After a while, the Polo slowed significantly. Dr Peterkin signalled and turned right on to a narrow road and he realised they were crossing the railway. He thought at first that she'd spotted a tail and was slowing, intending to confront him, but although she did stop it was to use her mobile. He crawled on, overtaking her, seeing the esplanade and the river beyond. A second later, he saw in his rear-view mirror that the Polo had turned into a parking area, and was cruising smoothly into a vacant slot. He continued a little way before coasting to a stop.

Dr Peterkin left the car. She took off her jacket, slung it into the boot, and shook out what looked like a white sheet. To his surprise, she slipped it on over her blouse and trousers, did up the front buttons, and pulled the sheet in at the waist with a dark belt. She exchanged her court shoes for a pair of sandals. He felt his pulse race. This was what he'd come for. He picked up the Canon and took several careful shots, then ducked down as Dr Peterkin walked past his car, carrying the flowers she'd bought at M&S. She took the footpath leading east.

The parking area was filling and the later arrivals had to leave their vehicles on the esplanade. Most people were already dressed for the occasion in long robes in a variety of colours, cinched in with contrasting sashes. One stunning woman with flaming red curls wore a hooded robe in green and purple and, round her head, a wreath of oak leaves. An enormous shaggy-haired man wearing a necklace of shells was dressed in a white robe and green tabard, and a headdress threaded with pieces of antler. Some of the assembly were young enough to be students, and Marek wondered if they were from the institute. Everyone was holding flowers.

He was relieved to see people in ordinary clothes as it meant he could mingle without drawing attention. He took as many photos as he dared, and then left the camera in the glove compartment. The patterned jacket incorporating his body camera would have to do the rest. He locked the Audi.

He had lost sight of Dr Peterkin but it no longer mattered. The others would lead him to where it was happening. He followed them along the footpath, past a sign that said 'Banks Caravan Park', and stumbled immediately on to a strand of beach, dotted with oval stones. A crowd was gathering, people exchanging words, acknowledging each other. The mood grew sombre. Some wiped away tears.

As he was the tallest there, he hung back, stooping his shoulders. He wondered whether Gerry had arrived. He'd recognise his distinctive flowing beard and plait anywhere. The man next to him, a thirty-something with a tangle of dark hair, glanced at him and then said, 'I've not seen you here before.' He had a gentle voice and childlike eyes. 'Is this your first time?'

Marek nodded. More seemed to be expected, so he added, 'I'm enrolled on the summer school. Dr Peterkin suggested I come tonight.' A blatant lie, and he waited for the earth to open up and swallow him.

'I'm Neil, by the way.'

'Mark.'

'So what draws you to Druidism, Mark?'

'I feel there's something missing in my life. Someone suggested I follow the course and see if that helps.' He hesitated. 'You?'

Neil gazed across the Tay, the water reflecting the darkening blue of the sky. 'I was in Iraq. Saw things no one should ever have to see.' He drew in his breath. 'Nothing helped after I came home. Then I ran across this group quite by accident, in Templeton Woods. I listened to what they were saying, and it seemed to make sense.' He shrugged. 'That's it, really. I joined and started studying.'

'At the institute?'

'Their home-study course. I don't have time to do it at uni as I work during the day. It was worth persevering, though. I'm an Ovate now,' he added proudly.

'The second level?'

'That's right. Many of the people here are Bards. First level. But see that lot there?' He nodded towards a group who wore identical robes, and cloaks in forest green. Some had painted their faces in red spiral patterns. 'They're Ovates,' he said.

Marek glanced at Neil's jeans and bomber jacket. 'But you're not in a robe?'

'It's in the wash. The baby was sick over it. Pity. Wearing it helps me to move into a ritual space, and shift energy. I feel shielded and protected, as if enrobed in the essence of the god and goddess.' He smiled. 'You've still to learn about this.'

'I hope I'll be worthy.'

Neil stared at him. 'Of course you'll be worthy. Look, no one knows how far he or she will journey on the Path. But take it from me. You *will* make a journey.'

He said it with such conviction and with such a look of serene anticipation on his face that Marek felt a stab of envy. He was starting to feel awkward in front of this tender-hearted man. 'Tell me about the robes, Neil.'

'Okay, so there's no such thing as an "authentic" Druid robe. Many people want something that looks like it might have come out of pre-Roman Britain but, for me, a robe is a combination of looking nice but being functional. So I can move, light candles, walk in a forest, be by the camp fire. That sort of thing. Some of the women have designed robes for members. There's an embroidery circle. They'll decorate your robe to your own design if you ask them.'

A dark-haired man, carrying a bundle of sticks under his arm and holding a lit wooden torch, was walking round the group. He was wearing a sheepskin jacket over an Aran roll-neck, and seemed to be well known, chatting and smiling. As each person took a stick, he touched the tip with his own, lighting it. The ends were covered in dark material which, Marek realised from the acrid smell, had been doused in tar.

As the flame flared on Marek's stick, the man stared at him in such a way that Marek thought he'd been recognised.

'I've not seen you here before,' he said.

'His first time,' Neil chipped in.

The man's gaze bored into Marek's, as though trying to read his thoughts. Then he smiled disarmingly. 'Welcome to our Grove,' he said, before moving on.

As if by a signal, a hush fell over the group. Marek peered over the heads and saw a burning torch being raised. A man with braided hair, and wearing a deeply hooded white robe, like a monk's, was holding it high. 'Light to you all!' he said in a rich voice.

'And light to you,' everyone chorused, lifting their torches.

Neil nudged Marek. 'He's a Druid,' he whispered. 'He's made the third grade.'

The Druid continued. 'At our ceremony this evening, I wish first to welcome our new members. Perhaps they could make themselves known to us?'

A small group raised their hands, grinning shyly. They were dressed in normal clothes.

'Welcome to our Grove,' the Druid said with a gentle smile. 'I hope that you, with us, will find what you are seeking.'

There was a murmuring of affirmation from the assembly.

'The reason we are here is to honour our beloved Archdruid, Judith Johnstone.'

A deep lamentation rose from the group, accompanied by the sound of sobbing.

'Was she the one in the scarecrow?' Marek whispered.

When there was no reply, he turned to look at Neil. Tears were standing in his eyes. 'Yes,' he said with a throb in his voice. He wiped his cheeks with his free hand. 'She was the Archdruid of our Grove. She used to preside over the ceremonies.'

'So what will happen now?'

'Someone else will have to do it.'

The man with the braided hair launched into a eulogy for Judith Johnstone, describing how she had started the Grove with a mere three companions. It now numbered over one hundred. She had worked tirelessly, not only to do the best for her university students, but also in service to the community and the environment. Marek listened intently. He'd learnt something that might interest Danka: not only had Judith been a Druid, she'd been an Archdruid and had conducted ceremonies.

Everyone moved into a wide circle and planted their burning torches in the sand. As they held hands, their heads bowed, a sudden wind harried the group, flapping at the hems of their robes and whipping the flames. Marek took Neil's hand, feeling the man grip his fingers hard. On his other side, a young woman grasped his hand, smiling shyly. He risked a glance around. Gerry was standing feet away. Marek resisted the urge to drop hands and run. He crouched into himself, hoping that his height and build wouldn't draw the man's attention.

The Druid finished his tribute. 'There is one further thing,' he said, as the circle broke up. 'It is becoming clear that this is no longer a safe place for our Grove to meet. We will need to find another location.'

There were groans, and shaking of heads. A discussion followed. Templeton Woods, an old haunt, was mooted, but many felt it too dangerous to return, making Marek wonder what had happened there. The more ancient Backmuir Wood was proposed but, if anything, members were even less keen. The Druid promised to let everyone know when and where they would next meet.

He held up his hand. 'The Wheel of the Year is turning and we must not forget that the next quarter day, the festival of Alban Hefin, draws near. This year it falls on June the twentieth. I will circulate the necessary information soon.'

Marek glanced enquiringly at Neil. 'The summer solstice,' Neil murmured. 'Alban Hefin means The Light of the Shore. But we may not be able to hold it here.' He glanced behind him and Marek caught the look of dread in his eyes as they darted back and forth, scanning the trees.

The comment that this beach, also, was no longer safe, intrigued Marek. 'What's been going on that you're having to move?'

'The locals don't like us.'

'Has there been trouble?'

'Nothing major. But there've been incidents.'

'Must be difficult constantly finding new meeting places.'

'Judith was great at that. She knew the ancient woodland. Some of the spots have been landscaped relatively recently and the energy isn't as strong there. When it comes to groves, the older, the better. Having oak trees nearby helps. But this beach is our favourite. We've been here all this year. The shoreline is where the three realms of Earth, Sea and Sky meet, and so the power is stronger. Judith was always able to get permission for us to light a fire.' He nodded towards the crowd, which was breaking up. 'Come on, let's give these guys a hand.'

They took their torches to where a fire had been started on the sand, throwing them in along with the rest. Out of nowhere, a man arrived with a milking stool and a clarsach. He was in ordinary clothes and wore a straw hat with oak leaves round the rim. Seated on the stool, he played a slow, haunting melody. The Druid turned to the river and read from a book in a language that Marek couldn't understand.

As the harpist finished playing, the Druid cast his eyes heavenwards and began to sing unaccompanied. Everyone joined in, their upturned hands raised, their eyes closed. The song, which sounded to Marek like the Gaelic psalm he'd once heard on the island of Harris, swelled until it drowned the rumble of the traffic on the distant road. Glancing around at the beach and the woodland, Marek felt himself transported to a time where people lived closer to nature, and respected it and each other; a time that, had it ever existed, had long since passed. The singing over, everyone gathered up their flowers and moved to the edge of the water.

'Gaia, queen of the earth and the river,' the Druid began, 'we humbly stand in awe of your might. Accept these gifts from your people, continue to give us your bounty, and look upon us with love.'

Those in front cast the flowers into the Tay, chorusing, 'Look upon us with love!' and stepped aside to make way for the people behind. The wind gusted across the water, serrating the surface. As the river flowed eastwards, it carried the flowers out to sea. Marek, strangely moved, watched the carpet of petals rise and fall with the waves.

He felt a light touch at his elbow. 'Hope you got something out of that,' Neil said kindly. 'Anyway, good luck with the course, and maybe see you next time?' he added with a question in his voice.

'Thanks, Neil.'

With a nod and a smile, Neil ambled away and joined the people leaving.

Marek trudged along the strand with the crowd, trying to make sense of what he'd seen. Of one thing he was certain: if Judith Johnstone had enemies, they weren't part of this Grove. As for the ceremony itself, he'd seen nothing that should offend the good citizens of Dundee, or even a practising Roman Catholic like himself. He thought of the Masses he'd attended in Warsaw's cathedral, with incense billowing up in cold clouds, and the service's central tenet of consecration and sacrifice, so different from the simple ceremony he'd witnessed here.

What had struck him forcefully, and something he was sure he'd remember long after the details of the ceremony were forgotten, were the expressions on the faces of these people. The last time he'd seen such looks of contentment was when he'd visited a convent in Perugia, in the hope of seeing a lesser-known fresco in a hidden chapel. He'd followed the mother superior along a corridor, craning his neck to peer through the high windows into the cloister. Nuns, young and clear-complexioned, strolled in pairs, some arm in arm, others reading aloud from books. But each had the same serene expression on her face. He'd left the convent with a feeling that, no matter how he lived his life, he would never find that kind of inner peace.

Deep in thought, he hadn't noticed the dark-haired figure at his side.

'Mr Gorski, I hope that when you come to write about us in your newspaper,' Dr Peterkin said primly, 'you will be kind to us.' She looked deep into his eyes. 'This is my life. Please remember that.'

She hurried on and joined the people in front, leaving him with the feeling that, not only had he defiled a sacred place by acting like a voyeur, but he had also in the process somehow dishonoured himself.

As he glanced around, hoping he wouldn't get the same rebuke from Gerry, he caught sight of something on the other side of the road. At a break in the trees, where the ground was higher, a line of figures stood watching the assembly. The sun had dropped behind them, silhouetting the figures in a sulphurous light. Their faces couldn't be seen but there was something in the way they held themselves that reminded Marek of an army, waiting for the signal to attack. He felt his skin prickle. He stopped and stared until, one by one, the figures turned away and melted into the darkness.

CHAPTER 12

Marek reached for the coffee pot. 'I've no idea how Dr Peterkin recognised me.'

Dania was piling into her breakfast. 'It's falling into place,' she said with her mouth full. 'That black dress in Judith's wardrobe. And those boots. She would have worn them to the meetings.' *She stayed out longer in the summer.* 'She wasn't attending university functions, but officiating at Druid ceremonies. How did you find the meeting place?' she added. 'It was Monifieth?'

'There's a beach there, right in front of Banks Caravan Park.'

Her head shot up. 'Did you say Banks?'

'Have you heard of it?'

'In Judith's diary, there were several entries with DM Banks. We thought it was the name of a person, but it must stand for Druid Meeting at Banks, or something. The last DM Banks entry was Saturday the twenty-eighth of May at eight p.m. May the twenty-eighth is when we found her body.'

'And the day my informant told me the meeting was cancelled. Remember he rang me? So no big mystery, then.'

Yet there was still one: LCM. In one of the entries, Judith had crossed out DM Banks and written LCM. Could LCM be another venue for the Grove meeting?

'Does the Grove always meet by this caravan park, Marek?'

'Neil told me there have been other places.'

'Did anything else happen? Anything unpleasant? No towns-people coming to watch?'

He added a piece of pickled herring to his bread. 'The only person watching was me.' He paused, the bread halfway to his mouth. 'Actually, no. I saw a group of people when we were leaving. I'm tempted to say they seemed harmless enough.'

'But?'

'There was something about them that I found disturbing. They just stood there, motionless.'

'How many?'

'About a dozen. Maybe fewer. Why do you ask?'

'My DI told me there have been incidents. A summer festival ended in a riot, and people were injured. The Institute of Religions and Belief Systems has been targeted.' She took a sip of coffee. 'It's shaping up to be our strongest motive for Judith's murder.'

'If that's why she was murdered, then it's disgusting.'

The anger in his voice surprised Dania. 'Sounds like these Druids made quite an impression on you.'

'I don't deny it. I'm not sure what I expected, to be honest, but they seemed genuine in their beliefs. Not like many of the Christians we see in church, who bow their heads in devout tran-quillity, and then go home and shout at their wives and thump their kids.'

'Are you going to write that in your piece?'

He lolled back in his seat. 'I don't know what I'm going to write.' He looked at her in a way that suggested he'd already decided. 'Not writing what I saw would feel like a betrayal.' After a pause, he said, 'I suppose you think I'm a bit of an idiot, taking myself off there.'

'Being an idiot is part of who you are.'

'Many of them couldn't contain their grief over Judith's death. Is there anything you can tell me about how she died?'

'Nothing yet, I'm afraid.' She glanced at her watch. 'Which reminds me that I'd better be off.' She scraped the chair back and made to leave the kitchen.

'Shall we go out this evening, Danka? It's Friday.'

'Maybe.'

He raised an eyebrow. 'Got a date?'

'I wish.'

'Well, perhaps we'll both get lucky. Isn't that what Friday nights are for?'

The incident-room door opened and Milo Slaughter strode in. He was in his trademark navy chalk-striped suit with the too-wide lapels. Without bothering with the usual greetings, he beamed round the room, brandishing a green-coloured folder eloquently.

'Good to see you, Prof,' Chirnside said. 'I take it you can now put us out of our misery.'

'I can.' Milo paused for effect and then opened the folder. He was like a showman, thought Dania. But maybe academics have to be like that, or else how can they keep their students' attention?

'The cause of death in the Judith Johnstone case is poisoning,' Milo said. '*Taxus baccata*, to be precise.'

'And in English?'

'Common or garden – and it *is* common in the garden – European yew.' He seemed greatly pleased with his little joke. 'Toxicology report that, not only did the victim test positive, she had enough in her bloodstream to kill an army.'

'That liquid in her stomach,' Dania said.

'Well remembered, DS Gorska,' he smiled. 'The liquid contained *Taxus baccata* to a high concentration.'

'Is it just the berries that are poisonous?' Honor said.

'Interestingly, it's the seeds within the berries and, even then, the outer husk has to be pierced. The berry bit is the only part of the fruit that is not poisonous, in fact. It's nature's way. Birds can eat the fruit and spread the seeds, unbroken, without ill-effect.'

'So are you saying she ate mashed seeds, Prof?'

'We found no evidence of seeds in her gut. But there are other parts of the yew that are toxic. The leaves, for example. And, as they dry, they become even more poisonous.'

'You said she hadn't eaten for several hours,' Dania said. 'So, given the quantity of liquid in her stomach, someone must have boiled up the leaves and made her drink it.'

'That's the conclusion I've come to.'

'Is death instantaneous?'

He looked at her kindly. 'There's no such thing as instantaneous death, in my experience. With *Taxus baccata*, the symptoms progress from a rapid heart rate to tremors in the muscles. The body convulses until, finally, the heart stops.' He lifted a finger, the way a conductor lifts a baton. 'Given the amount in her system, she may not have experienced all these symptoms. Death may have come quickly.'

'I don't suppose she could have drunk this stuff by accident,' Fergus said.

'I very much doubt it. When the body is under stress, cortisol and adrenaline are produced. Cortisol makes blood sugar levels rise. We found elevated levels of all these in her system.' His voice was stern. 'She knew what was happening to her.'

That look of horror in the woman's eyes. Judith's kidnapper wouldn't just have given her cup after cup of a strange-tasting tea. He'd have described to her what he was doing. She would have known she was going to die.

After a pause, Chirnside said, 'Thanks, Prof. I know you burnt the midnight oil on this one. We appreciate it.'

'The fine details are in the report. Don't hesitate to get in touch if there's anything you want to ask.' With a nod to the assembly, he left the room.

Dania broke the silence. 'Judith died late afternoon or early evening on the Friday. My guess is that her killer worked backwards. He knew when he wanted to dress her as the scarecrow, and he poisoned her less than six hours before. So she'd still be floppy when he put her on to the sticks.'

'Where do yew trees grow?' Chirnside said, wiping his face.

'In churchyards, don't they? It's easy enough to collect the leaves.'

'Maybe they grow in Backmuir Wood,' Fergus said. 'We can ask around.'

'No,' Chirnside said firmly. 'I want the details of how she died to remain in this room. It's to be kept from everyone, especially the press. Is that understood?'

Like everyone there, Dania knew why he was so insistent. If the killer thought the police were still scrabbling around in the dark, not knowing why Judith had died, he might become careless and leave evidence lying about. Yet, the only careless thing he'd done so far was not remove the traces of adhesive from the Honda's number plates. But the question that kept eating away at her was: why hadn't he disposed of the body? He could have buried it deep in the grounds in Backmuir or Templeton Woods, or even gone up the A9 into the Highlands. Why display it in the middle of a field where it would be found in a matter of hours?

Chirnside's voice broke into her thoughts. 'I want that driver. Understand? If it means taking Dundee apart, piece by piece.' He clenched his fists. 'Find the wee *shite*.'

* * *

146

'Sergeant Gorska. My office. Now.' Chirnside turned on his heel and marched out.

Dania glanced up from her computer screen. Hearing the DI's tone, the other officers threw her sympathetic looks.

'Don't let him get between you and the door,' Honor murmured as Dania brushed past.

The door to Chirnside's office was open. He was standing facing the window.

She knocked. 'You wanted to see me, sir?'

Without turning, he said, 'Take a seat, Sergeant.'

She sat behind the desk and waited.

'I understand you've been looking through MisPers.'

It came as no surprise that he'd know this, as a record was kept of who logged in, and when, and what files they requested. The surprise was that he wanted to talk to her about it. Even more surprising was that he was angry. She wondered whether his own particular form of anger management was talking to the window.

'That's right, sir.'

He turned. 'May I ask why?' He eyed her in a way she didn't much like.

'I interviewed Jenn McLaughlin yesterday afternoon, and—'

'You did *what?*'

She looked him full in the face. 'I showed her the photo of the Honda and asked her if she recognised the driver. We got talking, one thing led to another, and she told me about her sister.'

He continued to glare at her.

'So, I was curious and looked it up when I came back to the office.'

'Except that the logs show that you looked it up yesterday morning. You said you went to see Jenn McLaughlin in the afternoon.'

There was no point denying it. Dania looked at a point beyond his shoulder.

'I'm wondering why you're wasting your time on this, Sergeant. You should be working on the Judith Johnstone case. What's your interest in Ailsa McLaughlin?'

She nearly said, '*What's yours?*'

The silence lengthened. 'Well?'

'Curiosity, sir. Nothing more. The other officers mentioned the Ailsa McLaughlin case when Jenn's name came up.'

'When was this?'

'The day we found Judith's body.'

'And are you enlightened now?'

Something told her she should act as though she'd lost interest. She shrugged. 'Ailsa and Kerry seem to have surfaced in London.'

'It's an open-and-shut case of teenage runaways.'

Yet she couldn't leave it alone. 'Strange that they left in only the clothes they were wearing, sir.'

He snorted. 'Teenagers. They rarely think things through.' Whereas before, his manner had been confrontational, he now seemed strangely defeated. He pulled out his chair and sat down. 'What are you thinking, Sergeant? That this somehow has a bearing on the murder of Judith Johnstone?'

'I didn't think there was a connection but, now that you've mentioned it, the girls were both members of the Dundee Grove.'

'Yes, I did wonder at the time whether that had anything to do with their disappearance.' He played with his pen. 'The day they were reported missing, the Saturday, I interviewed several of the Grove members. Most of them remembered seeing the girls at the meeting.'

'Which meeting?'

'The one the day before. Friday April the twenty-ninth. The Grove met in Monifieth.'

'Ailsa and Kerry were at that meeting?'

'And that was the last time anyone saw those girls.' His voice was brisk. 'Until the texts started coming from London.'

'I didn't know they'd been at a Druid meeting. There's nothing on record.'

'We had confirmation they were in London before we got that information. The file was closed.' He said it with finality in his voice.

'Yes, sir.'

'I suggest you stick to the case in hand, Dania,' he said with a conciliatory smile. 'The newspapers are climbing all over this police station, and we need a result on Judith Johnstone.'

'Yes, sir.'

'By the way, Sir Graham tells me you called in on him.'

'Yes, it was about the concert for the Poles.' She made her voice casual. 'Do you know Sir Graham well?'

'Our paths cross from time to time. We're both on the committee for this memorial. You found the hall all right, did you?'

'I wouldn't, if I hadn't been looking through the trees. It doesn't always pay to keep your eyes on the road,' she added dryly.

His manner had softened. 'I know what you mean.'

'He has some interesting artwork on his land.'

'You got the guided tour, then.'

'Sir Graham seems very proud of it.'

'Not really my taste.' He paused, and from the expression on his face, she knew the interview was over. And so was his anger.

As she left the office, something in what he'd said rang a loud bell. It wasn't until she was back at her desk, and looking through the database, that she had it.

Friday 29 April. The Grove met in Monifieth. And Ailsa and Kerry were at that meeting.

And, on Friday 29 April, Judith had crossed out DM Banks in her diary, and written LCM.

But, since members of the Grove had recalled seeing the girls at the Monifieth meeting, the fact that Judith had crossed it out hadn't meant that the meeting had been cancelled. It only meant that she herself hadn't attended. Instead she'd gone to LCM. So who, or what, was LCM?

The pieces still didn't fit, and she was convinced that many were still missing. But, although she couldn't say why, her gut was telling her that something had happened on Friday 29 April that held the key to the murder of Judith Johnstone. *And* the key to the disappearance of Ailsa and Kerry.

CHAPTER 13

Marek was in the bathroom, rubbing something sweet and musky into his neck. 'Are you nearly ready, Danka?' he shouted into the corridor.

Dania sauntered in, straightening her blue satin jeans. '*I* am. But are *you?*'

He continued to apply the cologne, running his fingers through his hair.

'What's that you're using?' she said.

'Lothair. A new one by Penhaligon's.' He looked at her in the mirror. 'I occasionally smell it on you.' He raised an eyebrow. 'You're not the only detective in the family.'

'Where did you buy it? I haven't seen a Penhaligon's anywhere.'

'A lady gave it to me,' he said, holding her gaze.

'And might we be seeing this lady tonight?'

'Not where we're going.'

'And that is?'

'It's Friday night. That means only one thing.'

The pub, the Bonnie Dundee, was a new drinking house within walking distance of Union Place. An excellent location, Marek reminded Dania, as he held the door for her. They could drink without worrying about driving. Not that that was a problem, as the places they frequented in the city centre were also within walking distance. But this was a favourite because it was usually full of Polish farm workers, who assumed that 'Bonnie Dundee' referred to their new home, the city of Dundee. Neither she nor Marek had the heart to tell them that it was named for the soldier, John Graham of Claverhouse, about whose bloody exploits they had learnt in their school history lessons.

The interior, like many pubs, was gloomy with dark corners, and had a woody, beery smell. It had been recently renovated, the publican going for a tartan theme. Every armchair and cushioned seat was upholstered in a different design, and great swags of material, which Dania had learnt were different Graham tartans, were draped across the walls. Claverhouse, whose image was on the sign outside, would have been gratified.

As they looked around for a table, she heard someone shout in Polish, 'Hey, Marek. We're sitting over here.' It was Antek, a broad-shouldered man made of lean, hard muscle. He had pale eyes and light brown hair, which he wore long in the front and short at the sides. He also had plenty of stubble, which – he'd confessed to Dania during a drunken evening of confessions – gave him a manly appearance that would make him irresistible to women. Dania wondered how well this worked, since she wasn't one of them.

Marek and Antek had been friends – or rather drinking companions, which often amounts to the same thing – since Antek had helped Marek out with a piece about the experiences of Eastern European workers in Scotland. From the state of the man, you would be forgiven for thinking he'd been here since early morning, but that was unlikely. Antek was a hard worker, doing more than his share on one of the local farms. It was simply that, on Friday nights, he made up for it by getting plastered in record time. The empty glasses littering the table told Dania that he'd been making up for it for some hours.

Marek made a sign to indicate that he'd get the drinks and then join him.

'Who's that with Antek?' she said, after they'd got through the scrum at the bar.

'I'm guessing it's someone who works at the same farm. See the way they're dressed?'

Both men were wearing blue boiler suits.

Marek ordered a couple of bottles of Tyskie, and they made their way to Antek's table.

Antek got to his feet and, grasping Dania's hand in both his, brushed it with his lips. He spoke in slow, heavily accented English. 'Ah, Marek, I am so glad you brought sister. You know how I love kissing women.'

'Do they stay still long enough?'

Antek punched Marek lightly on the shoulder, and the men hugged, clapping each other on the back.

Antek's companion made no effort to stand. He looked as if someone had stolen his parking spot.

'This is Willie, by the way,' Antek said. 'He is from around here.'

'Hi.' Willie lifted his beer glass, disturbing the balance of the table and making it wobble. As far as Dania could tell, he was drinking Guinness. He had the same muscular build as Antek but, where the Pole was fair, Willie was dark, with brown eyes and heavy black hair. She wondered if he always drank beer the same colour as the rest of him.

Marek pulled out chairs. 'This is my sister, Dania, and I'm Marek.'

'Pleased to meet you, Willie,' she said.

'So, are you going to match tomorrow?' Antek said with almost religious fervour.

Dania knew that, like many Polish men, he lived and breathed football. Dundee United, it seemed, were playing at home.

Marek glanced at her, as if for confirmation.

'It's okay,' she said, 'I'm working tomorrow afternoon. You go and enjoy the match.'

Willie paused in the act of bringing his glass to his mouth. 'What line of work are you in, then?' He had a deep, husky voice.

'I'm a police officer.'

This either killed the conversation, or moved it on to safer ground. Willie downed half the Guinness in one go. 'You look like a detective,' he said, setting his glass on the table.

'Does it show?'

His gaze slid to her breasts and then back to her face. 'You working on the scarecrow murder, then?'

'I can't tell you what I'm working on.'

'That means you are. It's all right, I'm not going to ask you about it.'

'I take it you work at the same place as Antek,' she said, motioning to the boiler suits.

'We all wear these. The laird supplies us with them.'

'Sir Graham?'

'That's him. Not all workers are as lucky. Most of them have to buy their own clothes.'

'Does he also supply you with headgear?'

In reply, Willie reached into his pocket and pulled out a crumpled blue baseball cap.

Antek had been following the conversation. 'We say to him that he put his . . . what do you call it?' – he exchanged a few words in Polish with Marek – 'coat of arms here.' He pointed to his chest and laughed.

Willie didn't find it amusing. 'The laird's a good man,' he said, throwing Antek a look of scorn.

Dania picked up her bottle. 'In what way? Apart from supplying you with work clothes.'

'He pays a decent wage, for starters. And he goes out of his way to get the European workers settled.'

'How, exactly?'

'When they arrive, he makes sure they get English lessons. So they know the technical words we use when we operate equipment, and so on.' He shrugged. 'It may not sound like a big deal, but it means everyone is up and running. The Poles appreciate it, from what I've heard.'

'Have you ever met Sir Graham?'

'We all have met him,' Antek chipped in. 'He has big parties in barn.'

'Parties?'

'That's right,' Willie said. 'Usually when we've finished a long job of work. He joins in as well. Gets to know us.' He grinned at Antek. 'He's always trying to learn Polish phrases, but this clown here just teaches him swear words.'

'He gives us lots of drinks,' Antek said, slurring the words. 'Vodka as well as beer.'

She could see the Pole tuning out of the conversation. 'When was the last party?' she said, looking at Willie. 'Last weekend? Friday, maybe?' Perhaps someone coming or leaving had seen Judith with her killer.

'No, it was last month.' He paused, and nudged Antek, whose eyes were starting to close. 'Hey Antek, remember the time those pagans arrived?'

Antek opened his eyes slowly. 'Uh?'

'Druids,' Willie went on. 'Dressed in these long robes. No, go back to sleep, it was last year, and you weren't here then.'

'The Druids came for a party?' Dania said, her voice faltering.

'They were going to the wood, I think. Backmuir. The laird's land is right next to it. We watched from the barn. They were shuffling along the road, chanting. The laird doesn't like Druids, we found out then.'

'What did he do?'

'Okay, so he orders them off his land. In no uncertain terms. But they carry on walking and banging their drums. So he instructs Aleck to run and fetch his shotgun.'

'Who's Aleck?' Marek said.

'Aleck Docherty, the laird's estate manager. Comes to the parties as well. Although he doesn't drink much, to be honest. Has one small glass and then goes home to his bidey-in.' Willie leant forward, dropping his voice conspiratorially. 'As soon as Aleck returns with the shotgun, the laird grabs it and fires it over the heads of the Druids.'

'Illegal, surely, if he was near a road,' Marek said.

'Yeah, but I think he owns the road. Anyway, he screamed after them, using swear words I never thought a laird would know. Told them what he'd do if he ever clapped eyes on them again. The Druids scarpered back to their cars.' Willie shrugged. 'They seemed harmless to me. Nutters, maybe, but what were they going to do in the woods? A bit more chanting? Hold hands in a ring round the trees?' His gaze bored into Dania's. 'That woman found in the scarecrow. She worked in that Institute of Pagan something or other, didn't she? I'm guessing she had something to do with Druids. Maybe she was one herself.'

There was a challenge in his eyes, but Dania remained silent. Antek's chin had dropped on to his chest and his breathing was loud and regular. Marek caught her eye and grinned. They'd have to pour Antek into a taxi at the end of the evening.

But Willie wouldn't let it go. 'So, what's your theory, Detective? Why was that woman killed and dressed up as a tattie bogle?'

'What's *your* theory, Willie?'

'Know what I think it is? It's a warning.'

'A warning?' Marek said. 'To whom?'

Willie looked at him as though only then realising he was there. 'To the other Druids. It's a sort of gamekeeper's gibbet.'

'Which is what, when it's out?'

'An old practice, not done any more, but I remember my dad telling me he saw it when he was a lad. The gamekeeper would string up vermin as a warning to other vermin. To let them know he was coming after them.'

'You're not seriously suggesting that's why someone did that to Judith Johnstone?'

'There are plenty of folk round here, not just the laird, who don't like those Druids. And maybe they think of them as vermin.' Willie nodded at the crucifix round Dania's neck. 'God-fearing folk. And thank God I'm not one of them.'

She set down her bottle. 'Let me get this straight, Willie. Are you saying that, whoever did this to Judith, thinking she was a Druid, might be considering targeting another Druid? Is that what you're saying?'

He took a gulp of Guinness. 'I'm saying nothing.'

They were joined then by friends of Willie's, and the conversation moved on to the forthcoming match at Tannadice Park. At the word 'football', Antek awoke, his energy renewed. He threw himself into the debate, looking and sounding completely refreshed. These friends, she learnt, weren't migrant workers but tenant farmers, who leased their holdings from Sir Graham.

'Does the laird have many tenants?' she said to Willie, who showed little interest in the heated debate about Dundee United's recent performance.

'He had more, but many couldn't cut it. As a result, there are several empty cottages on the land.'

157

'Are you thinking of leasing and running a farm yourself? It's surely the next rung on the ladder.'

'It's crossed my mind. But it's a grind, and I'm not sure I want that kind of responsibility. What I'm doing suits me fine.' He looked steadily at her. 'What about you? You after your boss's job?'

'What makes you think that?' she said, surprised by the directness of the remark.

'Watching detective serials on telly.'

'And you think police life is like that?'

'Isn't it?' he said, smiling suddenly. He finished his Guinness, pushed his chair back, and got to his feet. 'I'm sorry, Detective, I have to be going. I'm up at dawn tomorrow.' He held out his hand, and she placed hers in his. He kissed it lightly and then bowed and said, in perfect Polish, 'It's been a great pleasure.'

It was nearly eleven before the party broke up. There were the usual goodbyes inside the pub, then at the door and finally on the pavement.

Antek, his head on his chest, was being supported by Marek. 'I can't leave him in a taxi, Danka. I'll have to take him to his flat.'

Dania knew that Marek could look after himself, but she said, 'I'll walk you to the main road and see that you get a cab.'

'You don't have to.'

'Someone might think you're both drunk and an easy target. Come on, I'll give you a hand.'

She grabbed Antek's free arm and slung it round her shoulders, and she and Marek half walked half dragged Antek, who was now singing – or what passed for it – the Polish national anthem. On the West Marketgait, she flagged down a taxi and helped her brother bundle the drunk Pole inside.

'I won't be long,' Marek said, climbing in beside Antek.

'Take your time,' she grinned. 'I'll be in bed by the time you get home.'

She watched the cab drive away, and then turned and walked briskly along the Nethergate. As she passed the Phoenix, she glanced into Tay Street Lane. There were no street lamps, but light from the Nethergate leaked in, outlining the high-sided buildings. She was about to hurry past when she thought she saw something shift in the darkness. Common sense told her to continue on her way. But curiosity got the better of her. She crept into the lane, her eyes slowly adjusting to the gloom.

There were murmured voices, too faint for her to make out the words, but they were coming from near the bins where she'd found the screaming child. As she reached the passageway, she felt something brush past her. She froze, pressing herself against the wall. A figure stumbled out of the lane. It was a young man in a padded parka and University of Dundee scarf. She waited until he'd reached the pavement, and then hurried after him.

He was weaving across the road, oblivious to the screech of brakes and the shouts through the wound-down windows. Pausing halfway, he fumbled in his pocket and then suddenly dropped to his knees. Her heart went cold. The wrong move and one of the vehicles hurtling past on either side would hit him. Dodging the traffic, she managed to get herself across and pull him to his feet. He tried to shake her off, and she saw then that he'd dropped something he was desperate to pick up, a small wrap of folded white paper. Ignoring both the blaring of horns and his pleas to leave him be, she dragged him the rest of the way to the safety of the pavement.

He was sweating and seemed strung out, his unfocused eyes staring into the road. He lifted a shaking hand and pointed, but the paper had disappeared, swept away in the heavy traffic. Then, crying softly, he leant against the street lamp and slid to the ground.

She was pulling out her phone when she became aware of a familiar prickling at the back of her neck. Across the street, a man in a dark hoodie was standing in the brooding darkness at the mouth of the lane. He was watching her, his face in shadow, his hands thrust into his pockets. There was something menacing in the way he stood motionless, eclipsed every now and then by a rumbling lorry. Although she couldn't see his face, she knew he was looking at her and not at the student. He turned abruptly and limped along the Nethergate in the direction away from West Marketgait.

She glanced at the whimpering student, torn between seeking assistance for him and following the hooded man. It was the limp that decided her. If this was the pusher Chirnside had warned her about, he would have to take priority. She walked slowly along the Nethergate, staying parallel to and slightly behind the hooded figure until he disappeared into South Tay Street. There was still no let-up in the traffic, but she had to make a move, or she'd lose him.

She was stepping into the road when she felt her arms gripped from behind.

'What are you trying to do, ma'am? Get yourself killed?' The voice was American.

She wriggled free and wheeled round to face him. He was a tall, thick-built man with sand-coloured hair.

'I'm a police officer and I'm tailing someone,' she said. She glanced into South Tay Street. The hooded figure was still visible but, if she didn't get across the road that instant, she'd lose him.

'Uh-uh, I wouldn't try it. Not if you enjoy life.'

And, as if the Fates had decided to conspire against her, a long line of heavy-duty vehicles rolled down the Nethergate, destroying any chance she had of crossing the road.

'There goes the ball game, officer,' the American said cheerfully. 'Say, you wouldn't like to have a drink with me, would you?'

'Sorry, maybe another time.'

A sudden gap opened up in the traffic. She dashed across the road and along South Tay Street, searching desperately to left and right. But the hooded figure had vanished.

And, she discovered, when she returned to the Nethergate, so had the student. And the American.

CHAPTER 14

'But you didn't see his face,' Chirnside said.

Dania shook her head in frustration. 'No, sir.'

'Or his hands?'

'He kept them in his pockets. At first, I thought he'd been in the Phoenix, but none of the customers said they saw him. The landlord told me he'd have noticed a man with missing fingers. No, I think he came out of the lane, where he'd been selling.'

'And he disappeared somewhere near the Dundee Rep, you said?' Chirnside narrowed his eyes. 'I wonder if he intended to double back and head for the west end. On Friday night, that area's teeming with students.'

'Interesting he came back to Tay Street Lane.'

'Aye. His patch must be round there.' A note of excitement crept into the DI's voice. 'We have a chance of finding him now, thanks to you. I'll let my drugs task force know.' He hesitated. 'Did he get a good look at you?'

'I was standing under a street lamp so, yes, he did.'

It was a while before Chirnside spoke. 'Maybe best not to go back there, Dania.'

'Yes, sir.'

Easier said than done, she thought, after he'd left the room. She walked past Tay Street Lane every day. But she shared his excitement. This pusher from Glasgow was obviously not afraid to peddle his wares in the centre of town. And that could work for them.

Although she'd told Marek she was working, Dania had the Saturday afternoon off. She could use it to recharge her batteries – the following week she had a couple of eighteen-hour shifts – but she made a start on her piano. Her intention was to work on Chopin's Prelude, Op. 28, No. 15, a possible candidate for the memorial concert in July. It was often referred to as the 'Raindrop' prelude, because of the repeating A-flat with its suggestion of the gentle patter of rain. Perhaps she should include the Polonaise in G minor, written by Chopin at the age of seven, and not published until after his death. It was only five minutes long, but it was delightful, with its fanfare lead-in followed by the light, dance-like melody. Unlike the 'Raindrop' prelude, it was not a piece that was well known, except amongst Poles. All the more reason to play it.

It would have been so much easier had the laird chosen the pieces himself, and she could practise without fretting. Thinking about the laird caused her mind to drift to the night before, and what she'd learnt, specifically about his supplying boiler suits to his workmen. Antek's and Willie's were identical to that in the photo of the driver with the grey beanie. Although, if all the workers on the laird's estate wore them and possibly went through them in large numbers, it wasn't going to help the investigation.

Willie had told her something else, to do with displaying vermin. What had he called it? A gamekeeper's gibbet. *To let them know he was coming after them.* She doubted such a device would deter vermin. Human 'vermin' was another matter, however. But, if this is why Judith Johnstone's body had been strung up, it meant she was only the first victim in the neo-Druid community.

Dania sat staring at the keys. Then she shut the piano lid and left the room.

An hour later, she was back at her desk in West Bell Street, peering at the maps on her screen. Copies of documents pertaining to land ownership had been requested from the Registry of Sasines after the discovery of Judith Johnstone's body, and had been downloaded on to the case file.

She only now appreciated how vast Sir Graham's estate was. There was land near Backmuir and Camperdown, all the way to Liff village and beyond. And an even bigger area north of the Coupar Angus. She clicked through the images, many of which were digital facsimiles of documents going back centuries, the elegant and mainly unreadable copperplate finally superseded by typescript.

There was something about the laird that intrigued her, something that didn't ring true. It wasn't just that lie about not knowing Judith Johnstone. It was the way he looked off to the side, behaviour she'd seen in people who had something to hide. She took another look at the maps and powered down her machine. Although she had no firm idea of what she was looking for, it was time to go hunting.

Dania remembered there were entrances to Backmuir Wood off the Liff Road from the time they'd met Jenn McLaughlin here. She parked the Skoda near Tiddlywinks Nursery School and sat for a while, running her hands over the steering wheel. An online article about Backmuir had told her that, although there was a web of trails, mainly through the northern part of the wood, the ground was boggy in places, so she'd brought Tony's stiff-sided leather boots. They were from his time in Special Forces, and were among the few things he'd left behind when they parted company. She changed out of her shoes and left the car.

The sun was in her eyes and she nearly missed the five-barred wooden gate. A plump, round-faced woman in a padded coat was leading a border collie out of the wood. She smiled at Dania, greeting her with a cheerful, 'Afternoon.'

Inside the gate, there was a map of the vast wood showing the trails spidering through it, and the areas of open ground. She studied the layout before choosing a route that led south towards the laird's land.

Huge conifers grew in dense clusters, their fallen needles cushioning the floor and making almost no sound. The vegetation consisted of aromatic ferns and grasses, and different species of tree, most of which she didn't recognise. Dead wood in the form of enormous stumps and fallen trunks littered the landscape. She walked for about half an hour before becoming aware that she was treading on drifts of fallen leaves. Soaring beeches grew here – trees she did recognise, as she'd seen them in the forests of Poland. She felt as though she'd stepped back in time.

The path widened into a small clearing. A couple of teenagers were sitting on a log bench, the boy playing with his phone, and the girl trying to keep his attention by rattling on like a self-winding machine. She gave up and flounced off. Only then did he seem to notice her, getting up and loping after her, calling her name wearily.

Dania sat down on the bench and breathed in the grass-scented air, listening to the sound of the forest – the occasional crackling of dry wood, a woodpecker drumming a tattoo on the bark of a tree, and a rustling from the undergrowth, followed by the bobbing of a rabbit's tail. A couple of girls jogged past, gripping water bottles in their sweaty hands. A minute later, her patience was rewarded: a pair of red squirrels scampered up the trunk of a tree and disappeared into the canopy of leaves.

She was wondering how much further she had to go to reach the southern boundary when something flashed past the corner of her vision. She peered into the woodland, seeing a reddish-brown shape blurring into the leaves. A roe deer? She left the path, and parted the branches. A fawn stared back at her. Something long and green was caught up in his ears, and trailed behind him. Not wanting to frighten the animal, she took a step backwards.

As soon as she heard the noise and felt the steel jaws snap on to her shin, she knew what had happened. She lost her balance and fell, trying not to land on her wrist. As she hit the ground, her leg lifted, and with it came the trap. She was familiar with gin traps, having encountered them in the forests outside Warsaw. Whoever had set this one had camouflaged it perfectly by covering it with sifted earth. She brushed away the soil, her heart pounding.

The device, which was badly rusted, was intended to trap a large animal. It was a design she recognised: a pair of toothed jaws, held closed by spring tension, opened above a flat plate when the spring was depressed, enabling the trap to be set. It would be sprung when an animal stepped on to the plate, and the jaws would snap together with considerable force. The only reason she wasn't howling with pain was that the teeth were sunk into leather that was thicker than normal. Her breathing steadied. Even so, she felt the pressure growing above her ankle.

She was reaching across to prise apart the jaws when she heard someone shout, 'For God's sake don't touch that.'

A shaven-headed young man in his twenties was standing staring at the trap. He was wearing a green jacket with a logo on it.

He gazed at her with dark, hooded eyes. 'If you try to open it, you'll lose your grip and it'll snap back.' He had a young-sounding voice when he wasn't shouting.

'But I just need to press this spring down.'

'Nah, you won't be able to do it.'

'Bet I can.'

She pressed down on the spring and the serrated jaws moved slowly apart, dragging pieces of shredded leather with them. She lifted her leg out, and released her hand. The jaws snapped together with a sickening sound.

The man eyed her with what could have been admiration. 'I've never seen a woman do that before.'

'Years of piano-playing makes your wrists strong.'

'I'll have to take that.' As he pulled the trap away, the chain appeared from under the soil. It was fastened to a metal stake disguised with leaves and bits of branch, and was intended to prevent the trapped animal dragging the gin away.

'Aren't these illegal?'

'Yeah, too right they are. This is the second I've found this week. There's someone putting them down. Dunno who. But when I catch him, I'm having him.'

'I remember gins from when I was a child. People used to trap animals for food.'

'They were made illegal here in the 1950s.' He eyed her critically. 'You're not British, are you?'

'I'm Polish.'

His expression cleared as if to say, 'Ah well, doubtless the laws are more lax in other countries.'

'Why do you think someone's set this trap?'

'God knows. For fun? Maybe he likes to hear animals scream. Or children. There are some sad crazies out there. If you want to catch animals live, you should use a humane trap which snares the leg and doesn't crush it. I've seen snares around too, come to think of it.' He gripped the stake and yanked it out. 'The gin I found yesterday was deeper in the wood. It's a run trap, intended to catch small vermin. About so long.' He indicated a length with his fingers. 'But this one looks like it's intended for the deer.'

She took her boot off and pulled down the sock. There were red marks where the jaws had done their work, but the skin was unbroken.

'Arnica gel,' he said suddenly. 'Yeah, good for bruising. Sorry about your boot. The leather's a bit wrecked.' He looked at her as if seeing her properly for the first time. 'I'm Euan, by the way.'

'Dania.' She gestured to the logo on his jacket. 'I'm guessing you work here?'

'I'm a forester with the Woodland Trust.'

'You work in Backmuir?' she said, interested.

'Mainly here. I was lucky to get the job. I live in Muirhead, up the road. Five minutes to get to your work must be a record.'

'What do foresters do?' she said, putting her boot back on.

'Protect the place.'

'Including the visitors,' she said, looking up at him.

His expression softened. 'Them as well,' he said, smiling shyly. He gripped her arm and hauled her up.

'Thanks.'

'Did you hurt yourself?'

'I had a bit of a jolt, that's all. A cup of tea and a little cry, and I'll be okay.'

He grinned. 'Where are you headed?'

'I planned to go right through Backmuir and out the other side.'

'I'll come with you, if you don't mind. In case there are more mishaps.' He hesitated. 'If that's okay with you?'

'Nice to have company. And you can tell me a bit about the trees here.'

'What were you doing off the path, anyway?'

'I saw something move in the bushes. I think it was a fawn.'

'We don't usually get fawns till late June. You were lucky to see it.'

'I think it was the deer that was lucky. It just missed the trap.'
Her shin was starting to ache.

He picked up the trap, and led the way to the path, holding
the bushes aside for her. 'So do you know much about this place?'
he said.

'Backmuir Wood? No. This is my first visit.'

'This is an ancient wood, about one hundred and forty acres.
Many of the forests round here were cut down to supply timber
for the jute mills. But this one survived.'

'The jute mills haven't, though.'

'Nah. March of progress, if you can call it that. The jute barons
planted exotic trees like giant redwoods and araucarias. You see
them around Dundee. And in Broughty Ferry. If you're interested
in trees, then visit Camperdown Park.'

'This place reminds me of the forests in Poland. They cover
about a third of the country, maybe a bit less.'

'A third?' he said in amazement. 'Wicked.'

'After the war, the government introduced a plan to restore the
forests that had been destroyed during the Occupation. It seems
to be working.'

'I'll have to go and see them then. When's the best time?'

'Autumn,' she said without having to think.

He threw her a smile. 'Yeah, like all forests.'

'The one to visit is Kampinos. It's northwest of Warsaw. We
used to pick mushrooms there when I was a child. The best ones
have a chocolate-coloured velvety top and a sort of honeycomb
underneath. I don't know the English word for them.' Her parents
knew where the mushrooms grew in profusion. It wasn't far from
the site of one of the mass executions. Her father had pointed
out the place, and had found a German machine-gun-shell casing
embedded in the stump of a tree. Finding spent casings from
machine guns was something her father was good at.

They walked in silence, and she was relieved to see that Euan knew the place well enough that he didn't need a map.

'Best to keep to the path if you're walking in this part of the wood,' he said. 'The ground can get a bit spongy.' He pointed ahead. 'When you see these oaks, you know you're near the southern exit.'

She saw the gate then, and the cars beyond.

'I hope you'll come more often,' he said, as they reached the car park. 'It really is a magical place.'

'You should charge an entrance fee, you know.'

He grinned. 'Perhaps you'd like to make a donation?'

'Okay,' she said, laughing.

'Seriously?' He fished out a card. 'This is the website. You can donate there.' He hesitated. 'I really am sorry you got caught in the trap. If you see anyone messing around with a gin, if you can't find me, go straight to the police.'

'Actually, I *am* the police.'

A look of alarm crossed his face.

'I'm off duty,' she said, familiar with the response. She was putting the card away when she saw the name. 'Euan Campbell?'

'That's right.'

It was a long shot, as there were likely many Campbells in the area, but she said, 'You wouldn't be related to Kerry Campbell, by any chance?'

'My sister.'

'And have you heard from her lately?'

'I get texts,' he said warily. 'She uses Ailsa's phone.'

'Listen, Euan, I've not been here long. I arrived just before your sister left Dundee so I don't know much about it. But I'm keen to hear what you think happened.'

It was some moments before he spoke. 'Kerry talked all the time about going to London. She'd failed to get into uni. Said there was nothing for her in Dundee.' He looked into the distance. 'Actually, that's not strictly true. There was one thing that interested her.'

'The Druid group. The one she went to with Ailsa McLaughlin.'

'You know about that?'

'I heard about it from Ailsa's mother.'

'Yeah, so on that Friday, Kerry disappeared. She didn't tell us where she was going. But she took my motorbike. She must have been in a hurry because she left behind my leathers and helmet.' He lifted a hand wearily. 'I know, it's illegal and all that, but it's done now, and I certainly didn't say she could take it. Anyway, that was the last we saw or heard of her until we got a text saying she was in London.'

'Was that like her? To take your bike without permission?'

'Totally out of character. She always asked, and I always said yes. And she was careful to take the helmet.'

'What was she like?'

'She had the sort of bubbly personality that made people think she was a bit of an airhead. But she was really smart,' he added defensively. 'Except she was always losing her phone.'

'And you think she and Ailsa went to London on the motorbike?'

'They may not have gone to London at all. They may be here. Or somewhere else.'

'Why do you say that?'

'When I phone, I always get voicemail. No one ever rings. I just get texts. Replying to mine.' He pulled out his phone. 'Here's the latest from Kerry. I got it this morning. The usual stuff about having a great time. But look what she calls me.' He thrust the phone at Dania.

She read the abbreviated message, not understanding much of

it as she'd never mastered text-speak with its accompaniment of emojis. But it began with, 'Hi Euan.'

'Euan.' She glanced up. 'That's your name, right?'

'Yeah, but she *never* calls me Euan.' He reddened slightly. 'She calls me Toodle-Bear. Has done ever since we were kids. But in all the texts we've had since she left, she uses my real name.'

Dania realised what he was implying even before he said it.

'This isn't Kerry, officer.' He played with the chain on the gin trap. 'Someone's taken Ailsa's phone and is sending these messages.'

Dania thought back to her conversation with Jenn. The girl's theory was that Ailsa and Kerry were being held somewhere against their will and forced to send those texts. If that was the case, then maybe using Euan's real name was deliberate on the part of Kerry, and intended as a signal that something was wrong.

'Did you tell DI Chirnside this?'

Euan's voice was hard. 'He didn't believe me. The case is closed as far as the police are concerned.' He threw her a hopeful glance. 'Unless you intend to reopen it?'

'I'm sure DI Chirnside has his reasons for not pursuing it,' she said unconvincingly.

Yet something wasn't right. Chirnside had told her that several witnesses had placed both girls at the Druid meeting in Monifieth on 29 April, the Friday they'd disappeared. But he'd not passed this information on to either the McLaughlins or the Campbells. None of them knew that the girls had attended a meeting of the Dundee Grove. An oversight on his part? Or was he afraid the families would assume the Druids were responsible for the girls' disappearance and take matters into their own hands?

'Have you got a picture of Kerry?'

He scrolled through his phone, and held it out. The photograph was of a baby-faced girl with moony eyes and a rosebud mouth. She had dark curly hair with a fringe that wouldn't lie straight.

'Officer,' Euan said, scuffing his foot on the path, 'I was close to my sister, and to Ailsa. The three of us hung out all the time. If Kerry and Ailsa are alive, then it would be wrong not to try to find them. Don't you agree?'

'Unless they don't want to be found. They're both adults.'

He waggled the phone in her face. 'Then how do you explain her calling me Euan?'

'I'm afraid I can't.'

'Yeah, fine.' He gave a curt nod. 'See you around, officer,' he added with a sneer in his voice.

Before Dania could reply, he had turned and disappeared into the wood.

CHAPTER 15

Dania crossed the car park, thoughts spooling round in her mind. The more she went through her conversation with Euan, the more she was forced to the conclusion that, as far as the missing girls were concerned, all was not what it seemed. Euan had examined the evidence and come to a logical conclusion. The problem was that there was more than one logical conclusion. The obvious one was that Kerry had simply decided it was time to be a grown-up and had called Euan by his real name. But what if Euan – and Jenn, for that matter – were right, and the girls were being held against their will, perhaps not even in London? Could the Druids be behind the girls' disappearance? Marek had found nothing suspicious about the group. On the contrary, he'd been impressed by what he'd seen.

Another possibility, and one she was more inclined to favour, was that, far from being the perpetrators, the Druids were the victims. Someone wanted to send them a message, had killed Judith, the head of the Dundee Grove, and intended to keep killing. Maybe Ailsa and Kerry were next. Would they, too, be given water boiled up with yew leaves and their bodies displayed prominently somewhere as a warning to the others? The thought was chilling.

She crossed the road, seeing more of the laird's metalwork

sculptures. Backmuir Estate stretched out towards the horizon in a patchwork of fields, punctuated with clusters of trees and bushes, with the odd barn or group of buildings breaking the monotony. Dirt roads formed a loose net across the land, allowing workers to bring tractors and other farm equipment into the fields. And, again, as she stood looking around, she felt that, from behind one of the huge trees or within one of the dense bushes, someone was silently watching her.

She was about to strike out across the fields when she noticed the single-storey cottage near a belt of thick-branched trees. It had a chimney at either end, and the state of the stonework and the missing slates suggested it had long since been abandoned. Careful to avoid the potholes, she approached the building from the back, stepping over the tiny vegetable patch overrun with weeds. She peered through the windows, seeing nothing through the dirty glass.

To reach the front door, she had to pick her way over what looked like a cratered battlefield, the charred grass and ash-reduced wood evidence of a recent bonfire. Rusty farm implements and broken bottles were strewn around, as were several ancient-looking plant pots containing dry earth. Her gaze drifted to the needles. No surprises there, given how off the beaten track the cottage was. There was no gate or fence, and whatever had passed for a front garden had disappeared under deep tyre marks. A tarpaulin lay bunched up by the wall, beside a pile of sawn logs.

The splintered front door was sturdy enough that it couldn't easily be broken, and a test of the latch revealed that it was locked. She made out 'WEN' in red paint but the rest of the word had worn away. The windows on this side were clean enough that she could see through them. Taking care not to let her cheek touch the glass, she peered into the cottage.

The interior was unbelievably filthy and consisted of one long room that did service as kitchen, bedroom and living room. An iron tub, the kind her grandmother had used, hung on the wall, suggesting that the room also doubled as the bathroom. The bed consisted of an ancient mattress and yellowing pillows without slips. The chamber pot confirmed her suspicions that there was no toilet, and she wondered idly if the occupant emptied the solid contents over the vegetable patch like her grandmother used to do. There was no fridge or washing machine, just the type of low sink you find in a scullery. A couple of saucepans and a kettle sat on the gas stove.

The furniture was either rickety and falling apart, like the bed, or thick and sturdy, like the dining table. A pile of crockery was stacked neatly on the table, which was long enough to seat eight people, ten at a pinch, although there were only the two chairs. A fraying needlepoint footstool seemed to have been kicked under it.

This would be one of the empty tenant cottages that Willie had referred to. With no bathroom and toilet facilities, she wasn't surprised that the tenants had given up. She wondered why Sir Graham hadn't upgraded it. Maybe, with the advent of the Polish workers, most of whom lived in flats in town, he was no longer reliant on tenants. She started to make her way back to the road.

She hadn't gone far when she noticed a figure approaching. He was a shambling giant of a man with a scarred face, and what was left of his light brown hair was flecked with grey. The shuffle of his breathing suggested he was in a hurry. Either that or he was a five-pack-a-day smoker. Seeing her, he stopped and stared.

'Hello,' she said cheerfully.

'Hello.' He looked past her towards the cottage. 'Are you looking for someone?'

She hesitated.

'Because if you are, you won't find them there,' he added with a pointed smile.

His soft accent was from further north. And his clothes, a clean soft-collared blue shirt and pressed moleskin trousers, weren't those of a farm worker. He was holding a Barbour jacket as though he meant to use it.

'I was curious and went for a peek,' she said.

'And did you find anything?'

'Nothing, I'm afraid.'

'Are you a member of the press?'

'I'm a detective.'

He straightened. 'I think you'll find the laird's away. And Backmuir Hall is on the other side of that field.'

'When did the laird leave?'

The man stroked his scalp. 'Ah, now you have me. It was Friday. I saw a taxi drive on to the Liff Road late in the afternoon. Sir Graham never takes any of his vehicles.' A look of envy came into his eyes. 'If I owned a Porsche, I wouldn't be leaving it at the airport.'

'Me neither. So where did he fly off to?'

'Paris, I think. He has a lady there.' The corners of his mouth lifted slightly. 'Lucky man.'

She smiled, trying to imagine the floppy-haired laird with a Parisian beauty, and failing. 'Does he often go away?'

'That depends on how you define "often".' There was an expression in the man's eyes that was hard to read. 'Aren't you going to ask me about the scarecrow murder?'

'Is there anything you want to tell me about it?'

'There's nothing I *can* tell you.'

She wondered why he'd raised it, in that case. Perhaps he was hoping she'd let slip how far on the police were in their investigation. But something made her say, 'You must have heard about the two girls who disappeared not long ago. Ailsa McLaughlin and Kerry Campbell.'

'Disappeared? Are you treating that as a missing person's case?'

'Should we be?'

'I think those girls ran away from home. They'd reached the age of majority, so there's nothing anyone can do about getting them to come back.'

'Ailsa's sister, Jenn, doesn't think so.'

'Jenn was devoted to her sister. I think she can't accept that Ailsa chose to go and live elsewhere.'

'Do you know the McLaughlin family well?'

'Everyone round here knows everyone else. It's the same in all rural communities. Listen to *The Archers*.' He extended his hand. 'I'm Robert Cranna, by the way, but everyone calls me Rabbie.'

'Dania Gorska,' she said, shaking his hand.

'Whatever you're looking for, detective, I hope you'll find it. But you won't find it on the laird's land.'

She looked deep into his eyes, wondering what he was trying to tell her without saying it.

'I'd get to your car, if I were you,' he said then. 'It's about to pour.' He stared at the clouds massing on the horizon. 'There's a rainstorm brewing. I give it five minutes.' With a nod, he headed for the main road, shaking out the Barbour and putting it on.

She lingered, watching his figure dwindle, thinking that, although he looked in his fifties, he had powerful arms. Powerful enough to hoist a limp body on to a pair of sticks. She was finding that she now made this calculation of every able-bodied man she met.

As she reached the field, the clouds dropped their water and, seconds later, ragged sheets of rain blew in behind her, covering her like a cloak. It was the kind of rain that never stops, and which she hadn't experienced since she'd been a child in Warsaw. Ignoring the ache in her shin, she ran towards the Liff Road, cursing herself for not bringing an umbrella. And yet the forecast had been for a sunny day. That's what comes of playing Chopin's 'Raindrop' Prelude, she thought, as the rain ran down her arms and dripped from her fingers.

Jenn was leaning against an oak. The Polish detective was running into all sorts of people today. First Euan Campbell and now Rabbie. From her vantage point in Backmuir Wood, Jenn had seen the woman talking to the forester, and whatever they were saying had left him fair scunnered. Might be something to do with the trap he'd been holding. He'd found the smaller one she'd set deeper in the wood, so that left just one more. Chances were, he'd find that too. And that would be the last of Aleck's gins. Euan had already removed most of her snares. Her experiments on decomposition following exsanguination might now have to be put on hold. Unless she could find live animals, she'd have to fall back on Plan B – studying decomposition in water. That morning, she and Aleck had visited the body farm to check on the progress of the vole. Putrefaction was well under way, with the swollen body leaking a foul-smelling sticky liquid. Aleck, who knew everything there was to know about bacteria and its effects, had been able to predict to the day when that would happen.

The detective had seemed in no hurry to get back to her car. Quite the opposite. She'd sauntered through the car park behind Backmuir Wood and crossed the road deep into the laird's land. Jenn should really have returned home to help her mum, but something made her follow the Polish woman. Interesting how she'd poked around outside Wendy's Cottage. Jenn knew all the laird's cottages, as Aleck had pointed them out the first time they'd driven around the estate on the old tractor.

So what was the detective talking about to Rabbie? Would it be to do with the murder of the university woman? Or was she enjoying a wee nosey stroll? Either way, she'd need to get a move on, as it was about to pour.

One good thing, though, was that Aleck seemed to be more like his old self, although Rabbie said he was still sleeping badly. That would account for the headaches he had on waking up. Paracetamol didn't seem to help. Maybe he wasn't drinking enough water. And he'd had a sudden nasty nosebleed during their walk through Backmuir, which had necessitated a stop and the administering of the first aid she'd learnt at school. She'd not yet had the opportunity to talk to Rabbie alone and find out what he thought was wrong with Aleck. Could it be the publicity surrounding the scarecrow murder? There'd been a fair few journalists on the laird's land this past week, wanting to interview him and disrupting the work of the estate. This could be stressing him out. She'd have to visit him more often and check that he was coping.

She watched until Rabbie and the detective disappeared from view, and then pushed herself off the tree and left the wood. She unlocked her bicycle and wheeled it on to the Liff Road. A sudden cawing made her glance into the sky. A flock of crows was wheeling and dipping somewhere above the laird's mansion. Her interest was piqued – a dead animal? Maybe a fox, or something bigger. She was tempted to make a diversion, but clouds were darkening the sky.

Throwing her skinny plait over her shoulder, she climbed on to the bike and headed for home. Just as the rain came bucketing down.

CHAPTER 16

Jenn was kneeling, watching Cleopatra feeding her kittens. The large feline had given birth a few days before in the cardboard nest that Jenn had designed. It was at the back of the abandoned shed, an excellent location, made perfect with the addition of straw, an old blanket and a portable heater. She'd placed food and water beside the nest, and replenished them daily. Once she knew that Cleopatra was near her time, she'd taken to locking her in the shed so she wouldn't do anything daft like trying to give birth in the henhouse. That would have been disastrous, as Cleopatra was terrified of hens.

The cat seemed quietly proud of her litter of six, although this wasn't her first. Jenn, who had known Cleopatra since she was a kitten, had been allowed to watch, keeping a respectable, and respectful, distance throughout. She'd observed what took place over the course of two or three hours, counting the kittens as they were born, and the placentas as they were pushed out and eaten. What was impressive was how the cat immediately took charge of her blind, mewing offspring. The kittens were identical to how their mother had looked when she was born: tiny black-and-white balls of fur that slept and fed and did little else. Their tiny ears, folded down at birth, were beginning to stand up, although their gummy eyes wouldn't open fully for a few more days. Birth was a fascinating process, although Jenn had always found death, and what came after, more fascinating still.

She had followed Cleopatra's pregnancy with interest, realising from the change in colour of her nipples and their thin discharge that she'd been impregnated, almost certainly by the foul-smelling tomcat who frequented Oaktree Farm. Her mum had shown little interest: she knew that the cat could cope well enough on her own – Cleopatra's nine lives had been seriously reduced but not eliminated – and, anyway, the woman had little time for anything that didn't put bread on the table.

Jenn was not long back from her Sunday-morning session at the swimming pool. Her hair was still a wee bit damp because, on fine summer days, she didn't bother drying it, but spread it over her shoulders like a yellow towel. She could do one hundred lengths easily now, and it was time to push the envelope. Maybe she could start with ten lengths more. She'd cycled back, approaching the Liff Road from the south so she could call in at Keeper's Cottage, but hadn't found Aleck at home. She'd caught sight of him in the forklift earlier that morning and had hoped he'd have finished whatever he was doing, but she had been unlucky. So she'd taken a cup of tea with Rabbie, who had been poring over his plant books. He'd been able to reassure her that he was keeping a close eye on Aleck and would let her know if there was any change. The man had seemed genuinely touched by her concern, and suggested she stop at Keeper's for a wee bitty, but she said she needed to get on home.

As she left Keeper's, she spotted a column of smoke in the distance, near the cottages. Either Aleck had finished with the forklift and was burning stuff on the estate, or one of the tenants was having a barbecue that was getting out of control. The sound of raucous crows was loud in her ears and, cycling up the Liff Road, she again caught sight of the swirl of black above the laird's mansion. One time, she'd been on this road at night and seen bats dipping and fluttering. The following evening, she'd crept through the laird's grounds and seen where they swooped out from under the eaves. They exited the hall in twos and threes, and then in larger groups, their numbers tailing off over the course of a couple of hours. Thinking about the bats, she realised she could trap them live. She knew how to do it with a large hairnet, a technique she'd seen on a nature programme. The thought of trapping live bats made her heart accelerate. There were all sorts of interesting experiments she could do with those leathery wings.

As she passed the field where the scarecrow had hung, force of habit made her glance into it. Probably everyone who travelled the Liff Road did the same. The police sign had gone.

At school, she and her classmates had followed the case of the murdered woman in the newspapers, their conversations rarely about anything else. The police seemed no further forward in their investigation, and she wondered if the Polish detective had got anywhere with that photo of the driver. She doubted it, as those sunglasses covered much of the face. And he was wearing gloves, which meant that, even if they'd identified the car, there'd be no forensic evidence. Although Nikki Alexander in *Silent Witness* would have found it, no question. Jenn's classmates had crowded round the photo, humming with excitement that Jenn had had a visit from a real-life copper who'd questioned her about the murder. That Jenn had been first at the scene of the crime had turned her into something of a celebrity, and girls who'd earlier turned up their noses at her friendly approaches now actively sought her company. Although she enjoyed her newfound status, she was smart enough to know that it wouldn't last, and it was simply a matter of time before her classmates went back to avoiding her or, more likely, ignored her completely.

She leant over the box and picked up one of the kittens. It sat on her palm, no longer than her finger. It was the largest of the litter and always the first to attach itself to its mother's nipple, and she wondered when it would start to push the others away. She brought it to her face, examining the soft fur, how the white patch under the neck was like goose down. Hardly any flesh on the thing, though. All in good time.

Cleopatra was watching her lazily, seemingly undisturbed by the theft of one of her babies. Jenn replaced the kitten, who latched on hungrily to a vacant nipple and sucked like a pig. Ailsa would have loved these kittens, she thought. After all, Cleopatra was her cat.

The temperature in the shed had risen to an uncomfortable level, and the cloying smell, a mixture of congealed blood and sour milk, was growing unpleasant.

Her mum was calling from the yard. It was time for Sunday Mass. Jenn got to her feet, pulling the drawstring of her trousers tight, and left the shed.

'I still think there's something suspicious going on,' Dania said, watching Marek putting the dinner plates away. Although she'd managed to walk up to Mass at St Joseph's, and back to the DCA for lunch, he was still insisting on treating her like an invalid and doing all the cooking.

She was regretting having told him about the gin trap. When he'd returned from the football match and learnt what had happened, he had assumed she needed a good dollop of TLC and had immediately cancelled his plans for Sunday. They'd spent the afternoon watching *Casablanca*, eating gherkins and snuggling up to a bottle of Wyborowa. As a child, she'd always been a wobbly mess watching romantic films, although it was something she'd outgrown. Marek, on the other hand, was greatly affected, although he managed to keep his face expressionless, even at the end. The DVD was his, one of a collection of 1940s films, which included *Random Harvest, Now, Voyager, Brief Encounter* and, his favourite, *The Third Man*. They'd talked about *Casablanca* afterwards, with its theme of love and wartime sacrifice. What they didn't talk about was the shameful performance of Dundee United the previous afternoon.

She'd just finished telling her brother about her conversation with Euan Campbell.

'Suspicious?' Marek said, turning to face her. 'In what way?'

'Euan claims the texts from his sister aren't being sent by her.'

'Cards on the table, Danka. What's going through your mind?'

'Ailsa and Kerry are being held somewhere. If Judith's death is meant as a warning to the Druids, the girls could be next. They were Druids too.'

'The gamekeeper's gibbet theory?'

She nodded.

'But they went missing at the end of April,' he said. 'A month ago. Why keep the girls for so long? They didn't do that with Judith.'

'Maybe whoever is behind this is waiting for a special occasion on which to kill and display two young girls together. Do the Druids have, you know, the equivalent of holy days?'

He ruffled his hair. 'I remember hearing something at the meeting. About the Eightfold Wheel of the Year. One of the festivals is Alba something or other. It means The Light of the Shore.' He looked at her thoughtfully. 'The laptop's in the living room. Shall I carry you?' he added, a smile forming.

'I'm not decrepit,' she said, getting to her feet and trying not to wince.

On the living-room sofa, he opened the laptop, giving her a glimpse of an article he was working on. He closed it down and brought up Google. 'Here it is. The Eightfold Wheel of the Year.'

She peered at the screen. 'There are eight special festivals in the Druid yearly cycle. Four are solar and four are lunar. Okay, so the summer solstice is one of them.'

'It's called Alban Hefin. There's a whole section devoted to it.'

'Is there a festival before then?'

'We've missed it. The spring equinox, or Alban Eilir.'

'Nothing in between?'

He scrolled down. 'Beltane. On or around May the 1st. In the northern hemisphere, anyway.' He glanced at her. 'Can you remind me when Judith Johnstone was killed?'

'May the twenty-seventh.' Dania lifted her legs on to the sofa. 'Maybe it's not Druid festivals we should be looking at but Christian ones.'

'Pentecost was May the fifteenth.'

She felt deflated. 'Okay, let's forget that theory.'

'Which one? That the girls are being held for a special occasion? Or that the girls are being held?'

'You think I'm wrong, don't you?'

He set the laptop aside. 'I think you're taking this too personally. Aren't detectives supposed to work with the evidence they have? Like scientists?'

'Ah, but it's getting the evidence in the first place. That isn't always done scientifically. The best detectives I've worked with succeeded because they trusted their instincts.'

'And what are your instincts telling you, Danka?'

'That these two girls didn't go to London of their own accord. They may not even have gone to London at all.' She gazed at him earnestly. 'And perhaps their disappearance has nothing whatsoever to do with the Druids.'

'Let's suppose they're here, then. Where might they be?'

'It's not easy keeping two girls for a month against their will. But it's not impossible.'

'A purpose-built basement somewhere?'

'Or a big rambling house in the middle of nowhere.'

'There aren't many of those around.'

'I know of one. Backmuir Hall.'

'Sir Graham Farquhar? The Much Honoured the Laird of Backmuir? You're not seriously thinking he's holding the girls?'

'Not seriously. But I'm thinking it.'

Marek was staring at her as though she'd lost her mind. 'Why?'

'He told me he'd never met Judith, but something he let slip convinced me he was lying. There's no hard evidence, of course. And I'm struggling to find a motive.'

'Are you sure you're not imagining this, Danka?'

'You'd have come to the same conclusion if you'd met him.'

'Actually, I interviewed him a few months ago.'

She plumped up the cushion behind her. 'In what connection?'

'I did a piece where I profiled his charity work. He's chairman of several local charities which, under his guidance, have raised hundreds of thousand of pounds. He's extremely well thought of. I've heard it said that, whenever he walks into a pub, he never has to pay for his drinks. When I met him, he came across as a genuinely nice man. A bit eccentric with those strange-coloured metal monstrosities, but one can hardly hold that against him.'

She could think of several killers she'd known in her time at the Met who'd also come across as genuinely nice men. 'What does he do when he goes down to London?'

'He owns property there, so perhaps it's for business reasons.' Marek's mouth twisted in a faint smile. 'Or maybe he's one of those gentlemen who likes a little privacy when he plays house with a little doll.' After a pause, he said, 'Shall I make tea?'

'Not for me, thanks. I haven't done my piano. Each time I come into this room, the leaflet on the mantelpiece reminds me that I need to practise.'

'Will you be able to work the pedal with your bad leg?'

'Are you offering to do it for me?' She nodded at the laptop. 'Anyway, you need to finish whatever it is you're writing.'

After Danka had settled herself at the piano, Marek slid the laptop over. His piece just needed the finishing touches, but he was finding it difficult to concentrate. His sister's preoccupation with these so-called missing girls was becoming unhealthy. Personally, he thought she was wasting her time and energy. They were in London or another big city, either living the high life, or living in a squat.

The furious opening bars of Chopin's 'Fantaisie-Impromptu' reached him. Danka never played anything other than the Rubinstein edition, considered by the master to be the composer's finished work. She was still trying to decide what to perform at the memorial event and was working her way through her repertoire and, in doing so, giving Marek the equivalent of a series of concerts.

He pulled his attention back to his article, made a few edits and sat back, staring through the window, remembering the Druid ceremony at Monifieth. His thoughts strayed to Friday night and Willie's comments that the grotesque and very public posing of Judith Johnstone's body was the start of something horrific. She'd been the Archdruid of the Dundee Grove. If the man's theory was correct, she was the obvious candidate for stringing up first. But who would be next? The Druid who'd conducted the ceremony? Or the gentle Dr Peterkin who'd caught him spying?

Danka had finished the 'Fantaisie-Impromptu' and had moved

on to the second movement of Chopin's Concerto No. 1, written, in fact, after his Concerto No. 2. Was she considering playing this at the concert? It really required an orchestral accompaniment. He paused to listen, remembering how, the first time he'd heard this masterpiece, he had been with his grandfather. The man had told him that, during the Occupation, when the playing of anything by Chopin meant certain death, Poles had defied the German decree and listened clandestinely. The reason this concerto held a special place in Polish hearts was not just for its romantically glorious music but because, at the premiere in 1830, it was Chopin himself who played it, the concert marking his final public appearance on the Polish stage. Soon afterwards, he left his country for Vienna, finally dying in Paris.

Danka was finger-perfect. Marek listened for several minutes, noticed his cheeks were wet, and wiped his tears away before his sister saw them.

He read through the article a final time. What would Danka make of it? he wondered. Instead of writing an exposé of the Dundee Grove the way his editor had wanted, Marek had found himself drafting something completely different, a piece extolling the virtues of a simpler way of looking at, and living, life, and asking the question: can we really argue with the promotion of harmony, worship of nature and respect for all beings? He'd even gone so far as to contrast the Druid ceremony with the Roman Catholic service he attended on a Sunday, knowing that this might land him in hot water. The priest at St Joseph's was likely to give him a heavy penance, which, in a previous century, would have included self-flagellation.

Marek had extracted a large number of stills from his body-cam, and selected those where the Druids' faces were turned away or were otherwise unrecognisable. He and his editor had discussed the use of the body-cam in advance of the meeting. The man had agreed that Marek's feature would be social research in the public interest, in view of the past incidents surrounding pagan-like meetings, and had granted his approval for the secret recording of images of the Druids without obtaining their consent.

The article was entitled: *Neo-Druidism – A Light For Our Times?*

He put it through the spell-checker. And then he emailed it to his editor. The man could publish it, or bin it.

CHAPTER 17

'You got caught in a gin trap?' Laurence said, a look of horror on his face. 'Those things are lethal. So what happened to your leg, Sergeant? Can I see?'

'There's nothing to show. A few teeth marks and a yellowing bruise. Marek bandaged it up. We didn't have that gel, as it happens.'

'So what did you use on your leg?'

'Vodka, of course,' Dania said, keeping her face straight.

He stared at her, and she could see he was trying to figure out whether she was joking. But all Poles know about the medicinal properties of vodka. And not just for rubbing. Drinking a glass or two helps the circulation and promotes the body's natural healing process. Or so Poles tell themselves . . .

'What were you doing in Backmuir, anyway?'

'I wanted to see it,' she said, not prepared to say more. She knew how her suspicions about the laird of Backmuir would sound. Interestingly, Laurence had shown no reaction when she mentioned Euan Campbell. Perhaps Campbell was a common enough name that he didn't associate it with one of the missing girls.

Her mobile rang. She listened without interrupting and then disconnected.

Laurence was grinning. 'Chopin's "Funeral March"? Nice ringtone.'

'Get your coat. We're meeting the DI there.'

'Where?'

'At Backmuir Hall.' She grabbed her jacket. 'It's happened again.'

Laurence made no attempt to slow down on the road to the hall, and they lurched on the potholed track so violently that Dania was in danger of losing her breakfast. He stared straight ahead, ignoring the giant sculptures and, because he drove as though he were competing in the Monte Carlo rally, they arrived before Chirnside.

They passed through the gateposts on to the gravelled area.

She saw it before Laurence did. 'Dear God,' she murmured.

He screeched to a stop. Without waiting for him to cut the engine, she opened the door and scrambled out. As she looked up, she felt the small hairs on the back of her neck rise.

A figure was hanging from the flagpole. His arms were out-stretched and his legs dangled limply, the leather shoes gleaming in the sun. His head drooped forward in a way that hid his face but allowed her to see that he was mounted on two crossed wooden planks.

Below the figure, a man stood staring at the crumpled saltire on the ground. He was wearing dark denims and a worker's jacket, green with age. He lifted his head, giving Dania a view of dishevelled brown hair and a weather-beaten face. There was an expression of numbness in the eyes.

She pulled out her warrant. 'DS Dania Gorska. West Bell Street Station.'

He clasped his grimy hands together, making no attempt to take the card. It did nothing to prevent their tremor.

'Are you the person who called the police?' she said.

'Aye. I saw the corbies from a distance.' His voice was hoarse. 'That number of birds means only one thing.'

'So you came to investigate,' she said when he seemed reluctant to continue.

His eyes narrowed. 'I'm the estate manager. Aleck Docherty. It's my responsibility to check whether there are dead animals on the land.'

'I'm sorry, I wasn't implying anything.'

'I called the emergency police number as soon as I saw him.' Shading his eyes with his hand, he looked up at the figure.

There was a sudden thrum of wings, and a huge shabby crow landed on the dead man's shoulder. With a rapid motion, it thrust its beak forward and ripped a piece of flesh from his cheek.

'We need to get him down, Laurence,' she said without turning round. 'Can you call it in? And get the professor here.'

She heard Laurence sprint gratefully to the car.

'Do you know if the laird's at home, Mr Docherty?' Rabbie had told her that Sir Graham had left on Friday afternoon. It was now Tuesday morning.

'He's not due back till later this week.' Docherty shoved his hands into his baggy denims. 'I haven't been near the hall for days. Without yon corbies, I reckon that man would have been up there till the laird returned.'

She stepped closer to the flagpole. Steeling herself, she looked up, and immediately wished she hadn't. Where the man's eyes should have been were two red-black hollows. Not only had his cheeks been ravaged, but also his neck where it bulged over the tight collar. His jaw hung slack. Bird mess streaked the jacket of his brown suit.

'I'll need you to come to West Bell Street and give us a statement, Mr Docherty.'

'Aye, I thought it.' He massaged his temples.

'Are you all right?'

He smiled emptily. 'I'm okay, lass.'

There was the sound of a car engine, followed by a door slamming.

Chirnside joined them, stopping short as he saw the figure. 'Jesus Christ,' he whispered.

'Do you think the same person did this, sir?'

He said nothing. He didn't need to. The shock on his face said it.

'I'm afraid he's unrecognisable,' she said. 'He's missing his eyes.'

'Have you called this in?'

'Laurence has.' She glanced towards the car. Laurence was standing staring straight ahead at the building, making no move to join them.

Chirnside seemed to have recovered himself. 'Who found the body? This gentleman here? Please don't touch that!' he added, as Docherty reached for the flag.

'I thought to get it out of your road.'

'Please leave it. This is now a crime scene.'

'Aye, of course. I should have realised.'

'Sir, perhaps Mr Docherty could go back with Laurence and give his statement, and you and I can wait for the team.'

But the DI had tuned out. He was staring at the man's shoes. They were expensive-looking brogues, in two tones of brown and beige.

'Sir?'

He walked over to where he could see the man clearly. He gazed upwards, and then again at the shoes, a look of disbelief on his face.

★ ★ ★

Milo Slaughter was squatting on his heels, inspecting the damage done by the crows. Now that the birds were no longer feasting, the flies had returned and he was having to swat them away.

'Not pretty, is it?' he said, glancing at Dania kneeling at his side.

Seeing the corpse's face close up, she noticed how pinched it looked, the result of dehydration after death causing the skin to contract. The smell, a by-product of putrefaction, was so strong that she could taste it on the roof of her mouth.

'Any sense of how long he's been up there, Professor?'

'Several days. I can't be more precise. Rigor's been and gone. Otherwise the birds wouldn't be able to have their dinner. And he's starting to bloat. See that bloody foam leaking from his nose?'

She steeled herself to look at the face again. 'Sir Graham left the Hall on Friday afternoon, Professor, so I'm assuming this man was killed and hoisted some time afterwards.'

'Given he's missing his eyes, I won't be able to determine time of death from the potassium eye test. But we can check the length of the blowfly larvae.' Milo paused. 'It's similar to the last. Mounting and displaying.' He nodded towards the wooden planks and bits of rope. The planks had been nailed together to form a cross. Rope had been wound several times round the victim's chest, and the wrists tied to the crossbeam in a similar way. 'Do you think it's a copycat? Someone who read about the scarecrow murder in the paper and wanted to try his hand at something similar?'

'It looks like a classical crucifixion.' She could see him waiting for her to say more. 'Can you tell if he died from asphyxiation? That's how you die on the cross, isn't it?'

'I'd say he wasn't asphyxiated.'

'In that case, would you be able to fast-track a tox test?'

'Are you thinking what I'm thinking, Sergeant? *Taxus baccata* again?'

'Unless there's evidence that something else killed him.'

Milo looked towards where Chirnside was standing with the SOCOs. The man seemed permanently glued to his mobile. 'Your DI's been a bit reluctant to come near this one. Can't say I blame him. You're made of stronger stuff.'

'A few years in the Met hardens you.' She looked squarely at him. 'You know, Professor, I took a lot of flak when I was in London. Not just the casual sexism, but also the fact that I'm a foreigner. Yet when it came to blood and bodies, I made sure I was up there, dealing with the dead and not passing out like the boys. I think I just got used to it.' She looked at the corpse. 'I'm guessing Dundee doesn't see things like this very often.'

'Just the usual beatings and knifings like the rest of the UK,' Milo said grimly. 'Do you want to check his pockets now that I've finished?'

She bent over the body, realising from the stink of excrement that the victim had soiled himself. A riffle through his pockets produced an unused handkerchief, a small mirror, a biro that looked like a fountain pen, coins, a metal credit-card wallet and an iPhone. There was a Yale but no car keys. She searched through the wallet.

'The name on his credit card is Dr Adam Frederick.' She looked questioningly at Milo. 'Another member of the university?'

'I don't recall the name. I think I'd know him if he were in the medical school.' He gestured to the man's wrist, half hidden under the sleeve. 'That's an expensive watch. I doubt many academics could afford it,' he added wryly.

She pulled back the sleeve and studied the blue-faced watch with the word 'Piaget'. Her gaze was drawn to the man's hands, the flesh torn but the fingernails immaculate.

She went over to the cross and squatted down beside it. Whoever had assembled it had drilled a hole in the top, slotted the metal halyard through, and hoisted the cross and victim like a flag. The other end of the cable was wound several times through the sturdy metal ring on the wall of the building. One obvious question was whether one person alone could have pulled the body up. Another obvious question was: why?

Milo got to his feet and beckoned to his assistants, who brought the trolley from the mortuary van. Chirnside followed them over.

'Inspector, in view of the advanced stage of decomposition, we'll do the post mortem this afternoon. I assume either you or the sergeant will be attending?'

Chirnside hesitated. She could see he didn't want to attend, and she was about to offer to go, when he said, 'I'll be there. You get back, Dania, and find out what you can about the victim. You know what to do.' He looked past her towards where Laurence and Docherty were standing waiting. 'A second one on the laird's land,' he muttered.

'You think it's the killer's hunting ground, sir?'

'Looks like it.'

'We know the victim's name now. He's a Dr Adam Frederick. A GP, maybe?'

A sudden shadow passed across Chirnside's face.

'Was he your doctor, sir?'

He shook his head. There was a hopeless expression in his eyes, as though not only had he been here before, but he knew this wasn't the end of it.

They were in one of the station's interview rooms. It was like all interview rooms – small, windowless and airless, and with regulation plastic chairs and grey metal table. Laurence, after a couple of glasses of Alka-Seltzer, felt able to join them.

'Would you like a cup of tea, Mr Docherty?' Dania said, trying to ignore the smell of unwashed clothes.

'No, thank you.' He seemed agitated. 'I'm not being charged, am I?' He was sitting on the edge of the chair, as though afraid he'd break it.

'Not at all. We'd simply like to talk to you about this morning.'

He rubbed his forehead with both hands. 'Aye, all right.'

'You said you're the estate manager. How long have you worked for Sir Graham?'

'Well, I'd have to check my records. About ten years, I'd say.'

'And before that?' Laurence chipped in.

'I worked on an estate north of Perth.'

'As an estate manager?'

'I was the gamekeeper. I looked after the game birds and animals for the shoot. And their habitat,' he added.

Dania glanced up from writing. 'What made you give it up to become an estate manager?'

'The pay was better,' he said simply. 'I got a place on a course and learnt the trade.'

'So let's talk about this morning. You mentioned you saw the crows. What time would that have been?'

'I didn't look at my watch. I spied the corbies from my cottage. When I went over there and saw the man hanging, I called 999 immediately.'

'Your cottage is nearby?' Laurence said.

'Aye, Keeper's Cottage, off the Liff Road.'

'When was the last time you were at Backmuir Hall?' Dania said. 'Before today, I mean.'

'Well, now you're asking. Let me see. It would have been Tuesday. Aye, a week ago.'

'And what were you doing there?'

He ran a hand over his chin. 'I went to see the laird. He'd asked to take a look at the estate figures.'

Docherty seemed calm enough but his eyes were avoiding hers. She'd seen that behaviour before in people who had something to hide and weren't practised enough in how to hide it. She decided on a gamble. 'You know Dr Adam Frederick, don't you?'

The gamble paid off. Docherty's gaze flew to hers. The expression on his face was one of mild panic. 'I've never heard of him,' he said too quickly.

'Why do you think his body was on the laird's land?'

'I've no idea,' Docherty gasped.

'Is he a friend of the laird's?'

'I don't know all the laird's friends. You'll have to ask that question of him.'

'Was Judith Johnstone a friend of the laird's?'

'Who?'

Interesting reaction. The press had gone to town on the story and, by now, the whole of Dundee knew the name Judith Johnstone. Dania had seen a transcript of Docherty's earlier interview, in which he'd been asked if he knew the woman in the scarecrow, Judith Johnstone. So why was he acting as though this was the first time he'd heard the name?

'She was the woman found in the scarecrow,' Dania said.

'Aye, now I mind.' He nodded, his attention on Dania. 'As I said, you'll have to ask the laird if he knows her.'

'She was a member of a Druid group. What do you make of that?'

'I ken nothing about such a group.'

'Don't you remember Druids meeting on the laird's land? Last year?'

He ran a hand over his eyes. 'I heard something about it.'

'Weren't you there?'

'I must have been on another part of the estate. I'd have remembered Druids.'

After a silence, she glanced at Laurence. He shook his head to indicate he had no further questions.

'I think that'll be all, Mr Docherty,' she said. 'We'll prepare a statement for you to sign, based on what you've told us, and we'll get you in to sign it. Now, though, I'll have someone drive you back to the estate.'

He pushed his chair back and stood up heavily.

'Thank you for coming in,' she said, getting to her feet. 'We may have further questions for you as the investigation develops.'

He nodded silently. His gaze moved over her face, as though trying to memorise her features. Dania wasn't sure she liked the look in his eyes.

She and Laurence accompanied Docherty to the reception desk, where the duty sergeant arranged for a car.

'So what was that about, Sergeant?' Laurence said, as they watched the man leave.

'How do you mean?'

'The third degree about knowing Adam Frederick. A bit harsh, wasn't it? The poor man's just found a dead body.'

'He was too cagey. I'm convinced he knows the man.'

'So why would he lie?'

'You tell me.'

'And Judith Johnstone. Just because he couldn't immediately remember who she was.'

'I find that hard to believe. But it's not that that's bothering me. He's lying about something else.'

'What?'

'The Druids on the laird's estate.'

'Docherty said he wasn't there.'

'And I find *that* impossible to believe. He fetched his shotgun and the laird fired it to scare the Druids away. He was there all right.'

She could see the doubt growing in Laurence's eyes.

'That's right, Laurence. Someone firing a shotgun over the heads of a group of Druids isn't something you're likely to forget. Is it?'

Yes, not only had Aleck Docherty lied, he had the build of someone who could hoist a woman on to a pair of sticks, and heave a man up a flagpole. Those massive shoulders would hardly have felt the strain. As the estate manager, he had the keys to hidden unused cottages on the laird's land, cottages where he could imprison people indefinitely.

And, as both the laird and the estate manager had lied about knowing Judith Johnstone, could they be working together? Perhaps two teenage girls were at that moment being held in an abandoned cottage, or even somewhere in Backmuir Hall.

CHAPTER 18

Dania ducked under the wind chimes and rang the bell of the large Victorian house. This was her first trip to Invergowrie, a village west of Dundee which had once been closer to the river, but land had been reclaimed from the Firth of Tay, pushing everything further from the water. Standing waiting for the door to open, she tried to imagine the view of the river from the top-floor dormer windows.

The front garden was in such immaculate condition that it was unlikely to be the work of the homeowners. A silver Volvo, gleaming in the afternoon sunlight, was parked in the wide driveway in front of a new-looking camper van.

The family liaison officer, a girl who looked about sixteen but had to be older, was gazing across the street at the low-walled garden which served as a roundabout. She had fluffy brown hair that came to her shoulders, and one of those faces that didn't need make-up. Dania had often wondered about the strength of character it took to fulfil this role. She was about to find out if this girl had it.

She heard hurried footsteps and a tall angular woman in tight-fitting leather-effect jeans opened the door. Her short dark hair, with the fringe almost covering the eyes, was cut in a style where the hair is shorter at the back. The collar of her cream shirt stood up to frame a face that was so expertly made up, she must have spent an hour on it. One heavily ringed hand, a bracelet hanging loose on the wrist, was clutching a mobile and, seeing Dania, she indicated with a smile that she was about to cut the conversation short. The smile faded as she caught sight of the uniformed police officer. She turned away and spoke hastily before ending the call.

'Mrs Frederick?' Dania said.

'Yes?'

'Mrs Adam Frederick?'

The puzzlement in the woman's eyes changed to alarm. 'Has something happened to Adam? Oh, he hasn't been in a train accident, has he? Or has something happened in Glasgow?'

'I'm Detective Sergeant Dania Gorska,' Dania said, holding up her ID. She smiled gently. 'This is Police Constable Bridget Walsh. May we come in?'

Mrs Frederick hesitated and then flung open the door. She stood staring as Dania and PC Walsh came into the hallway.

'Is there somewhere we can sit down?' Dania said when the woman made no move.

'Of course. I'm sorry. I'm being rude.'

She led them into an open-plan living area, all polished pine flooring, scatter rugs and floral air freshener. Two white leather sofas formed an L-shape.

'Do take a seat,' she said.

Dania and PC Walsh took the nearest sofa, but the woman remained standing.

'Please sit down, Mrs Frederick,' Dania said, gazing up at her.

'Do I need to?' she said with a little laugh. When Dania remained silent, the woman sank on to the adjacent sofa. She stared wildly from one officer to the other.

'I have some very bad news, Mrs Frederick. And it will come as a shock. I'm sorry to say that your husband has been found dead.'

The woman's expression froze. Her bony hands flew to her mouth and she started to shake. 'Are you sure it's Adam?' she blurted. 'There hasn't been some mistake?'

Dania removed the photos from her bag and held them out. 'He was wearing this watch. And these shoes. Do you recognise them?'

Mrs Frederick lowered her head and gazed at the photos. Then she jerked her head back and squeezed her eyes shut, as though by this action she could squeeze out the horror of discovering that her husband was dead. She rocked backwards and forwards so violently that Dania was afraid she'd fall off the sofa.

PC Walsh sprang to her feet and sat down beside Mrs Frederick, slipping an arm round her shoulders. By rubbing her arm and murmuring something that Dania couldn't hear, she managed to halt the rocking. Gradually, Mrs Frederick opened her eyes. The expression of grief in them made Dania look away.

Her gaze fell on the silver-framed photograph on the mantelpiece. It was of a couple on their wedding day. The bride, in a tight-fitting lace dress with a boat-neck collar and white roses in her hair, was smiling radiantly for the camera. It was Mrs Frederick, younger by about twenty years. But it was the groom who commanded attention. With his charming smile and intelligent eyes, he was totally unrecognisable from the man hanging from the flagpole. His brown hair was thinning, and Dania put him roughly ten years older than his bride.

When she looked back, Mrs Frederick was dabbing at her eyes with a lace-edged handkerchief. PC Walsh gripped her free hand.

'How did it happen?' Mrs Frederick said, her voice sullen.

'I'm afraid I can't go into details. Your husband was found on the Backmuir Estate.'

The woman's gaze bored into hers. 'But that's not possible. He's in Glasgow. At a conference.'

'Are you up to answering a few questions, Mrs Frederick? We can leave it until another time if you'd prefer.'

'What sort of questions?'

'Can you tell me when your husband left to go to Glasgow?'

'It was . . . last week . . . Thursday. No, Friday. That's right. I was away myself that day.'

Dania caught the expression on the PC's face. The girl was signalling with her eyes that continuing wasn't a good idea.

'Mrs Frederick,' Dania said, 'is there someone you'd like to ring? Someone who can come and stay with you?'

The woman stared at Dania. Her eyes filled and she squeezed them shut, causing tears to spill down her cheeks. 'My sons,' she whispered, clutching at her throat. 'How am I going to tell them?'

Dania started to get to her feet. 'I think it's best if I come back another time.'

'No,' Mrs Frederick said firmly, surprising Dania with her determination. 'Please sit down, Sergeant. I want you to tell me how he died.'

'We haven't determined the cause of death yet.' Pity for the woman rose in her gorge. Sooner or later, someone would have to tell Mrs Frederick what had happened to her husband.

'Very well, then,' Mrs Frederick said, wiping her eyes. 'Ask the questions you need to.' She straightened, as though affirming that she was ready to face whatever else the world was going to throw at her. Dania felt a creeping admiration for the woman.

'Shall I make a cup of tea?' PC Walsh said with a kindly smile.

'That would be nice, officer. I'll show you where everything is.'

'There's no need. I'm sure I'll find it.' She left the room.

Dania pulled out her notebook. 'You said your husband left last Friday to go to Glasgow.'

'He was to attend a medical conference.'

'And what time did he leave?'

205

'I can't be sure, as I wasn't here. I went to Edinburgh for the day.'

'When was the last time you saw him?'

'At breakfast. I left straight after.'

'Did you go by train?'

'I took the car.'

'And how was your husband going to travel to Glasgow? Do you have a second car?'

'We've just the one. And the camper, which we use for holidays. No, Adam said he'd take a taxi to the railway station. He does that when he goes away. He leaves me the Volvo. I need it to pick up the boys.' Her voice broke on the word, but she got herself under control.

'And Friday, when you were both away? Did the boys come home themselves?'

Mrs Frederick looked vacantly at Dania, as though wondering what relevance this question had.

'I'm simply trying to get a complete picture,' Dania said with an encouraging smile.

'The boys have after-school clubs. They go to Dundee High. I was back in time to pick them up.'

'And do you know which cab company your husband would have booked?'

'We always use the same one. Mackay Taxis. Adam rings them well in advance.' She picked at the lace on her handkerchief. 'He always takes the train from Dundee. Although Invergowrie has a station, the trains to Glasgow aren't brilliant. If you miss one, it takes ages for the next to come along. He hates waiting more than five minutes for anything, which is why he always goes from Dundee. He will have gone after his morning surgery ended.'

'And when would that have been?'

'It ends at twelve-thirty. Adam's a stickler for punctuality and he never goes over. I always have lunch ready for twelve-forty-five.'

'Is his surgery nearby?'

She looked at Dania in surprise. 'It's at the back of the house. He has his own practice,' she added, anticipating Dania's next question.

'He practises privately?'

'Always has. This house was left to him by his father, who was also a doctor. His father had it purpose-built, with a waiting room and dispensary as well as the office. The patients come in round the back. There's a small area where they can park their cars. The drive was made wide enough.'

'And your husband definitely had patients to see on the Friday morning?'

'He's always booked up, Sergeant. Lately, he's been busier than ever.'

'Do you have access to his patient list?'

The question was badly put, Dania realised. Mrs Frederick's response came as no surprise.

'I'm afraid I can't let anyone see that,' she said in a defiant voice. 'Adam always said that I shouldn't. It's against the Data Protection Act.'

'Of course.' Dania laid it to one side. There were ways of getting access to the data. 'What sort of suitcase would your husband have taken?'

'Oh, the little red wheelie.'

'You're sure?'

'I packed it myself. I always do.'

'Did he take a coat?'

Mrs Frederick looked vague. 'He sometimes wears a trench coat in summer, but it's still on the peg.'

'Could I ask you to forward me a recent photo of your husband?' Dania said delicately.

'A recent photo?' the woman said, her voice trailing away.

'It would help us enormously.'

'Sergeant, the fact that you're asking me these questions tells me that my husband died in suspicious circumstances. Am I right?'

'I'm afraid so.'

'Was he murdered?'

'We think he was. But I can't tell you any more right now.'

Mrs Frederick took a breath. 'I don't know what sort of photo would be suitable. Perhaps I could show you what I have.' She got to her feet and tottered to the sideboard in her stilettos. With a few sharp tugs, she opened the bottom drawer, and dragged out a thick album. 'I have these on my iPad but I get them printed and mounted, too, in case something happens to the tablet. I don't really trust computers.' After searching through the pages, she tapped a photograph. 'This was taken last year. We were on holiday in Capri.' She swivelled the album round to show Dania.

Dr Frederick was in a light-coloured polo shirt, smiling broadly. Behind him, beyond the beach, was the rock formation for which Capri was famous, although Dania couldn't remember its name. The photo had been taken in close-up and showed him chest upwards. He was holding the strap of the rucksack slung over his shoulder, the sunlight glinting off his wedding ring.

'Will that do, Sergeant?'

Dania smiled. 'It's perfect. Here's my card with my email. Could you send me the digital version?'

The woman's eyes were shining with tears. 'We love Italy. We'd planned to retire to Capri.' She gestured to the photo. 'That was the last time we went there.' Tears streamed down her cheeks, her expression conveying better than words that she realised that, from then on, whenever she talked about her husband, her conversations would include the phrase, 'that was the last time'.

PC Walsh arrived with a tray. She set it down on the sideboard and handed round mugs of tea. Dania sipped thoughtfully, admiring the way the girl was able to comfort the grieving woman. It was a skill she herself would never have been able to master although, God knows, she'd had enough practice.

'One last question, Mrs Frederick,' Dania said. She caught PC Walsh's warning look. 'And then I'll leave.'

She opened her bag and took out the photo of the man in the boiler suit and grey beanie. It was a long shot, but worth trying. 'Do you recognise this man, Mrs Frederick?'

The woman gazed at the image. 'Does this have anything to do with the death of my husband?'

'It may do.'

She brought the photo to her face, her hands trembling. After a few moments, she said, 'I'm afraid I can't help you, Sergeant.'

'Thank you, all the same.' Dania got to her feet. 'PC Walsh can stay for as long as you need her.'

Mrs Frederick gazed up at Dania, a look of hopelessness on her face. Now that the detective's questioning was over and the fact of her husband's death had sunk in, she'd depleted her reserves of strength.

Dania addressed herself to PC Walsh. 'Perhaps you could help Mrs Frederick. She's going to email me one of her photos. And can you go with her to pick up her sons from school?'

'Of course.'

Mrs Frederick was still looking at Dania.

'You understand that I'll need to talk to you again, Mrs Frederick?'

The woman nodded numbly.

'I really am most dreadfully sorry.' It always sounded trite but Dania couldn't leave without saying it.

Mrs Frederick lowered her head and sobbed loudly. PC Walsh gripped her hands and murmured into her ear, making Dania wonder again how the girl could bring herself to deal with such grief when there were other ways of making a living.

She let herself out after nearly tripping over the shoe rack in the hall. It was tempting to take a quick look round the back, but she would have to pass the living-room windows.

As she reached the pavement, she became aware that someone was watching her. Across the gravel, on the first floor of the neighbouring house, a net curtain had been drawn back. She shielded her eyes, catching a glimpse of a youngish woman with streaked blonde hair and a look of anticipation on her face. Something in the way she inclined her head made Dania think they should have a little chat. She nodded at the woman whose mouth curved into a smile.

The path consisted of concrete slabs with weeds wilting between the cracks. Dania walked up to the front door and rang the bell. Nothing happened. She waited, allowing time for the woman to come down the stairs, and then rang again. Still nothing.

She walked back to the pavement and looked up at the first-floor window. The woman had vanished.

It was nearly five before Dania reached West Bell Street. The first thing she noticed on entering the incident room – apart from the atmosphere of renewed energy, something that always happens after a second murder – was the large-scale map of the Backmuir Estate. The two murders had already been cross-referenced. It didn't surprise her – the similarity in the way Judith Johnstone and Adam Frederick had died had left no one in any doubt that the cases were linked.

Dania checked her email. PC Walsh had wasted no time. A couple of clicks, the attachment opened, and the image of Adam

Frederick filled the screen. Dania called to everyone to cluster round.

'So that's what he looks like,' Laurence said softly.

'Yes, it's amazing how removing the eyes makes you almost unrecognisable. We'll need to get copies of this photo made.' She lifted her voice so the others could hear, and went through her interview with Mrs Frederick.

'So far, the last known sighting of Adam was by his wife, at breakfast last Friday. We'll have to check with Mackay Taxis whether anyone picked him up. According to her, it would have been after twelve-thirty p.m.'

'I'll do that,' Honor said.

'And we need to check with Dundee railway station. If he left Dundee, he'll be on CCTV. If not, we'll need to get hold of his schedule for that morning and find out which of his patients saw him last.'

'We contacted his bank and credit card company,' Fergus said. 'No large sums deposited or withdrawn.'

'What about his phones?'

'Still checking the landline. The last call he made on his iPhone was on Friday morning at eight-fifteen a.m. To the School of Medicine at Glasgow Uni.'

'He rang the organiser of the conference, confirming attendance,' Honor said. 'I had a good chat with her.'

'What was the conference about?' Dania said.

'Everything you ever wanted to know about the brain. Turns out the brain was our Dr Frederick's specialist subject.'

'What did they think when he didn't turn up?'

'They rang his mobile a couple of times. We clocked the missed calls and the voicemail messages.'

'They didn't think to ring him at home?'

'I asked the lady professor that and she said they only had his mobile. They reckoned something more important had come up. The reason they didn't pursue it was that he wasn't giving a paper or anything like that.'

Fergus thrust his hands into his pockets. 'It's a pity we found his iPhone switched off. Otherwise, we could have tracked his movements. We're not getting any breaks in that department.'

Dania twisted a strand of hair round her finger. 'It's too early for Forensics to tell us anything.'

'I guess you haven't heard what happened,' Honor said, grinning. 'Some journalist tried to get too close to the crime scene and Kimmie saw him off with a few choice words.' The girl shook her head. 'Got to hand it to the Aussies. They know how to say it like it is.'

Kimmie was brutal when it came to preserving her crime scene. Dania could well imagine how it would have gone. 'Has anyone been able to track down the laird?' she said.

'The DI said he'll ring him,' Fergus said wearily. 'Just as well that gamekeeper saw the crows. Otherwise Sir Graham would have come back to that corpse on his flagpole.'

'Unless he put it there himself,' Honor said.

They stared at her.

'Why do you say that?' Dania said.

'No reason, except that I've always thought a great way of diverting attention away from yourself is to divert it towards yourself, if you see what I mean. Both victims were found on his land.'

'Any evidence for that theory?'

Honor shook her head. 'Nope.'

Dania glanced at her watch. 'The autopsy should be over by now. I wonder if it's worth going up to Ninewells. It'll be six before I get there, and that's assuming the traffic's light.'

'They'll have gone home,' Fergus said. He closed his eyes. 'Do you think we've seen the end of this, or will he do it again? That's what I'd like to know.'

'What *I'd* like to know,' Honor said emphatically, 'is why the perp didn't take the good doctor's watch?' She went over to the incident board and tapped the photo of the Piaget. 'See this? I looked up how much this cheeky little number costs. Hardly any change out of fifteen grand.'

'*How* much?' Fergus said.

'Even second-hand, it would be worth a mint. So why leave it there?'

CHAPTER 19

A phone call to Ninewells confirmed that the autopsy had ended an hour earlier. Chirnside hadn't returned to West Bell Street, leaving Dania to conclude that he'd gone home. She toyed with the idea of returning to Invergowrie and confronting the nosey neighbour, as experience told her that someone who lived behind twitching curtains was likely to have seen something. But experience also told her that the public rarely welcomed evening visits from the police. It could wait until morning. She powered down her computer, picked up her bag, and left.

As she walked along the Perth Road, she went through the events of the day. Specifically Aleck Docherty's testimony. Her boss at the Met had been keen on staff development, and had urged her to attend a course on reading body language. She'd thought it lightweight and dismissed it as a waste of an afternoon, but then she had started to put it into practice. The estate manager, she was convinced now, was hiding something. And yet he seemed an unlikely murderer. She'd met many, and he didn't fit the mould. And now they had a second murder. Tomorrow's exercise would be to establish a link between that and the death of Judith Johnstone. Yet something bothered her. And she couldn't get it. It eluded her, slipping away each time she closed on it.

She let herself into the flat. Marek wasn't home yet. She poured

214

herself a small glass of Wyborowa and took it into the living room, where she searched through her collection of Rubinstein's recordings.

Lying on the sofa, she sipped the ice-cold liquid and listened to the Scherzo No. 2, Op. 31. Of Chopin's four scherzos, this was her favourite, with its rich melody and mad dash towards the end. She'd tried it herself, but there were one or two passages which required her attention and she wanted to hear how Rubinstein interpreted them. She closed her eyes, seeing the score as she heard the music. After listening to the piece twice, she finished the vodka, rose, and opened the lid of the piano.

She started to play the piece, but found her mind pulling her to the events of earlier in the day. When that happened, there was no point doing anything other than going with it. It was as she shifted into the *con anima* section that she stopped in the middle of the bar, and stared at the wall. She sent Marek a text saying that something had come up, and not to wait for her.

Five minutes later, she was on the Perth Road, heading towards West Bell Street.

Honor looked up as Dania hurried into the incident room. 'Thought you'd gone home, Sarge,' she said. She was wearing her baseball cap back to front, the sign that she was about to leave.

'That Piaget watch,' Dania said, shrugging off her jacket. 'Remember what you said about it being expensive? You wondered why the perp hadn't taken it?'

'That's right.' Honor's gaze moved over Dania's face. 'So what are you thinking?'

'The list of Judith's effects. They've been put online.'

'Yep. Sydney gets one of the secretaries to do it.'

Dania pulled a chair across to Honor's desk. 'Let's have a look, shall we?'

'Okey-dokey.' Honor tapped away and, a few seconds later, the list appeared on the screen. Dania recognised the items: woven shoulder bag, keys, hairbrush, Specsavers case, chocolate bar, make-up bag, purse, card wallet, notebook, mobile. Added to the list was what Judith had worn when her body was found, namely her underwear and the scarecrow's clothes.

'What are you looking for?' Honor said, frowning.

'There's no watch.' Dania stared at the other woman. 'Judith was a busy academic, to say nothing of organising meetings for a group of Druids.'

'I get you now.'

'Mind you, she may not have worn a watch. She could have taken her time from her mobile. But let's go with the watch for now. Why wouldn't she be wearing it?'

'Maybe she left it at home that day. We can check that.' A couple of clicks later, a longer list appeared, itemising the contents of Judith's cottage by room.

They went through the list systematically, even pulling up the photos taken by the SOCOs. There was no watch.

'She could have left it in her office,' Dania said warily.

Honor retrieved the data and photos from Judith's office at the institute. The result was the same.

'Okay, suppose she was wearing it when she was kidnapped,' Dania said. 'What does that tell us?'

'Maybe it broke in the struggle and the time it happened is significant. The perp might not have wanted us to know.'

'Okay, what else?'

Honor pulled off her baseball cap. 'Can't be anything to do with it being valuable because he left the Piaget on the doctor's wrist.'

'So do you think he's a trophy-taker?'

'If he is, we'll need to get a profiler in. The DI won't like that.'

'Why?'

'He doesn't trust them. The last one we got in, about a year ago, turned out to be a bit of a disaster.'

'In what way?'

'He turned out to be the perp.'

'I see.'

'But, if you're right, then something will have been taken from our doctor. Not his watch,' Honor added unnecessarily.

'Right now, though, we're going to have to move quickly to establish his last known.'

'My shift doesn't start till midday tomorrow, but I'm willing to come in at eight and we could make a start on the CCTV from the railway station. It's just come in.' Honor looked speculatively at her. 'What say you, Sarge?'

Dania smiled. There was something genuine about Honor, the sense that you could trust the direction she wanted to go in. 'I'm up for it,' she said.

'You don't fancy a coffee right now, do you? There's something I'd like to run past you.'

'Fine. Where do you want to go?'

Honor put the cap back on her head, adjusting it so it was back to front. 'You're not allergic to cats, are you?'

Half an hour later, Honor was pushing through the door of Purrfect, a café on Castle Street.

'Purrfect?' Dania said, following her in. 'What kind of a place is this?

'It's a cat café. Not been open long.' She glanced over her shoulder. 'Have you been in one of these before?'

'I used to walk past one in London.'

'And you didn't go in?'

'I was always in a hurry.'

The interior was full of squashy old sofas covered in patterned cushions. Pen-and-ink drawings of cats lined the parts of the walls that weren't fitted with box shelves. In these shelves reclined half a dozen cats of different varieties, all specialist breeds. There was an area reserved for customers who wished to drink their coffee and just watch the proceedings, but those who'd elected to play with the cats either had them on their laps or were taking toys out of a box in the middle of the room and trying to get the animals' attention. Dania had expected the place to reek of cat litter but was pleasantly surprised: the café smelt fresh and airy, as though someone had run over everything with baby wipes.

They took their cappuccinos to the back and set them down on a low table. Honor made herself comfortable on the sofa, crossing her legs and giving everyone a view of her unlaced blue and green trainers. Although the girl's clothes were always on the smart side, she drew the line at the sorts of shoes female detectives were expected to wear. Her feet, she'd once confessed to Dania, were unusually wide and only men's trainers would fit.

A black cat with white tips to his longish hair padded over and sprang gracefully on to Honor's lap. The worried expression on the girl's face vanished as she petted the animal. 'This is a Maine Coon,' she said. 'He and I are old friends.'

Dania sipped carefully. The coffee, which was too hot to gulp in mouthfuls, was excellent, and tasted exactly as its name suggested: orange mocha. The mugs were stamped with pictures of cats and, instead of the usual mess of chocolate on the cappuccino's foam, the sprinkles were in the shape of paw-prints.

A fat marmalade cat appeared from nowhere and wove her sinuous body round Dania's legs. 'So, how did you find this place?' she said.

'Through a mate of mine. He's a cat lover, too. The big plus point is that it's open till ten.'

'Have you got a cat at home?'

'Nope. Landlord won't allow it. Which is why I come here. There's no food prepared on site, by the way. So I'm sorry if you were expecting home baking. The owner gets the biscuits and cakes from a special bakery, where they're made with cat themes.'

'This looks like a fun place,' Dania said, trying unsuccessfully to pick up the marmalade cat.

'At the weekend, there are special kiddies' hours.'

'What happens when the cats have had enough?'

'See that flap? It leads to an enclosed area with bowls of food.'

After a pause, Dania said, 'I wonder how the DI got on at Ninewells.'

Honor shook her head. 'I feel sorry for him, Sarge. He's nearing retirement, and yet he gets this shitty murder case.' She set the Maine Coon on a cushion, where it wound its bushy tail round itself, closing its gold-green eyes. 'And, believe me, it *is* shitty. *Dundee* is shitty. If they ever give Scotland an enema, this is where they'll put the tube in.'

'It's not that bad, surely.'

'I've had a spell on the drugs task force. I know what I'm talking about.' She paused. 'I heard there's a new man in town. From Glasgow.'

'The pusher with the limp?'

'Things have taken a turn for the worse since he arrived. The entire task force is out hunting him. But he's slippery.'

'So no luck yet?'

'None.'

'How long have you worked with the DI?' Dania said after a brief silence.

'I've been at the nick for two years. He's a great guy. Old school, does things by the book, but, hey, what's wrong with that?' There was venom in her voice. 'He doesn't deserve the title some of our colleagues bestow on him. Mr Plod.'

'That's unfair,' Dania said. She knew that Honor was referring to Fergus, who'd used the term once or twice in her hearing.

'Annoys the crap out of me. He does a lot for the community. Always grafting away. I think he wants to stand for the local council when he retires.'

'So, he doesn't plan to spend it on the golf course,' Dania said wryly.

'And here's another thing. He reckons women are better at teamwork. He's a supporter of getting more of us into the Force. Did you know that?'

'I might have guessed. He treats me better than I was ever treated in London.'

'When I arrived and one of the lads made some sexist comment, he nearly pulled the guy's head off and handed it to him. Did it in front of everyone too. I've had no problems since.' She stroked the sleeping Maine Coon. 'These last few weeks, though, he's been acting different.'

'In what way?'

'Hard to put your finger on it. I'd say he's preoccupied with something. I'm guessing it's his folks.'

'Has he ever been married?'

'Not as far as I'm aware. He's living with his mum and dad, God love him. Not sure how many opportunities come your way under those circs.' She smiled crookedly. 'Maybe the job peels his banana and that's enough.' She set down her coffee mug. 'Okay, so here's what I wanted to run past you. You remember that comment I made earlier, about the laird hoisting the doctor on to the flagpole? Well, I wasn't completely joking.'

Dania nodded encouragingly.

'I've been doing a lot of thinking about this case. And I've done a bit of digging around. Judith Johnstone was killed eleven days ago,' she said, leaning forward. 'Professor Milo thinks it was around six p.m., give or take.' She dropped her voice. 'Okay, so that same evening, at five past nine, Sir Graham boards a flight from Edinburgh, bound for London. He takes a taxi from Backmuir Hall at six p.m.'

'Did he volunteer this information?'

'Not in so many words. I had to press him for the details. I thought it strange he couldn't remember the name of the taxi company. At the very least, he should remember what time his flight was. Behaviour like that always makes me suspicious. So I got the details for myself. Taxi company, and flight times. The taxi people confirmed he'd booked the cab for six p.m. And I managed to speak with the airline.'

'So the laird did board the plane.'

'Yep, but the point I'm making is that he could have killed Judith and put her on those sticks *before* he left.'

'Too risky, surely, doing it in broad daylight. People from Liff village who work in the town would be coming down that road. I think he would have waited till dark.'

'Okay, then, so maybe he had a helper who did the hard graft. Someone who's built like Godzilla. Aleck Docherty, for example. I interviewed him too.'

'What did you make of him?'

She ran a hand over the Maine Coon. 'Strange man. Lost his temper. And he was shifty with it. Didn't always give straight answers and, when he did, they contradicted what he'd said before.'

'Much the same as when I talked to him. Does he have an alibi for the time of Judith's death?'

'Our problem is that *no one* has an alibi for the time of Judith's death. Docherty said he was out working on the estate most of that Friday. We checked and, yep, a few of the workers remembered him. But you know how bad people are about timings. "Some time in the afternoon" is usually as good as it gets.'

'He lives with someone, doesn't he?'

'Robert Cranna. Also known as Rabbie. I managed to talk to them separately.'

Robert Cranna. The man Dania had met when she poked about the estate. 'Are they a couple?' she said.

Honor shrugged. 'Hard to say. They sleep in separate rooms, from something Rabbie told me. When I asked him if he could remember hearing Docherty getting up in the night that Friday, he said, no, he'd slept like a baby. Of the two of them, Rabbie seems to have the brains. He's quite a cool customer. Not like Docherty.'

'Honor, I can't help feeling we're going about this all wrong.'

'I always feel like that when we've no motive. It's like we're at sea, swimming in the dark, not knowing whether we're going towards the shore or further out into the inky vastness.' She lay back against the cushion. A Siamese jumped on to her legs. She didn't stir while it crawled over her chest and on to her shoulder. Another Siamese sprang up on to the sofa and settled on her lap, purring loudly while she stroked it. 'I have a strong feeling that the laird's in this somehow, Sarge.'

Interesting comment. Had Honor not made it, Dania would have made it herself.

'What I can't get over is the way the victims have been killed and posed,' Dania said.

'It's just god-awful. Things like this don't happen here. Do you think it's the Illuminati?'

'Honor, have you ever heard of a gamekeeper's gibbet?'

'Can't say I have.'

'I heard the term from one of the laird's workmen. The gamekeeper traps vermin and displays them to let the other vermin know they're next.'

'Cripes, that's taking serial killing to a whole new dimension.'

'Look, can you check something for me?' Dania said, watching the Siamese shift around on Honor's shoulder. 'The laird's movements *last* Friday, the day Professor Milo thinks Adam was killed. I need the same information you had before. Flight time, taxi time. And whether Sir Graham did actually board the plane. And anything else you consider important.' She took a gulp of coffee. 'If Professor Milo can establish the doctor's time of death, we may discover that Sir Graham had the opportunity in both cases. Maybe he's one of those killers who doesn't like to be around when the bodies are discovered.'

The girl sat up, causing both Siamese to spring on to the floor. 'Consider it sorted, Sarge. Although motive may be a tad harder to establish.' She picked up her coffee mug. 'I may be overstepping the mark here,' she said warily, 'but have you heard from Tony recently?'

Dania had been careful not to mention her private life to any-one at Dundee, but the world inhabited by the police was not large. Honor still had friends at the Met.

'This may be none of my business,' the girl went on, sipping and watching Dania, 'but I heard he came out. Stop me if you don't want to talk about it.'

'There's nothing to talk about. You've got it right. Tony was gay.'

'Must have hit you hard. I know how I'd feel.'

'These things happen, Honor. I've moved on.'

'How did you two meet?'

'One of the sergeants in my team knew him. A group of us went out for a drink.' She shrugged. 'Tony and I hit it off.'

Honor was looking at her as though she didn't quite believe her. 'I guess this is why you came up north, huh?'

'One of the reasons.' Dania smiled. 'I have a brother here.'

'Is he like you?'

'Not really. He's an old-fashioned romantic and refreshingly unashamed of it.'

Honor half closed her eyes. 'You don't think you can be a romantic and a copper at the same time?'

'I don't.'

After a pause, the girl said, 'Cards on the table, Sarge, what's our priority in solving these murders?'

'I doubt we'll get anything from Forensics. We got nothing on Judith and I'm betting we'll get nothing on Adam. Our priority is to find what links them.'

'You don't think they're random victims?'

'With these sorts of killings, they're never random victims.'

'Maybe the good doctor was involved with the university, and knew Judith that way.'

'It's possible. But Professor Milo said he'd never heard of him. And he's likely to know.'

Before Honor could reply, the early evening news came on. At the sound of the DCI's west-coast rasp, both women turned to look at the wall-mounted screen. DCI Jackie Ireland was announcing to the assembled mass of journalists that the body found at Backmuir Hall was that of Dr Adam Frederick. When asked if there was a serial killer on the loose in Dundee, she replied with a thin, wintry smile that the press should avoid jumping to conclusions in the absence of hard evidence.

'Have you met her, Sarge?'

'Only briefly. She was in a hurry about something, so we didn't talk long.'

'Yep. That's her. She has two speeds. On and Off. Did you know she used to be in the military?'

Dania studied the power-dressed woman in her early fifties. She had heavily lidded eyes and stiff hair cut in a sharp style. 'It doesn't surprise me.'

The DCI was fielding questions with an expertise that Dania could only dream of. Maybe that was the key skill you needed to get to the top. She herself would have lost her temper at the insinuation that the police at West Bell Street were sitting on their hands.

'I know that gobby journalist,' Honor said, nodding at the pushy woman who'd just delivered a stinging comment at their lack of progress. 'What a cow.'

Someone was asking the question that must have been on everyone's lips: had Adam Frederick been killed in the same way as Judith Johnstone? Was it another scarecrow murder? DCI Ireland side-stepped that one by simply saying that there was nothing more she could tell them at this stage, but the public should be assured that the police were following a number of leads. Which Dania knew was the stock answer when the police were making little or no progress.

Honor finished her coffee. 'I'd like to work more closely with you, if that's okay, Sarge,' she said suddenly, picking up the Maine Coon. 'Sort of be your wingman.'

'Not DS Finnie's?'

The girl looked directly at her. 'I watched how you did it on your last case.'

'Fine, Honor. I'd like that.'

'So, after the CCTV tomorrow, what next?'

'We need to look at the doctor's life. Every aspect of it.'

'Crack open his secrets, eh?'

'Wide open.'

And, looking at the determined expression on the girl's face, Dania reckoned that, if anyone could do it, it would be Honor.

It was after seven before Chirnside inserted the key in the front-door lock. Although he'd rung his parents to say he'd be home late, he expected them to wait for him to make a start on supper.

So it was with some surprise that he breathed in the vinegary odour of fish and chips.

His parents were in their armchairs, bent over cardboard boxes, eating.

His mother smiled up at him. 'Yours is warming in the oven, son.'

'Thanks, but I'm not hungry,' Chirnside said, sinking on to the sofa.

'You need to eat,' his father said. He'd somehow managed to dribble tomato sauce down the front of his oversized beige cardigan.

Chirnside couldn't face the thought of food. He could still smell the cutting room on his clothes. 'I'll take a shower first.'

'As you like.'

He trudged into the bathroom, catching sight of himself in the mirror. His face was a mess. He ran his fingers over the skin, feeling the new spots erupting and picking the scabs off the old ones. His hair badly needed a trim. Maybe he could get his mother to run the scissors over it. She had a steady hand, despite her years, and would do it gladly. She would do anything for him, he knew that. Her life hadn't been easy, married to a bully of a man who seemed to take delight in putting her down. But she'd stuck by him and had made it work somehow, leaving Chirnside full of admiration for her strength of character.

He made the water as hot as he could manage and stood under the jet, soaping his body and what was left of his hair, and trying to blot out the memory of what he'd seen that afternoon. Like the others in the dissection room, he'd worn a mask, but it hadn't prevented the nauseating, sweet stench of decomposing flesh from seeping through his pores, into his lungs, and on to his hair and clothes so that he carried it everywhere. And, as if that weren't enough, he'd had to endure the prof droning on about not being able to establish a firm time of death. The length of blowfly larvae suggested Friday afternoon or evening, but that was the best he could do. He'd found a contusion on the front of the head, under the hair, consistent with a blow. Not hard enough to cause internal bleeding, but it would have rendered the doctor unconscious. And there were no signs of a struggle. It would be the same as last time, the prof had said confidently – plant poisoning, given the smell and abnormal quantity of liquid in the stomach.

So what the hell was happening? First Judith, and now the doctor. Poisoned. But who was doing it? And why? Chirnside reached for the soap, but it slid out of his hand and slithered about on the floor. Damn and blast it. He should install one of those liquid dispensers. Except that his father would object. The man objected to all his son's suggestions for improvement. As though the cost would break him. Maybe he should go ahead and do it anyway.

At the thought of squaring up to his father, Chirnside's energy left him. He sank to the floor, letting his head rest against the wall, savouring the sensation of water hitting his chest. With his eyes closed, he went through the events of the day. He'd come straight from Ninewells, not calling in at the station, and there were things that needed to be done as a matter of urgency. Maybe he should eat something, and then go to the nick and see where they were. Dania would have made sure everything was up on the board. She was a good lass where that was concerned. Where everything was concerned. They were lucky to have her. As he'd said to the DCI, the Met's loss was Dundee's gain. The only thing that worried him was her interest in those missing girls. He'd warned her against wasting her time, and the logs showed she was no longer looking at the case records, but something told him she wouldn't be letting it go. He'd have to keep an eye on that. He needed her attention on these murders.

He turned on to his hands and knees, feeling the hot water on the back of his neck, and slowly hauled himself upright. Taking care not to slip, he stepped out of the shower, and towelled himself dry. In his bedroom, he bundled the clothes he'd worn that day, including his vest and pants, into a bin bag ready for taking to the dry cleaner's. Christ, he could still smell the stink on them. Maybe he should throw them out. The suit was shiny with age but it was the only one that actually hung right. He dressed in casual clothes, pocketing his wallet and phone, and returned to the living room.

His parents had finished their supper. His father had a lit Dunhill between his lips and was sucking thoughtfully as he listened to the eight o'clock news. As the newsreader reported the finding of a body at Backmuir Hall, his father and mother turned to look at him. The expressions on their faces were accusatory, as though he himself were responsible for the murder. They must have read his own expression correctly, because they said nothing.

'I'll get that fish supper,' he said, remembering it was still in the oven.

There was a faint smell of grease in the kitchen. His mother had taken the food out of its wrapping and put it on a plate to warm. But she'd turned up the heat too high and the plate burned his hand, making him drop it. The fish and chips fell on to the floor, mingling with old crumbs and fresh mouse droppings. If he could only persuade his parents not to drop food on the floor, which deterred the mice from hopping into his traps, then things would start to look up. He suddenly found himself no longer hungry and, after scooping everything up, threw it into the bin.

He suddenly remembered that he hadn't called Sir Graham. He pulled out his mobile, flicked through the Contacts list, and hit Dial.

CHAPTER 20

Jenn was loitering in the corridor, breathing in the familiar odour of school disinfectant and waiting for the lesson to start. The previous day had been one of those in-service days, where pupils were off school. Her classmates, deliberately excluding her from the conversation, were chattering about how they'd spent their time in the nail bars or the Starbucks in the Overgate. She only half listened, as her mind was on Aleck. As it was so often now.

The day before, she'd run into Rabbie in Backmuir Wood, where the man was busy with his snazzy new camera. The Woodland Trust, grateful for having the services of a plant biologist, had leapt at his suggestion of cataloguing plants and flowers for free. But then Rabbie did a lot of things for free. When he wasn't cataloguing in the wood, or issuing books at the library, he was working on the laird's garden venture.

Rabbie had told her that Aleck was not long back from the police station where he'd been interviewed about the man on the flagpole, and the poor old thing was in a bit of a state. When she'd learnt that a second victim had been found hanging outside Backmuir Hall, she had understood why those corbies had been screaming above the laird's mansion. The news that the victim was a doctor was something she'd heard that morning at the Olympia Centre. Two bodies on the laird's land, and the laird nowhere to be seen, one of the ladies had said. Aye, the farms were fair buzzing with it all. And it was left to that poor gamekeeper to find the doctor and call the police. They'd glanced furtively at Jenn and then switched to talking about the EU referendum, a favourite subject of theirs.

The Big Day was just over a fortnight off and they were still undecided as to how to vote. One said she would vote to leave just to stick it to Cameron and his posh cronies. Another said that, if the UK left, her farm would go under because the Polish workers would have to return to Poland, so she was voting to stay. Interestingly, none of the women believed the silly nonsense that, if the vote was to leave, the NHS would get an extra £350 million a week. They had debated the referendum at school, so Jenn was up on the arguments, but she wished the whole thing were over and life would return to normal.

As she'd been towelling herself dry, she recalled Rabbie's reaction to the new murder, and how his mouth had twisted in disgust that the police had given Aleck such a hard time. But she'd seen enough police dramas to know that the person who finds the body is the first to be suspected. Although, in this case, Aleck had a reason for being there. It was his duty to remove dead animals from the estate. Of course, he could have been going up to talk through the figures the laird wanted to go over. She'd been through the data with Aleck, explaining what he should draw the laird's attention to, what was needed for this tax year, and what could be carried over. She'd rehearsed him until he was word-perfect. He'd been grateful, but she could see his mind was on other things.

Now, more than ever, she was convinced there was something he was deliberately keeping from her. And it was something big. And, whatever it was, Rabbie was in on it. Aleck avoided her gaze and when she dropped hints to Rabbie, so did he. What did the two of them know that she didn't? She decided her best course of action was to work on Rabbie, and try to persuade him that, whatever he and Aleck knew, the knowledge would be safe with her. She had spent much of the previous day with him in Backmuir Wood, having offered to help him with the cataloguing. They worked well together, and he seemed to take a delight in her interest, showing her which plants didn't like direct sunlight and grew in the shade, which preferred marshy ground and which needed light, dry soil. She made notes on his notepad, while he took the photographs. He'd gone so far as to say that, when the pamphlets were published, he would ensure that her name was in the acknowledgements. He was good like that.

And yet, although she waited until she thought the time was right before broaching the subject, it was clear she'd blown it. Rabbie clammed up, saying only that Aleck needed space, and that a time would come when she would understand why his behaviour had changed so much lately, and that he would have to go away for a while. But, far from reassuring her, Rabbie's words served only to plunge her deeper into a state of despondency.

It was mid-morning and the incident room was packed. The DCI had brought more officers on to the team and there was a welcome renewed buzz of activity. The crime-scene photos from Backmuir Hall were up on the board, and Chirnside was draw-ing connecting lines with a marker pen, apparently ignoring the argument that was developing behind him.

'I still think we should get the maths boffins in and see if they can draw any conclusions from the locations of the bodies,' Fergus said, his arms crossed. 'There's a guy in the States who's developed this piece of software. He used it to analyse the Jack the Ripper murders.'

Dania's frustration was growing. Fergus had waited until the room was packed before launching his attack. It had started off as a friendly bit of banter, but she hated futile arguments, because she always ended up losing her temper. It was a weakness and, although she recognised it for what it was, she could rarely do anything about it.

'There are only two murder sites,' she said caustically. 'It's not statistically significant. It's a complete waste of time. And money.'

'So, what, you're saying we should ignore the fact that they were found close to one another?'

'I'm not saying that at all.'

'Are you a statistician, Dania?' Fergus said, tilting his head.

'I know enough to be able to tell you that this isn't the way to go about it.'

'Ah, a strictly by-the-book copper.' He was enjoying himself. He pointed both forefingers at her and said, 'Don't you ever get flashes of inspiration?'

This was fighting talk. Anger surged through her. 'Excuse me?' she said, her voice rising.

'That's enough,' Chirnside said, putting the top back on his marker pen. 'DS Finnie and DS Gorska, my office. The rest of you, if you're going to gawp, I suggest you gawp at the incident board.' He marched out.

Fergus held back, motioning politely with his arm that Dania should leave first. She felt like slapping him.

As soon as they were in his office, Chirnside turned on them. 'What the hell do you think you're playing at, bickering like wee bairns? Eh? A great example you're giving to the others.' He took a step forward. 'From now on, you behave professionally. Got it? Or, by God, I'll have you transferred out of this station. Do you understand?' There was no mistaking the menace in his voice.

Dania exchanged a glance with Fergus. 'Yes, sir,' she said. 'But we didn't mean anything by it.'

'She's right, sir,' Fergus said. 'We often bat ideas back and forth.'

Chirnside looked unconvinced. 'Right then, DS Finnie. Organise teams to scour the villages around Backmuir Hall. Someone must have seen something. And make sure you speak to all the farm workers.' As Fergus began to protest, he added, 'Yes, I know there are hundreds, so there's no time to lose.'

Fergus nodded and loped out of the room.

'Did you manage to ring Sir Graham, sir?' Dania said, after the door had closed.

'Aye, his plane gets in this afternoon. He'd heard nothing, of course, so it came as something of a shock.' As though anticipating her next question, Chirnside said, 'The DCI's put in for the court order. Once we have it, we'll know who the doctor's patients are. And we'll get closer to knowing who saw him last on the day he was taken.'

Honor had checked with Mackay Taxis and learnt that, on Friday 3 June, there had been no reply to the knock at Dr Frederick's door. And, yes, the cabbie added tetchily, she'd been at the door at 12.50 p.m. on the dot, the time Dr Frederick had booked the taxi for. She'd tried ringing both at the front and the back. The place had looked pretty empty. And, yes, of course she'd waited. But not for long, as she has a business to run, ken?

Dania and Honor had spent the early part of the morning sifting through the CCTV from Dundee railway station. Even allowing an hour-each-way margin of error, they saw no one resembling the brown-suited Adam Frederick. The red wheelie case made the search easier, but the only person dragging one around was an elderly woman, and it looked more orange than red. Honor had insisted they examine the entire day's recordings in case the good doctor had taken himself into the town centre and opted for a later train. Dania had gone along with it. At the end, she felt as though her eyes were pointing in different directions. But at least they could now confirm that Adam Frederick hadn't taken the train. Not to Glasgow. Not anywhere.

'Mrs Frederick is at Ninewells this morning, making the ID on her husband,' Chirnside said.

'You're kidding,' Dania gasped. 'With that face?'

'I'm told the lot at Ninewells can work miracles in making people look presentable. Anyway, the prof said she'll see him through a window, from the side.' He looked at Dania. 'I'm putting you in charge of interviewing family and friends. I know you've already done a preliminary interview with Mrs Frederick, but we need more answers.'

'I'll go first thing this afternoon, sir.'

He nodded, smiling sympathetically.

She returned to the incident room.

Honor was at her desk, reading *The Courier*. As Dania approached, she folded back the pages and held it out. 'There's something that might interest you, Sarge. I guess, had Dr Frederick not been found hanging on a flagpole, this might have been on the front page.'

The title leapt out at Dania: *Neo-Druidism – A Light For Our Times?*.

The double-page article, she realised, was the piece Marek had been working on. There were several photographs, chosen so the faces would be unrecognisable. The exception was Marek himself. A small image of him appeared at the top of the article.

'His name's like yours,' Honor was saying. 'That's your brother?'

'That's my brother.'

'Don't take this the wrong way, but he's drop-dead gorgeous.'

'How would I take that the wrong way?' Dania said, starting to read.

'Does he have a girlfriend?'

'Are you offering?'

'What does he like to do? Does he like cats?'

'He likes to tango.'

'Hmm. Men taking control of women.'

Dania glanced up. Honor was staring into the distance, smiling dreamily.

Dania and Honor managed to push through the crowd of noisy reporters and reach the porch without things turning nasty. Dania raised her hands for silence and delivered the standard message about having nothing further to communicate, and the reporters should apply to the Press Office for regular updates. The reporters looked unconvinced.

Dania had hardly taken her finger off the bell when the door opened a crack. Seeing the detectives, PC Walsh opened the door wide enough for the women to pass through, and bundled them inside.

'How is she?' Dania said in a low voice.

'She nearly collapsed at Ninewells. The press were all over the place.'

'Looks like they followed you here.'

'Some of this lot were already waiting when I arrived. I've just this minute given them a statement on behalf of the family. With any luck, they'll take themselves off soon.'

PC Walsh was a good choice, thought Dania. She was the right combination of sensitive and strong, which was exactly what the job needed.

'This is DC Honor Randall, by the way.' Dania turned to Honor. 'PC Walsh is the family liaison officer.'

'It's a pleasure,' Honor said automatically.

'Likewise.'

The formalities over, PC Walsh took them into the living room.

Mrs Frederick was sitting on the sofa with two teenage boys. She was in a light blue tracksuit and her feet were bare, showing bony toes tipped with red. Her lipstick looked hastily applied and she hadn't bothered with eye shadow or mascara, probably because she was constantly wiping her eyes. Her hair was tousled, the fringe plastered to her forehead. She glanced up as the detectives entered, an expression of emptiness in her eyes. The dark bruises under them made her look ten years older.

Dania introduced Honor, and Mrs Frederick lifted a hand, indicating they should sit down. The three officers took the other sofa, PC Walsh sitting at the end nearest Mrs Frederick, and hunching forward in a protective attitude, as though ready to ward off those questions she deemed too distressing. Dania's gaze strayed to the boys who, she assumed, given the same dark hair and angular features as Mrs Frederick, were her sons. They were dressed casually in jeans and sweatshirts and expensive-looking trainers. The younger one looked as though he might have been crying and avoided Dania's gaze, but the older was at the angry stage, with restless eyes and a scowl Clint Eastwood would have been proud of.

'Mrs Frederick,' Dania said, 'we have to ask you a few questions. We need to know a little more about your husband.'

'Why haven't you caught the bastard who killed my dad?' the older boy said, thrusting his head forward.

'We're still early in our investigation.'

'Well get your finger out,' he said nastily.

'Matthew,' his mother said wearily. 'Mind your manners.'

'What good are manners at a time like this, Mum?'

She stared at him, uncomprehending.

'How did you and your husband meet, Mrs Frederick?'

236

She transferred the stare to Dania. Then her expression softened and she looked more like herself. 'It was at a May Ball. We were both up at Cambridge, you see. Adam was already fully qualified as a medical practitioner but had returned to do a one-year course. We were watching the fireworks display from the Backs. It was terribly romantic. Things sort of went from there.'

'What did you study?' Honor said.

'I read Arc and Ants.' The woman smiled apologetically. 'Archaeology and Anthropology.'

'Did you and your husband keep up with your university friends?'

'Sadly, no. We've been to the odd reunion but it's never the same. Many of our close friends have moved abroad. We relocated up here and Adam went into practice with William, his father. He took it over when William died.'

'Mrs Frederick,' Dania said gently, 'can you think of anyone who might have wanted your husband dead?'

Her eyes filmed over. 'No one. He was a doctor.' She picked at her eyebrow, and Dania noticed that her rings and bracelet were gone.

'I know you can't give me the names of your husband's patients, but do you know if any of them had a grievance against him?'

'What kind of a grievance?'

'Maybe they didn't agree with his diagnosis.' Seeing the woman's expression harden, she added, 'It does happen, Mrs Frederick. There are people who form their own opinion of what's wrong with them and try to get their doctor to come round to their way of thinking. They can become angry if they feel they're being denied treatment. Did your husband ever mention anything like that to you?'

'Never. He kept his professional life to himself. As he should do. I knew neither the names of his patients nor their conditions. And I didn't want to know.'

'What was your husband like as a person? Did he have any hobbies?' When nothing was forthcoming, Dania added, 'What did he do when he wasn't working?'

The woman's eyes filled with tears. 'He was a good man,' she whispered. 'Thought only of the welfare of his patients. When he wasn't holding a surgery, he made regular house calls. You don't get that with the NHS.'

'Did he know Dr Judith Johnstone?'

A look of horror came into the woman's eyes. 'Was it the same way?' she said in a strangled voice. 'A scarecrow? No one's telling me anything, and there's almost nothing in the paper.'

'No, Mrs Frederick,' Dania said firmly. 'He wasn't dressed as a scarecrow. The reason I ask is that, when we have two killings so close together, we have to consider the possibility that they're linked.'

'As far as I'm aware, he didn't know her. He never mentioned her name.'

'Did he have links with the university?'

'Well, they gave him a gong a couple of years back for his work on brain function. He's an international expert,' she added with pride in her voice. 'It was a nice ceremony. In the Caird Hall.'

'Did he have anything to do with the town?'

She hesitated. 'He'd been to the odd meeting. About the city's problems.' She glanced at her younger son. 'He was concerned about issues facing young people today.'

Her glance at the boy was not lost on Dania. 'What sort of issues, Mrs Frederick?'

'Oh, you know, unemployment, drink, drugs. Sir Graham is the leading light in this city where those are concerned. Adam told

me he's set up committees to try to address them. He asked
Adam to serve on one or two.'

At the mention of the laird's name, Dania felt Honor stir. 'Did
your husband know the laird well?' the girl asked.

'Only so far as this committee work went.'

'Have you ever met him?'

'Never. I'm not sure I know what he looks like.'

'Who are your friends here in Dundee?' Dania said. 'Can you
tell me?'

'I'm afraid that's impossible, Sergeant. Some of our friends are
my husband's patients. As I said before, I can't reveal their names.'
After a pause, she said, 'Is there anything *you* can tell *me*? About
what has happened?'

'It's too early in our investigation. What I can say is that we
know your husband didn't take the train to Glasgow.'

'You don't have to be Sherlock Holmes to work that out,'
Matthew said with a sneer in his voice. 'He was found at
Backmuir Hall.'

'Where someone is found and where they're killed aren't always
the same place,' Dania said.

'Murder site versus dump site.' He chewed his fingernail. 'Yeah,
I know all about it from Ian Rankin.'

Mrs Frederick picked at her eyebrow. As she lifted her hand,
Dania stared at the fingers. 'Mrs Frederick, did your husband
always wear a wedding ring?'

'Of course. It was inscribed with our initials. As is mine.' The
woman looked at her thoughtfully. 'Why do you ask?'

Dania smiled. 'No particular reason.' She studied the boys. The
older one glared at her resentfully. Yes, thank you, Matthew, I've
already met you. No, it was the younger one, who refused to meet
her eyes, who intrigued her. That glance his mother had given
him when she mentioned the problems facing young people. He

looked about fifteen. Old enough to have those problems. Was that why he was avoiding Dania's gaze?

Something made her ask, 'Who lives in the house next door?'

'That's Mrs Reilly,' Matthew said. 'She's a, you know . . .' He caught his mother's glance and stopped. 'You thinking of interviewing her?' he added.

At the question, the younger boy's head shot up and a hunted expression appeared on his face. He shifted as though his seat had suddenly become uncomfortable.

Dania got to her feet. 'I know this has been difficult, Mrs Frederick, and I do appreciate your speaking to us.'

The woman nodded numbly.

Dania glanced at Honor. 'We'll see ourselves out.'

They left Mrs Frederick staring tearfully at her hands.

As Dania closed the front door, the rising wind set off the chimes. Most of the reporters had gone, and those that remained threw questions at the detectives, but drifted away when nothing was forthcoming.

'Why the interest in the wedding ring, Sarge?' Honor said, watching them leave.

Dania examined the long metallic tubes. They were threaded with lilac-coloured butterflies, and were shivering and making a tinkling sound. 'Because, when we found him,' she said, tapping one of the tubes, 'Adam Frederick wasn't wearing one.'

CHAPTER 21

'What did you make of the boys, then?' Honor said when they were on the pavement.

'I'm determined to talk to the younger one. He knows something. It may not be relevant. But he knows something.'

'So, back to the nick?'

'Let's see if Mrs Reilly's at home for visitors.'

This time, there was a response to Dania's ring. The door opened and the blonde woman she'd glimpsed the day before put her head round the side. Seeing the detectives, her face broke into a smile and she opened the door wide.

She was taller than average, with a lean muscular body that suggested her spare time was spent in the gym. Her black leggings and sleeveless top were covered in sparkles, although the top was a size too small and struggled to contain her breasts.

'I was wondering when you'd call on me, Detective Inspector,' she said in a husky Scottish voice. Her soft brown eyes were expertly lined in black, with long lashes thick with mascara. Close up, her complexion was flawless; she was one of those lucky women who needed only a trace of foundation.

'I'm Detective Sergeant Dania Gorska. And this is Detective Constable Honor Randall.' They produced their warrant cards. 'We'd like to talk with you, if that's possible, Mrs Reilly.'

'Of course. Do come in,' she said, stepping back.

She led the way down a narrow corridor and through a door on the left.

There was little in the room other than a three-piece suite crowding round a two-bar electric fire, and an old television in the corner. The dark carpet had seen better days, as had the cream-coloured flocked wallpaper, which showed lighter patches where pictures had once hung. The only thing on the wall was a Jack Vettriano print of a woman in a dressing gown, staring out of a window. A vase made of cloudy yellow glass stood on the television, the scent from its white freesias filling the room.

'Would you like something to drink?' Mrs Reilly said. 'I've got some cava in the fridge.'

Dania took out her notebook. 'We're on duty, I'm afraid.'

'In that case, please make yourselves comfortable.'

The detectives took the settee while Mrs Reilly settled herself in the armchair. She sat back, crossing her legs, and looked at them expectantly. 'I'm assuming you've not come here for a blether, officers.'

'It's about Dr Frederick,' Dania said.

'Yes, I heard it on the news. And I've seen the reporters.'

'Did you know him well?'

'Well enough. I spoke to him a couple of times when I was in my garden, and he was in his.'

'What about his wife and children?'

'She's a nice lady although, between you and me, she's a bit of an airhead. But she always says hello when she sees me. The boys are typical teenagers.' Mrs Reilly sniffed. 'Whatever their parents are paying that posh school of theirs is money down the pan.'

'Oh?'

'No manners. The older one anyway. Manners are supposed to make the man, aren't they?' She hesitated. 'The younger one is different.' She smiled as though sharing a secret with herself. 'He knows when to say "thank you".'

'Can you remember where you were last Friday, Mrs Reilly? That's June the third.'

'I had a guest, so I was here at home.'

'A guest?'

The woman gazed at her. 'I offer a particular type of personal service, which is greatly appreciated by men of a certain age.'

Dania was skilled at keeping her expression neutral. 'And what time were you performing this service on Friday?'

'Various times.'

'With the same guest?' Honor said, blinking.

'This particular guest books the entire day. Actually, Friday's my day off, but I made an exception this time.'

'We're particularly interested in the period between twelve p.m. and one p.m.,' Dania said.

'Ah yes, we were definitely upstairs.'

Honor shifted in her seat. Dania could see the girl was wondering how much of this she should be writing down.

'I was at the bedroom window, pouring him another whisky,' Mrs Reilly went on. 'He likes a small glass and a good rest before trying it again. He's in his mid-seventies, you see. Most times he visits, he's happy with a chat and a cuddle, where I stroke his private parts. But, on the rare occasions when this makes his wee man stand up, he's so delighted he goes for a repeat performance. Anyway, as I said, I was at the window when I heard an unfamiliar sound. I looked out and saw a strange car coming into the Fredericks' drive.'

'Strange in what way?' Dania said.

'It wasn't the usual type of car that comes to see Dr Frederick. I know what sounds they make. Which is why I noticed this one. It was one of those old cars you don't see much on the roads these days. I don't know the make.' She shrugged. 'I'm a woman.'

'What colour was it?'

'A sort of emerald green.'

'I don't suppose you could estimate more exactly the time it arrived, could you?'

The woman shook her head.

'Was it nearer one p.m., for example?'

'Hard to tell. But it was the doctor's last patient,' she said with confidence.

Dania glanced up from writing. 'How do you know?'

'Because, a short while later, I heard the car start up again, and it came back down the drive with the doctor in it.'

The detectives stared at her.

'You're sure?' Dania said softly.

'Whoever arrived in that green car, Sergeant, left with him.'

'How long was there between the car arriving and the car leaving?' Honor said.

'Not long. I'd say a matter of minutes. I was putting ice into the whisky when I heard the engine again.'

'Can you show us which window you were looking through?' Dania said.

'Surely.' She sprang to her feet and led the way into the corridor.

Dania and Honor followed her as she took the narrow stairs on her toes, two steps at a time.

The bedroom was crowded out by a queen-sized bed covered with a white linen bedspread. A dressing table stood in front of the window. On the bedside table, next to a jumbo-sized jar of Vaseline, were two mannequin heads, one wearing a dark wig, the other a wig in orange-red. There was such a strong scent of lemon air freshener that Dania wondered how the woman's clients were able to perform.

Mrs Reilly went to the window. 'You can see everything from here, Sergeant.' She stepped back, motioning to them to take a look.

The drive curved round sharply and nothing of the back was visible.

She peered over Dania's shoulder. 'Whoever was at the wheel turned the car round behind the house, where the surgery is, and came back down the drive.'

The hedge between the drive and Mrs Reilly's garden was low enough that, from this angle, it would be possible to see the passenger, although not the driver, of any vehicle leaving the house. The angle, however, was too steep to give a view of the registration number.

'So you didn't see who was at the wheel when the car arrived?' Dania said, turning to the woman.

'I'm afraid I wasn't looking. But when they left, the doctor was sitting in the front passenger seat. He was holding his red suitcase on his lap. I think he was dozing. He had a baseball cap over his face.'

'What was he wearing?'

'A brown suit. He wears it a lot. He'd obviously forgotten to cancel his taxi, because it came a short while later.'

'You were still at the window when the taxi arrived?'

She pressed the palms of her hands together. 'Cyril had found a new lease of life and was pumping away gently behind me. When he does it standing up, I have to brace myself against this dresser or I fall over. I got a good view of what happened. The taxi driver tried the front door. Then she went round the back. When she returned, she had a face like fizz. Although I couldn't hear anything, I could see she was mouthing a few expletives. And then she got into her car and drove off.'

'What do you think was going on?'

'The doctor had forgotten to cancel his cab. Someone came to collect him. I thought nothing of it.'

'Why?'

'I knew he was going to a conference. David told me.'

'Who's David?'

The woman looked directly at Dania. 'David Frederick. His son.' Her gaze strayed to the garden below. 'This house used to be owned by the Fredericks. It was built as a sort of granny flat for the old lady, the current Dr Frederick's grandmother.' Mrs Reilly gestured to the hedge that divided the gardens. 'The reason the privet is so low is so they could see when the old lady was in her garden. And look there.' She pointed towards the back. 'There's a gate. They'd use that to pop over from their garden into hers.'

'Convenient,' Honor said.

'You've been very helpful, Mrs Reilly,' Dania said. 'We may have a few follow-up questions, if that's all right.'

'Well, you know where I work,' the woman said without a shred of irony. 'But I'm not sure I can tell you any more.' She glanced at her watch.

'Expecting someone?' Honor said.

'A guest.' Mrs Reilly's eyes lit up. 'This one's good to me. He buys me fancy shoes.' She gestured to her shiny spike-heeled sandals. 'I've got red ones like Judy Garland's. He likes putting them on me and then taking them off. The only downside is that he's a wee bit obese. I have to give him oral relief.'

'We won't hold you up any longer,' Dania said. 'One last question. Did you socialise with the Fredericks? Did they have you over to dinner?'

The woman's wide mouth went slack.

'You see, we're trying to get a handle on who their friends are.'

'Well, I've noticed cars draw up of an evening, and I assumed they were friends come to dinner, but of course they would never invite someone like me. So, no, I can't help you there.'

Dania wondered about Mrs Reilly's circumstances. The absence of photos suggested she had no family. Not even someone who might once have been Mr Reilly. Honor caught her gaze and signalled that she was ready to go.

They followed the woman downstairs.

'You've got an interesting accent, Sergeant. Is it German?'

'It's Polish,' Dania said, remembering how the same remark to her mother would leave a bitter taste beneath her tongue.

'You'll be interested in the results of our referendum, then. How do you think the vote will go?'

'I'm afraid I've really no idea.'

The woman opened the door, stepping back so they could inch past.

Wheezing up the path was a jovially huge roly-poly man, with blue eyes and feathery white hair. He was wearing patched workman's trousers, and a flannel shirt open at the neck. As he passed, Dania caught his sour cheesy smell. He didn't give the detectives a second glance.

'Hello, sweetie,' Mrs Reilly said in a caressing voice.

'Hello, cupcake,' they heard him reply as the door closed.

'Quite a foxy lady,' Honor said, grinning. 'I'm used to collaring underage Kings Cross toms, who offer knee tremblers. With that athletic build, she's wasted on old men.'

'They might not agree with you.'

'I wonder what she charges.'

'So what do you think?' Dania said as they reached the Skoda.

'That green car's the best lead we've had to date.'

'Sounds as though the doctor was overpowered at the back of the house and bundled into it. Whoever did it was confident enough to get close to him. That suggests he knew his assailant, which explains the blow to the front and not the back of the head.'

'And then the perp put the red suitcase on the doctor's lap and rammed a baseball cap over his face.'

Dania opened the car door. 'Not leaving the suitcase behind made it look as though he'd gone to Glasgow, so his wife wouldn't raise the alarm when she returned from Edinburgh. That gave him time to dispose of the doctor and take his body to Backmuir Hall.'

'Well planned, then,' Honor said, getting in at the passenger side. 'Got to hand it to him.'

Dania started the engine and put the Skoda into gear. 'It's the motive that's getting me.' She pulled away slowly. 'Both for the doctor and for Judith.'

'Okay, so Mrs Frederick said her husband didn't know Judith.'

'We can't trust that statement, Honor. But here's something. We know the laird set up committees to tackle issues like drugs and drug-related crime. We also know that Judith was involved in student-welfare issues. If the doctor was invited on to the laird's committees, maybe Judith was too.'

'They might have met that way, sure. But I don't see the relevance. Why kill two people who are on the same committee?'

'It's the only connection we have so far.'

'Did you catch Mrs Frederick looking at her son when she talked about all that?'

'I was more interested in David's reaction when his brother mentioned Mrs Reilly.'

'Yep,' Honor said, grinning. 'Furtive wasn't in it. Hold on. You don't suppose? I mean, you're not suggesting—'

'He knows when to say "thank you". Those were Mrs Reilly's words.' Dania smiled. 'I wonder what he was thanking her for?'

When there was no reply, she risked a glance at Honor. The girl was looking at her with an expression of amusement in her eyes.

Sir Graham Farquhar paid off the taxi, which had stopped a short way from his house. Seeing the posse of reporters rushing towards him, he decided that the best course of action was to give a brief statement.

'Good evening,' he said, striding towards them.

'Sir Graham, can you tell us what you think is happening here?' someone shouted.

'I'm just back from a few days in Paris, where I heard the dreadful news. I'm afraid there's nothing more I can tell you at this stage.'

As he made to go, a woman's voice shouted, 'Did you know Dr Frederick?'

'I've nothing further to add.'

Ignoring the questions hurled at him, he pushed past the crowd and let himself into the hall. He left the suitcase in the corridor and went into the study, which had the advantage of looking out on to the back. Reporters camping on your doorstep was the unfortunate price you paid for having a corpse on your land, but at least they hadn't ringed the building. Except that, knowing how tenacious the press are, it was simply a matter of time. He flopped down into the armchair, leant back and pulled up the footrest.

He'd been in the bathroom in Paris's Le Bristol, tweezing the hairs out of his nose, when he got Blair's call about Dr Frederick. The emotion in the detective's voice was somehow magnified over the ether, and it had taken him a while to calm the poor man down. He could imagine the rumpus at the police station. A second body turned the investigation into more than the sum of its parts. That's if television police dramas were to be believed.

A great weariness descended. He was too tired to pick up Tippex from his neighbour in Muirhead. He rose and, pouring himself a double Talisker from the decanter on the tallboy, took it to the armchair. Whisky was a drink in which he was increasingly taking solace. He sipped for a while, and then downed the rest.

Closing his eyes, he steeled himself to whatever the Fates had decreed for him.

Marek was aware from the sound of movement in the flat that Danka was in. He was taking his jacket off when he heard her speaking to someone in the kitchen. He paused. Had she brought a guest home?

He was about to go in when he heard her say, 'I've got to run, Tony. Marek's back.'

Tony? She was keeping in touch with him?

He made a noise in the corridor, and shouted, 'Did you remember the Wyborowa, Danka? I totally forgot.'

'I didn't hear you come in,' she said, poking her head round the door. She smiled. 'And, yes, I've stocked up on vodka. It's in the freezer.'

'Fantastic.'

'We need to celebrate your big splash in *The Courier.*'

'Ah, yes,' he said shyly.

'Although I think we could do something a bit fancier, maybe at the weekend.'

He followed her into the kitchen.

'Kitchen or dining room?' she said. 'Your choice.'

'Let's stay here. It means we don't have to keep coming back for things.' He reached into the freezer and took out the vodka. 'I heard you speaking to someone and thought you'd brought a guest home,' he said, pouring and handing her a glass.

'I was on the phone to Tony.'

Marek's gaze met hers. 'You're still in touch with him?'

'Evidently.'

'Why?'

She drank down the vodka before speaking. 'Why not? We're still friends.'

'Best way to be, I suppose.' He frowned. 'The divorce has been finalised, I take it?'

'That was done before I left London. It's in the past.'

'But Tony isn't.'

'As I said, we've remained friends.'

There was something in the way she held her shoulders back proudly that brought a dull ache to his chest. He had been gutted when he'd heard the marriage was over. He and Tony had hit it off from the start. Not only could the man match him vodka for vodka, he had the same mischievous sense of humour as Danka, which is why Marek thought they were such an excellent match. Tony was tall and handsome, with a roguish smile. Every woman's dream. Was his sister still in love with him?

'Has he found someone, Danka?' Marek said softly.

'I think so. I can't imagine him staying single for long.'

'You need to do the same,' he said, raising an eyebrow.

'I've only been here a few weeks.' She smiled. 'You need to give me a bit of time.'

He downed the vodka, and poured another for them both.

'So tell me about it,' she said, laying the table. 'Your article.'

'Have you read it?'

'Of course. I'm no expert, but I'd say it was prize-winning stuff. So, what sort of reaction has there been?'

The vodka had made his mind relax and he told the story beautifully. Since the morning, his editor's phone hadn't stopped ringing. Radio Tay and Radio Scotland wanted him on, and there had been interest from a couple of chat shows on STV. More interestingly, he'd had a phone call from Dr Peterkin.

'The lady you interviewed?' Danka said. 'So what did she want? To offer you a place on the course, after all?'

'She wants to see me. I've arranged to meet her.'

He watched Danka's lips curve into a smile. 'A date?' she said.

'A drink.'

'Why not a date? She's a beautiful woman.'

'How do you know she's beautiful?'

'She came to Ninewells to identify Judith Johnstone.'

After a silence, he said, 'You know, when you told me last night that another body had been found, I couldn't believe it. Something very nasty is going on, Danka. Dundee's seen nothing like this.' He hesitated. 'Can you tell me if this second murder was like Judith's?'

'There'll be a press briefing tomorrow. So, when are you going to be on the radio?'

'I've no idea. My editor is arranging everything.'

She looked at him strangely, but said nothing.

When dinner was over, they stacked the plates and left them to soak in the sink.

'Are you going to practise tonight, Danka?'

'I'll get up early tomorrow. Shall we listen to some music?'

'Gladly. What will it be?'

'*Tosca*, I think, but just the first act.'

In the living room, he selected the 1953 EMI recording with Maria Callas and Giuseppe Di Stefano. Callas was the only soprano he could listen to without getting a migraine, and this recording was considered by many to be her best.

They were sprawled on the sofa, listening to the love duet, when Danka said, 'Can I ask you something, Marek?'

His eyes were closed. 'Mmm?'

She got up and went into the corridor. When she returned, she was holding a photograph. It was of a man in a short-sleeved polo shirt, standing in front of Capri's famous rock formation, the Faraglioni.

'Do you recognise him?' she said.

'Why do you ask?' Marek glanced up. 'Is this the man who was killed?'

'The picture will be in the papers tomorrow but, yes, this is the man who was killed. His name's Dr Adam Frederick.'

Marek stared at the photograph. 'You wanted to ask me something,' he said without looking up.

'Did you see him at your Druid meeting?'

His head shot up in surprise. 'You think he was a Druid?'

'Was he?'

He dropped his gaze back to the photo. 'There were many people on the beach that night, Danka. I didn't see everyone's face.'

'You see, I'm trying to establish what connects Judith Johnstone to Adam Frederick.'

'And you think they were both Druids?'

She ran her hands down her jeans. And he knew what she was going to ask him. 'Marek, am I right in thinking you were wearing a body-cam?'

'I might have been.' It was a stupid remark, because it was obvious he must have been.

'May I see the footage?'

He hesitated. 'It's with my editor.'

'Do you think he's likely to let me view it?'

'I doubt it. We have a policy about images taken with body-cams.' He could see the muscles in her throat tightening. If they kept this up, she was liable to say something they'd both regret. 'You can always get a warrant, Danka.'

This was definitely the wrong thing to say.

'So you're refusing?' she said, her face set in anger.

'Not me. The editor,' he said lamely. After a pause, in which she glared at him in such a way that he was forced to say something, he added with more than a trace of asperity, 'Why not apply for a warrant?'

'Because we'd never get one. There's no evidence to suggest that Adam was a Druid.' There were spots of colour on her cheeks. 'It really would help the investigation if I could see that footage.'

'And if you find the doctor on it, and you act accordingly, at some stage you'll have to declare where the information came from.' He closed his eyes. 'We agreed at the outset that we'd try to help each other, but not do anything we shouldn't.'

'Will you ask your editor? You can at least do that.'

'I can try. He keeps that sort of thing in his safe, in case you're wondering.'

She looked away, and he was impressed at how quickly she got her temper under control. 'Thanks,' she said. 'I wouldn't have asked but, if someone is targeting these Druids, we need to do something about it. Warn them, perhaps.'

He felt a sudden uneasiness as he thought of the gentle Dr Peterkin, and Neil, the former soldier with the childlike eyes who'd wished him luck on his summer course. Were these people in danger?

'I'm off to bed,' Danka said. 'I'll see you at breakfast.'

He sat staring at the photo long after she'd gone. He was already wondering how he would tell her that she wouldn't be viewing the footage. His editor would never allow it. And Marek had no intention of asking him. It would feel like a betrayal.

He continued to gaze at the photo. Dr Adam Frederick smiled out at him. Marek remembered him well. The last time he'd seen him was at Monifieth. The man had given him a long wooden torch and then had touched the tip with his own, lighting it.

CHAPTER 22

'Why can't you tell us if the murders of Adam Frederick and Judith Johnstone are linked?' the journalist with the thick-framed glasses was demanding.

Dania, standing at the back of the room they used for press briefings, glanced at her watch. It was now 11.30 a.m. and the meeting showed no signs of ending. The reporters were giving the DI and DCI a hard time. Dania didn't envy them. Briefing the press required skirting the minefield of questions and giving out enough information that might move the investigation forward and address the public interest, while keeping back whatever might help the killer evade justice. Chirnside was sitting in an attitude of defeat, and not making a very good fist of dealing with the queries. DCI Ireland was faring better. She fielded the questions the way a tennis pro swats back the ball. Dania and Honor had come along in case anything helpful came out of the questioning, but it was increasingly looking like a waste of their time.

The first thing Dania had done when she'd arrived for work was to check the crime-scene photographs, specifically the close-ups of Adam Frederick. She'd rung Kimmie, who had looked through the victim's effects, even rummaging through the pockets. They were left in no doubt: there was no wedding ring.

Honor was fidgeting. She wanted to get back to the incident

room where they'd left Laurence looking through the traffic cameras. The three of them had spent the morning scouring the major roads between Invergowrie and the Backmuir Estate. Whoever had taken Dr Frederick would have had to cross the A90 to get to the hall, and the most direct route necessitated taking the A85 and skirting the roundabout at Dundee Technology Park. Their problem was the lack of hard data. An old car in emerald green wasn't the most helpful of descriptions. They'd discussed the type of old cars you still see on the roads and, with the help of the Internet, had drawn up a list, complete with photographs. But all they'd achieved was the discovery that, in the space of an hour, Honor could work her way through two boxes of toffees.

Dania caught the girl's eye and signalled they should creep out.

In the incident room, they found Laurence frowning at the screen. He looked up briefly, and shook his head. Dania decided to leave him to it. He was better at this type of work than most, as he had that completer-finisher streak that meant he didn't cut corners. No wonder Fergus had wanted him.

She steered Honor to her desk. 'While Laurence is grafting away, Honor, let's you and I try something else.'

The girl leant forward conspiratorially, a gleam in her eye.

'Are you still monitoring Judith's emails?' Dania said.

'Well, I never really monitored them. The techie at the uni let me see a few, but that was all. He didn't give me full access.'

'Did you get on well with him?'

'Oh yes, like, I mean, he's hot. Got these big bedroom eyes.'

'We could ask for a warrant to get access to their server, but that'll take time. Or . . .' Dania let the sentence hang.

'We could ask *him*. But why the sudden interest?'

'I want to see the email list that Judith set up for the Druid Grove.'

The girl's expression cleared. 'Ah, I get you now. You think the doctor might have been on it?'

'It's worth checking.'

'Do you really think he was a Druid?'

'We need to rule it out.'

'We could ask Mrs Frederick.'

'She may not know.'

Honor grinned. 'No secrets between a husband and wife, eh?'

'What we could ask Mrs Frederick is whether her husband was out the night before he was killed. Although, if he visits patients, that may not tell us very much.'

'So what happened the night before?'

'The Druids met at Monifieth.'

Park Place had the advantage that it was within easy walking distance of West Bell Street, which was just as well, as it was a narrow road with double yellow lines on both sides. Roughly halfway along, behind black iron railings, was the Scrymgeour Building, a three-storey structure in red ashlar, which housed Dundee University's Computing Centre. To Dania, it looked like a Victorian institution for young offenders.

She and Honor pushed through the double wooden doors into the reception. It was staffed by a young woman with puppy eyes and long hair swept over one shoulder.

'We'd like to talk to Mr Zack Hedison, the systems manager,' Dania said, showing her warrant card.

'I'll check whether Dr Hedison is in.' The woman picked up the phone.

A few moments later, a man in a red shirt, black satin waistcoat and black leather trousers sauntered along the corridor. He had white-blond hair combed high off his forehead into a duck's tail.

Seeing the women, his face broke into a huge grin. 'I'm Zack Hedison. How can I help you ladies?' His gaze lingered on Honor's face a fraction longer than politeness allowed, making Dania suspect that things had moved on from simply looking at emails.

'Dr Hedison, I'm Detective Sergeant Dania Gorska. I think you already know DC Randall. Can we talk in your office?'

'Sure. Please follow me. And call me Zack.' He led the way along the corridor into a small, overheated room. There was nothing there except a desk, moulded plastic chairs, and a table at the window on which sat a blue Tassimo coffee machine. No filing cabinet. No shelves groaning with manuals. The paperless age had arrived.

'Please take a seat,' he said, indicating the chairs. 'So, what can I do for you?'

'It's about Judith Johnstone,' Dania said.

'Uh huh,' he said, leaning back.

'Is her account still open?'

'As far as I know.' He tapped at the keyboard. 'It's scheduled to be closed at the end of the month.' He glanced up enquiringly. 'But I can keep it open if you like.'

'Please, would you? Now, I'm particularly interested in the mailing lists she set up. Can you help us with that?'

'Sure. Any list in particular?'

'How many did she have?'

'Quite a few. Most academics set up a list for each of their courses. Then there are lists to do with their research. Here, take a look.' He swivelled the screen round to face them. There were several groups. Fortunately, Judith had been one of those people who gave them meaningful names.

'It's this one,' Dania said. 'Grove.'

'Grove?' Zack repeated, gazing at her.

She knew that, as systems manager, he could look through the emails at his convenience, so she saw no point in hiding anything. 'Judith was a Druid,' she said. 'And that information is classified.'

His gaze sharpened, but he said nothing.

'Could I see who's on that list?' When he hesitated, she added, 'I really do need to. It's part of our murder investigation.'

The last thing she wanted was to threaten him with a warrant, but she'd guessed correctly that he wanted to help. He moved the screen back and, tapping rapidly, said without looking up, 'Do you want a printout, or a file?'

'A file, please.'

He inserted a USB stick and, a few keystrokes later, removed it and handed it to her. 'It's a long list. And only a few of the members have entered their full names. See here?' He turned the screen round again.

The email addresses were listed, one per line.

'Is there anyone you're looking for?' he said.

'Adam Frederick.' She scanned the list. 'But his name isn't here.'

'Ah, he's the one who was found hanging?' He checked something in another window. 'He's not got a university account.'

She saw it then. And froze, staring.

'You've got a strange look on your face, Detective Sergeant.'

A smile flickered on his lips. He had large hazel eyes that exuded warmth. She could see why Honor was so smitten.

'This one here,' Dania said, pointing to Ailsa McLaughlin's name. 'Can you tell me if there's been any recent activity on her account?'

A slight frown appeared on his face. For a second, Dania thought he would refuse her request, but then he said, 'I know that name from somewhere.'

'Maybe the papers, or the radio. She's a schoolgirl who went missing a while back.'

'When, exactly?

'She was last seen on April the twenty-ninth.'

'A few messages have arrived in her mailbox since then.' He glanced at her. 'Do you want to read them? Okay, I can see by your face. Let me have that stick and I'll transfer them.'

Dania held her breath. This was more than she'd hoped for. But she was too impatient. 'What do they say, Zack?'

'Read them for yourself,' he said smoothly. 'But I suggest you come round to this side. Saves me having to keep turning the screen round.'

She moved her chair next to his, close enough to get a waft of his citrusy cologne. Honor sat on his other side, her thigh touching his.

The emails were messages from Judith and were mostly about what the Grove would be doing next, and where they would be meeting. Some had links to reading material. Dania did her best to hide her disappointment.

Honor pointed to Ailsa's email address. 'This isn't your usual Gmail or Hotmail account. It's a Dundee Uni account.' She glanced at Zack. 'How come a schoolgirl has an account with you?'

He shrugged. 'We set them up for sixth-formers at the request of a staff member. I'm guessing it was Judith Johnstone who asked.'

'Ailsa was enrolled on a course in the coming session,' Dania said. 'And I think also on the institute's summer school.'

'That'll be it, then.'

'And can you tell me if there have been any emails *sent* from this account since April the twenty-ninth?'

A few moments later, he sat back, blowing out his cheeks. 'Nothing. She's not logged in to check her mail. And she's not set her mail to be forwarded to another account. The last time she logged in was *on* April the twenty-ninth, and it was to send a message to Judith Johnstone. Here, take a look.'

Ailsa was thanking Judith for all the advice she'd given her, and was greatly looking forward to her course at the Institute of Religions and Belief Systems. She hoped she'd be seeing her in the evening, at the meeting of the Grove.

'She was a Druid as well?' Zack said with a question in his voice.

'What about the other girl who went missing with Ailsa? Kerry Campbell. Does she also have an account with you?'

He checked. 'No. But that doesn't mean she's not on any of the mailing lists with a Hotmail or other account.'

'Can you do something for me, Zack?'

'Your wish is my command,' he said theatrically.

'Can you keep Ailsa McLaughlin's account open for now? And is it possible to flag it up in such a way that, if she logs in, you're notified?'

'Not difficult for a man of my limited talents,' he said with a sclf-deprecating smile. He tapped away. 'Done.'

Dania gave him her card. 'Will you contact me the instant it happens?'

'Sure.' He held up a hand. 'Wow. Talk of the devil. A message has just landed in her mailbox.'

They stared at the screen. 'I'll be damned,' Honor said. 'It looks like it's been sent to the entire Grove list.'

'That's the thing about email lists, honey-bun. People reply without thinking. They rarely cull the list to remove old addresses.'

The message was from someone called Murdo. There was to be a meeting of the Grove on Saturday 11 June at 8 p.m. The venue was still to be announced.

Dania stared, her mind in turmoil.

'You've got that strange look again,' Zack said. 'It's like a rabbit in headlights but without the terror.'

'Thanks,' she said automatically. She got to her feet. 'We need to be going.'

'So soon? I was hoping to offer you coffee.' He nodded towards the Tassimo. 'That's my latest acquisition. I like experimenting with the settings.'

She smiled. 'Maybe another time.'

He stood up. 'I'll hold you ladies to that.'

He picked up a carrier bag and accompanied them along the corridor. Before they parted company, he slipped the bag into Honor's hand.

'So, what's in there?' Dania asked when they were outside.

The bag contained two large tins of toffees.

'You've been busy, honey-bun.'

'He told me he could smell toffee on my breath and must have guessed I like the stuff.'

Dania was about to make a comment that he must have been standing very close to smell her breath, but decided against it.

'Pity about that,' Honor said glumly.

'What?'

'I was hoping we'd find clear evidence that Adam was a member of the Grove.'

'His email address might still be in there. Do you think, when people join the Grove, they give their real names?'

'Ailsa did. But I see what you're saying. They may make up a name and a special email to go with it. Not everyone wants others, even Druids, knowing who they are.'

'The obvious way to establish whether the doctor was in the Grove is to ask one of the members. But that may not help us if he went incognito. Or in disguise.'

'We're back to getting hold of his laptop, Sarge.'

'And that means waiting for the court order.'

'I think I know what the hold-up is. We've locked horns with that magistrate before. She's nasty-fussy when it comes to protecting private records, specially of people who aren't connected with the case.'

'And Mrs Frederick won't tell us anything.'

As they walked down Park Place, Honor said, 'Sarge, I didn't want to say anything back there, but why the interest in Ailsa and Kerry? They're not missing. They're in London.'

'That's just it,' Dania said. 'I don't believe they are.'

'Because?'

'Let's say it's a gut feeling. And I always act on those.'

'And what action is your gut telling you to take?'

'The obvious one.' She looked at Honor speculatively. 'Have you ever attended a Druid meeting?'

They'd reached the Nethergate. 'Shall we get a sandwich somewhere?' Dania said.

'Yep,' Honor said. 'I need to reboot myself.'

'Where do you fancy?'

'The nearest eating place is the Cup O' Kindness. They do great pulled pork.'

Dania remembered the Cup O' Kindness from when it had been a hotel, one of those Grand Old Dames decorated in Art Nouveau style. It had since fallen on hard times and only the exterior could be described as grand. The ground floor had been remodelled: the lounge and reception were gone, the bar had been expanded, black and chrome furnishings installed and walls painted grey – which seemed to suit the young clientele – and wide picture windows put in. The extensive kitchens meant they could serve meals as well as drinks. What went on upstairs in the former hotel's bedrooms was anyone's guess. She'd heard they were to be stripped out and the first floor transformed into a casino, but no one believed that, and the rumour mill continued to grind. The current whisper was that the whole building was about to be converted into deluxe apartments.

The caramel smell of real ale, mingled with the odour of roasting meat, greeted them as they entered the room.

'What are you having?' Honor said.

'Soda water.'

'Two soda waters, please.'

The barman was a great brute of a man with stubbled cheeks and a shaven head. 'Coppers, eh?' he said, gazing at them without blinking.

Honor eyed him suspiciously. 'Excuse me?'

'Well, when two fit-looking women don't order alcohol, they must be coppers on duty. I get many of you lot coming in for our specials. Two pulled porks, is it, then?'

'I suppose so,' she said in a small voice.

Dania picked up the drinks. 'Have you ever thought of becoming a detective?'

He winked. 'Take a seat, officer, and I'll bring the porks over.'

They took a table by a window. The clouds shifted suddenly, and sunlight streamed in, spangling the wall opposite.

'I thought I looked quite normal,' Honor said. 'Is it that obvious we're coppers?'

'It's stamped on our foreheads.'

Minutes later, the pulled pork sandwiches arrived. The women ate quickly, without speaking. Dania was anxious to get back to the station and make a start on the addresses on the Grove's email list.

'I got that information you were after, Sarge,' Honor said, wiping her fingers. She dropped her voice. 'The laird's movements on the day the doctor was killed.'

'What time was the flight?'

'Nine-thirty p.m.'

'And the taxi?'

'It arrived at five-thirty p.m. The cab driver remembers taking him, and the airline confirmed he was on board. Given Professor Milo's best guess for time of death as the Friday afternoon or evening, it doesn't really tell us anything.'

'Except that he's not ruled out as a suspect.'

'I can see you're a pint-half-full lady.'

'Even when it's three-quarters empty.' Dania took a gulp of soda water. 'Did we find anything on the doctor's phones?'

'The usual domestic stuff on the landline. We traced the calls on his iPhone to people making surgery appointments, but we couldn't find the last appointment on the day he was taken.' She finished her drink. 'So, what's our next move?'

'We need to keep looking for the link between Judith and Adam. It's our only way into this thing.'

'I notice you use their first names.'

'It's easy to stop thinking of the dead as people otherwise.'

'And these missing girls? You think they're in the mix somehow?'

'I'm sure of it.'

'What does the DI say?'

'He thinks I'm wasting my time.'

And, from the way Honor avoided her gaze and looked deep into her soda water, Dania suspected she agreed with him.

'So, shall we go?' Dania said, finishing her drink.

'Yep.'

As they reached the door, it opened, and they nearly collided with a tall figure.

'Marek!' Dania said.

Seeing her, his mouth formed into a smile.

'Honor, this is my brother, Marek. Marek, my colleague, DC Honor Randall.'

Marek reached out and took Honor's hand. He bowed, and then lifted her hand to his lips, his eyes never leaving her face.

'Pleased to meet you, Detective Constable,' he said, releasing her. 'But surely you're not going?' There was disappointment in his voice.

'I'm afraid so,' Dania said.

'In that case, I won't keep you.' He held the door open, smiling.

'Wow,' Honor murmured when they were outside.

Seeing the expression on the girl's face, Dania decided that, given a choice between a night with Zack or a night with Marek, it would be a close-run thing.

Marek watched the women leave, and then ambled over to the bar and bought a pint of beer. He took it to a table at the wall, and shook open the day's *Scotsman*. It was always useful to see what the opposition were printing, and he set aside time every day to skim the paper. He was lifting the glass to his lips when he became aware that he was being watched. Across the room, a dark-haired man was looking at him as though trying to place him. Marek recognised him instantly. It was the former soldier he'd met at the Druid meeting. He was wearing the same bomber jacket.

'Neil,' he said, lifting a hand.

The man's expression cleared. He picked up his drink and hurried over.

'Mark, is it? How are you getting on? May I join you?'

'Of course.' Marek hesitated. Perhaps this was the time to come clean. 'It's Marek, actually. Marek Gorski.'

Something about the name must have registered, because Neil said slowly, 'Gorski, Gorski.' His expression changed. 'It was you who wrote that article about our Druid Grove. In *The Courier*.'

Marek waited for the inevitable recriminations. If anyone had a right to accuse him, it would be Neil.

'It was fantastic,' he said, wide-eyed and almost breathless. 'I loved it.'

Marek nearly dissolved with relief. It would have hit him harder if he'd let this man down. 'Thank you,' he said, smiling. He lifted the glass to his lips. 'What did you like about it?'

'It was even-handed, for one thing. Not the usual crap I've read about modern Druids. And I loved the way you described the event, the singing, and how we threw the flowers into the sea. It brought it all back to me. I think it will do wonders for the Grove's reputation.'

'Well, *I* think it was a crock of shite.'

The voice came from the adjacent table. A couple of men in ill-fitting suits were sitting nursing their drinks. The one who'd spoken was a bald man with no neck. He wore a gold earring and had an obviously fake tan.

'You're entitled to your opinion,' Marek said, keeping his voice even. It wasn't the first time he'd encountered disapproval of something he'd written – God knows, the articles he was currently writing about the EU referendum could best be described as inflammatory – and he'd learnt that the way to deal with it is not to attempt to defend yourself.

'Well, let me tell you something,' Gold Earring snarled. He paused after each sentence, like a comedian waiting for applause. 'You don't know what you're talking about. A light for our times? What's that supposed to mean?'

'I think this gentleman is qualified to write about what he saw,' Neil said, springing to Marek's defence.

'It's okay, Neil,' Marek murmured. 'I'll handle this.'

'Qualified? You carry on like that and you'll get your head broken.'

'What did you say?' Marek got to his feet. He was conscious that the room had fallen silent.

Gold Earring pushed his chair back. 'You're one of them, aren't you? No wonder you wrote about them in such glowing terms.'

'Whether I am – or am not – a Druid is no concern of yours. But I am a member of the fourth estate, and that means I am committed to writing about what I see.'

The man came round the table and stood in front of him, seemingly unfazed by the fact that Marek dwarfed him. 'You immigrants are a real pain in the proverbials, you know that?' He gripped Marek's arm, and thrust his face into his. 'It'll soon be time for you all to leave.'

Marek stared at the hand until the man took it away.

Gold Earring's mate, a tall blond-bearded man, threw down his drink and stood up. 'Let's go, Gavin. He's got the message.'

'I just don't like the way these journalists think they're royalty,' Gavin said more quietly.

When it was clear he wasn't going to budge, his friend came round the table and, grabbing his arm, bundled him protesting out of the building.

'Cossack,' Marek muttered.

'Are you okay, Mark?'

He turned to see Neil standing staring at him. He was trembling slightly.

'I'm fine.'

'You could have taken them both, no question.' After a silence, he said, 'Well, I'd better be going. It was good to run into you. Maybe we'll see you at a meeting?'

'I'm seriously thinking about it.'

Neil offered his hand, and Marek shook it, appreciating the warmth of the grip.

After the man had left, he made his way to the bar, seeing the nods of approval to left and right. He was glad it hadn't come to blows, but he felt hollowed out by the encounter.

'A vodka,' he growled to the barman.

'Anything to go with it, sir?' the man said, glancing at the packets of peanuts.

'Yes. Another vodka.'

As he sat scanning the pages of *The Scotsman*, his mind harked back to the encounter with Gavin, and the man's threat if he carried on with his articles. But what he kept returning to was the comment about immigrants. *It'll soon be time for you all to leave.*

Yes, it was that that rankled.

CHAPTER 23

'How are we supposed to know which of these email addresses is Adam Frederick's?' Laurence was saying. 'There are over one hundred members on this Grove list.'

They were crowded behind Laurence's desk. As soon as they'd returned to the incident room, one look at his face told Dania that he'd failed to find an old green car anywhere on the traffic cams. The litter of coffee cups suggested that, having skipped lunch in an attempt to crack the problem, he'd now had his quota of caffeine for the month. She hoped that, where he'd failed with the cameras, he might get somewhere with the doctor's address.

They'd eliminated the addresses with names attached but those formed only a small percentage. 'Look at this one,' she said. 'Wotan. How many people are baptised Wotan?'

'How many people are baptised, full stop?' Honor asked.

'We could try something radical. I'm thinking maybe it's in code. Based on an anagram of his name. Or something medical. Perhaps to do with the brain.'

'We could try Tech,' Honor said brightly. 'They have all sorts of software goodies. Maybe one of them will see it as a challenge and be inspired to solve this for us.'

The head of Tech had the temperament of a jellyfish, but her mild-mannered assistant was the smartest techie there, and Dania knew that Laurence was keen on getting to know her better. It might turn out to be a win-win.

'Laurence,' she said, 'why don't you go and charm – what is her name? – Louise, yes. Give her this.' She reached into Honor's carrier bag and took out one of Zack's tins of toffees. 'In my experience, all techies have a sweet tooth, and this offering might persuade her to drop whatever she's doing and work on this for us.' She could feel Honor about to intervene. 'I'm sure DC Randall will make the sacrifice this one time. For the good of the investigation. Won't you, Honor?' she said, turning to the girl.

Honor kept her expression neutral.

Laurence licked his lips. 'Well, if you think I can be of help.'

'I do,' Dania said promptly. She jerked her head towards the door.

He didn't need telling twice. He sprang out of his chair.

After he'd gone, Honor glared at Dania.

'I wouldn't cry too much over the loss of your sweeties,' Dania said smoothly. 'I'm sure there'll be more where those came from.'

Honor's look of outrage turned into a grin.

The door opened and Kimmie breezed in. 'G'day,' she said to no one in particular. She glanced around and, seeing the women, moved towards them in loose-limbed strides.

'I hear you nearly killed a reporter at the crime scene,' Dania said.

'Strewth, you don't believe in verbal foreplay, do you?'

'I take it you know DC Randall.'

'Yeah, we go back,' Kimmie said with a broad smile. 'I've left my report on the DI's desk but he doesn't seem to be in.'

'Is this the report on Backmuir Hall?'

'I can fill you in now, if you like.'

'You're going to tell me you found nothing worth writing home about.'

'That's about the size of it.' She piled her hair on top of her head and then let it drop. 'First off, the area around the crime scene is gravel, so footprints are one mother of a nightmare. There was nothing we could get from the flagpole or the halyard. Some dabs, but they were too smudged and/or overlaid to be of any use. The chemical reagent gave me a few partials but I eliminated them as Sir Graham's. He told me he raises that blue and white flag occasionally.'

'You've got his dabs?' Dania said in surprise.

'I got them yesterday.'

'And the wooden planks?'

'Totally clear of prints. Which is unusual. It's as if someone wanted to remove all trace. What I did find was evidence they'd been coated in bleach. Must have been done not long before the poor bugger was strapped to the thing, as there were also traces of bleach on his clothes.'

'Anything unusual about the wood?'

'They're hardwood boards you can buy in Homebase. Which is where I suspect the perp got them. The nails too.'

'And the flag?'

'No traces of anything except bird shit.'

'What about the stuff in the victim's pockets?'

Kimmie shook her head.

'So what did you make of Sir Graham?' Dania said, studying the girl.

'Charming man, if you like someone with garlic on his breath. He offered to show me those awful metal things. His latest magnum opus looks like gigantic female genitalia.' She glanced at her watch. 'Woops, I've got to dash. The report'll be online by tomorrow, if you care to see the details.' She waved a hand and breezed out.

'I guess we sort of expected a nil return,' Honor said, 'given that's what we had with Judith. So, what now? Do we go to Plan B?'

'I suppose so.'

'What *is* Plan B?'

'No idea.'

Which wasn't strictly true. An idea was forming, but it was nothing Dania could let Honor in on.

Half an hour later, Dania was driving along the rutted road towards Backmuir Hall. Her quest, she'd told Honor, was simply a loose end: she was visiting the laird to ask him for more detail about Adam's and Judith's roles on his committees. What she didn't reveal to the girl was the real purpose of her visit.

Although it was late afternoon and still bright, there was a light on in Backmuir Hall. She parked the Skoda behind the Porsche, and crunched across the gravel. A window was open on the ground floor and the sound of a piano reached her ears. She paused to listen. It wasn't a recording; someone was playing the Mason & Hamlin.

She recognised the music as the Rondo in Beethoven's Piano Sonata No. 21 in C major, but played much more slowly than Beethoven had intended. The pianist was still learning the piece, given the number of times he stopped to practise certain bars. Although Chopin was her great love – she was a Pole, after all – she went weak at the knees at Beethoven's compositions, specifically the second movement of his Piano Concerto No. 1, a piece she'd had to play for an exam. She'd worn out both the keys and her parents, practising those trills. At the end, the examiner had told her, whilst awarding her an A, that it was less about proficiency and more about expression, something she came to appreciate the more she played.

She wondered if she should wait until he'd finished, but decided against it. The front door was open. This time, however, she found the bell pull hidden within the ivy. As she tugged at it, she heard a discordant jangling from deep within the house. The music stopped.

A moment later, Sir Graham appeared. 'Sergeant Gorska, to what do I owe this honour?' He stepped back. 'But do come in, do come in.'

He ushered her into the living room. The light, she noticed, came from the Anglepoise on the piano.

'As you can see, Sergeant, I've been doing a little practising of my own.' He waved a hand as though to signify it was of no importance. 'But how are you getting on? Have you decided what you're going to play at the memorial concert?'

'Not completely, but I'm narrowing it down.'

'Splendid, splendid. Now, may I offer you a drink?' A gleam came into his eyes. 'A little Żubrówka perhaps?'

'I'd love to Sir Graham, but I'm on duty.'

His disappointment was almost palpable. 'A small one just before you leave, then?'

'I'll still be on duty.'

'Ah well. Such is life. So how can I help you? But I'm forgetting my manners.' He gestured to the room. 'Please, do make yourself comfortable.'

'Thank you.' She sat on the edge of the sofa, not wanting to be swallowed up in it.

Sir Graham took the adjacent armchair. He sat hunched forward, hands clasped loosely in front of him, an expectant expression on his face.

'It's about the murder of Dr Adam Frederick.'

For an instant, a fleeting look of panic crossed his face. 'The reporters only left this morning,' he said, rubbing his forehead. 'I can't understand why the poor man's body was displayed here.'

'Did you know Adam?'

This time, Sir Graham made no attempt at pretence. 'Indeed, I knew him well. He was chairman of one of my committees. An excellent chairman too, I should add.'

'Which committee was this?'

'The one dealing with drug-related crime. He was on other committees, but it was as chairman of this one that he made the most impact.'

'In what way?' she said, taking out her notebook.

'He had many practical suggestions. I think it's called thinking outside the box.' Sir Graham threw her a crooked smile. 'I don't know if you've ever sat on a committee full of townspeople, Sergeant, but they can be hard work. If you're really unlucky, you get people who just want to sound off. That's fine as far as it goes, but of course it never goes far enough. You need people of ability, leadership and vision. Adam had those qualities. As did Judith, in fact.'

It was the lead-in Dania had been looking for. 'And was Judith on that same committee?'

'She was vice-chairman. Her role was to liaise with the university.' He played with his hands. 'I must say, Sergeant, that I had hoped the university would do more in this area, as their students are the ones greatly at risk. But I suppose all educational establishments are strapped for cash.' He threw her a tired smile. 'It's been left to the local council to foot the bill.'

'Did Judith and Adam know each other well?'

'As chair and vice-chair, they must have. They will have discussed the agenda beforehand. From what I remember, they worked extremely well together. You could say they were the driving forces on the committee.'

Dania tried to choose her words, but in the end couldn't find a good way of saying it. 'Did they see each other outside the committee?'

'Good heavens. What are you suggesting?'

'I'm wondering if they socialised, that's all. You see, I'm trying to find out what links them. Other than their committee work.'

'I have to confess, Sergeant, I only saw them at committee meetings. If they were, well, seeing each other, to put it delicately, I wouldn't know. But I saw no evidence of anything untoward.'

'When was this committee established?'

'About three years ago.' He raised a tense face. 'Maybe a little less.'

'And who else was on it?'

'Well, people came and went, as I'm sure you'll realise.'

'Would you be able to give me a list of who's on currently?' She saw him hesitate. 'It may help the investigation,' she added, smiling in what she hoped was a reassuring manner.

'I'm sure there won't be a problem. We occasionally find ourselves photographed for the local newspapers so the information must be in the public domain by now.'

'And would I be able to see the agendas and minutes?'

'I don't see why not,' he said thoughtfully. 'Nothing we do is secret. If you could wait a moment, I'll make copies of everything for you. There's a copier in my study.'

'Thank you, Sir Graham.'

He left the room.

As she waited, she wondered what was different from the last time she'd been here, and then realised that the bundle of energy known as Tippex was missing. Probably out chasing rabbits.

A while later, Sir Graham reappeared, clutching a plastic folder. 'I've collated everything for you, Sergeant. You can take it away and peruse it at your leisure.' He lifted his hands in a gesture of supplication. 'Now, are you sure I can't tempt you to a drink?'

'My day hasn't finished, I'm afraid.'

'Pity,' he said, sounding as though he meant it. 'No matter. Maybe another time?'

'Of course. And thank you,' she said, holding up the folder.

'Let me see you out.'

At the front door, she let him kiss her hand, and then strolled towards the Skoda. Conscious that he was watching, she climbed into the car, threw him a wave, and started the engine. A minute later, she was rounding the bend, out of sight of the hall.

A little further on, she cruised over to the side of the road. She cut the engine and got out.

She listened, hearing nothing in the quiet stillness of early evening except a gentle rustling in the undergrowth, and the sound of birds.

Keeping to the edge of the road, she stole back towards the hall, running through various excuses in her head should she meet the laird. But, as she took the curve, she heard the piano again, played more vigorously.

She dropped down behind the Porsche and crept round the side of the house. The flagpole was on her left, minus its flag, which was still with Kimmie. As quietly as she could, she made her way towards the straggle of bushes at the back. There was a path wide enough for a car to pass. And tyre marks that told her a car had passed along here recently.

It was the realisation that Sir Graham took taxis to the airport that made her conclude there had to be a garage somewhere. Of course he wouldn't leave the Porsche out while he was away. Yet nowhere had she seen anything that remotely resembled a garage.

She followed the path until it disappeared behind the bushes. To the left was the screen of trees and, beyond, the laird's rose garden. Ahead was a two-storey redbrick building.

It had two sets of double doors. The ones on the right were wide open, giving her a view of a space large enough to take the Porsche. There was a bench at the back with greasy rags and an old-fashioned oil can. She tried the doors on the left but they were secured with a Yale lock.

The two spaces were separated by a wall of unevenly placed bricks which finished roughly eight feet above the ground, well below the high ceiling, as though the dividing wall had been an afterthought and the builder couldn't really be bothered.

There were foot- and hand-holds everywhere. A glance outside, and she started to climb. She needed only to get up a couple of feet to see over.

As she poked her head over the top, she heard barking. Tippex rushed in, yapping furiously.

'Shush, Tippex,' she said anxiously.

At the sound of her voice, the terrier sat with its paws up. She turned back to the wall. The yapping started up again.

'Will you shut up?' she commanded.

Each time she spoke to Tippex, he assumed the begging position. He returned to making a racket when she continued to climb.

She needed only a couple of minutes. Peering over the top of the wall, she made out the shape of a car. As her eyes became accustomed to the gloom, the lines and detail resolved themselves. It was a four-wheeled convertible in a dark green colour and, although she didn't recognise the make, it looked like the sort of car people drove in the 1930s.

Her heart beating wildly, she pulled the phone out of her pocket and set it to flash. But she needed a better angle. She dropped down into the empty garage, hurried to the back and pulled herself up the wall. Tippex went berserk and dashed round in small circles, yelping loudly.

Straddling the wall, she took several photographs, checking the quality and adjusting the settings. She was pushing the phone into her pocket when she heard the sound of an engine, followed by a car door opening and slamming shut. And footsteps.

'Tippex! What's all that noise about?'

Hearing his master's voice, Tippex rushed out, barking.

'Into the car. Now! Or you'll get run over.'

Dania lay along the top of the wall, not daring to move. There was the sound of a car starting and then, to her dismay, the Porsche reversed into the empty garage. If the laird climbed out, he would see her, and no end of explanation would get her out of this. There was no time to lose. The car was easing inside. She swung her leg over the wall and, clinging to the top to steady herself, dropped down beside the green car, losing her balance and falling against it. Pain shot up her shin, reminding her that the wound from the gin trap still hadn't healed. Fortunately, the sound of the Porsche's engine masked the noise of the fall.

The engine died. A car door opened, and closed. Tippex was yapping furiously.

'What's got into you, old man?' she heard the laird say. 'Go on, outside with you.'

With a deepening sense of unreality, she heard the garage doors pulled shut. She was plunged into darkness. Before she could appreciate what was happening, there was the sound of a key being inserted into the lock, and the lock turning. The doors were rattled once or twice; she heard footsteps on gravel, and then Tippex's barking, which stopped suddenly at a sharp word from the laird.

CHAPTER 24

Dania leant against the Porsche, thinking through her options. She'd spent the last half-hour systematically checking the walls of both garages, and had come to the depressing conclusion that there was no way out. Both sets of doors were locked and, unless she could find a way to open them, she was trapped. All was not lost, however, as, by the light of the phone's torch, she'd discovered that the doors had been fitted with the hinges on the outside.

She debated with herself as to whom to call and, in the end, settled for Honor. The girl shared her suspicions about the laird and Dania reckoned she'd keep this episode to herself.

The phone answered after two rings. 'DC Randall,' came the voice.

'Honor, it's me, Dania.' As briefly as she could, she explained where she was and what she needed Honor to do.

'Cripes,' Honor said. 'What were you doing in there?'

'I'll explain everything but, right now, I need to get out of here. It's just a matter of time before the laird finds my car parked not far from the hall. And he'll start to ask himself what it's still doing there.'

'I'm on my way.' The resolve in the girl's voice was good to hear.

Dania sat on the bench and settled herself to wait, wondering what the oil and dust were doing to her lungs.

A while later, she heard footsteps. She put her ear to the door. 'Sarge? Can you hear me?'

'Loud and clear.'

There was a scraping sound from low down. 'Okay, I'm removing the screws in the bottom hinge. Problem is they're a bastard to shift. Hold on. I've brought the WD40.'

A minute later, Dania heard her say, 'Right, that's the bottom hinge off. I'll try to move the door out a bit and maybe you could slip through. If not, I'll have to work on the top hinge.'

With the sound of wood moving over gravel, the door began to shake and, in the growing light, a pair of workmen's gloves appeared, gripping the edge.

'Get ready to move,' Honor said. She gave the door a yank, and the shaft of daylight widened. 'Can you slip through?'

'I think so.'

Dania got on to her hands and knees and, holding her breath, squeezed through with difficulty.

'Great,' Honor said, grinning. 'I won't have to take the door down. Not sure I'd be able to get it back up, to be perfectly honest.' She replaced the hinge and tightened the screws. 'Seems a pretty insecure arrangement. I doubt his insurance company would pay out if his car was nicked by someone who took the door off.'

'Quite.'

They inspected the hinge.

'It looks okay,' Dania said. 'I'm sure he won't notice that some paint has flaked off. Right, let's get out of here. But first, I want a quick look round the back.'

'What for?'

'The garage doesn't run the whole length of the building. There's something behind it.'

Honor glanced round. 'Okay, Sarge, but let's be quick. It's spooky here. The hairs on my neck tell me that something's in that woodland.'

They hurried behind the garage to the back of the building, which was nothing more than a barn that had seen better days. The high wooden doors were unlocked. Dania tugged them open, and peered inside. To the left, beside a gas cylinder that was secured to the wall with a chain, was a small metal table with welding equipment. The shelving unit behind it held an assortment of leather aprons, jackets, gauntlet-type gloves and protective helmets. Tools, wire brushes and rags were stuffed into the bottom shelves. The place reeked of paint.

'Cripes, he's well set up here. That's a state-of-the-art electric arc machine.'

'How do you know?'

'My brother's a welder.'

'That stuff over there must be what he uses to spray his artwork.'

Aerosols and paint tins were lined up against the wall. Stacked next to them were sheets of sandpaper and heavy-duty plastic, and old blue boiler suits.

'Gawd, take a gander at this violet colour,' Honor said, peering at one of the tins. 'It's positively migraine-inducing. I'd rather have food on my face than wear anything in that. Now *this* is more my colour.' A plastic sheet spattered in pale metallic gold paint was lying crumpled in the corner. She ran her toe over it, smoothing it out.

Dania slipped on a pair of latex gloves and riffled through the boiler suits.

'You looking for anything in particular, Sarge?'

'A grey beanie.'

'Like the one worn by Judith's abductor?'

'There are only baseball caps here.' She straightened. 'Okay, let's go.'

They left the barn, and dragged the doors shut.

Keeping to the bushes, they crept past the hall to where Dania had left the Skoda. Behind it was Honor's Ford Fiesta.

'I'll see you back at the station,' Dania said, getting into the Skoda. She sent Marek a text to say that something had come up and she'd be home late.

A quarter of an hour later, she hurried into West Bell Street station. Honor was already at her desk. There were several other officers in the room, and Dania signalled to the girl to follow her into the corridor.

Without a word, she pulled out her phone and showed Honor the photos of the green car.

'Woah, Sarge,' the girl murmured. 'That is totally brilliant.'

It was after eight when Marek heard the front door open. He glanced up from the laptop. Danka strolled into the kitchen and hung her bag on the door hook.

'I'm sorry I'm so late, Marek.'

He gazed at her clothes. 'What on earth happened to you? You've got stuff all over your jacket. And your knees.'

'It'll brush off.' She flopped down in the chair opposite.

Something in her expression warned him against asking questions, and he wondered if a time would ever come when they'd be able to share freely with each other the details of what they'd done during their day.

'Vodka?'

She shook her head. 'I've got a bit of a headache.'

He filled a glass with water, and added ice and lemon. 'Drink this.'

'What would I do without you, Marek?'

He waited till she'd put the glass down. 'I've got something to show you, Danka.' He swivelled the laptop round and pushed it towards her. 'This is the footage of the Druid meeting.'

She looked at him in amazement. 'Your editor agreed to let me see it?'

'I didn't ask him.' He studied her. 'I kept a copy of the film for myself.'

'What made you change your mind?' she said, after a silence.

'You're my sister, and blood is thicker than vodka. If someone is murdering people because they're Druids, he needs to be stopped. I know you'll do the right thing as far as this film is concerned.'

'Thank you. So how do I use this?'

'Here, I'll show you.' He placed his chair next to hers. 'You pause it with this. And slow it down, or speed it up, like this. You'll soon get the hang of it.'

He watched as she started the film and let it run. And, as he followed the scene at the Monifieth beach, he lived it all again: the Druids in their coloured robes, his conversation with the gentle soldier, Neil, the lighting of the torches and the chief torch-bearer's greeting, 'Welcome to our Grove.' And the lament for the murdered Judith Johnstone, the song like a Gaelic psalm, and the final throwing of the flowers into the sea. He closed his eyes, remembering how he'd envied the simplicity of the ceremony and the look of peace on the faces of those attending.

'The people there?' he heard Danka say. 'On that ridge. Were they the ones you were talking about?'

He opened his eyes, seeing the image frozen at the line of people silhouetted by the setting sun. 'Yes. Fortunately there was no trouble.' He hesitated. 'So, did you find what you were looking for?'

'I couldn't see anyone who looks like Adam Frederick.'

After she'd gone to bed, Marek admitted to himself that he hadn't played fair. He had raised his sister's hopes only to have them dashed, because he wanted her not to be angry with him. But perhaps it would have been better had he not shown her the film, because he knew she would never have found the doctor. She'd seen part of his torso, and his hand holding the torch, but the lens of the body-cam was simply too low for her to see his face.

CHAPTER 25

'You mean you can change these so they all have the same green colour as the car in my photo?' Dania said.

'You're looking at an expert in the use of Photoshop, Sarge.' Honor nodded at Laurence. 'This whizz-kid practically invented it.'

With deft mouse movements, Laurence pulled up each image in turn and changed the paintwork of every car to the same shade of green. There were six in all: a Morris Minor, Triumph Herald, MG TD Cabriolet, Lincoln Premiere, Wolseley Hornet and the one in the laird's garage, which Laurence had told them was an Austin 7 Pearl Cabriolet 1935.

None of these had appeared on the traffic cams, but what Dania would settle for was a firm ID on the Austin. Anything to lift the gloom they were feeling, given that, despite Laurence's best efforts and Honor's toffee sacrifice, Louise from Tech had got nowhere deciphering the Grove's email addresses.

'You're a genius, Laurence,' Dania murmured.

'I'll get these printed off.' He hurried out of the room.

Honor lowered her voice. 'Sarge, suppose you find that the Austin's the car that picked up the doctor. How are you going to explain to the DI that you knew Sir Graham has one? Or explain it to Sir Graham himself, for that matter?'

'I'll worry about that when the time comes. I'm making this up as I go along.'

Half an hour later, Dania pulled up a little way from the house. It was quiet outside the Frederick place, which meant either that PC Walsh had chased the reporters off, or they'd found a better story elsewhere. Dania left the car and strolled along the street towards Mrs Reilly's. It was a warm day, and shredded clouds filled a sky that was nearly blue.

The door opened after the second ring and Mrs Reilly appeared, clutching a mobile. She was barefoot, in tight jeans and a loose-fitting red t-shirt, and her blonde hair was scraped back into a severe ponytail. No mascara today, but her wide mouth was carefully made up in matt pink lipstick.

'Sergeant,' she said in surprise.

Dania smiled cheerfully. 'I'm not disturbing you, am I, Mrs Reilly? I thought Friday was your day off.'

'No, you're not disturbing me at all.'

'I've something to show you. May I come in?'

'Of course.' The woman opened the door wide and stepped back. 'Do go through, Sergeant.'

The living room smelt strongly of furniture polish, and Dania suspected Friday was cleaning day.

'Mrs Reilly,' she said when they were seated, 'you mentioned an old green car driving Adam Frederick away last Friday.'

'That's right.'

'I've brought along some photos, and I wondered if you'd look through them and tell me if any of them might be the car you saw.'

Mrs Reilly studied each photo carefully. 'This is it,' she said, holding out the one of the Austin.

'That's definitely the car?' Dania said, making her expression doubtful. She'd played this game with the public before. If they were undecided, then a look of encouragement from a police officer could sometimes make them 'remember' something that wasn't true, causing endless problems down the line. She needed the woman to be 100 per cent sure.

'No doubt about it. I mind that purple hood now that I see it again. It's the kind of car American gangsters used to drive.'

This convinced Dania it was Sir Graham's car that had taken Adam Frederick away last Friday lunchtime. A court, however, would rule it circumstantial, as the laird couldn't be the only person in the UK who owned an Austin 7 Pearl Cabriolet 1935. What she needed was supporting evidence that Sir Graham had visited the doctor on that day, and at that time.

'Thank you, Mrs Reilly. You've been very helpful.'

'Is that all you wanted to ask?' Disappointment, tinged with relief, appeared on the woman's face. She glanced at her watch. 'Maybe you could stay for a quick cup of coffee?'

'I won't, thanks,' Dania said, registering the gesture as one of politeness rather than sincerity. 'I need to get back to the station.'

'Well, maybe another time.'

'Could I use your loo before I go?'

'Surely.'

Dania followed her into the corridor. At the end of the hall-way, an open door led into the kitchen.

'It's down there on the left, Sergeant.'

'Thank you.'

'Please let yourself out when you're done. I need to get on with tidying up upstairs.' She tapped at her mobile as she turned away.

The tiny loo consisted of an old-fashioned chain-pull toilet and a cracked wash-handbasin. The window was open, giving Dania a view of the low hedge between Mrs Reilly's garden and that of the Fredericks.

As she was wiping her hands, she heard a noise outside. She glanced through the window. The gate between the gardens swung open and David Frederick, dressed in skinny jeans and a hoodie, slipped into Mrs Reilly's garden. He paused, looking around furtively, before creeping towards the rear of the house.

She guessed there was a back door out of the kitchen. She also guessed that the teenager was heading towards it.

The kitchen stank of fried fish. To say that the place was in need of modernisation was an understatement. The brown-stained sink, chipped wall cupboards, and freestanding gas oven were beyond redemption. Only the large fridge-freezer looked recently bought. She slipped in beside it, out of sight.

She heard the door open and close.

'Hello, David,' she said, stepping out from her hiding place and putting herself between him and the door. 'Do you remember me? I'm Detective Sergeant Gorska.'

He stood as though paralysed. His eyes darted round the kitchen, and then towards the back door, as though weighing up whether he could make a run for it. Seeing him close up, she was struck by the smoothness of his skin, and guessed he hadn't been shaving long. He had the look of a boy growing too fast.

'Shall we have a little chat?' she said. 'Mrs Reilly's not expecting you, is she? I mean, Friday's her day off.' She paused for effect. 'Or maybe you know that, and that's why you're here.'

The hunted look on his face and the way his shoulders sank told her that her hunch was correct.

'Let's take a little stroll. We don't want to be overheard.'

He nodded, his body language making it clear that he was defeated, and he knew it.

She took his arm and led him out into an unkempt garden, all coarse grass and neglected flowerbeds. It disappeared into thickly packed trees. They walked through the woodland until she was sure they were out of sight of the house, and stopped at a large chestnut encircled by a wooden bench. She released his arm, and motioned to him to sit down.

'How old are you, David?'

'Sixteen.' He looked at her defiantly. 'Old enough, okay?'

But not old enough to be interviewed without an adult present. So she wouldn't interview him. They would have a friendly tête-à-tête. She smiled. 'I'm guessing your family don't know about the recreational visits you pay Mrs Reilly.'

'It's none of their business,' he muttered. He chewed a thumbnail. 'I'm not doing anything illegal.'

'Look, David, I'll be honest with you. I'm not in the slightest bit interested in what you and Mrs Reilly get up to in the privacy of her house.'

'She says she likes it,' he blurted.

'Many prostitutes tell their clients that.' She regretted her words, seeing his look of disappointment. 'Although I can well imagine that you'd be more vigorous than most of the men who buy her services. Do you come here every Friday?'

'As often as I can. She sends me a text first.'

'I'm wondering where you find the money.'

He reacted as though he'd been touched with a cattle prod. 'I only took the cash the first time, okay?'

'From your mother's purse, I'm guessing. And she found out, yes?'

He stiffened, and she knew she had him. 'So what do you do now, David? Use a credit card? Hmm?'

'I don't pay for it any more.'

'Oh?'

290

'She lets me have it for free. Says she likes showing me what to do.' There was a look of pleading in his eyes. 'You won't tell Mum, will you?' he added in a little boy's voice.

Dania took his hand. 'Right now, the only thing I'm interested in is finding your father's killer.'

'I want that as well. I haven't been able to sleep since it happened.'

'Then maybe we can help each other.'

He chewed his nail, his gaze never leaving her face. 'How?'

'I need to know who his last patient was on the morning he disappeared. I don't want to see medical records or anything like that. I just need a name.'

'He has a calendar on his laptop,' David said hopefully. 'Mum and Matthew are out seeing the solicitor. You could come and take a look.'

'I can't go into the house without a warrant.'

'I could invite you?'

'That would still be problematical.'

He sat up. 'Tell you what, I'll bring the laptop out here.'

She glanced at the bulge in his jeans. 'You could leave it with me while you go up and see Mrs Reilly. Then you could take it back to the house. How long do you and Mrs Reilly usually take?' she added delicately.

He looked away. 'That depends.'

She was tempted to ask on what, when he said, 'Do you promise not to tell Mum?'

'All right. As you've pointed out, you're old enough,' she added, smiling.

He smiled back and she saw then that he'd be stunning once he filled out.

'Okay, wait here,' he said.

He returned a few minutes later with the laptop. 'I've powered it up. Dad never uses a password. He hasn't a clue how to set one,' he added with the contempt of youth for their technologically challenged parents.

'That's great, David. Leave it here on the bench. You'd better go up. Mrs Reilly's waiting for you.'

'How much time do you need?'

'I've no idea.'

He thought about this, nodded quickly, and left, running.

After he'd disappeared, she slipped on a pair of latex gloves and lifted the lid of the laptop. She'd expected to have to search for the calendar, but it was open at the day's date: 10 June.

She scrolled back as quickly as she could without making mistakes. The days from 9 June back to 3 June were blocked out with the single word, GLASGOW. This would be Adam's medical conference. But there, on the morning of 3 June, was his last surgery appointment – Sir Graham Farquhar!

She felt a surge of excitement. Finally, something solid. So, had Sir Graham arrived in his Austin with the express purpose of kidnapping and subsequently murdering the doctor? The Porsche would have been recognisable to everyone in the vicinity, but perhaps he rarely used the Austin, and certainly never for his doctor's appointments.

She scrolled back further. And, on Thursday 2 June, she saw the entry that told her who, or rather what, Adam Frederick was: DM Banks, 8.00 p.m.

She stared at the screen, hardly able to control her breathing. Then, almost without having to think, she searched for 29 April. If the entry for 2 June had astonished her, what she saw for 29 April left her dazed – LCM, 8.00 p.m.

29 April: LCM. The same entry that Judith Johnstone had in her paper diary . . .

Dania was still gazing at the screen when she heard footsteps. She laid the laptop on the bench, set the calendar to 10 June and slipped off her gloves.

David arrived, slightly flushed. She felt the moist warmth off him as he sat down.

'Well, did you find what you were looking for, Sergeant?' he said, breathing audibly. 'Did you get the name?'

He'd be able to read it for himself. And she wanted to see his reaction. 'Sir Graham Farquhar,' she said.

'I've never heard of him.'

'He's the laird of Backmuir. Not only was your father treating him, they served on committees together. To do with issues of importance to the town.' She looked into David's eyes. 'The night before your father was killed, do you happen to know if he went out?'

The boy scratched his chin. 'He went to the Druid meeting.'

'You know he was a Druid?' she said, astonished.

'It was our secret. Mum and Matthew didn't know.'

'How long had he been one?'

'About six months.'

'Did you meet any of the Druids? Did your dad bring them home? Or give you any names?'

David shook his head. 'He kept all that to himself.'

'How did you feel about it?'

The boy looked into the distance. 'He explained what it was about, and it made perfect sense. He said it was a way of living closer to nature, and to people. Appreciating simple things. Leaving the shit in the world behind. There was an article in *The Courier*, a day or so ago, about it. The guy who wrote it had it more or less right.'

'Do you think you'll join the Grove?'

'I'd really like to, but they wouldn't have me,' he said, playing with his fingers. 'And I'm not sure I'd make it. I might find the Path, but I'd be straying from it all the time.'

'Then it sounds just the thing for you.' She hesitated. 'If you feel that strongly about something, don't give up on yourself.'

He looked at her appreciatively. 'You're not the sort of cop I expected.'

'And what kind is that?'

'The kind that goes all preachy about what I'm doing wrong.'

'We all do things wrong, David.' She gestured to the laptop. 'I shouldn't have looked at your dad's calendar without authorisation. I wouldn't like anyone knowing that.'

'And I shouldn't have gone up to shag Mrs Reilly,' he said with a sheepish smile. 'I wouldn't like anyone knowing that, either.'

She slipped her hand into his. 'Tell you what, David. You keep my secret.' She leant into him. 'And I'll keep yours.'

Dania was climbing into the Skoda when her mobile rang.

'Sarge?' Honor said. 'Where are you?'

'About to leave Mrs Reilly's.'

'We've had a call from Ninewells. Professor Slaughter said the tox report's in. He's about to come over to West Bell Street but I reckon that, if you're still at Invergowrie, you could drop in.'

'I'll do that.'

'I'll call him back and let him know.'

'Thanks,' Dania said, cutting off Honor's question. The girl wanted to know if Mrs Reilly had recognised the Austin, but now was not the time.

Fifteen minutes later, Dania was pushing through the doors of Ninewells Hospital. She was directed to Professor Slaughter's office, the route taking her through the kind of maze the ancient

Greeks would have been proud of. She knocked at the door and was directed inside by a familiar booming voice.

'Ah, Sergeant Gorska,' Milo said, getting to his feet and extending a hand. He was in shirtsleeves with his tie at half-mast.

She put her hand in his, and he pumped it hard. 'Thank you for coming over,' he said with an easy smile. 'You've saved me a whole heap of time.'

'I'm glad.'

'Please do take a seat.' He shuffled through his folders. 'I'm sorry this has taken as long as it has, but we've finally identified what killed Dr Frederick.' He opened a folder and scanned the page. 'It's water hemlock. Sometimes known as poison parsnip. I've a picture here.'

He handed across a photograph of a plant with small white flowers arranged in an umbrella shape.

'It's extremely poisonous, Sergeant. It contains cicutoxin, which causes seizures almost as soon as it's swallowed. Other symptoms include nausea, vomiting, abdominal pains, tremors and confusion.'

'And what actually causes death?' she said, staring at the plant and wondering where she'd seen it.

'Respiratory failure and/or ventricular fibrillation. They occur just hours after ingestion.'

'Is it the flowers that are poisonous?'

He traced down the page. 'Cicutoxin is found in all parts of the plant but is concentrated in the roots. And it is at its most potent in spring.'

'Looks like our killer knows what he's doing. Does water hemlock grow locally?'

'As the name suggests, the plant likes wet meadow or marshy areas. And there are plenty of those around here.'

'Is there anything else you can tell me?'

He shook his head, and she saw from his expression that he didn't envy her. 'I know it sounds like an unpleasant thing to say, Sergeant, but I'm guessing that two victims poisoned in almost the same way must make your job slightly easier. The difficulty, of course, is tracking down the poisoner before he strikes again.'

She stared at him. 'Professor, if you were going to poison two people, wouldn't you use the *same* poison the second time round? Specially if you saw how well it had worked on the first victim?'

'You have a point there. The first was poisoned with yew leaves, if I remember. It can't be because the killer's supply ran out. The churchyards are full of yew trees. I've even seen them in people's gardens.' He frowned. 'In your previous cases, did you come across serial killers who varied their method of killing?'

'The ones who did usually did it because they had to. Circumstances prevented them from always using the most direct method. So, for example, firing a gun in the middle of a city is a much riskier prospect than firing it in the countryside. Some serials are opportunists, and are good at using whatever's to hand. But the killings of Judith and Adam weren't opportunism. They were meticulously planned, and that includes the method of poisoning.'

He lifted his hands and let them drop. 'Well, you know more about these things than I do. I wish you luck.'

'I'd better be getting back. May I take this?' she added, indicating the folder.

'Indeed. It's yours.'

'Could I ask you to keep this under wraps?' she said, remembering Chirnside's insistence on secrecy regarding the nature of Judith Johnstone's murder. The press still hadn't got wind of what killed her.

'Of course,' Milo said. His gaze moved over her face. 'So how are you getting on with the case in general?'

'We seem to have ground to a halt.'

His face broke into a smile. 'When one avenue fails, Sergeant, try another.'

'The problem is that I've been doing that, and they're all dead ends.'

Although not quite all, she thought, as she left the office.

'A Druid?' Laurence said. 'His son told you that?'

They were standing near the door where the coffee things were kept. Dania had finished giving Honor and Laurence an account of her conversation with Mrs Reilly. And what David Frederick had told her, saying only that she'd run into him outside the house and he'd readily volunteered the information.

'I'll have to let the DI know about Sir Graham's car, and that he was the last person to have seen Adam alive,' Dania said, 'but until I speak to the laird, I think we should keep that quiet.'

'Yep,' Honor said promptly.

'Shouldn't you have checked it out with the DI first?' Laurence said nervously. 'I mean, before you poked around the laird's garage?'

'I was using some initiative. Anyway, I haven't been able to find the DI.'

'Other cases have been coming in thick and fast,' Honor said, switching off the kettle. She dug a spoon into the coffee jar. 'The DI dropped in earlier and said he'll have to divide his time. We're too short of DIs in this nick,' she added, pouring water into a mug. 'But he's called a briefing for later this afternoon.'

It was a briefing Dania had no intention of making.

The incident room was filling. The trickle of officers returning suggested that Fergus and his crew had finished their interviewing. And the looks on their faces suggested that the exercise had been a colossal waste of time. They started the process of entering statements and cross-referencing them, tapping at their keyboards with a marked lack of enthusiasm. She caught Fergus's eye. He threw her a desperate glare, and carried on typing.

She walked over to the incident board, and opened Milo's folder.

'You got something for us, Sergeant?' Fergus said eagerly.

'The tox results on Adam Frederick have come in.'

This got the room's attention. Briefly, she went through what the professor had told her. 'What I find interesting,' she finished, 'is that the killer used a different poison the second time round.'

'Maybe it's a copycat,' someone said.

'A copycat wouldn't have known that plant poison was used on the first victim,' Fergus said. 'I take it we're keeping this from the press? Like with the yew leaves?'

'Absolutely. And there's another thing. I've found something that links Adam and Judith. They were both Druids.'

A few jaws dropped, but no one asked Dania how she'd come by the information. 'What about you, Fergus?' she said, before anyone thought to press her for details.

'As straw-clutching exercises go,' he said with a tired smile, 'it was one of the most successful. We got absolutely nothing, which is precisely what I thought we'd get. No one in the villages around Backmuir Hall saw or heard anything.' He went back to typing. 'I've been at this for too long. I need to bank a full night's sleep.'

'Don't we all,' someone said.

Dania took Honor aside. 'When the DI arrives, will you bring him up to date about the tox report?'

'Will do. But don't you want to do it?'

'I intend to talk to the laird before he leaves.'

'What makes you think he's leaving?'

'When he's away, it seems always to be at the weekends. Look, if the DI asks where I am, can you say you don't know?'

Honor nodded, and Dania could see what was going through her mind – she was taking an enormous risk striking out on her own and not keeping her boss in the loop. But Dania knew of Chirnside's friendship with the laird, and suspected he'd block the direction her enquiry was taking.

She slipped away before anyone else noticed.

CHAPTER 26

Dania steered the car successfully from side to side, feeling a quiet triumph that she now knew where the potholes were. She rounded the bend and saw the Porsche parked beside the flagpole.

Sir Graham sauntered out of the hall and watched, unsmiling, as she pulled up a little way behind his car. He was wearing a lightly checked suit and moccasin loafers.

'Sergeant Gorska,' he said with a small bow. 'To what do I owe the pleasure?'

'I was wondering if you've time for a chat, Sir Graham. There are things I need to ask you.'

'But of course. Please.' He indicated the front door. 'Do go through into the living room.'

Tippex was curled up on the sofa, panting as though he'd chased every rabbit on the estate. He lifted his head as Dania entered, but made no attempt to move.

When they were seated, Sir Graham said, 'So, what would you like to ask me?'

She noticed he didn't offer her vodka. 'It's about Adam Frederick,' she said, taking out her notebook. 'I understand you were his patient.'

'That's right,' he said slowly.

'Can you remember when your last appointment with him was?'

300

'Goodness, now you're asking.' He blew out his cheeks. 'It would have been in April, I think.'

'Not more recently than that?'

'I can tell you exactly. Let me fetch the journal from the study.' He threw her a smile. 'All the details of my life are in that journal.'

He rose and left the room. From her seat facing the door, she saw him cross the corridor and disappear into the room opposite. He reappeared moments later, carrying what looked like a gigantic ledger. He laid it on the coffee table and leafed through it. Although it was upside down, she saw that it was a page-a-day journal, crammed full of entries in different-coloured inks.

'Ah, here we are. My last appointment was on Thursday April the twenty-first.'

'Sir Graham, Dr Frederick's calendar shows that you had an appointment with him on June the third.'

The date must have registered because he said, 'But I wasn't here. I left for Paris that day.'

'You left for Paris in the evening. A taxi arrived for you at five-thirty p.m. and your flight from Edinburgh was nine-thirty p.m. Your appointment with Dr Frederick was for midday.'

He stared open-mouthed. Then a fleeting smile of reassurance crossed his face. 'Yes, of course, I remember now. I'd made the appointment but realised I was running late. So I cancelled it.'

'Cancelled it?'

'I emailed Adam first thing.' He hesitated. 'You look doubtful. Here, let me show you.' He pulled his mobile from his back pocket and flicked through it. 'There we are,' he said, holding out the phone.

Dania read the email quickly. 'And where were you that morning?'

'I spent the day here.'

'Alone?'

'Alone. I had things to do before I left.'

'Do you own an Austin Seven, Sir Graham?'

'I do, as a matter of fact. What does that have to do with anything?'

'Can you remember when you last drove it?'

'Now that I definitely can't remember. It really was too long ago.'

'So you didn't drive it on June the third?'

'Good heavens, no, I'd have remembered that. I hardly ever drive it. No, I drive the Porsche if I need a car. I admit I've taken the Austin to the odd vintage-car rally, but I would never drive it to a doctor's appointment.'

She rested her gaze on his. 'I didn't say you'd driven it to Dr Frederick's. I simply asked if you'd driven it on June the third.'

'Well of course I assumed you meant I'd driven it to Adam's house, as that's what we were talking about.' A bead of sweat slid down the side of his cheek. 'Look, what is this about, Sergeant? Are you suggesting I drove the Austin to Adam's house on the third, kidnapped him, drove him here and strung him up on my flagpole?' When she said nothing, he added, 'But that's preposterous. Why on earth would I?'

'Adam was a Druid. Did you know that?'

There was a glimmer of recognition in his eyes. Yes, the laird had known.

'Did you know that Judith was a Druid too?'

The silence lengthened.

'What are your feelings towards the Druids, Sir Graham? Would you be happy to let them meet on your land, for instance?'

'Well, of course I'd have no objections.'

She looked at him for a few moments, as though trying to gauge how genuine he was. 'Is that why you fired a shotgun over their heads last year?' she said.

He got briskly to his feet in a way that concluded the interview. 'I mustn't keep you, Sergeant. I'm sure you have much to do.'

She hesitated, and then stood up.

'Let me show you out.'

'No need. I know the way.'

'As you wish,' he said with a tilt of his head.

As she reached the living-room door, he said, 'I must remember never to forget, Sergeant, that you are first and foremost a detective.'

She looked squarely at him. 'Goodbye, Sir Graham. Thank you for your time.'

She left the building wondering what, if anything, she'd achieved. Of course, the laird would deny everything. It had been a waste of time. But then, as she went over the interview, she realised that, actually, it hadn't.

From behind the bushes, Jenn watched the Polish detective's car turn on to the Liff Road and accelerate in the direction of Muirhead. So, the woman had been visiting Sir Graham again. Twice in two days. At least, she hadn't got herself locked in his garage this time. That had been a close-run thing. Just as well she had a mate who knew how to take hinges off a door. Had she not arrived, Jenn would have fetched her tools and freed the detective herself.

It wasn't hard to guess what had brought the woman to the garage. It seemed a strange thing to do, take photos of the laird's vintage car. Maybe it wasn't taxed and someone had reported it on the road. Jenn had never seen it driven, although Aleck had told her that the engine was much louder than that of the Porsche, and you had to do something called double-declutch. One advantage was that, if you had problems, you could start it with a handle. Easy enough, he'd smiled ruefully, provided you remember to keep your thumb out of the way so it doesn't get broken when the engine fires.

She'd managed to look in on the body farm, and had updated her notes and made a sketch in her exercise book. Decomposition was now at the active decay stage. The vole's tiny body was swarming with maggots and was completely flat, the body fluids having drained away and turned the surrounding grass dark and withered. She would describe this to Aleck when she next saw him.

It was nearly five, and she needed to get home as her mum would be back. She trudged through the woodland until she reached the Liff Road. She'd left her bicycle at the farm and taken a walk, as there were things she needed to think through. But it had been a mistake as she found her energy leaving her. A restless night was all it took and she was wrecked the next day. She had lain in bed waiting for the alarm to ring, and watched the light leaking in round the bedroom curtains. There had been no point going swimming. She thought of Ailsa, who'd not been a great one for getting wet; dipping her toes in the sea was about all she was prepared to do. When she'd first gone missing, it had dominated Jenn's life, consuming her every waking thought. Now, as the weeks wore on, she realised she was coming to terms with not having her sister around. Was that a good thing? Was she being uncaring? On Sunday, she would talk to the priest about it.

Dania ran into Honor outside the incident room. The girl steered her into the nearby ladies and gave her a run-down of Chirnside's briefing. There remained the feeling that the case was going nowhere and DCI Ireland was now considering offering a reward for information leading to a conviction. Chirnside seemed not to appreciate the significance of the Druid link between Judith

Johnstone and Adam Frederick and, banging his fist on the table for emphasis, stunned everyone by stressing the need to establish whether Adam had life insurance, or had left a will. They reckoned he'd lost the plot. Even Fergus, a consummate politician, challenged greed as a relevant motive for the doctor's murder.

'So how did you get on, Sarge?'

'The laird admitted he owned an Austin Seven but claimed he couldn't remember when he last drove it. And he said he'd cancelled the surgery appointment at midday.' She leant against the wash-handbasin. 'But he knew that both Adam and Judith were Druids. On that subject, have you heard from Zack about the Grove meeting tomorrow?'

'Yes well, about that, he's been in touch.' The girl looked at a point beyond Dania's shoulder. 'It's been postponed.'

'*O, cholera jasna!*' Dania said, slamming her hand against the dryer and setting it off.

'I assume you're swearing in Polish.'

'It's not particularly obscene. For that, you need to apply to my brother.'

'The reason for the postponement is that there's a live chat show tomorrow evening on STV, *Tayside Voices*, I think it's called, about the Dundee Grove. Some of the Grove members are on it.' Honor was looking at her strangely. 'What were you expecting to learn from the Druid meeting, Sarge? Did you think our killer would be there, sizing up his next victim?'

'I didn't think that, no,' she said wearily. 'The reason I wanted to go was to see if Ailsa McLaughlin or Kerry Campbell would show up.'

CHAPTER 27

'So I met with Rose yesterday afternoon,' Marek said, staring through the kitchen window.

Dania was checking her text messages. 'Rose?'

'Dr Peterkin. She's on the show tonight. We decided to meet and talk about what we would and, more importantly, what we wouldn't say. I hope you'll be watching,' he added, turning to face her.

'Of course. And I've set the telly to record so you can see yourself all over again.' What she wanted to ask was whether he knew anything about the next meeting of the Grove. Chances were that, given the late cancellation, the date and venue hadn't yet been decided.

'I need to get ready, Danka. I've to be at the studio by four p.m. at the latest.' He hesitated. 'Why don't you come along? There's a room where families can sit and watch. And there'll be drinks afterwards.'

'I'm not sure.'

'I thought you had the evening off.'

'Would it offend you if I stayed home?'

'No, of course not. I thought you might find the process interesting, that's all. Although I keep forgetting you were interviewed yourself when you worked at the Met.' He paused. 'I'm guessing that things aren't going well with the case.'

'The leads simply haven't materialised. I have a feeling I know who the killer is, but the problem is finding the evidence. I'll do my piano this afternoon. Playing has always helped me think straight.'

'I thought I heard you early this morning. One of the nocturnes, wasn't it?'

'Opus Forty-Eight, Number Two.'

'Is that the one you intend to play at the memorial concert?'

'Possibly. It's in a minor key. It may be too melancholy for the citizens of Dundee, although Poles love that kind of music.'

'Yes, it just melts them.'

'I'll have to decide soon so the laird can print the programmes. But, look, don't worry about me.' She tapped at her watch. 'Go and get changed.'

He gave a mock salute, and left.

When he returned, he was dressed smartly in a navy suit and red tie, his hair tousled from being towelled dry. Seeing him, she wondered why he hadn't yet found a woman with whom to share his life. The thought crossed her mind that the flat was over-crowded, and perhaps it was time for her to start looking for a place of her own.

'I'm not sure what time I'll be back, Danka. It may be late.'

'Not a problem. Anyway, best of luck,' she said, hugging him. 'I know you'll be brilliant.'

He pulled a face. 'That's what my editor says, but I'm not so sure. It depends on what questions we're asked.'

She noted his use of 'we' and realised that, more and more, he was thinking of himself as one of them. What would the Polish priest at St Joseph's make of it?

After he'd gone, she lay on the sofa, toying with the idea of getting a takeaway later, when her mobile rang.

'Dania, it's Fergus.'

She noted the stress in his voice. 'Yes?' she said, sitting up.

'Where are you?'

'At home.'

'We've had a call. There's another one.'

'Oh God. Where?'

'Liff village. The churchyard. I'm about to get over there. If you can walk up to the Perth Road, I'll pick you up.' Without waiting for a reply, he ended the call.

Fergus screeched to a halt, leaving the engine of his Volkswagen Golf running while Dania scrambled in beside him.

'There was a treasure hunt in the church grounds,' he said, pulling away and doing a U-turn to the accompaniment of blaring horns. 'It was the kids from Liff Primary who found the body.'

Dania closed her eyes. '*Jezus Maria*,' she murmured.

'I've rung the Slaughterman. He's getting his people together.' Fergus glanced at her. 'I suspect, with all the kids and teachers there, the site's been well trampled.'

'Did you call the DI?'

'He isn't on duty today. I left him a message. Look, can you call the station controller and get the uniforms sent out? I didn't have time.'

'No problem,' she said, pulling out her phone.

They reached the Marketgait and turned left at Dudhope roundabout. Dania had a strong sense of déjà vu as they followed the twisting Lochee Road until it became the Coupar Angus. They passed the greenery of Camperdown Park and Templeton

Woods, and arrived at the traffic lights at Tiddlywinks Nursery School as they were turning green.

The Liff Road meandered left and right and then, as it turned sharply, Dania saw a knot of people standing in front of low iron railings. Behind them was a stone church with a decorated tower and slender spire.

Fergus pulled up further on, not wanting to block the entrance.

As they left the car, a young woman with red-gold hair and striking brown eyes hurried forward. She looked sick with fear. 'I'm Yvonne McGlynn,' she said, sounding out of breath. 'I'm a teacher at the primary school.'

Dania and Fergus introduced themselves. 'Was it you who found the body?' Dania asked gently.

The woman shook her head. 'It was wee Stuart.'

'And where is he now?'

'His parents have taken him home.'

'And the other children?'

'They're away home too. We don't teach on a Saturday but the children and parents come in for this.' She squeezed her eyes shut. 'The children all saw it,' she said in a wail. 'This was supposed to be a treasure hunt. A special treat at the end of term.'

Fergus waited until she opened her eyes. 'Miss McGlynn, can you tell us where—'

'Round the back of the church,' she said, pointing down the wide path. 'You can't miss him.'

A thin-framed man who stank of body odour stepped forward. His hair was peppered with grey, and there was rage in his dark eyes. 'Is this another one like yon scarecrow?' he said fiercely.

'I'm sorry, but we need you to stay on this side of the railing,' Dania said firmly. 'And please don't leave until we've had a chance to take your details.'

There was a murmuring from the bystanders, which sounded

like general agreement. Police cars, their sirens blaring, could be heard speeding down the Liff Road. Dania nodded at Fergus and they hurried into the church grounds, following the path, which was wide enough to accommodate a car. Ahead and to the right lay the graveyard.

The path swung left, giving them a view of the tree with low, wide branches. Lolling against the trunk, his arms extended, was the figure of a man. He was wearing shabby jeans and trainers, and a blue and black striped t-shirt, stained at the armpits. His wrists had been tied to the branches, palms outwards, fingers gently curled, but his body was otherwise untethered. His head hung forward, exposing an incipient bald patch through the messy brown hair and, in this position, his face wasn't visible.

'How long do you think he's been here?' Fergus said.

'Impossible to tell.'

'We need Forensics. I'll call them again.'

She stepped forward, intending to crouch and get a look at the man's face, when she saw his left hand twitch. The fingers went rigid and then curled limply again.

'Never mind Forensics!' she shouted. 'Call an ambulance! He's still alive!'

The trolley raced through the corridors of Ninewells's Accident and Emergency department. Dania, running alongside, was trying to communicate to the worried-looking junior doctor that the victim may have been poisoned and should have his stomach pumped immediately. The doctor seemed to absorb this information but laid a firm hand on her arm when she tried to follow him into the emergency room.

As she paced the corridor, she wondered if the ambulance paramedic had saved the man's life. Hunched over in the vehicle, she'd watched him perform various procedures before clamping an oxygen mask over the man's face. To her repeated requests for information, he'd simply shaken his head in frustration. All he could tell her was that the man's lungs seemed not to be working properly. He was alive but in a critical condition.

There'd been no time to establish the victim's identity. As he'd been cut down, she had caught sight of a bad complexion, pimples around the nose and a steep forehead. And a sticky-looking red patch on the back of his head. She'd left Fergus to get statements from the muttering crowd.

She stopped pacing and peered through the window into the emergency room, seeing equipment and wires and people in blue scrubs. The man was being ventilated via a tube through the nose.

There were sudden hurried footsteps. Chirnside arrived, his face ashen. Listening to his wheezing, she concluded that he could probably use some oxygen himself.

'His name's Derek Strachan,' he said in a faltering voice. 'His wife's been notified. She's on her way.' He placed both hands on the window and stared into the emergency room, a stunned expression on his face. 'What's going on, Dania?' he whispered. 'Why is someone doing this?'

'We'll know more when we've had a chance to interview him.'

'You think he'll survive?'

'I'm hoping so. The paramedic told me it's his respiratory function that's impaired, but his heart seems to be beating normally. Surely that's good news.'

The DI shook his head, as though unable to believe anything that was said to him.

The doctor hurried out of the emergency room. He had red hair and an old–young look, which would inspire confidence in some but not in others. 'Are you family?' he said to Chirnside.

311

'DI Chirnside, from West Bell Street Station. Is there anything you can tell us, doctor?'

'The muscles used in respiration are showing signs of paralysis. It's touch and go, I'm afraid. We've pumped out his stomach,' he added, nodding at Dania, 'but we've no idea what's in there. Anything you can tell us would be extremely helpful and might save his life.'

'Two other victims were killed with different plant poisons,' she said with a glance at Chirnside. 'It's likely this is part of the same series.'

'And have you any idea which plant it is?'

She shook her head.

'A poisonous plant narrows it down. I'll get one of my colleagues on to it.' He was about to re-enter the room when she grabbed his arm. 'Is he conscious? We really need to speak to him.'

'That's out of the question.'

'I just need a few minutes. Please.' She brought her face close to his, hoping he'd read the appeal in her eyes. 'He may be able to tell us who did this to him.'

'It wasn't an accident, then?'

'You've seen the wound on the back of his head.'

The doctor chewed his lip. 'Okay, if he comes round and is able to speak, I'll call you in. But it may not be any time soon.' He nodded at Chirnside and left.

'Can you stay here, Dania? I need to get back to the SOCOs.'

'Of course.'

'I'll send someone along later to relieve you, but it's vital we try to speak to him. And Mrs Strachan's likely to arrive any minute.' He patted her arm. 'You know what to say. The usual words of sympathy.'

'I'll do my best, sir.' She watched him lumber down the corridor, thinking he'd aged ten years.

She took one of the chairs in the corridor, and settled in for a long wait.

Fifteen minutes passed, and the doctor emerged.

She sprang to her feet. 'Any news?'

'He's still unconscious.'

'But he's stable?'

The doctor frowned. 'We found a pacemaker identification card in his pocket. He's been fitted with a rate-responsive.'

'Rate-responsive? What does that mean?'

'The pacemaker has sensors that detect changes in physical activity and automatically adjust the pacing rate. It's probably what saved his life. Many plant poisons interfere with the normal electrical pacing of the heart, and his device tried to keep his heart going. However, there's likely to have been tissue damage.'

'His assailant didn't wait until he died before tying him to a tree,' she said, half to herself.

'It's possible he went into a catatonic state when the poison was administered. It would be an easy mistake to assume he was dead.'

'Bottom line, doctor. Will he live?'

Before the man could reply, they heard a woman's voice. 'Doctor?'

A petite woman with a heavy curtain of dark hair was hurrying towards them. She was accompanied by a hospital official.

'I'm Mrs Strachan,' she said with a tremor in her voice. 'Where's my husband? I want to see him.'

'I'm afraid that's impossible,' the doctor said.

'But I *have* to see him.'

'He's not yet conscious.'

She pressed her face against the window. 'Dear God,' she murmured. She seemed suddenly to become aware of Dania.

Dania pulled out her warrant card. 'Detective Sergeant Dania Gorska.'

'They told me in the village that someone had tied him to a tree.' The woman grabbed the doctor's arm. 'He has a pacemaker,' she said in a breathy voice.

'We know that, Mrs Strachan.'

'When can I see him?'

'I can't tell you. Now, I'm afraid I have to go.' He disentangled himself gently and returned to the emergency room.

Dania softened her voice. 'Can I get you something, Mrs Strachan? A coffee, maybe?'

'Coffee?' The woman seemed distracted. She bit her lip, as though unable to make up her mind. 'Yes, yes, that would be nice,' she said, staring through the window.

'Milk and sugar?'

'Yes.'

Dania took the official to one side. 'Is there a coffee machine nearby?' she said. 'I'm liable to get lost, and I don't want to have to lay down a trail of coloured beads.'

He smiled. 'You're in luck, it's not far. Follow me.'

When she returned, she found Mrs Strachan sitting upright on one of the corridor chairs. As Dania approached, she glanced up, wiping her eyes with her fingers.

'There we are,' Dania said, handing her a cup. 'One coffee with milk and sugar.' She sat beside the woman and sipped slowly, wondering why coffee from machines is always too hot to drink.

'Have you any idea what happened?' Mrs Strachan said, in between sips.

'All I can tell you is that we had a call into the station that Derek was in the churchyard, tied to a tree.'

'And he was unconscious?'

'He'd been hit on the back of the head, I'm afraid.' She wondered how prepared the woman was to talk about her husband. 'Do you live in Liff village, Mrs Strachan?'

'We're further along on the left-hand side. Past the church.'

'Were you at home this morning?'

'I was, but after lunch I went shopping in Dundee with my daughter, Becky.'

Dania glanced at her. 'And where's Becky now?'

'I left her with a neighbour. She's only six. I couldn't bring her here to see this,' she said, gesturing to the window with her coffee cup. She let her head drop.

'Can you think of anyone who'd want to do this to your husband?'

'Absolutely no one. Ask around the village. Everyone likes him.'

'What does he do for a living, Mrs Strachan?'

'He works for the local council.' There was a look of anguish on her face. 'He's a good person.'

And, as Dania sipped her coffee, she recalled the same words being spoken about both Judith Johnstone and Adam Frederick. They were good people too.

It was nearly ten before Dania climbed the steps to the flat. As she pushed open the door, she knew immediately from the darkness that Marek was still out.

She hung up her jacket, switched on the living-room light and threw herself on to the sofa. The cheese and pickle sandwich she'd eaten at the hospital hadn't agreed with her and she wondered if she was going to throw it up.

She'd left Fergus, who had arrived to relieve her, sitting gloomily outside the emergency room with Mrs Strachan. The prognosis was not good: Derek was still in a critical condition.

Dania dragged herself off the sofa and into the kitchen. A glass of Wyborowa would settle her stomach. She was pouring herself a large measure when she remembered Marek and the chat show.

She took the vodka into the living room and switched on the television. The programme had long since finished, and she wondered idly why Marek hadn't returned home. He must still be at the drinks reception.

She selected the chat show and hit Play. There was a boy band on first, and she fast-forwarded, overshooting the start of Marek's segment. When she eventually found him, he was on the sofa next to someone she recognised as Dr Peterkin. But this was a very different Dr Peterkin from the nervous woman who'd made the identification of Judith Johnstone. She was confident, and it didn't take Dania long to appreciate that her confidence stemmed from having Marek at her side. Whenever she replied to a question, she glanced at him for confirmation, which was duly given with a nod or a smile. Her clothes were surprisingly sexy, a figure-hugging dress in a cream shade and matching stilettos.

The show host had just asked her about the Institute of Religions and Belief Systems.

'The course is designed to become a living, breathing way of life,' Dr Peterkin was saying with decision in her voice. 'It will transform the student through a steady series of initiations and extracurricular challenges provided by their life experience into the person they wish themselves to be.' She turned her head and faced the camera. 'At the end, the graduate will have acquired the tools to live a conscious, clear and powerful life.'

'Is it really that simple?' the male host said, leaning forward and gazing at her. He looked as captivated by her quiet intensity as Marek was.

She flushed with pleasure. 'All the graduate needs to do is to integrate the lessons into his everyday reality. There is only one question he should ask himself: how far will I journey along the Path?'

'Mr Gorski,' the host said, shifting to face Marek, 'this seems to be pretty much what you wrote about in your article. Have you taken your first step along the Path?'

Marek smiled self-deprecatingly, running a hand through his hair. He was about to answer, when a man's voice could be heard shouting. Suddenly, something was hurled on to the stage. Whoever had thrown it was an excellent shot because it hit Dr Peterkin on the shoulder. The missile exploded on contact, showering her and Marek with red liquid. She looked in dismay at her dress, and then lifted her head and stared into the audience, her expression changing to one of fear.

'Get that slag out of here,' a huge voice shouted. 'And send the bloody foreigner back to wherever he came from!' The camera swung away from the stage and panned round the audience, focusing on a stocky little elephant of a man with dark hair slicked into furrows. Seeing the camera trained on him, he took a menacing step forward.

Dania heard the host's voice. 'Get security!' The camera swung back to the stage as more missiles, which couldn't all have been thrown by the same person, hit Dr Peterkin, Marek and the host. Marek sprang to his feet and, grabbing the stunned Dr Peterkin by the shoulders, steered her rapidly off the stage. The camera returned to the audience. There were now almost a dozen people on their feet, some grappling with uniformed security guards. Dania watched in astonishment as members of the audience in the rows behind climbed over seats and joined in. Over the shouting, the host's voice could be heard announcing almost farcically that, due to circumstances beyond his control, he was having to cut short the interview.

'Beyond his control' was an understatement, Dania thought, watching as the security men were overpowered. One of the audience, an oldish man with a grizzled face, must have seen the cameraman recording the scene because he made a lunge for the equipment. A second later, the picture skewed, there was a crashing sound and the screen went blank.

She ran into the corridor and pulled the phone out of her bag. Her call to Marek went to voicemail. She sent him a text, asking if he was okay, and to get in touch immediately.

She returned to the living room, her mind churning. Something made her rewind to the section where the fight became a free-for-all. She rewound and fast-forwarded until she found what she was looking for – a man, a few rows behind, standing watching the proceedings, his arms folded, a smile of approval on his face.

At least now she had the answer to one of her questions: the laird of Backmuir hadn't left Scotland this weekend. He'd decided to stay in Dundee.

CHAPTER 28

Dania bowed her head automatically as she listened to the Polish priest speak the words that transformed bread and wine into the body and blood of Christ. Her mind, however, was elsewhere. After a restless night, she'd woken early and, unable to drift back to sleep, had decided to attend the 6.00 a.m. Sunday Mass attended by the Polish farm workers.

There'd been no reply to her gentle knock at Marek's door. She'd peeked inside, seeing the curtains open and the bed not slept in. Her hunch had been correct: he'd not come home last night. Normally, this wouldn't have worried her, but she suspected that, after rescuing the fragrant Dr Peterkin, he had returned to the studio and joined in the fighting. She'd tried phoning and texting him again without success. The temptation to ring round the hospitals was enormous, but that was probably a step too far.

She joined the queue for Communion, aware that she had been glancing around the church in the hope of seeing him there. As she received the host, she caught the expression of disapproval on the priest's face, and wondered if he, too, had noted Marek's absence.

When the service was over, she didn't linger, but slipped away while the priest was speaking to one of the Polish workers. Such disrespect would doubtless increase the length of time she spent in the sulphurous fog of Purgatory, but she had enough to do in this world without worrying about what would happen in the next.

'Anyone seen the DI?' Dania said over the hubbub in the incident room.

Honor looked up from her screen. 'He's not in yet, Sarge.'

'Any news from the hospital?'

'No change.'

Dania flopped down at her desk. 'If we could only get a name from him.'

'You're assuming he saw his attacker.'

'Why would he not see him? The man intended to kill him, as he'd killed Judith and Adam. Why bother hiding his identity?' Her gloom lifted. 'This is our biggest chance to solve this, Honor. We're so close. Don't you feel it?'

'What I feel, Sarge, is dog-tired. My shift at the hospital didn't finish till three a.m.' She shrugged. 'Someone has to get the shit jobs. I wouldn't mind so much if the pay were better. No one told me that policing is such an underpaid occupation.' She gestured to the screen. 'We've got the statements entered and cross-referenced. There's nothing much there.'

'What about the children on the treasure hunt?'

'Laurence and I spoke to them. They seem pretty okay about it. I guess they see worse things on telly.'

'Imagine if they'd found him with his eyes pecked out.'

'I still think they see worse things on telly. The parents and teachers couldn't tell us anything either. The parents were pretty angry, which is understandable.'

'Do we have the last-known sighting of the victim?'

'He was mowing his lawn, Sarge. Does it every Saturday

after lunch, according to his neighbour. His wife takes the car to Dundee.'

'And this neighbour saw him yesterday?'

'He heard the sound of the electric mower. Glanced out of the window and there was Derek. The guy couldn't be sure of the exact time, but he'd not long since heard the two o'clock news.'

'That's probably as exact as it goes. Did he say when he heard the mower stop?'

'He went upstairs to take a leak. When he returned, he saw it in the middle of the lawn, which is unusual as Derek always puts it away. Even more unusual is that the lawn was only half mown.'

'If Derek was taken in full view of the street,' Dania said, rubbing her forehead, 'his assailant took a huge risk.'

'Yep. But maybe he had no choice.' Honor paused. 'By the way, did you watch *Tayside Voices* last night?'

'I recorded it.'

'The uniforms made dozens of arrests after that punch-up. The DCI is furious. We have a whole heap of interviewing to do, which we don't really have the manpower for.'

'Did the uniforms, by any chance, arrest Sir Graham Farquhar?'

'Cripes? Was he there?'

'I saw him watching the fight, although the camera was knocked over before I could see if he joined in.'

Honor snorted. 'Wouldn't a laird have a lackey do the fisticuffs for him? I'd put my money on that Docherty guy. He's built like a brick shit-house.'

Dania lowered her voice. 'If the laird was in the recording studio, then he wasn't in London.'

'So I won't have to check his flight from Edinburgh Airport this time.'

'And if he wasn't away yesterday, I don't need to tell you what that means.'

'Let me guess.' Honor's eyes were gleaming. 'He had the opportunity to kidnap Derek Strachan and string him up in Liff churchyard.'

'And if he did, he must have been supremely confident. I saw him only two days ago and effectively accused him of murdering Adam Frederick.'

'Talk about brass neck.'

'The question, though, is: was Derek a Druid?'

Dania let herself into the flat. The clattering noise from the kitchen told her that Marek was home.

He appeared wearing an apron and holding a wooden spoon. 'Danka,' he said in surprise. 'I thought you'd be back before now.'

She struggled out of her jacket. 'I feel like bashing you over the head with that,' she said, gesturing to the spoon.

'Bad day in the office?'

She made to grab the implement, but he lifted it out of reach. 'What's got into you?' he said more seriously.

'I saw what happened last night. I've been texting and ringing. Why the hell didn't you reply?'

'Ah, I switched my phone off before the show.' He turned away. 'I must have forgotten to switch it back on.'

'All day?' she said, following him into the kitchen.

'I've been a bit preoccupied.'

'Doing what? I rang your office and they said they hadn't seen you. I was about to call the hospitals.'

'You don't need to worry about me,' he said, chopping vege-tables with the speed of a master chef. 'I can look after myself.'

'So where have you been?'

He laid the knife down and faced her. 'I spent today with Rose.' He hesitated. 'And also last night.'

'Dr Peterkin?'

'She was in a terrible state so I took her home. There's not much more to tell. We were covered in paint and we tried to wash it off.' He shrugged. 'One thing led to another and we ended up in bed.'

Dania's lips twitched. 'Well, I'm relieved to hear you were in such good hands.'

'Oh yes,' he murmured, a half-smile on his face.

She glanced at the array of food on the working surface, and wondered idly how long it would be before the lovely Dr Peterkin would be the beneficiary of his culinary expertise.

'And what about you, Danka? How was your day?'

'I spent most of it taking statements from those idiots who threw paint at you. Do you know the Scottish word "stramash"? Well, I learnt it today.'

'A stramash?' He stared at her. 'Is that what happened after Rose and I left?'

'There were a few broken heads, so we'll be charging them with GBH. I could have done without it, to be honest. We have a third victim.'

'Displayed, like on a gamekeeper's gibbet?'

'Except this one's still alive.'

His eyebrows shot up. 'So you're close to finding the killer?'

She said nothing. He went back to chopping vegetables. And, as she watched him, she realised with a sudden dismay that, given the lack of firm evidence, finding Derek's killer – and that meant finding Judith's and Adam's – turned on whether Derek lived or died.

It was Tuesday before all the statements from Liff village were entered on to the database. It hadn't helped that the press had got hold of the story and were hanging around the village like a bad smell, generally getting in the way of the investigation. And, as everyone at the station had predicted, none of the residents had seen or heard anything.

DCI Ireland had called Dania in and informed her that Chirnside had phoned in sick and, as they were short-handed and she had no DIs to spare, the station would be relying on Dania to keep the murder investigation on track, and also to make things work somehow with Sergeant Fergus Finnie, with whom she'd had a word and from whom she'd extracted a promise not to behave like a complete bampot.

As Dania was working through the newly entered statements, her phone rang.

'Sergeant Gorska?'

'Professor Slaughter. Thanks for calling.'

'I've heard from Toxicology. Thanks to your insight, we were able to get on top of this one. Derek Strachan was poisoned with aconitine. It's present in the species *Aconitum napellus*, commonly known as aconite or monkshood. You find these plants in gardens, as well as woodland.'

'How poisonous is it?'

'Very. The toxin is absorbed easily through the skin. Simply picking the leaves without wearing gloves can lead to poisoning. Every part of the plant is dangerous if ingested, but the root is the deadliest.' A pause. 'The quick work by the emergency-ward doctor may have saved Mr Strachan's life. If he hadn't pumped out the man's stomach, he'd be dead by now.'

'Thank you, Professor.'

'Good luck, Sergeant.' He rang off.

She was thinking through the implications when her phone rang again.

'Sergeant?' came Laurence's anxious voice.

'Yes?'

'You need to get yourself down here. He's regained consciousness.'

As Dania rushed through the swing doors into the emergency ward, she knew she'd arrived too late. Laurence was in the corridor with Mrs Strachan, patting her shoulder and looking everywhere but at her. The doctor was speaking to her but it was clear she wasn't listening. She was bent over, taking deep, gulping sobs, her hand over her mouth.

'Is there someone we can call, Mrs Strachan?' the doctor enquired gently.

The woman seemed only then to notice him. She straightened and shook her head. 'I need to go home.'

'DC Whyte will take you,' Dania said, looking at Laurence, who seemed relieved to be given something to do. 'And he'll arrange for a family liaison officer to stay with you.'

Mrs Strachan gazed in apparent incomprehension, and then nodded. She let herself be guided down the corridor.

As soon as they were through the swing doors, Dania said to the doctor, 'What happened? I heard he regained consciousness.'

'He opened his eyes, but I'm not sure how much he could see, to be frank. I got your DC to call his wife. Pity she didn't arrive in time. Anyway, I realised he was trying to say something.'

Dania felt her heart race. 'And did he succeed?'

'He seemed very anxious to get the words out. I put my face close to his and asked him to repeat what he was saying.'

He hesitated. Dania thought she would burst with impatience. 'And?' she said, gripping his arm.

He shook his head. 'I'm really sorry.'

CHAPTER 29

Dania had spent the previous day with the team. Once the gloom over losing their best chance of solving the murders had lifted, they pored over what little solid evidence they had, and tried to turn it into a working hypothesis.

Kimmie had filled them in on what she and her team had found. There were many small footprints on the path, which she reckoned had been made by the children on the treasure hunt. Interestingly, there were no tyre marks, new or old, suggesting that Derek had been carried into the church grounds. She had snooped around the woodland behind the building and noticed several paths leading either to the nearby roads or deeper into the trees. Oh, and she'd discovered the treasure, hidden under a holly bush. It was a small wooden box full of chocolate coins, which she'd returned to the school, suggesting to the teacher that, in the good Christian tradition, all the kids should take a share. But she'd found nothing else and was unlikely to, unless the ropes that had tied Derek Strachan could give up their secrets, which she doubted.

The timing was their best clue: between roughly 2.00 p.m. and 2.15 p.m., Derek had been taken. He'd been mowing the lawn in full view of the road. So had he been lured into a car? Unlikely, as there had been people on the road at that time and no one could remember seeing him getting into one. Had he left to meet his killer, then? Also unlikely, according to the neighbour who saw him do the lawn every week, not stopping until he had finished, and then putting the mower away in the garden shed, which he locked after him. The only time he varied this procedure was when rain stopped play, which hadn't been the case last Saturday because, as the neighbour helpfully explained, 'the sun was fair crackin' the flags'.

Derek's body had been discovered a few minutes after 3.00 p.m., the time the treasure hunt had started. Roughly forty-five minutes after his abduction. That left his killer little time to take him somewhere, bring him back to consciousness and administer the poison. Ergo, the place he'd been held had to be nearby.

Which was why Dania was now driving down the Liff Road.

The street on which Mrs Strachan lived was an odd mixture of old and modern houses. The Strachan's could best be described as a tired-looking building with badly plastered walls. The garden consisted of flowerbeds along the side of the house, a low privet hedge that separated it from the neighbour's, and a sloping lawn, easily visible from the road. A weathered bench stood against the wall.

Dania had considered leaving it another day before calling, giving the woman time to grieve, but this was now a murder enquiry.

There was no reply to her knock, and she was on the point of turning away when she saw a thin, bespectacled man in sagging trousers wheezing down the path of the house next door. He shuffled along the road and up the Strachans' drive. She held up her warrant as he reached her, but he paid it no heed.

'If you're looking for Lesley,' he said, out of breath, 'she's at the church.'

'Mrs Strachan?'

'Aye. She goes there every Wednesday afternoon to collect the hymnaries and tidy up.'

'I see,' Dania said. 'Thank you.'

He seemed not to want to let her go. 'I'm guessing this is about Derek,' he said. 'I've given the police my statement,' he added politely but importantly.

'You've been very helpful.' She stepped past him and started briskly down the path.

'I've been thinking about how someone could have kidnapped him.'

She stopped, and turned round. 'Go on, please,' she said softly.

He gestured to the woodland behind the lawn. 'I can show you. Lesley won't mind.'

Before Dania could reply, he tottered across the garden. She followed him past a shed with heavily creosoted walls, towards the trees.

'If I'd wanted to do a spot of kidnapping, I'd hide myself here, behind this shed,' he said, watching her reaction.

She saw immediately that, if Derek Strachan had chanced to step behind it, and someone was waiting for him, he could have been overpowered and dragged into the woodland without anyone noticing. It was a theory. And probably how she would have done it herself. But why would Derek come over to these trees?

'Anyway, I thought you should see this. Now, I'm afraid I have to go,' the man said. He shuffled back across the lawn.

'Thank you,' she called after him. It struck her that, had he not gone upstairs to relieve himself, he might well have seen what had lured Derek away from his lawnmower.

She pushed through the trees, seeing well-trodden paths leading away in different directions. Mrs Strachan could wait, she decided. She took one of the paths that veered left. A minute later, the woodland started to thin. And suddenly she saw them in the distance – the red–stone turrets.

She made the mental calculation. It would take about five minutes from Derek Strachan's garden, through the woodland to Backmuir Hall. No more than that. Even dragging a semi-conscious man.

The wooden door under the gable of Liff Parish Church opened with a loud creak. There was little in the small hallway other than a table piled with hymnaries, and stone stairs that spiralled into seating galleries on the first floor. On either side of the table, doors led into the nave. Dania took the one on the left.

The centrepiece of the raised chancel at the back of the room was an impressive organ with decorated blue pipes. Wide galleries supported on simple columns stretched round three sides. The rich smell of polish hung in the air, suggesting that Mrs Strachan was doing a fine job.

Dania had thought that the woman would be keeping herself busy, but she was sitting in a gated wooden pew at the back. Her head was bowed, and the sunlight filtering through the diamond-paned windows caught her hair. She'd made no response on hearing the door, making Dania wonder if she was expecting someone.

Dania opened the gate and took the seat next to her. The woman lifted her head wearily and, seeing the police officer, gave a faint smile of recognition.

'Your neighbour told me I'd find you here, Mrs Strachan.'

She stared straight ahead. 'It's a place I come when I need to think.'

'Are you up to answering a few questions? I'll understand if it's too soon.'

'No, no, I want to talk.'

Dania glanced around. 'Did the family liaison officer not arrive?'

'I sent her away. I didn't need her.'

Mrs Strachan was putting on a brave face. 'Can you tell me a bit about Derek?' Dania said, after a pause.

'What is there to tell? He had a successful career doing what he'd always wanted. Which was helping people. But it was a difficult job and he didn't talk about it much. Said he didn't want to tread it through the house.'

'How long had you been married?'

'Too long.'

Dania shot her a look. 'Weren't you happy?'

'I was about to leave him.'

The silence hung between them.

'I was on the point of telling him,' Mrs Strachan said finally. 'But he was a fragile person. Too fragile for me to bring his world crashing down.' She ran a hand down her flowery skirt. 'You see, he loved me. I knew that.'

'And he didn't suspect?'

'He'd have spoken to me if he had. He was like that. A great believer in talking things through. That's what made him such a good councillor.' A note of pride crept into her voice. 'Sir Graham particularly asked for him when he set up all his committees. Derek was often away in the evenings at meetings.'

Dania stared straight ahead. It was a hunch, but worth a try. 'Can you remember if he had any evening meetings in April?' she said slowly.

'I can check for you. Hold on.' Mrs Strachan pulled out her phone. 'We have one of those shared calendars.' She flicked through the pages. 'Yes, here. Friday April the twenty-ninth.'

April the twenty-ninth . . .

She held out the phone.